RED X WOLF

DAMSELS OF DISTRESS

DAKOTA KROUT

MOUNTAINDALE
PRESS

This book is dedicated to my sister Chandra, short of stature but immense in presence, a person who constantly seeks mastery in each new skill she chases.

CHAPTER
ONE

Lily Red's breath created small clouds of quickly evaporating moisture in the crisp forest air—the *only* sign she left behind while making her way through the underbrush of the Wyld. She was comfortable here, perhaps even more than when she was at home. *Certainly,* Lily was more at ease than when she was in the Heart of the Wyld, the only true city her people claimed on the island of Canu Moch.

Slinking softly across the mossy surface of the forest floor, Lily was forced to slow down as the ground became overly wet and muddy; as if it were trying to trick her into leaving behind footprints. But there was no room for mistakes—not today. If she managed to return home carrying all three of her prizes, not leaving a single trace which could implicate her, Grandmother had promised a special present.

The sun had just dawned on her eighteenth birthday. Not only was this a significant milestone for any youngster, it was an actual magical moment just waiting to happen.

Lily let out a light, slow breath to try and regulate her heartbeat as she alighted on the tip of an exposed boulder. Deciding it was finally time to take a pause, the redhead quickly inspected the three items she had acquired, starting with the trophy fish she'd taken this very morning from the lazy people who lived along the coast, only a scant few hours through the forest from her own home.

"I don't understand why we even *bother* interacting with the Coastals. They have no respect for... well, anything. Nothing they do makes any sense whatsoever. Every day, they have a competition to see who can bring home the most impressive fish, yet then didn't even notice I had taken it? What's the point of being the best if you don't get your reward?"

As far as Lily could tell, not a single person who lived in the Coastal city-state worked to develop their system-granted skills, to advance their class, or had any ambition at all—beyond simply finding the most pleasurable way to move through life. Rolling her eyes, she amended her thought. "Pshh. More like *coast* through life. By the *system*, even their nation's *name* is lazy. 'We live on the coast? Let's call ourselves Coastals. Wow, what a great idea'."

Pulling on the line, she pulled the fish up to eye-level and inspected it with slight disgust at how it had been treated. "Were they *really* going to eat this after basically just... just *hacking* it apart? They ruptured the internal organs, scales and bones were shattered and driven into the meat... what a waste. Maybe a *third* of the poor creature will end up being edible. That is, without having to pick something out of my teeth. What a waste.

To be fair, even one-third of the fish was going to end up being a dozen pounds of meat more than she could eat in a day. It was just that *enormous*, typical of the creatures along their coastline. Letting go of the line, she pulled a face as the dead thing flopped and almost pulled her off balance. Even hooked on the upper end of her backpack, the lengthy body still nearly touched the ground as she crept along.

Pursing her lips in annoyance, Red was once again reminded of *why* she was so very devoted to increasing her current system-skills and pursuing the class her grandmother had been training her for since she was a child. Standing at four feet and eleven inches tall as an adult, she was at the *minimum* a foot shorter than the next shortest adult on the island. "That won't matter when I'm officially a Scout. No one'll give my height a second thought; my skills being top-notch is all anyone will care about."

Her lack of vertical growth had been a source of *constant* annoyance her entire life, earning nicknames she despised, such as Lil' Red—admittedly not terrible, as she could pretend they were shortening her first name, Lily. 'Little Red' was what her Grandmother called her, which was fine coming from *her*. Lastly, the worst people in the Wyld had come up with the most *infuriating—*

"Bah!" Physically shaking her thoughts off with a full-body shiver, Lily forcefully pulled her thoughts away. She *refused* to let herself be sucked into a spiral of annoyance. Not today. Not on her birthday. Still, as her mind had shifted from the city-state of the Coastals, to those living in the city-state of the Wyld, Lily found herself looking at her second trophy: a rare type of rabbit which lived deep in the Wyld woods.

It had been difficult to hunt, as the timid creatures only emerged from their burrows before dawn, and their ears were so sensitive that it was nearly impossible to catch one unaware —especially without a Full Class with corresponding skills. It was a testament to her training and constant preparation that she'd managed to take this one just as it fully surfaced, having sent an arrow up in a long, parabolic arc as soon as the tips of its ears emerged.

Lily had made the arrow herself, specially designed to be as silent as possible during its flight. Having had plenty of warning that this task was coming, she'd prepared five owl-feather fletched projectiles, and was delighted she'd only needed one. Inspecting her handiwork with a critical eye, she finally allowed herself a ghost of a smile as she looked over the careful skinning and dressing she'd completed before wrapping it in leaves and hanging it from her small Scout's backpack. Technically, she hadn't earned the right to carry such an item yet—as she didn't have the corresponding class —but her grandmother being the *best* trainer on the island afforded her some liberties.

She dropped her hands to her sides, accidentally creating her first audible noise of the day as her knuckles came down on the metal helm she'd taken from one of the roving guards of Bleakrock nearly a week prior. Her fingers trailed lightly over the intricate metal work, and her mood slowly began to lift. While it had been challenging to find a way to take the trophy from someone standing on a wall over forty feet above her, it had been a *good* kind of challenge.

Eyes slightly out of focus, she thought back over the heist.

At one point, the third and final city-state on the island, Bleakrock, had been a towering mountain. Over the centuries, the people living there had been tasking the residents of their nation to hollow out the prominence, eventually mining it down until their towering city walls hid whatever they were doing. Even so, both the residents of the city-states 'Coastal' and 'Wyld' separately agreed there was likely now an enormous pit behind the unbroken walls surrounding the exact center of Canu Moch, yet there was no way to confirm this rumor.

Bleakrock had taken an absolute-isolationist approach after clearing a wide swath of land around their territory in an attempt to make it impossible to approach without being noticed. They *never* allowed visitors, and anyone who entered their walls was never heard from again.

For Red, this had made it all the more satisfying to sneak close to the walls more than fifty miles north of her home; bright red hair pulled into a tight ponytail, piercing green eyes focused on her target... going completely unnoticed while laying still for several hours. She'd remained in her position until, just after the sun reached the midpoint of the sky, one of the guards had broken their protocol and removed their helmet, setting it on the wall to wipe away sweat accumulating on their brow.

Going from unmoving to flashing into motion was one of Lily's specialties. An arrow with an attached grapnel had sunk through the eye socket, swiftly reeled in as it sent the armor flying. Lily had yanked back, reeling in the thin line like a coastal landing a fish, until the helmet was eventually delivered to her hands.

The best part?

The guard had clearly and vocally assumed a bird had knocked his helmet out of his hands and was furious the creature had taken it over the wall. Even while he peered down, trying vainly to find where it had fallen, she had slipped back into the woods without a single person laying eyes on her.

It had gone... *perfectly.*

While she wanted to take all of the credit for such a successful hunt, her Basic and Advanced Class skills had most definitely done their part. Red's left eyebrow twitched upward as the thought ran through her mind, and she allowed a real smile as she softly chuckled at herself. "What am I even thinking? I worked hard for those skills, and I've been training to maximize how well I've used them since I was *ten*. No matter what anyone else says, I shouldn't minimize my successes just because I have fantastic skills."

Putting the index and middle fingers of her right hand together, she swiped them down her left arm, from the crease of her elbow to the edge of her palm. Combined with her intention, the action caused golden words to begin temporarily scrawling across her skin—words she was intimately familiar with at this point, as they'd first begun appearing on her tenth birthday.

Basic Class: Prodigy Pathfinder
Basic Skill: Wilderness Whisperer: Level 10/10.

You have a [Perfect] innate understanding of the environment around you, allowing you to move across most types of landscape with [Perfect] grace and silence, and you can read natural signs and tracks with [Perfect] accuracy.

Advanced Skill: Natural Huntress: Level 10/10.

Having spent more than 95% of your life in a forest, you have slowly become one with it. In a forest environment, your senses are [Perfectly] enhanced, you may now sense the presence of animals and trespassers with [Perfect] precision, even at great distances or through dense foliage. Your movements become an extension of the forest, allowing you to set up [Perfect] tracking mechanisms and ambushes which are [Perfectly] impossible to detect.

Breakthrough Skill: Permanently locked.

You did not unlock this skill before accepting an Advanced Class.

As she read, the words vanished; only to be replaced with the next lines of information. Her eyes lingered on the Breakthrough Skill, wondering—not for the first nor the last time— what she could've unlocked if she'd managed to achieve Perfection in her Advanced Skill before she turned fourteen and unlocked her Advanced Class. She had been assured over and over that it was the correct decision, as she could've been trying for nearly a decade to unlock the third skill in her Basic Class, and still fail, as so many had before.

Still… she took a deep breath and squared her shoulders. "I already have a Basic Skill with *three* modifiers and an Advanced Skill with four. I need to stop being greedy."

Her eyes traveled back along her arm, taking in the information on the Advanced Class she'd unlocked at fourteen.

Advanced Class: Flower of the Forest
Basic Skill: Wyld Rose: Level 10/10.

Having started your training at four years old, you already have a decade of experience utilizing the weaponry of the Wyld Scouts. Thanks to your voracious learning and constant practice, the system has decided to further enhance your capabilities. You have System-enhanced [Perfect] accuracy with bows and bow-type weapons. You have System-enhanced [Perfect] skill with knives when it comes to killing and butchering creatures you hunt. The use of live traps becomes an innate knowledge, and you may be struck with inspiration when attempting to use them.

If targeting another person, the System enhancements will be reduced by half, leaving them as [Moderate] modifiers.

Advanced Skill: Roots and Thorns: Level 7/10.

This is a passive ability which [Proficiently] enhances your awareness of dangers to yourself and those you are attempting to protect. You can [Proficiently] sense impending threats, whether from natural predators, enemy combatants, or environmental hazards. When fighting in rough terrain, your chosen weapons will [Proficiently] act as if they are unimpeded.

Breakthrough Skill: Locked.

Reach level 10 with your advanced skill to unlock!

"Not bad… better than most thirty-year-olds, if Grandma is to be believed. *Forty*-year-olds if we're talking about a *Coasty*." Red shook her head and snorted at the thought. With her three prizes in hand, she once more began roving through the woods, until finally the familiar sight of Grandmother's house appeared through the foliage.

The structure was made of wood, just as everything else in the Wyld was. Grandmother's house blended seamlessly with the surrounding forest, adding a layer of camouflage; as well as simply being a testament to the forestry skills of the Scouts who had built the place to act as a training ground for future generations.

Not only was this place important to Lily, it was important to the Wyld, as well as the island as a whole. Grandmother's house was built around a Class Shrine, necessitating year-round protections. While every person was welcome to access the small structure within the structure and unlock their class or the ever-rare Breakthrough Skills, it was *deadly* important to keep out animals.

The system was extremely level-handed; *anyone* who touched the shrine could enhance themselves based on their life experience, as well as the age of maturity for their race. This meant even something as simple as an adult squirrel scampering up onto the Class Shrine could end in disaster when the cute creature became a ferocious Ascended Beast, or a beast became a true Monster.

Lily was proud of her grandmother, the only person on Canu Moch who was trusted to guard a Class Shrine on her own. It was a not-so-subtle reminder of how the person who'd trained her since she was a child was one of the most competent, skilled, and deadly combatants on the entire island. The young woman walked to the front door, pushing it open and allowing an inviting aroma of fresh-baked bread mingled with the smoke from an oak-wood fire to wash over her.

"Welcome back, Lily." Her grandmother's voice reached her in the next moment, not a hint of surprise in her tone. "Right on time. As expected."

"Master Scout. As directed, I've completed the three tasks assigned to me-"

Lily's words stopped abruptly as her grandmother looked up sharply and waved off the incoming report. "None of that, not today. Look at me, see how wide these eyes are? They're perfectly capable of seeing you've completed your task. From this point forward, at least until tomorrow, I'm not 'Master Scout'. I am only a proud grandmother. Happy birthday, my Little Red."

Though she winced slightly, Lily knew Grandmother wasn't teasing her. "Thank you. I hope I've reached the standard you've hoped for me."

"Oh, *pshh*, you did that *years* ago." Walking over with a plate of sliced bread, Grandmother traded Red for the fish and rabbit, pointing at a wash bucket as she glanced at the streaks of mud Red had on her hands, feet, and face. "Wash up now, it's almost time for dinner. I'll have the rabbit added to the stew, and the fish fried up as an appetizer in no time flat. While I'm doing that… I don't suppose you'd like to unlock your Full Class?"

Grandmother smiled knowingly and threw open a door leading deeper into the house. A silver light immediately shone through the opening, the reflected sunlight half-filling their living space. "After all, no one has earned it more than you."

Lily let out a sharp gasp, a single glance confirming this was no joke. With reverent steps, she walked to the center of the domicile, into a small room housing a diminutive plinth. "Heh… just my size."

Legend stated that each of the Class Shrines appeared exactly the same across the world, being small structures with only enough room for a few people to comfortably stand in. They were always clean and perfectly white, impossible to alter, damage, or fully close off from the world around them for some reason. Though she had never seen how they appeared on the mainland, and likely never would, the fact that all those on the island had the exact same appearance lent credence to the story.

Without further hesitation, Lily slapped her hand onto the plinth in the center of the room, and her mind was filled with the voice of the system.

Codex Arcane Ledger access requested.

C.A.L. is assessing…
Age verification: 18 years. 0 months, 0 days. Conditions for Full Class advancement met.

Assessing skill use and level. Combined skill levels: 37. Determination: 92nd percentile.

Scanning brain waves to account for knowledge and desires in Full Class selection process. Requirements met for: 12 Full Classes.

Comparing skill use and desires... 92nd percentile of skills shows a subconscious desire to continue progressing. Waking brain is in alignment with subconscious. Determination made.

Full Class Unlocked!

Full Class: System's Scout
Basic Skill: System's Whisper: Level 1/10.

This is a composite skill which [Minimally] enhances your trained skills of navigation, stealth, camouflage, survivalism, archery, and environmental awareness. As you have already honed these personal abilities to an exceptional degree, system guidance will come into effect whenever you are outdoors. The guidance will manifest as a subtle glow [Minimally] highlighting any of the actions you are attempting, as well as flashing a warning when the actions are failing or when your attention needs to be drawn to a specific area.

Requirement to advance to level 2: Travel across the entirety of Canu Moch—or a similar sized landmass—from coast to coast, without being seen by a single predator or human. You are not allowed to bring food or water.

"Wow." She breathed out in awe as she looked over her new class and skill, wincing only slightly as she saw the difficulty and specificity of her advancement requirement. "That's... *awesome.*"

After sharing her class and skill with her grandmother, the Scout trainer's eyes went distant and hard for a long moment. "I'm excited for you. Though it only has two modifiers, and others may disparagingly call it 'only' an Uncommon skill, never think of this as anything other than a *powerful* ability which has been granted to you. It's absolutely a testament to your training and dedication that the system itself will be aiding you in your tasks. If it had noticed a glaring flaw in your abilities, you would likely have instead gained a skill which would have helped to cover those weaknesses."

The older lady went silent as she stirred chunks of rabbit meat into her stew, thinking through a few things. Red decided against interrupting her train of thought, as this was a fairly common occurrence. Eventually, Grandmother looked up and met her eyes. "You are going to have to use every single one of your enhancements to get through even the *first* skill upgrade, and you won't even know if you succeeded or failed until you reach the coast on the opposite side of the island. This will test your stealth and camouflage mastery to the limit."

The elderly woman paused and stirred, contemplating the stew. "No food or water allowed means you'll need to practice your survivalist skills even harder... perhaps slaying a predator from a hidden vantage would count as you not being seen by them? Ha, just like that, you have a plan for getting protein on your journey!"

As excited as Lily was to begin improving herself once more, she forced herself to calm down and set the table. "We can start a new training regimen. *Tomorrow.* Tonight, I just want to spend my birthday with my grandmother."

The hard eyes softened, and the pursed lips twisted into a doting smile. "For you, anything. Oh! I nearly forgot! A reward for completing your tasks. A gift from me."

Placing a package on the table, the elderly Scout waved for Lily to tear it open. She did so, revealing a bright crimson hooded cloak, which would cover her from head to toe when worn and fully closed. Trailing her fingers over the material, Lily blinked in shock as she realized it was the softest material she had ever felt. A gentle tug revealed that the fabric was surprisingly resilient. Looking up in slight confusion, she met the smile of her protector and mentor with her personal confusion.

"It's *enchanted*," Grandmother casually mentioned, earning a gasp from the new System's Scout. "No matter how filthy it gets, it will be easy to clean. It won't tear easily, and if it *does* get damaged, it will heal itself over time. As for the color…"

"Red?" Lily had been wondering about that choice. "In the forest?"

"Well, the fact of the matter is…" There was a victorious smile on the elder's face now. "Out of all of the people I've trained, there's only *one* I have enough faith in to say 'she can wear bright red in a forest and still be hidden better than anyone else'. That's *you*, my darling. In case you were wondering."

Reaching out and caressing Lily's face to wipe away a single tear of joy, Grandmother warmly stated, "Happy birthday, my Little Red."

TWO

A SOFT LIGHT was pulsing around the bushes Lily was staring at, patiently waiting for the person hiding there to get bored and finally stand up.

It had been two full years since she'd gained access to her Full Class and her System's Whisper skill. In that time, the Scout had grown accustomed to the world itself speaking to her through shifting colors and strobing light of varying intensity. Now she was so familiar with it that she trusted her skill *almost* as much as her training.

So, when the smirking face eventually peeked out of the bush and looked around, a soft chortle escaping the trespasser's mouth, she was fully unsurprised. The man was a Coasty; for some reason, they'd been pushing into the Wyld's territory more frequently recently. They weren't breaking the treaties between the city-states by cutting down trees, nor were they poaching animals. No, this was something more... *annoying* than simple law breaking.

Recently they had decided sneaking into the woods and avoiding capture for as long as possible was a *hilarious* game. The event boiled down into a simple question: how long can you stay in the woods without being dragged home? Apparently, the longer they went without returning, the more they would 'win'. The bet was hours of work, or just the friends of the person in the woods paying for their fine, with a little extra thrown in on top to make up for the player not being able to catch their own meal that day.

While tensions between the three city-states existed, none was outright hostile to the others so long as they didn't break any important laws. Trespassing into the woods was a violation, but as the fine was only a few fish—something even the most *common* household along the coast had an overabundance of, the game was starting to be played far too often. If they got bored or scared, as long as they had taken care not to damage anything in the woods, all the Coasty would need to do to be escorted safely home was get the attention of a Scout.

Technically, Lily had no reason to get them home, no responsibility for their lives. She was *not* a Scout employed by the Wyld—a constant source of frustration—but her Full Class Basic Skill would constantly **ping** her with the location of anomalies such as the Coasty, thanks to the environmental awareness aspect which the ability came with. If she didn't bother to get him out of here, it was going to keep flaring light at her for the rest of the day.

She watched with tired eyes as the fish-reeking man took a few steps forward, only for him to let out a scream of fear and surprise as a net suddenly shot up from the ground, closing around him and yanking him into the air. His fear turned to laughter as she stepped forward, seemingly appearing out of nowhere in her bright red Scout's cloak.

"It's you! I found *Little Red Riding Hood*!" The man howled with laughter as her grim-set mouth turned into an actual frown. "Do you *know* what kind of multiplier I get on my bet because of this? I'm going to eat like the mayor for a week! You win this one. Take me home, oh scary Wyld Scout."

"Red... riding hood?"

"Yeah, you know." The man gestured at her outfit.

"Because that's a full-body cloak for you, but for anyone else, it would just be a hooded riding cape."

She watched on in… not disbelief—as she understood Coasties had no self-control in the slightest—but mild disgust at the *minimum*, as he leaned back and used her meticulously hand-crafted net trap as a hammock.

Lily shifted slightly on her heels, using only a single kick to destabilize the stake holding the rope taut. A moment later, the man let out another yelp as he crashed to the ground, the net holding him in place as the falling rope pooled atop his now-bruised body.

"Hey! Abyssal rude of you. How about some *profession-alism?*" The man grumbled as he ineffectually pulled on the ropes to try and get himself free. Red wasn't having any of *that*. After a yank on the loop to close the net more tightly around him, she walked over and adjusted his feet, forcing them to poke through the holes at the bottom of the net to allow him to walk.

"Let's go." Without another word, she gave a sharp tug on the rope-turned-leash and began navigating the two of them through the woods. As soon as she set her mind on the location she wanted to return this man to, a streamer of light appeared in the air—which only she could see—weaving around trees and through bushes to show the best, safest path to her destination.

"Oh, come on! Don't be like that! Chat with me a little, wouldn't you? All the other Scouts at least *talk* with us on the way home." When Lily didn't respond, the man grumbled in annoyance behind her, "Whatever, I know you're getting paid for this. I'm job security for you Wyldlings. You should be *thanking* me."

Red's pale face tinged slightly as her annoyance simmered and began flaring into actual anger. Yes, this was a task which should've been completed by the Scouts hired by the Druidic Grove of the Wyld. No, *she* was not being paid for it. She would receive none of the credit for 'rescuing' a Coasty lost in the woods, none of the compensation for going out of her way and losing hours of training. Instead, she would be spending the next half day being taunted by this lazy person, then his lazy friends, and *still* need to return and finish her tasks.

The sad fact was, one of Grandmother's rivals had made it on to the council. Even with Red being more qualified than literally *any* other Scout her age, perhaps even some even a decade her senior, she had been trained by Grandmother. Reynard had been the *second*-best Scout trainer on the island for decades now, and he had never forgiven Grandmother for beating him by all available metrics with *every single* trainee.

Lily, as the poster child of the successful methods, not to mention being her own flesh and blood, was a far easier target for his ire than Grandmother herself. After gaining her Full Class two years previously, Red had attempted to gain a paid position with the Druidic Grove, showing perfect results on all the testing requirements. Stealth, situational awareness, survivalism, *everything*.

Lily had completed all of the tests perfectly, and was calmly waiting for the job offer, only for the new councilor to block her acceptance on the flimsiest of excuses: a six-foot-tall longbow was standard issue for all Scouts employed by the Wyld...

...and she was too short to effectively use the weapon.

Even though using the longbow had never before been a requirement for the post, the councilor argued she was unfit for the position if she couldn't even use the equipment everyone else did. With so many other *viable* candidates, her offer had been canceled without further discussion. To add insult to injury, as she walked out of the Heart of the Wyld, the only city in the Wyld, and therefore the only area with designated testing equipment, Reynard had called out to her and casually made an announcement.

"You should try again when you're older. You'll definitely get a job with us when you grow *up*."

The blatant insult had caused the other Scouts in the area —all trained by him when they were younger—to burst into laughter. The joke spread like wildfire, and now Red was a laughingstock among her peers, even though her skills surpassed theirs in almost all areas. Perhaps *because* her skills were so much better.

"Oww! That one had *thorns*!" The netted man whined pitifully as a branch snapped back on him, causing Lily to blink furiously and glance about as her attention came back to the present. "Can't you be a little nicer? Life's a game; what's the point if we don't enjoy playing it?"

"Stay on the path, don't stray or roam, lest the forest decides you shan't go home." Lily stopped so abruptly the man walked into her and rebounded, falling on his butt and letting out another pained grunt. She turned her piercing stare on him, bright green eyes narrowed as she tried to reign in her rising temper.

"We are not playing a *game*. You're trespassing, and I'm *not* a Scout hired by the Wyld. My only obligation is to ensure you don't damage the forest. I could accomplish this by tying you up and leaving you for anyone else to find, or maybe for the bears. Frankly, you're already lucky you walked into my trap. My *live* trap. Some of the other ones are not so… forgiving."

The man let out a muted *eep* and recoiled from her, though after a moment he looked her up and down and grinned as if she were only teasing him. "Yeah, maybe, but that's why I came looking for *you*. Everyone's heard how you specialize in being able to capture pretty much anything alive and unharmed. I've heard how many tokens you make on securing animals for people to tame and turn into pets."

Red couldn't even be upset about his words, as the annoying man was correct. There was a *huge* market for young foxes, rabbits, and other fragile creatures who weren't too difficult to be trained up by young people with classes such as Beast Tamer. She *should* be happy word was spreading so far, as she hadn't been sure how effective her minimal attempts at getting out the word on her services had been.

Still, no matter how lucrative each individual job could be, it wasn't the same as having steady income. There were only so many young, rare beasts, not to mention youngsters who wanted to train them.

Lapsing back into her preferred silence, she pulled the Coasty to his feet and prodded him with the hilt of her short sword. Lily could practically hear the man roll his eyes as he started walking again. "Seriously, you're no fun. Like, at all."

No matter how much he grumbled, Red didn't bother responding any further. She stayed several feet ahead of him, the rope connecting them together sometimes being the only reason he knew where to go. Even with such a short distance between them, the man often called out to her fearfully, having lost sight of the Scout in the dense underbrush.

Red suddenly halted, flashing lights from the system highlighting the area, specifically one creature *almost* perfectly hidden by the old growth forest. With a practiced, fluid motion, she unslung her bow and nocked an arrow. Just before she released, the rope Lily had wrapped around her arm went taut, and she was nearly pulled off balance as the netted man stumbled.

The target in the distance turned to look at them sharply as the bundled person dropped to the ground, loudly moaning over his misfortune. Red didn't hesitate any further, launching the arrow smoothly even with the disturbance.

Over the last few years, she'd grown to love owl-feather fletching, and had replaced every arrow in her quiver with them. So, as her projectile traveled from her to the animal, the shaft didn't make even the slightest whistle as it pierced the air. A soft *puk* reached Lily's ears just before the deer fell forward, suddenly visible as it slapped bonelessly to the ground. She let out a soft breath and nodded at the creature. "Clean kill. I'm glad you didn't suffer. I'm sure Grandmother will be pleased to add you to our larder."

"*Ahh!*" The man screamed as he heard the distant crash, only to be forced to his feet and into a stumbling walk as Red began moving again. "We're going *toward* whatever that was? What if it's a mountain lion?"

Besides letting out a soft snort of derision, Red didn't bother responding to the inane question. Approaching the kill, she knelt beside it, knife already in hand. For just a moment, the blade glinted in the filtered sunlight, catching the eye of the Coasty, who watched on with a mix of horror and fascination.

Then she plunged the blade into the carcass, cleaning the deer with efficient, methodical movements. As if the forest was holding its breath, the only sound in the area was her knives separating hide from flesh. The scent of blood quickly mingled with the earthy aroma of the forest, and soon Lily was wiping her blade and hands on the fur of the animal to clean off the already-sticky liquid.

When she was done, Lily jammed a meat hook into the deer's neck, tossed a rope over an overhead branch, and hoisted the creature off the ground. After tying it off, she reached for the other rope—still connected to the net holding the Coasty. "Let's go."

Only when the man refused to move did she bother looking at him, slightly annoyed, but calmer now that she had secured dinner for the next several days. The Coasty was pale, his eyes wide and fearful as he looked at the bloodstained fingers holding the rope. As Lily stepped forward to inspect him, worried he'd been stung by some venomous creature, he flinched back, turning his head and gagging. "N-no! Don't touch me! You capture pets for spoiled children, I didn't realize you were so *cruel!* Please don't hurt me; I'll stay out of the forest—"

"You're joking right now. Right?" Red scoffed as she stepped back and pulled on the rope, forcing the man to move his feet. "I'm glad you've decided to stay away from my home, which is the *correct* thing to do. But I'm not being cruel, I'm getting ready for dinner. Don't you catch fish and eat them? Do you *see* an ocean in the forest? How did you *think* we got our food?"

"It's just so… so *violent!*" the man whimpered as he struggled weakly against the ropes. "Fish practically throw themselves into our nets, and by the time we're home, they don't thrash around and bleed all over the place. *We* don't kill them, the *air* does!"

"Un. Be. Lievable." This time, when Red pulled on the rope, the man meekly followed along, thankfully keeping his thoughts where they should be: in his own head, with his mouth closed.

THREE

RED STOMPED AWAY from the coastal community, her hands clenched and the hood of her cloak up as a shield against the laughter and taunting coming from the people behind her.

After dragging the terrified man through the woods and back to his village, she had begun delivering a scathing admonishment to him for his reckless trespassing into the territory of the Wyld. Unfortunately, as soon as they'd broken free from the tree line, his cowed attitude had undergone a drastic, unpleasant shift. Suddenly, he was all smirks and taunts, and when the other villagers came into sight, he joined them in laughing at the 'ridiculousness' of his situation.

They had laughed at him because he'd been 'caught by a child', but he'd rebutted by pointing out his winnings would be multiplied because of it. The casual insults weren't even directed at Red, but they flew through the air so quickly that she couldn't help but be caught in the crossfire. Her words, instructions, and threats were drowned out by the shouting and laughter, and to her great annoyance, someone had stepped forward with a knife and cut through a few loops of her net before she noticed and managed to shove them away.

"Thanks for bringing me home, Wyldling!"

"At least I've got some busywork to look forward to," Red grouched as she walked away, lamenting her damaged net. She'd considered throwing a few punches, knocking out a tooth or two, or perhaps sneaking back and taking the annoying intruder's entire 'winnings' of fish for herself. However, she managed to restrain herself. Lily fully understood that she could overpower all of them, likely at the same time, if she didn't mind putting holes in them. But... even as embarrassed and angered as she was now, she knew better than to take this too far.

Reporting it to the leadership of the Wyld would earn her only sneers and taunts, and the Coastals didn't even have a clear group of leaders, only the best fisher of the month—their monthly elected mayor—who was in charge alongside the best *dancer* of the month, the co-mayor. As the roles were arbitrary, and no one would take the position more than once every three months, extracting a promise from them to police their own people would amount to nothing.

Suddenly, all of her anger turned to exhaustion, and she slumped slightly as she continued walking. "This is *not* how I wanted to spend my twentieth birthday."

When she had first gotten her Full Class, she had thrown herself into training and expanding her skill to the utmost. Unfortunately, just shy of a year and a half later, she'd hit a wall. The upgrade requirement had become impossible to complete outside of very specific situations, and like almost every other adult, she had finally reached the limit of what she could do with training. With a tired sigh, she swiped her fingers along her left arm, looking down at the level up requirement which hadn't changed in seven months.

Full Class: System's Scout
Basic Skill: System's Whisper: Level 9/10.
This is a composite skill which [Masterfully] enhances your trained skills of navigation, stealth, camouflage, survivalism, archery, and environ-

mental awareness. As you have already honed these personal abilities to an exceptional degree, system guidance will come into effect whenever you are outdoors. The guidance will manifest as a subtle glow [Masterfully] high-lighting any of the actions you are attempting, as well as flashing a warning when the actions are failing or when your attention needs to be drawn to a specific area.

Requirement to advance to level 10: identify a significant threat to the residents of Canu Moch—or a similar-sized settlement—and report it to the local leadership before anyone else has reported it.

"A single level away from earning a new skill, and I'm locked out of earning my next one unless I figure out a way to burn down the forest without getting caught. Maybe I should lay on a rock and hope to detect a volcano before it erupts?" Though she didn't want to be so bitter about this requirement, it was hard for her to have her path forward be *completely* outside of her ability to control. It wasn't something she could train, learn, or do. She had to be in the right place at the right time, then move faster than anyone else when it came to reporting it.

The last part she could do, she knew that for a fact. Lily had no doubt she'd be able to move through the forest faster than anyone—other than perhaps her grandmother, who never left home. Protecting the Class Shrine was more than a job, it was a full-time career. Not only keeping the area safe, but also providing access to the infrequent visitors who came to this out-of-the way shrine due to family tradition or the like; instead of the more central ones the main settlements had been built around.

In an attempt to get over the frustrations of the day, Red changed her direction slightly, quietly seething over the fact any further improvement had to be left to the whims of fate. Instead of immediately returning to the forest, she decided to walk along the eastern side of the island, where the coast turned into rocky cliffs overlooking the ocean.

Caught in the throes of her intrusive thoughts, Red let out a snort of derisive laughter. "Who knows? Maybe I'll spot a tidal wave in the distance and have enough time to report it before it drowns us all."

At first, she plodded along the coastline, but eventually began to feel anxious about wasting her time walking when she could be, at the minimum, using this time to train. The rocks were slippery from the spray of waves crashing below, providing an opportunity to test her balance in a new way. Slowly at first, but picking up speed as she became more practiced, Red sprinted along the stones, climbing them, jumping between them, bounding off steep, jagged cliff walls to reach safe landing spots that would've otherwise been out of her reach.

Half an hour after she began, she'd traveled nearly two miles down the coast, never staying at the same elevation for more than a few seconds at a time. She'd reached a tall cliff with an oversized boulder providing a nice area to relax in the sun for a few minutes; just enough time for her cloak to dry and her thin sheen of sweat to evaporate. The breeze was strong, blowing the scent of the ocean over her and causing her clothes and hair to fly in steady streamers behind her.

Red lay down for a moment, taking in a deep breath, letting it out... and waking up an hour later as a strange sound reached her ears. Blinking salt and sleep out of her eyes, she cursed herself for her lethargy. "Abyss, I need to get back to that deer before the birds get at it. I need to trade the pelt for some barter tokens if we want a chance at replenishing our cheese this month. By the *system*, did I forget to—"

The strange sound came again, and the light of the system highlighted the direction it had originated. To her surprise, it didn't come from behind her or even farther back in the woods. No, it came from in front of her and... below?

Crawling forward, she looked over the edge of the boulder, blinking a few times as her mind tried to figure out what she was seeing. "Why are there so many clouds so close to the ocean?"

She knew what it was; her brain simply didn't allow her to accept what she was seeing. When she saw the people swarming over the area under the 'clouds', everything *clicked* in place. Scores of ships were sailing toward the shore, far too well built and maintained to be something the Coasties had come up with. Putting herself in a slightly dangerous position, she hung out over the edge of the cliff and looked down, where the first of the ships had already landed and was starting to unload.

Just like that, the source of the mysterious sound which had woken her up came into view: dozens of armed and armored raiders clamoring out of their boats and onto the shore in the hidden cove, each of them either wearing a wolf-head helmet; or at least with a large stylized wolf head painted onto their armor. Red felt as though a pit had opened in her stomach. To her great dismay, she recognized them. Even among all the raiders out there, this was no ordinary group…

…this was *Wolf Warband.*

They were a huge, deadly force of raiders who would appear suddenly, ransack entire *cities*, then vanish without a trace. Rumor had it they were based in an incredibly harsh environment to the far north, where constant storms raged and made sailing safely nearly impossible. Every few years, a new story about them would crop up, as they ran out of food or other resources and invaded yet another country.

But… Canu Moch had never been attacked. By anyone. Sailing to their island was only done by the most desperate of merchants, and even *then*, there was no profit to be had. The Coasties had fish, and what sane seafaring merchant wanted to load up on fish? The Wyld had wood and meat, neither of which made for a good haul back to a far distant homeland, as the work required would be far too much. Bleakrock? They didn't trade whatever resources they were mining or creating, so as far as she knew, they *would* be worth raiding, but she couldn't imagine anyone cracking that nut.

Lastly, everyone on the island was paid in barter tokens, or with direct barter. They didn't have precious metals or gems. What use was there for the shiny coins of the mainland, besides breaking them down into arrow tips or fishing hooks?

As the warband unloaded and started pulling off supplies to make camp, Red realized in a flash that meat, wood, and fish might be *exactly* what these invaders were after. Whatever storm had blown them here had clearly left them far from an area they could stock up on provisions. They had a hungry, angry look about them, as if they'd been on half-rations for weeks. Red gulped when another understanding dawned: these brutes didn't need to worry about the islanders being unwilling to trade using coinage.

They would *take* what they wanted. Lives would be lost, her people would be in terrible danger. All of them would. Everyone on the island... had a significant threat to their lives.

"This is it!" Red whispered to herself as she shimmied backward on the boulder. Internally, she had to keep reminding herself she was nervous and unhappy with the situation. She didn't want anyone to get hurt, to lose their homes or lives. But... *but...* another part of her was repeatedly and gleefully pointing at this situation as the intervention of the system itself, which had apparently been trying to warn her for nearly half a year about the incoming invasion.

Standing and turning, she leaped off the boulder and landed heavily on the cliff, ready to race into the woods. Instead, she went very still as her sudden arrival caused an unfamiliar man to whirl around and drop into a fighting position. Red's mouth dropped open as she took in the visage of the massive warrior standing between her and the safety of the woods.

He was a dozen feet away, but appeared much closer due to his sheer size. His chestnut-brown hair was mostly covered by a white wolf head turned into a helm, both of which brought out the dangerous intensity of his icy blue eyes. Each of his muscles were as sculpted as the rugged contours of a mountain range, and the sunlight pouring over the coast caused shadows to dance over his body as he took two startled steps toward her with athletic, predatory grace.

Dangling from his hip was an oversized cudgel, simply a stout branch which had been dipped in metal on one end. The weapon was probably three feet long, but it looked practically minuscule compared to his nearly seven-foot-tall frame.

Before Lily could draw her bow and put an arrow in the air, he had shifted from casual walking to *hurtling* at her, hands half-lifted as though to tackle her to the ground. Only the lights of the system flashing bright red warnings reminded her to move in time, and she swept down and under his outstretched arms, spinning around and immediately sprinting toward the woods.

"No! You're the first person I've seen! The oracle says you must tell me-" The gravelly words were panicked, a thick accent making them difficult to understand in his rush to speak.

She didn't bother to hear him out, nor did she slow down as she took advantage of a slight parting in the underbrush to slip into the woods more easily. A moment later, her caution paid off as the barbarian crashed into the woods right behind her, his much, *much* longer legs allowing him to reach a straight-line speed she could only dream of.

For a moment, Lily was frightened, but as she wove around trees, she realized she was in her element. The forest was her domain. Her home. Although she could hear him behind her, his steps heavy and his passing clearly demarcating a path of destruction, a thrill ran through her as her eyes lit with excitement. "Finally... a *real* challenge!"

She spun and sprinted, catching him off guard with her sudden shifts. As the minutes passed, Lily led him deeper into the forest; sometimes even flapping her bright red cloak deliberately to catch his eye, all in an effort to draw him farther from the coast and the others. By the way he growled like the wolf he was clad in, she knew her taunts were effective. He began to use his cudgel like a farmer's scythe, crushing through bushes and ferns in his path as his frustration grew.

As Lily realized she'd gone from hunter to hunted for the first time in over a decade, her eagerness to test herself almost caused her to become distracted. The thrill of it was *amazing*, made better by the fact that she knew he'd never be able to catch her. Almost laughing at the man, she called out, "Come and get me, if you *can!*"

His face turned nearly purple with rage, but just as Lily became certain she could lead him into some of her traps, the enormous man behind her must have realized the futility of his pursuit. He was alone, deep in the forest, chasing someone who clearly knew what they were doing.

From her chosen hiding spot, Lily watched the enormous man scan the surroundings and fail to find her. For a moment, she thought about drawing his attention, but he turned back to the coast and shouted at the sky, "It matters not. *Warn* them. Let the entire island know Wolf Warband is on the hunt, and come to understand that soon there will be no place you can hide. You tell me to come and get you? Then I *shall*, you crimson forest sprite!"

Red remained still for a few minutes after he had disappeared from sight, planning out her next moves. Then she was running. Before all else, only one thing mattered at this moment:

Warning the Wyld of the incoming threat before anyone else could.

CHAPTER

FOUR

RED DARTED THROUGH THE FOREST, a flash of crimson in the trees easily mistaken as a cardinal flying low to the ground. The trees in this part of the Wyld were young, used as trading material to the other city-states. As she sprinted, they slowly shifted toward larger, taller, more ancient versions.

Even as she murmured softly to herself, Lily made sure each step was calculated, every footfall precise and agile, honed as they were through years of training and system guidance, "It's at least an hour in any direction at a dead run to reach the nearest Coasty town. The raiders will probably wait until everyone is off the boats before setting out, so I could have as long as two hours before those *wolves* are noticed."

Eyes flashing with excitement, she lengthened her stride. "I can *definitely* report this first. There might be thousands of invaders, but a hundred Scouts properly spread through the Wyld will easily make their numbers-"

The system flashed a light so deeply, *dangerously* red that it was nearly black. Instantly shifting her stance, Lily dropped to her knees and slid across the mossy ground as a tripwire flung a branch through the air where her head would've been. She leaned back as it whipped past her face, barely avoiding a trap designed to take down forest deer. Pushing off with her hands, she turned the dodge into a backspring, then shifted forward to continue sprinting along—though now paying much closer attention to her surroundings. "*R~right*. Let's not accidentally die on the way to earning a giant reward."

With her mind back on her senses, she realized the Wyld around her was alive with the sound of its inhabitants. With the adrenaline fading from her system, and her heartbeat approaching as level as possible, Red once more began slipping through the greenery, a sanguine shadow not adding a single decibel of noise to the cacophony of nature. Her eyes keenly scanned the path ahead, her body flowing to anticipate each root that might trip her, swaying out of the grasp of every branch reaching out to snag her cloak.

It was the duty of a proper Scout to respect the ever-changing nature of the Wyld. Even after having traversed these woods thousands of times, each journey needed to be treated as a new challenge—clearly shown by nearly having her head taken off only a short while previously.

As her focus narrowed, System's Whisper swung into full effect, highlighting the most direct route to the Heart of the Wyld, as well as softly pulsing a faint glow only she could see across potential hazards or medicinal herbs she would've otherwise missed. Still, now wasn't the time to earn extra barter tokens.

With a simple mental push of intent, a good chunk of the glow faded away in response to her deciding not to see valuables. Now with fewer distractions, Lily was able to more clearly see a concealed rabbit hole on the path, a rock which would slip if her foot came down on it, a low-hanging branch held back by a thin string waiting to spring out at her. Each one of them was easily avoided as she weaved through the dense undergrowth at speed others would be hard-pressed to match on open and flat terrain.

Though she'd been using her Full Class skill for years now,

she was still amazed by how much *more* the system saw than she did. At level nine, the skill did more than just guide her, it was a *Masterful* extension of her senses, literally *and* figuratively.

Now at the halfway point to the city, Red finally found a well-trod path, and her speed increased again. Ahead, a deer paused and glanced over, watching her pass while continuing to chew on a mouthful of acorns. Squirrels scattered at her passing, scurrying up trees and chattering at her in annoyance at being disturbed. Peaceful creatures were everywhere, leaving only one real obstacle she had to watch out for:

People.

She sprinted past other Scouts, people out for a quiet forest jaunt, and the occasional chuckling Coasty who was being guided back to the edge of the island. That last one filled her with no small amount of smugness, as the expressions of pure annoyance on the Scouts hired by the Druidic Grove easily matched hers from early this morning. Even though *they* were paid for performing the service, it was a chore no one wanted to be assigned. Coasties had a way of succumbing to starvation, dehydration, and exhaustion, which had to be carefully managed this deep in the woods—left to their own devices, they would destroy themselves and the forest around them.

Though she wanted to tell the Scout not to bother, as the island was being invaded, Perfecting her skill took precedence. Not to mention, they likely wouldn't listen to the outlandish warning without proof.

Finally, the forest began to thin. This deep into the Wyld, the trees were wide enough around that up to ten people would have to join hands in a circle around them to fully embrace the trunks. The dense canopy above made it difficult for any smaller plants to survive, reducing tripping hazards and allowing her to move without fear of misstepping. Finally, Red burst from the tree line, maintaining her sprint even as she wove around startled individuals, rushing into the Heart of the Wyld.

The dividing line was stark. One moment, towering old-growth trees with gnarled roots and canopies so thick they blocked out the sky. The soft hum of the Wyld was ever-present: rustling leaves, chirps of hidden birds, the quiet rush of wind through the leaves. As the city came into view, most people seeing it for the first time were confused, as though seeing an optical illusion—for good reason. At first glance, the city seemed like a part of the forest, as though it had grown from the very soil itself.

The old trees weren't cleared for construction; instead, their natural curves were embraced, used as the skeleton for the city's sprawling design. Vast platforms, woven from thick, resilient vines and reinforced with planks of wood, formed the foundations of tree borne homes. Rope bridges stretched between these arboreal structures, swaying slightly in the breeze. Beneath, between towering roots, ground-level buildings sat nestled into natural clearings, their roofs covered in moss and flowering plants to blend seamlessly with the surroundings.

People bustled about, moving easily between levels of the city. A young woman carried a basket of herbs across a bridge, her feet steady on the swaying ropes, while a man below rolled a cart laden with carved wooden tools. Children darted through the underbrush, their laughter rising as they weaved between the trees and climbed ladders leading to the treetop dwellings.

Red could see the ingenuity of her homeland in every detail: windows were cut carefully into tree trunks, framed with vines that served as both decoration and shade. Water collected from the near-daily rain was funneled through a series of bamboo-like channels into shared cisterns. Gardens spiraled upwards around trunks, cultivated layers of vegetables and herbs growing with the sunlight streaming through the gaps in the canopy. Near the city's edge, a series of nets formed a vertical farm, where berries and fruits hung in easy reach.

Though her chest was heaving from exertion, her eyes were alight with excitement as she burst through a berry patch, juices splattering her skin as she drew closer to success. Dashing along the ground-level paths, she ignored the annoyed shouts following her—not to mention the few concerned Scouts who had started chasing after her—in her rush straight to the center of the city where the Druidic Grove was always in session during daylight hours.

There was one final obstacle blocking her entrance to the oldest-growth area of a set of huge trees grown into a ring to create a massive meeting area: a pair of guards who saw her coming and moved to stand in her way.

Scoffing at the futility of their actions, Red shifted left, then right, managing to run straight between the two guards as they dove in opposite directions. With the System's Whisper showing her path as all clear, she burst directly into the clearing nestled between the six oldest trees in the forest.

Skipping all pleasantries and formalities, Red announced the reason for her arrival between short, sharp gasps of breath. "*Invasion!*"

"What in the actual-" The nearest councilor flinched away from the sudden intrusion and shouted, and he likely would've fallen, were it not for whatever benefits their full class afforded them.

"This is *highly* irregular!" another of the men yelped. "Guards!"

Fully undeterred by the surprised reactions, Red took a deep breath and tried again. "Barely a few hours ago, I witnessed dozens of ships landing along the cliffs on the eastern edge of Canu Moch! As I turned to bring this information back to the leaders of the Wyld, I engaged with a man who must've been their leader. He wore a white wolf pelt helmet and stood nearly seven feet tall. Going by the gear they wear, as well as the insignias on their ships, the invaders are members of *Wolf Warband*!"

Her pronouncement hung in the air, slowly fading as her voice echoed among the tree trunks. For a long moment, all was silent, then Lily noticed the councilors begin to exchange looks. Certainly, there was some unease on their faces, but that was quickly overridden by skepticism deeply etching their expressions. To Lily's dismay, the first of them to speak was none other than Councilor Reynard.

He leaned forward, lips curling into a condescending smile as he lowered his stance until he was nearly crouching. "Thanks for the warning, *Little Red*. I am excited to see what proof you bring us for these outlandish claims. Certainly, *I* don't have to remind you, nor anyone else present, of how our island has no resources worth stealing, is decidedly far away from any mainland, and has never before had the shadow of invasion fall over us. So again… show us your proof, and we will act *immediately*!"

His words had been practically dripping with derision, and as he finished his little speech, he looked over and made exaggerated faces of concern at his peers. Red's jaw dropped as she saw his response to her words, then clenched as she worked to ignore his ridicule in favor of getting her warning taken seriously. "Is this a joke, Councilor Reynard? Do you take your office seriously *in the slightest?* I saw them with my own eyes. Armed, organized, and just as you correctly stated: a threat like we've never faced. I managed to get into the woods and lose my pursuers, and came straight here to-"

"Does this have anything to do with your most recent application to the Scouts of the Wyld being rejected?" Reynard interrupted her callously, his eyes narrowing as a slight snarl curled his lips. "I understand you are *upset*, but we certainly cannot disrupt the peace of the Wyld based on the word of such an… *underdeveloped* 'Scout'. I know you want to make yourself seem more important, but being the little girl who cried wolf is *not* the way to go."

"I… cannot *believe* what I'm hearing." Red seethed as her hand twitched toward the short sword at her side. "You'd let your failure to best my grandmother as a trainer put the entire Wyld at risk? The entire island? I'm telling the truth! There are hundreds, possibly thousands of warriors swarming onto our shores even now. If we don't act now, and begin moving to fend them off, it'll be too late."

The area erupted into conflicting discussions, quickly petering off into doubtful murmuring as Councilor Reynard stepped forward and made soft shooing motions at her. "My apologies if I was *short* with you. Thank you so much for your… vigilance, Lily. We will *certainly* make sure to discuss these wild claims. I'm sure, to you, everything looks like a *huge* threat. Who knows, we might even send out a real Scout to verify your words. For now, you will keep your *tall* tales to yourself, and you will not lead our people to unnecessary panic. Go home. Stay there until you hear from us."

Leaning forward, he spoke in a softer voice, just loud enough to reach Red and the nearby Scout guards who'd stepped up to escort Red away. "That's right. Wee, wee, wee… go all the way home, and stay there, *little pink piggy*."

Hearing her most-hated nickname come from a person who was at least partly in charge of the entire city-state shocked Red to her core. Lily had never been able to find the source of the insulting moniker, but now she believed she was staring right at it. Canu Moch translated as 'singing swine', which was believed to be the first creature the original residents had seen when they landed on its shores. Because of their position of honor in everything to do with their culture, *insults* based on pigs were more insulting than almost anything else.

The Scouts around her began outright laughing, repeating the councilor as they grabbed her shoulders to lead her out of the clearing. "Come on, lil' piggy. No roast beef for you today."

"Show her to the market at the minimum, boys." Reynard chuckled as the two men he had clearly trained himself began forcing Red out of the area. His laughter died in his throat as Red *moved*, unsheathing both her short sword and cleaning knife, dodging around the grasping hands and slamming the pommel of her weapons into the back of both the Scouts' heads at the same time. They dropped like rocks, unconscious in an instant.

"If you want to tell me what to do, Reynard, put me on payroll." Red's voice was laced with bitterness as she flourished her weapons and slammed them into their scabbards. "I've already accomplished what I came here for."

Lifting two fingers on her right hand, she slapped them to her left shoulder and pulled down across her arm, causing her status to appear on her bare skin. For a moment, the text glowed gold... only to be completely overwhelmed as pearlescent light erupted from it: the mark of a skill achieving level ten—*Perfection*.

"In case you're wondering," she stated over her shoulder as casually as possible, walking toward the exit under her own power, "My task was to be the first to warn the leadership of the Wyld of a threat to their continued existence. Now I'm off to begin leveling up my *new* skill."

As she left the encirclement of trees, not a single sound followed her as she stepped out of the Heart of the Wyld.

FIVE

RED LEFT the city behind her, back into the woods where she truly felt she belonged. She took a moment to collect herself and read the new skill she'd earned. As her eyes roved over the words, the fury-distorted glare shifted to soft wonder as her eyes filled with tears of joy. "Years of effort... it was all worth it."

Basic Skill: System's Whisper. Level 10/10.

This is a composite skill which [Perfectly] enhances your trained skills of navigation, stealth, camouflage, survivalism, archery, and environmental awareness. As you have already honed these personal abilities to an exceptional degree, system guidance will come into effect whenever you are outdoors. The guidance will manifest as a subtle glow [Perfectly] highlighting any of the actions you are attempting, as well as flashing a warning when the actions are failing or when your attention needs to be drawn to a specific area.

NEW! Advanced Skill: System's Echo: Level 1/10.

System's Echo is an active skill which allows you to [Minimally] yet innately notice life forms as well as rapidly moving objects in a range of 10 x [1] meters around you for 3 x [1] seconds. Cooldown: 5 minutes -

(30 x [1]) seconds. Upon reaching Perfection, this skill becomes permanently active.

Requirement to advance to level 2: Avoid an otherwise lethal attack or encounter by relying solely on this skill.

"I got an active skill? I got an *active skill*! No one gets active skills, except powerful combatants or wizards!" Barely able to contain her glee, she read over the information once more, counting the number of modifiers carefully. "*Four* level modifiers? I've never heard of *anyone* getting four entire modifiers on their Advanced Skill! I don't think even Grandma has four...!"

Without further ado, she activated the skill for the first time, and suddenly knew where *absolutely* every living thing around her was. The sudden deluge of information didn't make her wince, flinch, or even feel slightly uncomfortable—clearly the innate portion of the skill at work. Like a bird flying for the first time, even if it was a new sensation, it just made sense.

Only a few seconds later, the wide blobs of colorful information in her mind vanished completely, and she felt an astounding sense of loss, as though she'd just been partially blinded. "Yeah... I already want to reach Perfection with this so it can be permanently active. It makes the world so... so beautiful!"

Gaining the new skill washed away practically all of the resentment she'd been feeling toward the Druidic Council, and Red took a moment to decide on her next steps. Settling into a box breathing pattern, she centered herself and aligned her thoughts. "I need to gather more information. I need to see what the Wolf Warband is doing, and bring, **psh**, 'proof' if I want anything to be done about it. Not going to bring it back here, though. I'll bring it to Grandmother. She'll know what to do."

With that thought in mind, Red began rushing through the woods once more, though this time at a far more sustainable pace. All of her practice with leveling her skills had been a massive benefit to this effort, building her endurance to an extreme degree by forcing her to constantly move across the island from coast to coast. It had also tempered her patience, while giving her a deep understanding of exactly how long it should take her to move from one point to another.

Now she was able to put that to good use, hurrying along to the most likely first target of the warband: the coastal village she'd already been to that morning.

As she traveled the forest, the sky—already hidden by the canopy above—began to darken as the sun slowly set. This didn't impair her even slightly, thanks to her Perfected System's Whisper highlighting her path forward. Even better, each time her new skill was off cooldown, Lily made sure to try it out again, marveling at the amazing clarity it brought to the forest around her.

No matter if it was a predator, prey, herb, root vegetable, or some other potent item which would otherwise remain hidden, she was able to get a feel for where it was, though it currently appeared as a smear of whatever its main color was. Even at level one, with the system granting her only minimal knowledge of the life around her, she noticed dozens of things she would've otherwise never even known to look for. This helped to pass the time, and before she knew it, Red was on the verge of stepping out of the tree line and onto the coast.

The first thing she saw was a pillar of cinder-lit smoke reaching into the heavens as if to alert the entire island that they were under attack.

"Looks like they weren't here for a friendly visit, but I never expected that to be the case," Red grimly determined, pulling her bow off her back and stringing it in preparation of hunting a few wolves.

She crept forward into the open area, constantly scanning

the landscape but always coming back to land on the chaos unfolding along the coast. Earlier today, the place had been alive with laughter, competition, and even taunting calls directed at her. Now?

Now it was burning.

With a single glance, Lily determined that she'd arrived only a short while after the invaders. They were still working their way through the huts set up along the beach and weren't yet heavily pursuing the fleeing Coastals. Enormous warriors were stepping out of the small buildings, carrying bracers of fish, enormous nets, and hundreds upon hundreds of earthenware jugs filled with the potent brew the Coastals seemed to drink constantly. Surprisingly, the few warriors who noticeably sampled the jugs were harshly reprimanded and sent to search the next huts after piling their loot in a central location.

Shouting drew Lily's attention over to a group of Coastals pouring out of the back of a building a raider had just entered. Their faces were drawn with fear, and they squealed like stuck pigs as the armed man casually stepped out of the house and began following them. Seeing her chance, the System's Scout lifted her bow and sent an arrow arcing into the air.

Thanks to her Wyld Rose skill, the projectile seemed to practically ignore crosswinds and even some gravity, reaching far, *far* farther than it otherwise should have. As she was attacking a person, the Perfected skill was only considered to have a 'Moderate' enhancement on it. Still, that was more than enough for the silent weapon to cross the intervening space and bury itself into the huge man's thigh. From this distance, she couldn't hear his shout of pain and surprise, but Lily was able to see him drop to the ground clutching at his leg.

Unexpectedly, the Coasties shifted their escape and began charging straight at where Red was now standing, in full view of anyone who cared to look. The expressions on their faces, though still fearful, were shining with hope as they stared her down like a herd of cattle charging a lion. More and more fleeing Coasties begin following after the main group, turning into a stampede of people rushing her. The surging crowd caught the attention of the raiders, and dozens of them began pounding after the slow, undefended island inhabitants.

"Oh, for system's *sake*!" Red grumbled as she lifted her bow once more, launching off arrow after precious arrow. She'd made them herself, sourcing the wood, capturing and plucking owls for the fletching, and using the tendons of the smaller creatures she hunted to bind it all together. Her arrows were excruciatingly well made, and she was almost always able to collect them after using them. Now, she was positive they were gone for good. "Why are you all coming here? You're going to get us all killed!"

Her arrows found their mark more often than not, tiny alterations in their flight always somehow managing to line up with the warriors who attempted to dodge. It helped some that she was aiming to incapacitate, not kill, else she was certain her shots would continually miss as the Perfected system assistance failed—this was a hunting skill, not one meant for warfare. The distinction had never felt so important before today, but then again, there were many first happening on Canu Moch this day.

People began streaming past her, shouting their thanks and quizzing her with dozens of confusing questions. Finally, an annoyingly familiar face filled her view, and Red had to dodge to the side as the man she'd led home that very morning tried to wrap her in a bear hug. "You came back for us! I knew you were one of those nice people, just like we always thought you were! All the things you said this morning were just for show, weren't they? Come here! What are you doing?"

"What am I doing? What are *you* doing?" Red pulled out another arrow and let it fly, barely managing to guide it into a raider's arm as he lifted an axe to chop at a fleeing Coasty. "Get out of my way, or they're going to start cutting your people down!"

"Oh, yeah. That makes sense." The man, infuriatingly enough, stood still for a long few seconds, clearly in deep thought. "Right. See you in the woods!"

Red, completely engrossed in her task, failed to understand his meaning immediately. Then her eyes went wide, and she looked over her shoulder for the man, who had already vanished. "No! Don't go into... where did you go? *System Echo!*"

Immediately, she was able to sense a bright, tan smear of color as the man literally crawled through a bush behind her, making her wonder if that was his normal method of getting through the woods. She blinked, realizing that was indeed how she had originally found him today...

Then a strange sensation filled her mind. Something was moving quickly only a few meters away from her, but it *wasn't* alive. She was moving before her conscious mind caught up, diving out of the way as a javelin as thick as her wrist pierced the air where she'd been standing only a fraction of a second before.

Skill increase! System Echo [Level 1 (Minimal) → Level 2 (Limited)]!

Requirement to advance to level 3: Successfully anticipate, then avoid or neutralize at least three separate, consecutive attacks which would otherwise be lethal; without engaging in direct combat. This must be completed within a single activation of System Echo.

The information poured into her mind, and she knew it would also appear on her arm if she had the time to look. Wide-eyed, Red followed the angle of the attack back, and back, and back... her gaze finally landing on a familiar brute of a man wearing a white wolf helmet. She went stock-still as he began charging up the slope, only breaking out of her adrenaline-fueled stupor as a chant from the other raiders rose into the air.

"Drwg Mawr. Drwg Mawr. *Drwg Mawr!*"

Deciding against facing the huge warrior again, especially in the open, Red took a few slow, steady steps backward. As soon as she was in the forest once more, she vanished from his view—easily discernible thanks to how his stare went from locked onto her to unfocused and searching. She lifted her bow, pulled back an arrow, and aimed the deadly tip at him… only for a hand to reach out of the darkness and grab her.

She fell back with a yelp as the annoying trespasser from that morning pulled her into the woods. "Whew! Glad I got there in time; there were invaders coming! I think I might've just saved your life. So, you know, now you owe me."

Lily chopped down at his arm with her left hand, smacking it away hard enough that she heard a slight *cracking*, then returned to the edge of the woods while pulling the arrow back into position.

"That would have only pinned your cloak to a tree! There must be words between us, crimson wisp of the forest." Apparently, the huge man had decided against following after her and was now walking away from the edge of the forest, while very carefully keeping his guard up. "I shan't harm you, on my honor! Show yourself, and we shall parley."

"Step into the open?" With a sigh, she lowered her bow and turned to retreat deeper into the forest. "You've got to be *kidding* me."

"Eee…!" The Coasty whined as he got into her personal space once more, using his undamaged arm to shove the other toward her face. "Look! I think you *broke* it!"

CHAPTER

SIX

THE NEXT FORTY-EIGHT hours of Red's life were nothing short of a crucible to forge her patience. Specifically: a trial by Coasties.

Leading a large group of unprepared, undisciplined, *ungrateful* coast dwellers through the Wyld tested her patience and skills to their absolute limits. What was a journey of only a few hours for *her* was an absolute nightmare for the people who'd only ever viewed the forest as a constant in the distance. To them, it was a place to trade for food, at best. At worst, it was a source of amusement when other people were forced to save them.

Frankly, Red was completely shocked by the sheer number and variety of times someone tried to off themselves through completely preventable, common-sense methods for just... just no reason whatsoever. The first several hours were filled by merely collecting the group, which had scattered in all directions. Dozens of people in earshot of each other were shouting for help, trying to find each other, and somehow walking right past each other by only a few feet.

Eventually, she needed to set a group down, physically *forcing* them to sit in a few cases, then went out and individually collected the others. After the initial task of collecting everyone, there'd been another half hour wasted as she gathered some of the people she had *already* collected once, who had ignored her directions and gone off to find someone they were missing. By midnight, they were less than a quarter mile into the forest, and most of the group had laid down wherever they'd been sat and were snoring.

Very loudly.

Red was about ready to rip her hair out when she checked the group one last time, finding that not a single person had bothered to stay awake to keep watch. She spent a sleepless night activating her new skill over and over, sending arrows whistling into the darkness to put down active threats to the sleeping people—such as pinning snakes to logs, and even dropping a couple deer so there would be a ready source of food upon their waking.

She butchered the deer out of sight, remembering the annoying man's reaction to the task, and started a few small fires in pits that she carefully dug out and circled with rocks. Lily set the meat up to cook, then waited patiently for the suddenly homeless people to sleep off the terror of their first night in the woods. At some point, Lily dozed off lightly, trusting in her training and skills to keep her safe for the last couple hours before sunrise…

… only to be awoken by a terrible stench. Nose twitching, Red hopped up and looked around, horrified to find how all the Coastals had relieved themselves wherever was convenient. In most cases, that meant the nearest tree or bush, with no attempt to bury the leavings. "Celestials, how'd these people ever survive until now? Disease must run rampant in their community."

Lily made a silent promise to herself that she'd never accept food or drink which had been prepared by a Coasty. She got up and took a deep breath, mentally preparing herself to hand out the cooked venison, only to find that both of the deer had already been fully devoured. There was a pile of bones next to each of the fires, with clear marks on them to show they'd been gnawed on. Even worse, less than half the group was even awake, meaning they'd go hungry even while the others had stuffed themselves so much they were groaning in pain as they rubbed their distended bellies.

Lifting her hands, she checked to see if they were shaking as much as she felt they should be. Deciding against wasting her breath telling them off, she walked around and began gently kicking everyone to get them on their feet. "Let's go, people! We've got a lot of ground to cover today, no one wants to be here when the warband gets bored on the coast and begins invading the Wyld! Get into a line, let's-"

"I'm hungry!" As soon as the first voice announced their discomfort, dozens of other complaints filled the air only moments later.

"I think I slept on my neck wrong."

"Where's the well? I'm thirsty. Actually, forget water, where's the booze? Last night was *rough*."

A huge number of people began clamoring for libations, and all Lily could do was stand there and stare as the group devolved into various factions all shouting about their issues and whose was most important. She tried yelling over them to get their attention, but found that her voice was lost among theirs extremely quickly. Eventually, she decided to simply let them argue until they were exhausted, losing another hour in the process. While she waited, she walked over to the most familiar of the Coasties and pulled him aside for a short conversation.

"You. Chuckles," she started with teeth grit so hard they were in danger of breaking. "Why'd no one think to share the food? Or save it? Two entire deer should've been plenty for everyone to have a good meal. Instead... *this*."

The man she'd known since the previous morning shrugged and let out a soft laugh. "Chuckles, huh? Not the worst thing I've ever been called. I'll roll with it. But hey, we're not exactly crazy prepper survivalists like you guys are, you know? Life's clearly different, *better*, for us."

"How is this disgusting behavior better? None of you can decide on anything, you destroy everything in your path, and you gorge yourself on whatever food is available. Celestial's sake, you make your homes out of *grass*!" Red finally lost her temper and began venting at the Coasty. "You say life is better? How can you think this is better? You're so unprepared! Do you *never* face any hardships?"

Chuckles merely shrugged once more and allowed a relaxed smile to break through the tired expression he'd been wearing. "This is what I'm talking about. Life should be simple. Fun. It could be, for everyone on the island, but all y'all Wyld people got sticks up your butt. Let's not even talk about Bleakrock, cuz, ya know, no one knows about them. Think about it for a moment... don't you know the island sits right in the middle of a massive fish migration path? There are warm currents flowing along the north and south shores, so why should there be hardship?"

Lily tried to think of an answer for the question, but Chuckles simply barreled on. "As for why we build our houses out of straw, grass, or leaves? Meh. We don't need anything super so-fish-ticated. We've got plenty of building materials, and almost everyone has a way to dry out their living space to be as comfortable as possible. We don't have boats or anything fancy like that. We don't need them, 'cause guess what? You need food? You just walk up to the edge of the sea, toss in a net, and bam! Full catch of fish almost every time."

Seeing a lifeline as he had brought up skills, Red grabbed onto it and asked almost desperately, "What about training? You have to have people who want more, who have classes that can become powerful! How are you supposed to get skills or training if-"

Waving her off, Chuckles shook his head and interrupted,

"Like I said, we've got everything we need. *Why* do we need more? Almost everyone gets skills and classes which are perfectly suited to us. It's all about quality of life, Red Riding Hood. I've got a swimmer class that lets me go through water faster than you can run on flat ground. I can float and relax in the sun the entire day without getting tired, and when I get out? I snap my fingers, and I'm dry."

"Your skills are all... leisure?" The very idea was deeply uncomfortable to the Scout, who'd spent both decades of her life training to be the pinnacle of her class. "But..."

Chuckles looked around the woods, shivering slightly. "Look, life is supposed to be about enjoying what we have. We don't want to fight and struggle in the woods. We've never been invaded before, so why's that something we should have prepared for? Generations of our ancestors lived exactly the way we do, and it's... I already miss it. Plus, look at these arms! Nets are heavy, and swimming is great exercise."

For the first time, Red managed to glimpse past the slight veneer of annoyance she always had when looking at the Coasties and actually inspected the man closely. He was covered in lean muscle, shaped in such a way to let him cut through the water easily. Somehow, in her head, she'd always pictured them as chubby little piggies, but the reality in front of her was different. "I suppose... I guess I understand it a little. But, out here, in the Wyld, it's not enough. You need more than a net and a plan to relax."

"Good thing we have you then, isn't it, Red?" Chuckles went in for a hug, which she easily avoided. "Ahh, had to try. Guess you aren't Red-y. Anyway, we've all heard the stories. Why do you think we get bonus points if we find *you* if we're lost in the woods? Because you're the best out of all the Wyldlings. The hardest to find, the gentlest when you return us to the coast. Everyone knows it; that's why we mess with you so much."

Red was left shocked, blinking rapidly as she took in this

new information. Before she could inquire further, the most argumentative among the Coasties finally went quiet, joining the others in sitting down and panting for air, sweat rolling down their face. To her surprise, everyone was looking at her, waiting to hear what the final decision would be. Just like that, she felt the stone around her heart crack slightly as she looked at these fun-loving fish eaters, while simultaneously feeling a weight of responsibility settle on her shoulders.

Taking a deep breath and standing straight, Lily began speaking loudly now that she was finally able to be heard. "Listen up, everyone. I'm going to do my best to keep you alive and in good condition until we get to the Heart of the Wyld. Some things need to change, and I have hard facts for you. Right now, we're just trying to survive. You need to understand that, when I tell you something, you need to *listen*. If you didn't get any food today, it's because the people who woke up first ate *all of it* with no regard for the rest of you. If you're thirsty, it's because you shouted over me when I tried to tell you there was a stream right over there-"

Immediately dozens of people stood and rushed into the underbrush, half of them missing the thin stream entirely and continuing deeper into the forest. Lily leaned back slightly, groaning as she put her hands on her head. "What have I gotten myself into?"

It was the duty of all Scouts in the Wyld to keep people alive when possible, and as the day slowly passed, Lily needed to remind herself of that fact near-constantly. The conversation with Chuckles had helped a lot, and the knowledge that the Coasties had such deep faith in her helped her keep her cool when she might otherwise have gently stabbed someone to get them moving in the right direction.

Any danger was blithely ignored, with the Coasties practically throwing themselves headlong at whatever would kill them fastest. "That's a *snake*, not a pretty ribbon! You! If you eat those, I'm leaving you here. It might not kill you, but you'll have constant diarrhea for at least six hours. What do you *mean* he ate them and said they tasted fine? Both of you, back of the group. I'm not making other people walk through your... trail."

Another issue was their absolute lack of training for moving through the woods. They stumbled over roots, flinched at every rustle of leaves, seeming on the edge of panic at all times—*except* when she was warning them about actual danger. Lily needed to constantly circle the group, keeping them together as if herding sheep on an open plain. While she did so, the Scout made sure to do her best to cover *almost* all traces of their passing, having no desire to be the one to lead Wolf Warband to the Heart of the Wyld.

Sustenance quickly became a major hurdle. Just as Chuckles had explained, the Coasties were used to nearly unlimited food and drink with a negligible amount of effort. What little time Lily had when not pushing exhausted people along was spent gathering food wherever possible. It didn't matter if it was meat, vegetables, or the very rare fruit, she needed to keep constant track of who'd recently been given food, or the same person would snatch it from her hands and into their mouth over and over.

They consumed everything in their path with no regard for the people for the hungry coming behind them, chewing with their mouths open and laughing as scraps fell to the ground only to be stepped on and made inedible for anyone else. Bizarrely enough, Lily needed to keep slapping leaves, flowers, moss, and even tree bark from hands, or force open their jaws if they were already chomping away. The Coasties actually had no idea what was inedible, what their bodies would reject violently.

Even with everything else they had going against them, perhaps the most concerning thing to Red was their absolutely casual relationship with fire. Far too many among them had a skill which allowed for the rapid drying of material, granting them dry wood and leaves with only a moment's focus.

On multiple occasions, she'd caught them starting fires for warmth, to try and cook something they'd skewered, or simply to have a little extra light as they walked through the permanent dusk the overhead canopy created. Time after time, she intervened, dousing flames and telling people *exactly* what would happen if their fire got out of control.

One day turned into two, but Lily persevered as stoically as possible—clearly observing how they would quickly expire without her help. She put in all effort possible to keep them safe and healthy: guiding them, feeding them, leading them to water... though her strong sense of duty stayed quiet when she contemplated digging a latrine for them.

There were some things she just wasn't willing to do.

They covered the terrain slowly, but eventually got deep enough into the forest where they found a clear path even the Coasties couldn't get too lost on. Once on firmer ground, they managed to pick up speed. With a deep sense of relief, Lily started murmuring a new mantra.

"Only a few hours until the Heart of the Wyld comes into view."

CHAPTER
SEVEN

LILY HAD her eyes on the dividing line between forest and city and kept needing to hold herself back from running forward and being done with this group for good. In fact, she was so focused that she almost didn't react in time when her System's Whisper skill suddenly flashed—so intently it nearly blocked her vision. Reflexively, she activated System's Echo and instantly understood what was happening.

The leadership of the Wyld apparently *had* decided to take her warning seriously. All around her were fast-moving objects, smears of brown and black coming toward her—the result of a central tripwire being stumbled over by someone behind her. Huge logs were swinging toward the path on either side of her, aiming to crush them between their trunks. Saplings which had been bent back and studded with sharpened metal were springing back into position. Lastly, an arrow aimed at her heart whistled through the air.

The only reason Red was able to react at all was her skill forcing her mind to fully understand the position of the things rushing toward her. Flipping her unstrung bow forward, she got it into position just in time for the arrow to *thunk* into the wood instead of her body.

"No!" The sharp cry followed on the wind behind the arrow, clearly a Scout who had thoughtlessly sent the projectile before realizing who he was attacking. Lily had no time to be angry about the situation, ducking, diving, and rolling as the saplings whipped around. She sprang into a backflip and tucked into a roll in midair as the logs ended their pendulous motion by slamming into each other with a thunderous *wham*-

-less than a foot below her airborne body. She landed atop the spent trap, whirling around to look at the people she'd been leading, only for her heart to sink into her stomach.

They'd been walking two by two along the path, and the first three ranks had been caught in the log trap. Six people had been pulverized, and even now blood was pouring out of their lifeless bodies and soaking into the forest floor. Three heartbeats later, the screaming began as the situation sank in, and the Coasties came out of shock.

Lily turned toward the Scout in the distance and roared, "Are you *kidding me*? I've kept all of them alive for the last two days, and not a single person is in the forest making sure *innocents* don't stumble into traps! You foul, *arrogant*, rank bast-!"

"Lily Red!" The man she was shouting at bellowed in return. "I knew you were mad at Reynard for refusing your application, but I didn't realize you were a traitor! How many people did you bring here? A group *that* size? You're going to lead Wolf Warband right to us! Our blood will be on your hands!"

"I *covered* our trail!" She raged in return, grasping the arrow embedded in her bow and yanking it out, barely stopping herself from stringing the weapon and sending the shaft back at its owner. "*I've* been out there performing the duty of a Scout, keeping people alive in the Wyld, while the rest of you have clearly been cowering here and setting up ways to kill off people running for their lives!"

"Are you calling me a coward-?"

"Yes I am!" Lily shouted back without a moment's hesitation, angry tears spilling onto her cheeks. "Or you would be out here, guiding people to safety!"

There were a long few seconds where nothing was said, the only sounds being Lily heaving for air and the Coasties behind her sobbing at the sudden violence and deaths.

Finally, the Scout in the distance reluctantly, begrudgingly, began speaking once more. "By the order of the Druidic Circle, the Coasties running through the woods are to be left to their own devices until the situation is resolved. They will serve us best by creating false trails for the Wolf Warband to follow, so our forces can slowly whittle theirs down."

Jaw dropping, Lily gasped in shock and horror at the words she'd just heard. Regaining control of herself, it still took several attempts before she was able to form words. "That order will kill more people than the invaders have."

"Wasn't my decision. I'm just doing what I'm supposed to do." The Scout sank back, vanishing into the woods before he could make a fool of himself any further.

Red's heart was pounding in her chest, absolute disgust with the leadership of the Wyld filling her like never before. She turned and began attempting to comfort the remaining Coasties, helping them bundle up their slain fellows so they could be properly carried along.

Even with all the heartbreak and horror they had suddenly been through, the Coasties still followed her into the wooden city, though they were silent and dispirited as they looked around with hollow eyes.

With each step they took, Lily attempted to breathe deeply and look for any silver lining in the situation. "We're here... after *that* feces-show introduction, they should at least be relatively safe for now. There will be food, water, and a place for them to sleep. I..."

She wasn't exactly sure what she would do next, but as her

spinning mind settled slightly, Lily realized there was a notification in her mind. Running her fingers along her arm, she took a moment to relish in the comforting sensation of having at least gained *something* from the debacle.

Skill increase! System Echo [Level 2 (Limited) → Level 3 (Rudimentary)]!

System's Echo is an active skill which allows you to [Rudimentarily] yet innately notice life forms as well as rapidly moving objects in a range of [30] meters around you for [9] seconds. Cooldown: [3 minutes, 30 seconds]. Upon reaching Perfection, this skill becomes permanently active.

Requirement to advance to level 4: Leading a group of at least nine people, coordinate and get them through a perilous situation using System's Echo, where your guidance is instrumental in the group surviving a potentially deadly threat without any of your group taking injuries.

"Thirty meters, huh? That covers a lot of space now." Red shook her head in frustration, knowing that, if she'd had the skill active only a few seconds earlier, she would've saved half a dozen lives. "I'm going to keep this active as often as possible... I can't believe that just happened."

"Hey. I hope you're not up here blaming yourself for what that future *villain* just did to us." Chuckles stepped forward and strode along with her, his longer legs allowing him to keep pace easily. "All of us totally understand the only reason we made it this far in the first place is because of you. Plus, you know, they lived a good life. It helps that they went out quick. No suffering. That's how all of us want to go... or maybe drowning."

"They shouldn't have died in the first place, Chuckles," Red muttered, unable to face him at the moment. "That's not our way. We're Scouts. We're supposed to keep people safe, guide them, protect them... not use them as bait, creating

false trails to keep ourselves safe using their suffering. This is…
it's wrong on a level I can't even explain to you, because you
aren't a member of the Wyld. You don't know our ways."

The Coasty went silent for a moment, then he reached out
and patted her on the shoulder. For the first time, she didn't
flinch away from his touch. "Maybe you actually have more in
common with us than you do with them. Maybe, when this is
all over, you come and try out our lifestyle on the coast?"

"No. Thanks for the offer, but that sounds incredibly
unappealing to me." Red's words started harsh, but she tried
to gentle them as she realized how she sounded. "I appreciate
your outlook on life more than I did even a few days ago, and
I'd even say I've gained some new perspective. But I want
more from life than just… coasting along. I don't know exactly
what it is I want. Not yet. I'm just going to keep getting
stronger and enhancing my skills until I figure it out."

A large group of people were walking toward them, only a
few of whom Lily vaguely recognized. They had mixed
expressions on their faces, relief and concern warring with
each other as they took in the sight of the newcomers. As the
two groups approached each other, Red tensed up, only to let
out a sigh of relief as she noticed the locals carrying pots of
stew, blankets, and clean clothes.

"We heard what happened." A matronly woman stepped
forward, gathering all eyes to her. "You poor dears, losing your
home like that! Come along, we've set up a large campsite for
everyone who makes it here. There's an area to get clean and
plenty of bedrolls set out under the sky. Let's get you fed and
comfortable."

Just like that, Red was able to transfer the care of the
Coastals to the townsfolk of the Wyld. Only a couple of
them even looked back or acknowledged her hard work.
Chuckles was among them, as well as a few of the others
she'd personally rescued from poisoning or another equally
arduous death. Even so, Lily didn't begrudge the others;

they'd gone through more hardship in the last forty-eight hours than they had in literally their entire lives to this point.

She simply watched them go until they vanished behind the tree line. As the last of them was hidden, Red finished her countdown and activated System's Echo at the new level for the first time. For a long moment, she merely stood still, trying to get used to the sheer amount of information pouring into her mind, as well as how the blurs of life now had distinct shapes to them instead of being only colorful streaks or blobs.

Then, she began the task of setting mental filters on the information, just as she'd once needed to consciously and regularly do with System's Whisper. Lily removed all traces of non-poisonous bugs to start, then moss and other plants with only a hint of vitality in them. By the time the skill ended a handful of seconds later, there was only a *fraction* of the amount of information to parse.

"Haaa." Letting out a long, slow breath, she resigned herself to several years of adjusting the feedback from the skill; until she got it exactly how she wanted it to be for each unique situation she'd find herself in. Opening her eyes, which she hadn't even realized she'd closed, Lily began walking toward the edge of the city once more. Her gaze roved the ground, looking for tripwires—not at all keen to reenact the situation from earlier.

As it turned out, her moment of respite was destined to be short-lived. A deep voice echoed across the open area between the denser forest and the cultivated city. "*Hold*! Lily Red, you are hereby summoned to account for your actions to the Druidic Council!"

Her left eyebrow twitched as she whirled around, scarlet cloak flapping with the motion. "They want me to account for *my* actions? Really? Excellent, I feel I have a few *choice* words for them as well."

"You are to surrender your weapons before entering the

clearing," the guard who had shouted for her imperiously stated.

Red scoffed at his demand, eyeing him up and down. "Is that something they said, or is this you trying to be petty because I knocked you out the last time you tried to grab me?"

"Little of this, little of that." He glared at her while gripping the hilt of his still-sheathed sword.

Lifting her arms away from her sides, Red walked toward him at speed. "You're welcome to try and take them from me. Otherwise, get out of the way."

Only a few minutes later, Lily marched into the council's clearing, all of her weapons still in their rightful place on her body. She looked around at the dark, thunderous expressions on the faces of the Druidic Grove, and opened her mouth to begin speaking.

Before she could get a single word out, Reynard shouted an accusation at her, his voice wavering between disbelief and fury. "You brought them right to us! I've already heard reports of your disregard for our orders, your smug satisfaction in putting us all at risk. You should have scattered those Coasties through the forest and bought us time to prepare for war!"

Red looked around at the others in the clearing, waiting for someone else to speak. No one did, so she simply scoffed and turned on her heel.

"Nope."

"What are you doing? Where are you going? Get back here and-"

Lily answered the councilor with a single, rude gesture over her shoulder, not bothering to look back. "You're leaving people to die. I find you derelict in your duty. *I'm* going out there to save as many people as I can, and you're welcome to show your true colors to everyone in the Wyld by trying to stop me."

She stormed out of town, honestly surprised no one came after her or tried to stop her. Once it was obvious she had shamed them into at *least* leaving her to her own devices, Lily took a moment to make a real plan.

"This is too much for me on my own. I need help." She adjusted her path to go east, walking between two trees she was extremely familiar with. "Over the river and through the woods. To Grandmother's house I go."

EIGHT

THERE WERE all sorts of reasons to speak with Grandmother and bring the invasion to her attention. First and foremost, being the greatest Scout trainer in Canu Moch required her to be the best Scout *on* the island. Beyond all the wisdom and skills she'd achieved over the years, there was one massive boon she had which no one else could claim.

She had gained access to her Full Class Breakthrough Skill.

This made Grandmother faster, stronger, more adept, better at training, and overall deadlier than any twenty other people on the island combined—enough to wrestle the leader of Wolf Warband and force him into submission. One time, after swearing her to secrecy, Grandmother had shown Red *exactly* what such a powerful skill afforded her.

Upon activating her power, the frail-seeming woman had suddenly vanished from Lily's vision. She hadn't become invisible; she'd simply moved so fast the young woman couldn't follow her with her eyes. Grandmother's skill gave her a multiplier to all of her physical stats, and at skill level five, she had five *times* more physical strength, speed, and dexterity than the most fit and powerful runner-up.

To the young Red's delight, her mentor had flashed over to a young tree, ripped it out of the ground—roots and all—then casually snapped the tree in half with her hands, not even bothering to bend it over her knee. Since then, Red had been devoting her life to being able to do something on that level. The memory had driven her for more than fifteen years.

Now, Lily's mind was buzzing with ideas and plans, each one more grandiose than the other. "Should I ask her to work with me on rescue operations? With her experience, we'd be able to gather dozens, maybe *hundreds* of Coasties before they die of dehydration or... other things."

She grimaced as the all-too-vivid memory of her charges getting smashed between tree trunk traps flashed through her mind. Trying to shake it off, she continued to murmur, "Or, maybe I should ask her to be involved with the war effort directly? If there's anyone who could fight that huge warrior in direct combat, it would be her. I mean, she'd never need to get that close, I bet she could snipe him with an arrow from halfway across the island!"

"Hmm... then again, there are a *lot* of warriors. Maybe we could go and set up a large variety of traps, far away from the city, and whittle them down?" She continued musing over these and several other perfectly acceptable ideas as she hurried along.

It wasn't a terribly far distance from the city to Grandmother's house, only an hour of running at a medium intensity. Still, once upon a time, Red had been annoyed by the stretch between her home and civilization. She had originally thought the entire reason Grandmother lived so far away was to manage the Class Shrine, but after her recent encounters with the politicians of the Wyld... she was starting to have her doubts.

Lily was only now starting to *appreciate* how far out of the way someone needed to go to bother them. There were plenty of other people who would *literally* fight for the honor of being in charge of guarding a Class Shrine. After seeing how vicious Councilor Reynard was, she was starting to put together a decent picture of what Grandmother's life may have looked like before Lily was aware enough to understand the intricacies and frustrations her grandmother must have had to deal with.

Still, the house was secluded, in another area of extreme old growth similar to the Heart of the Wyld itself. Lily had loved growing up between the freedom of the forest and the recessed Scout training area Grandmother had cultivated behind the house. It was enclosed on all sides by natural-seeming stone, though she'd never been able to wheedle it out of the older lady whether it truly was natural or not.

Ever since she was young, she had gone back there to watch dozens upon dozens of Scouts get expert training, learn how to use new tools, track prey, and set traps. It wouldn't be incorrect to say Lily knew this area of the forest, her home, better than anywhere else.

That was why, as she grew closer, Lily immediately understood that something was terribly, terribly wrong.

Smoke was rising from the chimney, but it was thick and black, as though someone were using wet wood instead of what had been properly stored in the shed outside. As she stepped closer to the house, Lily seemed to pass over some invisible line. On the other side of it, no birds were singing, no animals were calling, and not even bugs were buzzing. Her trained eyes swept over the area, quickly picking up the signs of a struggle.

A *massive* struggle.

The earth just outside the door had been deeply gouged, as if someone had taken a shovel and somehow managed to scoop up and overturn dozens of meters of topsoil at once, throwing it into the air and splattering it across the wood paneling. Branches were broken, and slightly farther from the house, entire trees had been shattered. Heart sinking, Red picked up the pace and rushed toward home.

"Did Wolf Warband already arrive? Grandmother! Please tell me you're okay!" Red slammed the door open, sword in hand, and immediately scanned the interior of the house. Bizarrely enough, for as damaged and unsettling as the outside had been, the interior of the house hadn't changed in the slightest. The fire was burning, roaring really, in the fireplace where it belonged. Sure, there was more wood piled in than she'd ever seen her grandmother use at once before, but maybe she was just cold?

No dishes were broken; no furniture overturned. In fact, the very person she had come to see was standing next to her massive stew pot with her back to Lily, slowly stirring the enormous cauldron.

Letting out a massive sigh of relief, Red sheathed her sword and stepped inside. "Grandmother! What happened here? I was so worried when I saw..."

With each step forward, her System's Whisper skill—which she'd been ignoring in her panic—pulsed ever brighter, finally shifting over to black and white strobing, a warning Red had never seen before, just as Grandmother began to turn toward her.

"What are...?" Lily went corpse-still as the person *imitating* her grandmother turned to face her fully. It was *absolutely* the face of woman she was looking for, though something was clearly horrifyingly wrong. All across the elderly woman's body, her muscles were twitching and writhing. The eyes which met hers were not the warm, loving, and knowing ones she remembered. They were cold and foreign, staring at her without recognition.

Her mouth opened, and a voice came out; a cruel facsimile falsetto mimicking Grandmother's normal voice. "Oh, there you are... child. I was just making some stew to recover my strength before I went to check on the Class Shrine. Would you mind getting the door open for me over there, so I can make sure everything is okay?"

Red's hand shifted toward her just-sheathed sword, the motion perfectly tracked by the black-sclera eyes of the imposter. Before she could properly draw her weapon, System's Whisper gained an auditory component for the first time in her life, literally *buzzing* at Lily as her entire vision shifted to static. A constant shifting of black and white warned her how she was about to attempt an absolutely lethal action. Instead of following through, she forced her hands to relax and tried to put a smile on her face.

It must've worked, because the creature—which had crouched slightly as though to spring at her—relaxed as well.

"Of course... Grandmother. Don't worry, I remember the correct combination of the locks and how important it is to open it correctly the *first* time, so as to not set off the traps you've put in place." At her words, the imposter's head snapped slightly to the side, not like a cute puppy hearing something interesting, instead being closer to the insectile motion of a praying mantis spotting a ladybug. "Especially all of the alchemical explosives."

Ever so slowly, Grandmother's head bobbed up and down, still in a position anyone normal would feel uncomfortable remaining in. "That would be just wonderful. See that you do so *immediately*."

"Might I just say, I can tell you've been working on your-self." Red eased herself across the room, not showing her back to the imposter for a second. "It's impressive how you managed to make your eyes bulge out and pull the skin taut. Really hides the few wrinkles you've been accruing."

As she watched, the face of her grandmother adjusted itself, coming closer to what it had been the last time Red had seen her. The muscles just under her eyes were twitching rapidly, as though all of the creature's focus had shifted to attempting to keep the face in place. "Yes, you know… as a Scout, I always have my eyes open wide. The better to see you with, my dear."

Seeing as how the creature was distracted and focused internally, its predatory gaze wandering off of Red and going distant in an attempt at better control of its body, she decided to keep pushing her luck. "I've never noticed how wonderful your control over your ear muscles are. Your ears are practically straight out from the sides of your head!"

Lily kept shifting her stance, trying to hide the hilt of her sword so as to be able to draw it without the creature being able to react in time.

The ears she'd just reference fluttered back and forth like a bird's wings, and the imposter showed a wide smile, with the skin around its mouth pulling back to show almost all of its teeth as it tried to assert control of the body it was in. "What can I say? All the better to hear you with."

"Oh, it seems I left my key outside." Red muttered as she pretended to jiggle the door handle, then shrugged and began carefully returning toward the door she'd entered through. "Must have left it in my pack. I'll be right back."

"Trying to leave so soon? But we just got reunited, *grand… daughter.*" The creature hissed, its face contorting grotesquely as it stepped forward slightly.

Red stopped moving, and so did it. Her mind began spinning up ideas, plotting out how she should fight this eminently dangerous *Monster.* She decided to treat it no differently than any other apex predator, keeping her motions small, her voice cadence even, showing no threatening movements while simultaneously not acting afraid. Even so, she knew a fight was coming. Her hand drifted ever so slowly toward her sword, trying to keep the motion as natural-looking as possible.

"You know, there's one other thing I'm noticing. Your mouth is so wide. I've never noticed what big teeth you have."

The creature leaned closer, its center of gravity lowering

as her grandmother's mouth opened unnaturally wide. Red could feel a dark chill, a draining sensation that sapped her vitality as the imposter stopped attempting to hide its true nature, lunging across the room at her with a screech.

"All the better to *eat* you with!"

NINE

LILY DOVE FORWARD, the sheer improbable act of dodging *toward* it being the only reason she managed to escape its wide grasp as it flew over her head. As it passed by her, the Scout looked up and scanned its body, searching for weaknesses, but only flinching as she got a close-up view of how the veins were pulsating with black blood—which added a strange, tattooed look to what could only be a Skinwalker.

As soon as the beast touched down, it spun in place and threw itself toward her once again, its movements accompanied by a nauseating crackling as its bones, cartilage, and tendons were adjusted and strained to the limits. Lily had managed to unsheathe her sword as she rolled to her feet and took advantage of the entity's telegraphed movements to lash out with a textbook-perfect slice of her short sword.

To her shock, the creature paused and allowed her sword to slam into its outstretched hand. Then it lifted its palm, showing Lily where her blade had cut through the skin, but failed to go much deeper than that. "Futile! You have but one option, red-headed step-child! Open the path for me. Grant me access to the Class Shrine, and you *may* even be able to escape with your life while I am distracted!"

"No!" Lily stabbed forward with her sword once more, only for the tip of the blade to barely sink into the hand which had already been cut. She swallowed a lump in her throat at having to deal with the horror of fighting such a vile beast—coupled with attacking her only relative's corpse; for that was what Grandmother had been reduced to: a puppet controlled by some foul, cursed being.

There was nothing left of the powerful woman she'd once known, who had raised her. Nothing beyond the *husk* she had left behind upon expiring. The Skinwalker let out a **hiss** more of agitation than pain, flickering back a few inches and lifting its palm once more—this time to show Red exactly why her attacks were useless.

As she looked on, the skin she'd just cut three times was pressed together, completely halting the flow of the black ichor which had replaced the blood previously pumping through the veins. Tiny fibers of skin wove out, joining together and sealing the wound—leaving it looking as though it had never been damaged in the first place.

"I *will* get access to it." The Skinwalker let out a hissing chuckle as it tracked Red's darting eyes, suddenly flowing to the side and blocking the only door offering escape from the building. "You can either facilitate my ascension and have a chance to escape while I am earning a new class, or I can feed on your life force and wait until I grow strong enough to penetrate the defenses on my own."

Lily threw herself to the side, ducking behind the large meal preparation island in the center of the open-concept room to give herself a little bit of cover. As her natural state was stoic and silent, she kept her mouth closed as she analyzed the creature, continuing to search desperately for a weakness.

"No, no, *deary*, I understand your thoughts." The Skinwalker mocked in its falsetto tone. "You think you have a chance against me, when the one who trained you did not. You think you can *escape*, perhaps get help? Allow me to dissuade you. First, I am faster than you, stronger than you, and far more cunning. Secondly… do you think I chose *now* of all times to make my attempt by *accident?* This island is being invaded. There is no help coming. There is only you and me. You will open that door. Or you will-"

The Skinwalker lunged forward with a scream, attempting to catch Lily off guard by interrupting itself, but her training shone through. Even in a state of shock and disgust, her diligence to combat and skill mastery was evident with every precise step, each calculated slash of her weapon, and every successful dodge.

The creature grew annoyed, so it tucked in its arms and legs and *sprang*; launching through the air like a cannonball. It hit the walls hard enough to turn the stronghold of a house into a massive drum, with the walls, floor, and ceiling shaking with every terrifyingly powerful impact. On the third successful dodge, as the creature hit the wall, every window in the building shattered simultaneously.

Laughing in ecstasy at the noisy destruction, the Skinwalker began taunting her once more. "Look! A tiny window only *you* could fit through. If you time your evasion just right, maybe I won't be able to grab your ankle as you dive through! *You should try.*"

"I fully understand that the only reason I'm still alive and uncaptured is that I'm not allowing you enough space to build up speed." Red growled as her knife launched from her left hand, slamming point-first into the creature's right eyeball and earning a scream of pain and frustration. "There we go… it seems you can't protect your sensitive sensory organs as easily as the rest of your flesh."

"*Foo~ool.*" The beast drew out the word as a long, warbling threat. "This body is immaculate. Physically strong, perfectly balanced! I've been playing with you, using this as an opportunity to get used to my new form… and you go and damage my new toy? Enough. Shhh, *shhh…* come closer."

The hunched body took halting steps toward her at a sedate pace, arms wide and to the side in order to react to whatever Red would throw at her. As it crept closer, lunging only a little to cut off escape attempts and to try and grasp her limbs, Lily found it becoming harder and harder to evade the slower, more precise grappling attempts. The entity was relentless, and as it came fully within range, it leapt at Lily with a speed it hadn't yet shown, hands grasping inches from her face and arm.

At this distance, Lily could feel the cold, existential dread that seemed to ooze out of it, her own vitality seeming to wither or be drained away.

"System's Echo!"

As Red activated her skill, the creature screamed and thrashed, falling to the floor as if having a miniature seizure. Its limbs lashed out, crashing through whatever object they touched and utterly pulverizing it. The table was reduced to splinters, a massive hole appeared in the floor, and a fist went right through multiple feet of wall, leaving a new peephole to the outside.

Lily stared on in horror as, for the first time, the information granted to her by the skill was too garbled and confusing to understand. Her grandmother's body was lit up from the inside, as though someone were holding a lantern to a thin sheet. It appeared as though a twisted, diseased man were hidden below that thin layer, and she could clearly discern his features as he glared and snarled at her.

Black lines of energy connected the man to the body he was possessing, more connections appearing over the several seconds the skill lasted. Yet, the black magic wasn't emanating from the man himself, but from an object hidden away to the side. Thanks to her skill, Red understood there was a totem in Grandmother's cauldron which was facilitating the possession. To her vision, it appeared as a tiny, perfect replica of the man hidden within the meat.

Strangely enough, it seemed the system highlighting his life energy caused the Skinwalker no small amount of agony. It clearly didn't seem to impact its strength or durability, but as Lily realized what was happening, she rushed toward the door and threw it open…

…only for the Skinwalker to cannonball into the wall next to her, grabbing the door and yanking it out of her fingers. The monster slammed it closed so hard that two of the three hinges popped from the frame. Then the beast backhanded her, sending her tumbling across the room and into a cupboard. Lily coughed out a mouthful of blood as the impact flowed through her.

The young woman reached up, dashing away the crimson fluid pouring from her nose as plates and bowls began raining from above and fragmenting on the ground around her. To Lily's great surprise and concern, just as the Skinwalker advanced on her, a new threat appeared in Red's skill-enhanced senses; a bare moment before System's Echo fully faltered.

She looked up as the creature lifted its right hand, flexing the fingers and causing thick, black talons to burst through the tips as it let out a harsh, quiet whisper. "I'm going to start by cutting off your *pink*~ies. If, after that, you still won't open the door, I'll work on your toes. Then your legs. You see, deary, I have large claws. All the better to *hurt* you with."

Just then, the stout oak door flew off its final hinge, a massive foot connected to a muscled leg hovering in the air where the wooden barrier had stood for a heartbeat. Though he had to stoop to enter, the massive form of Drwg Mawr then stepped into the room and reared up to his full height. His eyes locked on the twitching, bizarre creature standing over Red. Shoving his left hand at the Skinwalker, the invader leveled his index finger at its heart.

"You. Stand aside. I've been hunting after that one for days. She and I must have words."

Hiss. The Skinwalker opened its mouth wide, showing a mouth full of knife-sharp teeth, which definitely hadn't been there only a few minutes previously. With a last warning look at Red, it cannonballed at the wolf-clad warrior.

"*Monster!*" Without hesitation and only a *hint* of surprise, Drwg Mawr swung up with his right hand, the thick, metal-shod cudgel striking the flying creature and diverting it straight into the ceiling. There was an explosion of splinters, and dust rained down across the entire room as the powerful blow had an effect which a bladed weapon couldn't replicate.

As Lily pushed herself to her feet woozily, the sound of bone crunching from the heavy hit was too much for her stomach. Between the light concussion she'd just taken, and the sickening sounds filling her ears, she turned and emptied her stomach on the floor, a mix of blood and bile. Doing her best to shake off the affliction, she moved into a defensive position and looked up just in time to see Drwg Mawr swing with his gauntlet-clad left hand, closing his fingers into a fist.

This caused short metal spikes to push forward, revealing a brutal weapon within what she had assumed was only a defensive item. In this shape, the gauntlet appeared like a massive wolf's paw, the stubby, metal claws acting more as force-focusing points than anything meant to cut. As the huge fist landed, Lily shifted to the side in preparation of evading the Skinwalker as it was sent reeling.

Instead, the creature let out a dark laugh as it took the hit on its chest, not being pushed backward even an inch. It grabbed Drwg Mawr's extended arm, cackling with glee as the warrior's eyes went wide. Then it twisted to the side, dragging the man along with it like a crocodile planning to drown its meal. The warrior spun through the air, slamming against an already damaged wall and causing huge cracks to spread along its surface.

"Unlike the first tasty nugget, *this* one must not have known who my body used to belong to, hmm?" The Skinwalker shrieked excitedly as it jumped forward at the downed warrior, sending a flurry of strikes into his chest. "I shall eradicate your *weakness!*"

An arrow slammed into the back of the creature's head, not a single sound giving away its approach thanks to its owl-feather fletching. Whether it was because of surprise, or the location targeted, the arrowhead bit deep, sinking into bone and causing the creature to stiffen, then fall.

It convulsed a few times, then went still.

"Whenever they ask, I always tell them..." Drwg Mawr groaned as he forced himself up, weakly reaching behind himself and pulling on leather straps. A moment later, his warped and dented metal cuirass fell to the ground—bent beyond usability. "This is *why* we wear armor."

An arrow slammed into the wall next to him, half an inch from his face, causing the warrior to jerk back in shock, stumbling and falling onto his rear. He looked up, finding himself staring at the gleaming tip of a perfectly-made arrow. Raising an eyebrow, he huffed through his nose and slowly spoke.

"Not exactly how I expected to go out, but at least I managed to take this fell creature with me. If you're going to shoot me... *shoot me!*"

CHAPTER
TEN

WITHOUT FLINCHING, Red let the arrow fly.

At the last second, she adjusted her aim, and the projectile slammed into the fallen body. The creature, which had been playing dead, screeched once more and threw itself backward so hard it left holes in the floor where its hands had been. Two more arrows sailed through the air, perfectly tracking the monster as it landed on the far wall, sinking its fingers into the wood and pulling itself along the vertical surface as the projectiles ineffectually sank into it.

"It's not *dead?*" Drwg Mawr shouted in surprise as he pushed himself back to his feet.

"Correct," Red affirmed as she launched another arrow, only for the Skinwalker to grab a frying pan off a hanging pan rack and whip it at her. The object moved so quickly the Scout couldn't dodge, so she pushed her bow in front of the pan. It struck just above the hole where she had caught an arrow while escorting the Coasties, and the entire bow *cracked*.

Luckily, it hadn't broken entirely, but it was damaged enough that Red only had another shot, maybe two at best, before it fell apart. She hesitated to send another arrow, giving the creature enough time to adjust itself and cannonball toward her. Red braced herself, trying to calculate which way she should dodge, only for Drwg Mawr to intercept the creature with a flying tackle of his own.

The two powerful bodies dropped to the floor and rolled, the huge man grappling the smaller frame of the monster with his left arm, metal claws digging into its shoulder as he punched continuously with his right. Instead of showing pain, the Skinwalker only laughed at the warrior's efforts and gripped his left arm with both of its hands. "No escape for you now, *deary!*"

Once more, its jaws opened wide, though this time a visible-if-wispy cloud of dark energy roiled outward, latching on to Drwg Mawr and drawing a bellow of pain from the man. He swung his left arm, trying to throw the creature off, but it matched his strength easily as it secured its grip; the elongated claws on the tip of its fingers digging into the meat of his forearm.

Lily sent an arrow directly into its gaping maw as it lunged forward to bite the raider, piercing through the softer tissue inside its mouth a split second before it chomped down.

The angle of the wooden shaft forced the Skinwalker to adjust, but it was unable to yank the arrow out of its mouth while both of its hands were in use. After a momentary struggle, it snarled and simply began to chew, breaking through the splintering shaft in moments. Its speech slightly distorted due to the sheer amount of wood in its mouth, the creature hatefully spoke at Drwg Mawr as more dark energy flowed outward, "Become... my... *strength!*"

The warrior faltered as the cursed power sank into his flesh, Red's eyes went wide as a mental **click** echoed in her brain—the signal that her active skill was off cooldown. Without waiting, she barked, "System's Echo!"

For her, the world became more colorful and full of information. For the Skinwalker, the active energy of the system upon it caused instant agony. It screeched and thrashed, hands losing their grip as it struggled to correctly control the body it was using.

"A bunch of people outside… they must be members of Wolf Warband, waiting to hear from Drwg Mawr." Red quietly and accurately assessed the situation. "Dark energy coming from the Skinwalker, but…"

She looked over at the huge stew cauldron her grand-mother had always kept bubbling, ready to provide a meal for any Scouts she was training, lost souls wandering the woods, or just a quick snack when Red came back from a mission. The behemoth of a cooking utensil came up to her chest, but once more what drew her attention was the tiny replica of the man wearing her grandmother's skin. "That has to be a cursed object, and it's somehow allowing this nightmare to continue!"

Rushing over to the cauldron, she gripped the top, burning her fingers as she yanked to the side. Charred stew, churning with chunks of meat and vegetables, sloshed across the damaged, dirty floor. One item which *didn't* belong also joined the mess, flowing directly toward the Skinwalker and warrior. Red, not caring for the state of her clothes in the slightest, sloshed through the mess after the object, carefully studying it.

It was a small totem, a glass statue perfectly capturing the image of a man. It was filled with some strange, swirling liquid… a powerful alchemical potion of some kind? Dark, cursed energy was roiling off of it, now visibly flowing through the air to the Skinwalker. Strangely enough, the monster shrieked in fear as the foggy energy came faster, its struggles becoming more frantic as Red's skill, as well as the energy impacted it; both seemed to cause it physical or mental pain.

Lifting her bow, Red pointed the last arrow she would get to fire with this weapon at the glass, drawing back the string and… pausing. Just as her skill ended, a bizarre expression of fervent expectation darted across the Skinwalker's face, capturing Red's attention. Releasing the string's tautness, she ensured her arrow stayed in hand, and instead leaned forward and shoved the glass object toward the Skinwalker with the top limb of her extended bow. As it skittered across the floor, closer to the fell creature, the monster gave Red the most striking reaction she had managed to draw till this point.

Growling in frustration and concern, the Skinwalker shoved Drwg Mawr to the side, sacrificing its ability to wrestle with the man in lieu of getting away from the object closing in on it. The warrior tumbled across the ground, weakly attempting to push himself to his feet. He was still clearly enervated from being suffused with the cursed power of the monster, though with each passing moment he rapidly recovered. Almost as soon he hit the far wall, the muscled warrior was able to push himself up and begin moving.

Lily had formulated a simple plan, and was now using her bow to keep the glass totem between herself and the Skinwalker. It took absolutely all of Red's focus, but she was able to dance around the cursed object and keep it moving toward the creature.

The monstrous existence was hurling itself around the room, trying to find an angle to jump at her and end the fight without interacting with the glass. It was a well-known fact that you absolutely *did not* want to touch a cursed object, which added an element of uncertainty and caution to Lily's movements—though she was ready to take a few risks if needed.

"Know what I think? I'll just figure out the door on my own." The Skinwalker growled at her as the skin across its entire body went taut, being pulled down around its ankles and shins. It crouched slightly, then launched forward using not *only* its power, but also uncoiling the skin that had been twisted down and around its legs; treating the twisted flesh like a spring.

Taking advantage of Red's reluctance to grasp the object

near her feet, it flew through the air as if propelled by a cyclone; destroying the wall it pushed off and causing the entire building to tilt. Its hands were outstretched, talons curled and grasping, as if the Skinwalker planned to dive straight into and *through* Red's torso. As the Scout attempted to evade, the stew she'd been standing on caused her foot to slip, leaving her off balance and unable to do more than try and fall out of the way.

"Hup! *Huuuwah!*" A deep grunt of exertion echoed in Red's ears as she fell backward, staring up at the ceiling as a metallic object glowing with heat swung through the space she'd been occupying.

Clang!

Drwg Mawr had grabbed the enormous wrought iron cauldron—which weighed well over a hundred and fifty pounds when *empty*—and swung it into the creature flying through the air as easily as though it were his cudgel. The Skinwalker rebounded back and up, impacting the ceiling and destroying it further, only to bounce down, hit the ground, smack the back wall, then ricochet toward them. It came to a rest several feet away, briefly stunned motionless.

Lily rolled to the side, half-coating herself in burned stew, and swirled to her feet in a rush. "Quickly, while it's unable to move, get it *in* the cauldron!"

Drwg Mawr didn't hesitate to follow her directions. Using the huge pot as a shovel, he easily scooped in about half of the Skinwalker before needing to resort to kicking it in the face a few times to stuff the rest of it inside.

Red took her bow and slapped the glass totem into the confined space, rushing to the cauldron's original position and grabbing the fitted lid. "Catch!"

She tossed the iron disk over with a grunt, using all her strength, and the warrior easily caught it with one hand as he pulled the cauldron upright with the other. Then he slapped the lid atop the cauldron and held on for dear life as the Skinwalker began screaming at such a high pitch that it could easily have been mistaken for a tea kettle reaching a boil. Drwg Mawr's huge muscles bulged under the strain of keeping the lid held in place as the pot shook violently.

"Release me! *Release me-e-e!*"

Then, the unmistakable sound of glass breaking echoed from the closed cauldron, and the creature went silent. Red and Drwg Mawr held their breath, hoping it was over, but after only a moment, a wail of fury and dread echoed out. The iron cauldron distorted as a fist impacted it from the inside, then again, then it struck the lid, and the warrior was nearly launched off his feet as he strained to keep the iron barrier in place.

A heavy silence fell after that, the creature's struggles ending after the final hit. After a moment, the quiet was broken by the labored breathing of the wide-eyed humans, who stared at the container, then each other.

Drwg Mawr was the first to speak. "Is it… over?"

"One way to find out." Red stepped closer, still somewhat wary of the huge man, and gently helped pry his fingers loose from their position. The lid didn't burst off the cauldron immediately, so she motioned for him to pull with her. Together, they dragged the enormous iron object over to its original position, setting it in its place above the still-burning fire.

Silently, they watched for a quarter of an hour as the metal continued to heat, but finally Red nodded gently and motioned at it. "It *has* to be dead. Otherwise, it would've at least made a sound by now."

"Should I…? I'll go check." Drwg Mawr stepped forward, grabbed a wooden spoon, and threaded it through the handle of the lid, popping it off with a sharp motion.

After a moment, he peeked inside, only to recoil back a moment later. "The creature is gone, but now there's a *man* in there! He's dead… but… *no.*"

"What!" Red drew her sword, even knowing how ineffectual it had been against the monster.

Drwg Mawr pointed a shaky finger into the cauldron, but when Red didn't step closer to look, he reached in with the spoon, stirring the contents. Before Red could become too disgusted, he pulled back, lifting a necklace with a clear symbol on it into the air. "I recognize this object. It's the same sigil worn by the man who killed my father. This is a *Huntsman*, someone twisted into monstrous form by some strange, cursed magic from a distant land."

The way he spat the title of the creature indicated that Red should understand simply by the name alone, but she could only shake her head and mutter, "A Huntsman? I don't understand what would twist a hunter so."

"You…!" The warrior turned, a dark, thunderous expression on his face, pausing as she lifted her blade to point at him. "Enough of that, for now. You fought with me, and you fought well. I have no desire to battle a comrade right now, no matter how temporary our alliance has been."

"Go ahead and keep telling yourself we're on the same side," Red evenly directed him, nodding along as if she agreed. "Are you going to tell me what this *thing* is?"

"It's not a story with a happy ending." Drwg Mawr stated, his accent coming to the forefront and turning his tone darker. "It is the reason we are here in the first place."

"It killed my grandmother. Please, let me know what I'm dealing with."

"What *we* are dealing with." Drwg Mawr corrected grimly as he glanced into the cauldron, then back at her. "What we *dealt* with. It's melting away even as we speak."

CHAPTER

ELEVEN

EACH OF THEM stepped away slightly, leaving enough room to make the other feel comfortable staying in the destroyed abode. Drwg Mawr was tall enough to lean back and half-sit on the remains of the kitchen island, while Red simply remained standing in a somewhat defensive position. No matter how much she owed the man, the fact that they were enemies remained, and that wasn't exactly something she could afford to forget.

Drwg Mawr began his story, making Red flinch at the sudden cessation of silence. To her surprise, the enormous brute of a man spoke softly, his voice weighed down by grief he made no attempt to hide. "We have never been here before, and for good reason. Our lands lay far to the north, through the sea of endless storms, where ice fills the ground, and snow is ever present."

Lily goggled at the start of his story, hardly able to believe how well-spoken this barbarian warrior was. Still, she contained herself and remained stoically silent as he continued.

"It is a harsh land which treats life as a force to be snuffed out. The terrain is unforgiving. What is not craggy stone is barren soil, often frozen over or only found deep beneath the snow. But, against the odds, my people have always flourished. This is in no small part thanks to the powerful classes and skills we earn for facing such austerity head-on, testing ourselves at every turn, honing our resilience. Our strength is drawn from adversity. As I'm certain you know, the system rewards those who dare to meet its challenges unflinchingly." A ghost of a grin appeared on his lips, fading away as his eyes turned distant once more.

"Many of our structures are underground, hewn from the very bedrock of the frozen continent. Generations of living below the surface have led to my people becoming impressive metalsmiths and stone shapers. But, for all our mastery over metal and stone, the land offers no bounty. Food is always a grave concern, and for the sake of generations both current and future, we are compelled to go out and *get* it." A slight hint of bloodthirstiness echoed in his tone, causing Red to tense up. Still, the huge man was staring at the ground instead of her, seemingly unconcerned with being attacked. "It was a life filled with honor and passion."

He went silent, long enough that Red surprised herself by prodding him to continue. "*Was?*"

Drwg Mawr blinked and looked up, meeting her eyes for the first time since he'd begun speaking. They were an intense, arctic blue, their color brought forward even more so by the black-blood stain on his otherwise pristine wolf-pelt helmet. He nodded and confirmed, "Was. Little more than half a year ago, a Huntsman much like *this* visited our shores. Never before had an outsider found their way to our fortress, so we were taken by surprise. It did not have the same type of magic this one did, instead being cloaked in shadows and able to suffocate the sounds it generated as it moved and fought."

"So the symbol on the necklace is the only consistent clue you have? You're just *assuming* it's a Huntsman?" Her words came out more hostile than she intended, though the warrior didn't seem to mind.

"I have full faith I am correct." He solemnly pressed a fist to his chest, a gesture she could only assume meant something to his people. Then he did something which shocked her to her core, drawing an 'X' over his heart. "I *swear* this was a Huntsman, cross my heart… and hope to die."

A flash of energy which could only come from the system appeared where he'd moved his fingers, flashing bright gold after a moment before dissipating as the air *thrummed* with power. Outside, thunder rolled through the cloudless sky, and the birds of the forest went silent as the system witnessed the oath.

Red shook her head slowly as her eyes wandered to his cheek, where a shimmering, pearlescent 'X' marked his cheek —the mark of a person who had sworn and fulfilled such oaths in the past. "You would invoke a system geas… just like that? For a story? What if you had been wrong?"

"Then I would have died." Drwg Mawr lifted an eyebrow at her. "It's right there in the wording of the oath. 'Hope to die'. It would have cut my heart into four equal chunks. This is a worldwide effect; surely you know of it?"

Inspecting him closely, she huffed out of her nose slightly before answering. "You just made a promise only people who have great need or no other choice would. There's practically only two groups of people I've *ever* heard of using that kind of system-enforced power: kings negotiating peace treaties and swearing to uphold them, or loan sharks forcing borrowers to repay with immense interest. No one in between. So, seeing it in action, so casually? Yes, that was quite surprising to me."

"If you do not say what you mean and mean what you say, how do you trust your people each day?" the warrior inquired with a deeply puzzled expression. "This is a common form of peeling back falsehoods and ensuring correct information. If I truly did not know this was a Huntsman, I would not have said it was."

"I *guess*." Lily pressed her lips together, half-waving her hand for the man to continue his story. A few a moment to collect his thoughts, he did so.

"As if orchestrating a grim spectacle for its own amusement, the Huntsman in our lands killed our previous war leader—my father—as my people were engaged in a moment of unity and deliberation, a moot. He had removed his battle regalia, to speak to his fellows not as a commander, but as a fellow. It was his undoing; it is *why* we wear *armor*! *Haaa...* even though he stood not alone, but amidst the elite of my people, not even a single man could react or interfere before a knife had been driven through his heart."

Drwg Mawr shook his head, like he was hardly able to believe the words coming out of his own mouth. "Then the aberration cloaked in human flesh unleashed carnage, slaughtering all those around him. Among all of us, I was the singular combatant capable of enduring its relentless onslaught. We traded blow for blow, and I earned many scars that day. I weathered its attacks until, piece by piece, I dismantled the Huntsman, severing and removing its limbs. As it thrashed about, refusing to die easily, we compelled the creature to explain its raid on our most fortified locale."

"We expected revelations of a vendetta, perhaps a sinister plot, maybe even a blood feud which compelled someone to use a cursed artifact to sow death among us. That much, we would have at least understood. But the truth was far worse."

Swallowing hard, the man looked up and met Lily's eyes. "It was *none* of that. The Huntsman was not driven by vengeance nor having its strings pulled by a puppet master in the background. Far more chilling, the Huntsman killed dozens of our elite and my father... because it was *bored*. Sheer ennui drove it, a compulsion to derive pleasure from the suffering of others."

"It was *bored*? It sailed through the Sea of Storms, killed your father and who knows how many others, just because it needed something to *do*?" The vehemence in Red's voice once more drew Drwg's eyes back to her, and he blinked in surprise as her intense stare bored into him. "If there is one thing I've never understood, it's the idea of killing for no reason. It *disgusts* me. Hunting for sport is a heavy crime in the Wyld, punishable by permanent exile from the forest—at the minimum. To hear of a person acting that way toward another? Unthinkable."

"Yes…" Drwg nodded slowly as he considered the fierce Scout who was practically shaking with fury on his behalf. "Yet, the tale unfolds further. His ennui didn't merely happen, but was instead forced upon him by a dark power. Once upon a time, the Huntsmen were merely *men*. Some queen in a distant land, a Witch cloaked in the guise of sovereignty, is hiding behind her crown to perform cursed experiments upon the most loyal of her people. She twists their minds and alters their bodies with cursed rites and forbidden alchemical formulae."

"As I said, it is not a tale with a happy ending," Drwg quietly stated when he saw Lily waiting for more. "Those who teeter on the brink of madness, becoming unstable or uncontrollable, she casts aside like broken playthings, not cleaning up the mess she has made of them, but instead compelling them to wander the world to sow death and chaos."

"But… why?" Red wondered with great confusion. "What possible purpose could there be for this… darkness?"

"Now we get to the heart of it."

Drwg's voice took on a sharper tone, which managed to pull Red out of the story somewhat and remember the situation she was in. She leaned back, her eyes flicking around the room as he recounted his tale.

"The Witch is consumed by her search for power, a pursuit which knows no bounds. As I'm certain you've been taught, following the path of hatred and malevolence taints your system-granted skills, your classes, and turns you into something... *else*. A Witch, or a Villain. The further they pursue this path, the more the taint of their soul impacts their physical form."

Red had heard of this phenomenon, though she'd never seen it in person. In fact, on Canu Moch, it had turned into a mere nursery rhyme to scare naughty children. "In a cauldron's eerie light, a twisted soul seeks an answer to their desperate plight. Darkness ascends, is fully embraced. Inner disgrace soon reflects from a twisted face..."

"Heed this tale, children, lest you find a similar fate, should you to darkness bind." Drwg finished the remainder of the nursery rhyme with a rueful chuckle. "Yes, originally I had considered this as a simple parable, but I have since learned the bitter truth of the matter. The cursed energy these things exude? There is no other answer. According to the Huntsman I... *interrogated*, this Witch Queen is seeking to unravel the mess of dark magics, attempting to find the recipe to perfect possession; to become the fairest of all, over and over again, as needed. As you have seen–"

Here, he gestured at the once-again-covered iron pot, "– she has managed to distill some portion of it. Yet, it left the Huntsman insane and unable to fully control the body it snatched."

"My grandmother." Red realized sadly, getting a grunt of acknowledgment in return for the unfortunate news. "It was attempting to gain access to the Class Shrine Grandmother protected. Perhaps it had gained enough power where it felt it would be able to ascend, to become a new type of even more terrible Monster."

"Hmm." Drwg hummed noncommittally. "That would *not* have been good for us."

"Agreed."

Finding common ground caused both of them to grin ever

so slightly at each other, though Drwg sobered quickly and finished his story. "As I was the one to best the Huntsman in single combat, I became the leader of my people, earning the title of 'Mawr'. Now, I have made it my life's goal to find this Witch Queen and destroy her *before* she is able to refine the dark art of possession into a tool she could wield with precision. Imagine, if you dare, a terrible Witch who has none of the physical characteristics of one cursed by the system, and can live forever by choosing a new host when the current one begins to fail."

There was silence for a moment, and Drwg let out a small snort of reluctant annoyance, "However... this left my people with some... *logistical* problems."

"You need to find her, and you need to be able to feed your people the entire time you're searching." Red glumly and easily pointed out the issues. "Most likely, you also desire lots and *lots* of wood for ship building and repair. If metal is no issue, and warriors are no issue... I suppose I can see why you're here."

"I don't suppose you would... make things easier for us?" Drwg put a hopeful expression on his face. "Not that they have been exactly *difficult* so far. May I ask... who builds an entire city out of grass?"

"*Coasties*," Red agreed with an annoyed sigh, though if the head tilt of the leader of Wolf Warband was any indication, her explanation was lacking. "You said 'Mawr' is a title?"

"Yes. My true name is Drwg. 'Big' in your language, and for obvious reasons." The warrior flexed his tree-trunk of a left arm, causing his muscles to bulge like a pile of acorns wrapped in canvas. As he shifted his position, his helmet's false eyes glinted like gemstones in the evening sunlight now shining through the holes in the walls and ceiling.

"Only the leader of Wolf Warband is allowed to carry the title of Mawr, or 'Bad', in your language. By doing so, I accept all the responsibility for the actions of my people, so long as they are carrying out my orders. It is meant to be a reminder of how I am under constant scrutiny. If I show signs of going down the path of a true Villain, with my class becoming corrupted, I will be put down like the rabid wolf I have become."

"Wait a moment." Red blinked a few times. "If that's true, does your full name and title translate as 'Big Bad'?"

"I am quite large, and I was ever since I was a baby. The first word my father spoke when he saw me in my mother's arms, was 'big'," Drwg confirmed with a proud smile. "From there, I proved to them that the moniker was the correct–"

"No. Pause. Does that mean you are the *Big Bad Wolf*?" Red chuckled at him, the sound growing as Drwg went stiff, and his eyes went wide.

"Oh. Oh no. This is going to… my people can never hear you say that. I would never live it down." Drwg winced as she merely continued to laugh, finally giving in and joining her with a sad chuckle.

"The Big Bad Wolf is hunting the Huntsman on the island of the Singing Swine, and has already destroyed the grass homes of one of the three little pigs. That is, one of the city-states." Red quietly put everything together, speaking aloud so she could see his face twitching. "This will *definitely* not cause any misconceptions while you seek this Witch Queen out."

Once she was done taunting him, Lily asked a few more clarifying questions after that, observing the man across from her as time slowly crept past. Conversation flowed more easily than she'd anticipated, and she soon found they had similar concerns and objectives, though their methods were in stark opposition. No matter how friendly the post-combat conversation was, she remained acutely aware of their fundamental positions.

The Big Bad Wolf represented the force which had invaded her home, and they were a threat to everything she loved.

Almost as concerning was the revelation she had as her practiced eyes continuously studied him. The wounds across his body were gone, fully healed at some point during their conversation. "Ah. So *that's* why you were able to fight against the Huntsman on your own and walk away. You have a skill which heals you over time?"

"I do." Drwg showed a wolfish grin. "I don't care who knows about it, either. There's nothing they can do to stop me from *doggedly* pushing onward. Anyway, this leads me to an *unfortunate* part of our conversation-"

Without waiting to hear another syllable, Red threw her bow at the leader of the invaders like a javelin. Even though not expecting the sudden brutality, the warrior still managed to get his left hand up in time to fully block the attack, causing his hand to cover his face for a brief moment.

In that fraction of a second, Red made her true move. With a fluidity of years of practice, she turned away, diving through the tiny window the Skinwalker had taunted her into trying to attempt escaping through. The man behind her would be unable to fit through the space, and the direction of her movement allowed her to hit the ground, roll, and dash forward past the startled members of Wolf Warband and into the forest without giving them time to react.

Strangely enough, even with the startled cries of the warriors and the natural ambiance of the forest, which had returned, one sound reached her ears and drowned out all the others.

A sigh of frustration from a huge set of lungs, as Drwg Mawr stood at the window and watched her vanish.

TWELVE

"Abyss, feces, drat, and system forebode!" Lily ran through all the curses she allowed herself to use, upset at herself for allowing the Wolf Warband to encircle the entire building before she made her escape. "What would compel me to dash in a *straight line* into the forest instead of attempting to throw them off? All they'll need to do is shoot an azimuth along my escape route, and they'll be marching into the Heart of the Wyld in *hours*!"

Her mind was whirling with pain and loss at the death of her grandmother, shock over the cursed alchemically-created Skinwalker, confusion from the bizarre story of the big bad wolf, and shame at her own failure at her choice of escape route. "I need to get back to the Druidic Council and warn them of the Class Shrine being captured by Wolf Warband. Abyss. Worse, they may *not* capture it! They might just leave it *undefended*."

Lily wanted to scream at all of the terrible things which had happened that day, but all that would do is bring her enemies down upon her faster. Instead, she simply allowed silent tears to snake their way from the corner of her eyes, letting them freely drip from her chin. "I can't go straight back. I'd never forgive myself if *I* was the reason the Wyld… stop. What *can* I do to help hold them off?"

As soon as she reshaped her chaotic, panicked thoughts into a question she could actually answer, they began to swirl in a single direction. With each subsequent breath, she worked to transform her pain and fear into a straight, sharp arrow, finally loosing it at a proper target. "This is the forest. The Wyld is *my* domain."

Inhaling deeply, she swiftly formulated a proper response to the invasion on her heels. She had already decided taking a direct path to the city was no longer viable, and so adjusted her route slightly; veering away from the Heart of the Wyld. Her feet carried her to one of the many hidden caches of trapping supplies she'd meticulously prepared. Every item represented hours of work, either something she had created herself or bartered her efforts as a Scout or live-trapper for.

The small arsenals were filled with large coils of rope, twine, and even the small length of wire she'd managed to collect over the years, as hauling such a load everywhere she went was practically impossible, not to mention inefficient. Instead, like all good Scouts, she had set up strategic locations which would allow her to create as many traps as needed, *wherever* she needed them.

At least, as many as she *usually* needed.

"Looking at the scale of this challenge… perhaps trying to trap an entire invasion force is too much of a task for my supplies?" Still, her skill in setting traps was unparalleled at her age, honed over literal decades of practice and close instruction by… Red cut that thought off, determined to grieve her loss when there wasn't imminent danger. Dashing away small trickles of fluid from her eyes that hadn't gotten the message, she reminded herself aloud, "Grandma would already be hard at work, so I can do the same. It's time to put all of this training to good use. She… she would have nodded at me and said, 'busy hands, quiet mind'. I'll grieve for her when I've done my duty."

As Lily arrived at the cache, she pushed aside the branches and leaves she'd carefully scattered atop the small hatch, pulling it open to reveal a pit approximately her own height filled with coiled ropes, well-folded nets, and dozens of other implements meant to make everything from *live* traps… to utterly lethal versions. She avoided the latter, something in her mind rebelling against wounding or killing other humans without knowing if they were guilty of some crime. "Can't know for certain who'll stumble into the trap, and I don't want to have a repeat of the Wyld's defensive plans."

For a moment, the memory of swinging trees zooming through the air like pendulums flashed through her mind. Lily blinked, finding herself flat on the ground, where she'd thrown herself only a moment before. "What…? Oh… waking nightmares. Wonderful."

Trying to steady her shaking hands, she grabbed coils of ropes and got to work.

If her strategy was *not* to decimate the ranks of the warriors trailing her, that left only a single alternative. She was going to entangle, delay, frustrate and annoy them, get them lost, lead them the wrong way, perhaps even pit them against the predators of the forest. "Hmm… maybe I'll gather some of those intestine-cleansing berries and see if I can't slip them into their supplies. Good. Operation 'morale destruction' is officially underway."

Her first task, she decided, was to set up the large net traps. Not only were those her favorites for dealing with creatures and wayward Coasties, it would also remove the largest burden from her shoulders. Rope was *heavy*, and nets were just braided rope. Also, she liked the clear message it would send: at any moment, they could be strung up and caged like an animal.

"Start making them paranoid, and they'll move slower.

The longer I can give the Wyld to prepare, the better for all of us." Red began moving along her well-trodden trail, adjusting the path where possible to make it seem as though there were many branching routes through the forest. Choosing strategic points along the most likely paths they would take—where the trees were large enough to support the weight of the nets and huge invaders—she began her work, rigging traps and camou-flaging them, her skills allowing her to do so *Perfectly*.

As each was completed, Lily made sure to move a goodly distance away, spacing them out over a wide area to capture as many people as possible.

Hurrying along the forest pathways, she embedded and wove traps with a judicious hand, peppering the correct path with plenty of nets, yet working to ensure they weren't a constant menace. Lily needed to orchestrate a delicate balance: if the forest was littered with traps constantly springing one after another, after another, Wolf Warband would only correctly assume they were going the right direc-tion. "Going by how loquacious Drwg Mawr was, I can only assume they're going to be cunning as well as ferocious."

One net was blended seamlessly into the underbrush, and she adjusted it until the movement of the leaves matched to the netting near perfectly. Another she placed on what seemed like a bare patch of packed dirt, using the color scheme of the braided string to blend the rope with the dirt and pebbles without a trace. Lily ever so slowly created a maze guarded not by walls, but by the illusion of an open path.

Trap after trap was laid down, each of them designed to ensnare up to half a dozen men at a time, hoisting them dozens and dozens of feet into the air. While the fall likely wouldn't be lethal if they cut their way out, it should certainly be enough to make them reconsider doing so—forcing their contemporaries to carefully undo the trap by finding and following the rope into the underbrush.

Every minute of extra time they spent freeing their fellow

warriors was an extra minute the citizens of Canu Moch had to prepare against them.

When she ran out of rope, at least from the first cache, she turned her attention to redirecting the trails more extensively. Using precise cuts, removing underbrush, Lily created detours which seemed like natural paths—but led directly to an assortment of pit traps she'd been using for years. None of the local animals would fall for the simple redirection, nor would any Scout who had spent any time improving their skills. "I can only assume seafaring raiders don't spend much time in the woods, so these should be effective for a while, especially if they decide to keep going after dark. Now, what else can I do...?"

Red spent some time ensuring the pits were properly concealed with thin layers of twigs and leaves, as well as making sure she chose only the traps which were deep enough to prevent easy escape, but not likely to be deadly against hearty warriors. At worst, those who fell in would need to find a Healer or spend a few weeks recovering from broken bones. Inspecting her work, she nodded and murmured to herself, "Good. Now they'll not only be looking for traps, but be forced to second-guess every step they take."

She worked tirelessly as the day wore on, afternoon slowly sliding into twilight. Even so, she kept her movements silent and full of purpose. Three caches were fully emptied of their non-lethal supplies before night fully settled over the island, and it became nearly impossible to safely set additional versions out.

Still... it *wasn't* too dark for a Scout with Lily's capabilities to safely move through the forest.

Retracing her steps along the route she'd created, Red decided she should check her work and ensure that her actions were creating unhappy situations for the raiders as expected. Guided by the lights of System's Whisper, she darted through the dense forest, a crimson ghost among the trees. Each time she felt the mental *click* of System's Echo coming off cooldown, she eagerly reactivated it and let the system flood her senses with new information. At the faintest hint of voices carried on the wind and echoing among the trees, Red would momentarily pause and see what sort of trouble the invaders had gotten themselves into.

As the night wore on, she couldn't help but allow herself a satisfied smirk, though she never let her guard down as she moved among the trees. Already, nearly *half* of her net traps had been sprung, snatching groups of wolfy warriors up into the canopy.

Earlier in the evening, their shouts of surprise and frustration had garnered a rapid response, with their companions managing to get them out of the trees with only a few dozen minutes of careful work. Unfortunately for those caught after true night had set in, they were left swinging after a duo of net traps set up in serial—the second only allowed to go off after the first had—captured the second group who were meant to rescue the first.

This had led to a general call being sounded for them to settle in for the night: the exact reaction Lily had been hoping for.

With the situation in the forest meeting her expectations, Lily decided it was time to turn back and bring the news to the people in the Heart of the Wyld. Her smile faded slightly, and soon she found herself procrastinating by making small detours to the series of pit traps along her path. Quick checks found that almost all of them had been filled by two or three of the large warriors, with most of the men in them loudly grumbling and trying to settle in for the night.

She knew they wouldn't get much sleep, as those unfamiliar with the forest would always be awakened by the calls of the natural inhabitants. "I've probably gained us at least another full day."

Eyes dancing with mirth as she barreled through the forest

silently, Red gleefully chuckled. "I'd call this a successful operation. Instead of marching straight for the city, their focus is
fractured as they expend time and energy on rescue operations. They can't even build up a full rage, since I'm *pretty* sure
none of them managed to get themselves killed."

She allowed herself a moment to picture the grumpy
warriors forming up again in the morning, formations spaced
out as they attempted to anticipate her next surprise. But
caution alone wouldn't help them much, not with the sheer
density of traps she had placed. "I wonder how they'll react to
the triple net in a row. They'll probably go off the path
entirely at that point."

A chuckle echoed out from her, instantly causing her to
stifle her mirth. Red softly cursed at herself. "What was *that?*
I'm better than that—small mistakes led to big, bad
outcomes."

Gathering her wits about her, Lily dashed through the
underbrush of the Wyld, constantly forced to rely on the light
of the system, due to not even the barest hint of moonlight
being able to filter through the dense canopy above. She
moved in large loops, often doubling back or choosing an
incorrect path intentionally just in case the invaders had
someone who could latch onto her smell—or something
equally annoying—to follow her directly.

Even so, Lily's path wasn't random. Every turn, leap, and
pause was calculated and meticulous. She knew the locations
of all of her own traps, what would set them off, and hoped to
lead any pursuer directly into them. With her speed, she
managed to directly sprint and leap across pit traps with ease,
leaving a trail which would bring anyone using a skill to find
her directly into a deep drop.

Not only did she need to avoid man-made obstacles, the
forest was also alive with nocturnal predators—clearly
currently active, going by rustling leaves, sudden shrieks from
prey animals, and quickly cut-off snarls. Half a dozen times

along her run, she was given warnings of danger from System's Whisper or felt their presence directly with her new skill. She ran like never before, fully confident in her practically system-guaranteed safety when the active skill was off cooldown.

Lily only began to slow down as she approached the Heart of the Wyld. Here, near the center of the forest, the air was cooler, the trees were farther apart... and the danger was much greater. She was nearing her destination, but her proximity came with an added danger: what was certain to be an abyssal *multitude* of lethal traps set by the defenders of the Wyld in preparation for the advancing warband. "Last time I was nearly caught by what had to be some of the first traps they set up. Now they've had an entire day and hundreds of people are working on them."

With her senses heightened to the utmost, she moved forward with extreme caution. She stayed decidedly *off* the main path, her paranoia eventually pushing her to climb a tree and move along the thick boughs.

This proved to be a wise decision, as she was able to find dozens and dozens of sharpened wooden logs tied to the trees, merely waiting for the slightest pressure on a tripwire down below to send them swinging. Spike traps on planks or visible from above, and Red lost count of them as she moved cautiously through the treetops—highly doubting that the Scouts would have left this path into the city unguarded.

Her careful movements proved justified once more, as she activated System's Echo and began picking out handfuls of scouts, hunters, and practically anyone with any kind of marksman skill in the trees around her. If her encounter the previous morning had been any indication, they likely had their weapons ready, and itchy fingers were just waiting to release a sharpened shaft in the direction of any sound.

Red went still, her foot in the air, as her vision suddenly flashed red. Carefully easing backward, she looked where she'd been about to step, finding a metal tripwire, so thin it was nearly invisible. "And where do *you* lead, Mr. Trap?"

Now that she had found the trigger, the rest of the mechanism was easy to pick apart with her eyes. She followed a long, taut piece of twine to about a dozen feet away, where six crossbows were stacked together waiting to launch their projectiles as a wall of unavoidable death. Carefully stepping *over* the trip wire, moving extra slowly to ensure she didn't make the branch bob with her footsteps, Red picked her way through the treacherous trees.

Eventually, she crossed over a point where the traps thinned down to the point of nothingness, and she was able to gaze forward to see the Heart of the Wyld. The long, terrible day was wearing on her, though the only external sign was how her chest heaved with exertion from the slow, careful motions after the wild sprint through the woods. Red felt at her arm, knowing the cold, clammy flesh wasn't a sign of hypothermia—the island was warm year-round. No, it was only a reminder from her body of the fact that the early hours of the morning had arrived, she hadn't eaten anything all day, and was rapidly approaching exhaustion.

Red dropped from the trees and walked into one of the now-only-two remaining cities of Canu Moch with an exhausted directive to herself.

"Let's get this over with."

THIRTEEN

Upon entering the city, Scouts appeared around her out of the darkness like wraiths. Luckily for her, Lily's bright red cloak and hair made her stand out, even when there was practically no light at all. They lowered their bows, and she let out a breath of air she'd been holding far too long. "I have news on Wolf Warband for the council. It's pretty dire."

Unfortunately, her exhaustion had finally caught up to her, making her serious concerns sound fairly deadpan and unimportant. The others looked around, one of them finally deciding to take charge and answer her. "The Druidic Grove is in the midst of an important session at the moment. I'm sorry to say, you can't go in to see them."

"What a shock." Red shook her head and rolled her eyes tiredly. "Whatever. Let them play their little power games. We've all seen what the results of that looks like, *haven't* we? Can I at least have a spare bed roll or something? I've been fighting for my life the entire day, and I'm pretty tired."

Her words and too-casual declaration earned a few raised eyebrows, but she was led to a small treehouse near the grove. There was space for only a single person to sleep, which was absolutely perfect for her. After closing the hatch to block unwelcome visitors, she laid the bed roll atop it and immediately dropped into a deep, thankfully dreamless sleep.

Eventually, Lily was awoken by a rhythmic *thumping* on the hatch below her, shaking her enough to finally force her eyes open. She rolled to the side, off the mat, drawing her short sword before kicking the mat out of the way and letting the hatch swing upward.

"The councilors will see you now," the man who woke her called up, having made a smart choice in using a long pole to do the knocking instead of invading her personal space so quickly upon waking. "I'm sorry for the previous delay and the current rush, but with the war going on, there's very little time we can allot for unscheduled meetings."

Lily simply nodded, brushed her tangled red hair out of her face, and slid down the ladder. Her fingers swept over the cloak she was wearing, face pulling into a grimace as she realized with a deep pang of loss that she'd never again see the person who'd given her the fine clothing enchanted to remain clean and whole.

Hunger, thirst, and her overexertion the previous day were sending loud signals that tried to capture her attention as she moved, but Lily knew she needed to complete this task so she could get back into the forest. A glimmer of sunlight sparkled through the canopy, low to the ground and far to the east, calling her attention to the fact the council may have *actually* been rushing to speak with her.

"They're seeing me at first light? Does this mean they're finally taking my warnings and information seriously?" Red quizzed her escort, who could only shrug uncomfortably at the —accurate—insinuation she was making of having been ignored previously.

Walking past the glaring guards at the entrance to the grove, Red swept her gaze around the circle of ancient trees, finding the councilors seated and appearing extremely haggard. The air was thick with the smell of nature and the subtle fragrance of potent teas being poured for the clearly exhausted leadership of the Wyld. She waited a few moments, counting the faces, before asking her first question of the day, "Where's Reynard? I'm sure he'll have some *comments* about my report."

The councilors shuffled awkwardly for a few moments, until one of them tiredly spoke up. "Scout Reynard has been shown to have ideals and opinions which do not mesh with our sacred duties and laws. As of approximately three o'clock this morning, he has stepped down from his position with the Druidic Grove in an effort to spend more time training with his contemporaries."

Red raised an eyebrow at the words, reading between the lines and fully understanding that her grandmother's nemesis had been removed from the council. "Not going to lie, it's about time. Still, I'm not here to gloat, but to pass on some very concerning news to all of you. From least to most important, I've figured out why the Wolf Warband landed on our shores."

"You..." A new leader spoke out as Lily's words brought every eye onto her. "You talked to them, gaining intelligence of this level... and it is the *least* important information you have to report?"

Lily nodded sharply, then worked to recount the events of the previous day as professionally as possible, doing her best to keep her voice steady, despite her inner turmoil making her gut churn. Everything from the encounter with Big Bad, the loss of her grandmother, the cursed Skinwalker, and finally the unknown status of the Class Shrine. She was bombarded with questions and quizzed for clarifications for the next hour, before they finally fell silent and worked to digest the information.

Multiple people placed their heads in their hands, half-full cups of tea cold and forgotten in front of them. When they did speak, to Lily's surprise, the response wasn't the dismissive or skeptical reception she'd braced for. Without Reynard to stand against her, there was no reason for them to doubt her coldly clinical report. Instead, she was met with somber faces and a series of words coming from their mouths she'd never expected to hear.

"Lily Red, on behalf of the Druidic Grove, we would like to issue a formal apology for the actions of our previous member." One of the exhausted councilors spoke, his words holding as much excitement as a pile of gravel in midwinter. "His mishandling of the warning you brought us, days before anyone else managed to replicate, cost us time we desperately needed. Frankly, it may have cost our lives. At the *minimum*, it placed the lives of thousands at risk."

Even more unexpected, a different councilor spoke up and took over as the previous one faltered. "Based on your experience, clearly well-practiced skills, and devotion to your craft even in the absence of remuneration, we would like to offer you a position."

Red's eyes widened at the words, her heart soaring momentarily as she finally gained the recognition she'd been seeking her entire adult life. She had been trying to become an official Scout of the Wyld since her eighteenth birthday, and had always been insulted and blocked by Reynard. Following the moment of elation, a small, jaded voice in her mind reminded her of the situation they were now in: it had taken a literal invasion for the leadership to step up and even acknowledge their mistakes. Did they now want *her* to fix those mistakes while under their thumb?

The spark of excitement burned out as quickly as it had come, and Lily needed to work to keep her facial expression neutral. "Thank you for the opportunity, but at this time, I don't believe becoming a Scout of the Wyld is the correct option for me. Without autonomy, I believe I won't be as effective against the invaders."

The councilors looked amongst themselves for a moment,

some of their faces holding amusement, others showing every bit of their sleepless night. One of the latter let out a sigh of annoyance, then clarified, "Good, because we weren't talking about you becoming one of our Scouts."

Lily opened her mouth slightly to respond, closing it in confusion as once more another member continued speaking where the other had left off. "Lily Red, there's an open position on the council, and we believe *you* are the one who should fill it."

Her jaw dropped slightly, and her thoughts went into overdrive as realization took over. A seat on the Druidic Council? At twenty years old? Taking a desperate step back from her emotions, she tried to analyze the offer for what it was. Lily could practically feel the weight of responsibility waiting to drop on her shoulders, balanced against the opportunity to influence decisions from practically the start of this war until its end.

"But then what?" she muttered to herself, too quietly for the people around her to hear. "What happens after the invasion?"

She tried to look past the point where they drove off Wolf Warband, but was still sitting on the council, day after day of making decisions and handling the minutiae of laws and regulations for thousands of people. Dozens of hours each day, sitting here. In the grove. Not the forest. Something inside of Lily violently rejected the idea, and unconsciously, she mirrored her thoughts by shaking her head.

"Lily?" One of the councilors gently prodded, "Are you ready to join us and save the island of Canu Moch?"

"No…" Her answer came out breathlessly, so she swallowed, squared her shoulders, and repeated herself more firmly, "No. As flattering as this proposal is, it's far outside the bounds of what I want my life to look like. This may be me being far too honest, but I've grown to dislike almost all of the leadership in the Wyld. I love this island, and the forest, but

I... I don't need the position and the finery. The trappings of control, at least to me, have a heavy emphasis on *trap*."

The last sentence was muttered very softly, as she didn't want to offend the people who were attempting to be gracious. The seated group broke out into murmurs, the chief emotion on display being anger and frustration.

"You would turn down a seat on the council? Pah. You really *are* just like your grandmother."

The jab at her recently deceased relative caused an instant shift inside Red. She went from calm and thoughtful to disgusted and scandalized in an instant. "I'm like Grand-mother? Thank the system for *that*. That's the nicest thing anyone on this council has said to me before *today*. You want to know the real reason I don't want to be here, *Franklin*? Because I know as soon as I sit among you, I'll be surrounded by *cowards*. People who were too afraid to stand up to one of their own, a man who was openly abusing his power, until a crisis situation forced their hands."

She shook her head, allowing her lips to naturally curl into a sneer as she swept her gaze across their faces. "Now you want me to dive into this mess and fix it for you? Or are you just looking for a scapegoat? Perhaps you're just taking on the youngest councilor ever, so you can blame *me* if things go wrong?"

Absolute silence filled the area, the councilors staring at her in open-mouthed shock, and Red balled her hands into fists, already turning to leave. To her surprise, the tense moment wasn't broken by angry words directed at her. Instead, a Scout with bloodshot eyes rushed into the area and dropped, coughing violently as he attempted to catch his breath.

"Councilors!" He hacked for another few seconds, "The Wyld... is *burning*!"

Every emotion Red was feeling at that moment fell away, being replaced with utter dread as if a cold iron dagger was being pressed to her throat. Giving her full attention to the heaving man, she waited as patiently as possible for the rest of the report.

Knowing his duty, the Scout got his breathing under control then spoke as quickly as he could manage. "The southern forest is fully ablaze, and a strong wind from the coast is driving it north at a running pace. Our recommendation is a full evacuation of the Wyld to the north."

"How did this happen?" Contrary to Lily's expectations, the council was moving rapidly and speaking powerfully. Already, several had rushed to the sides of the grove to begin giving orders to various runners: the evacuation of the Wyld was to begin immediately.

"Sir! We believe the warband has decided against pushing through the forest and dealing with our traps." The Scout practically growled as he thought of the invaders. "It seems they're on a mission for absolute eradication of our people-"

The council, guards, and Lily were currently walking out of the grove, planning to join in on the evacuation immediately. However, as the Scout spouted his vitriol, she shook her head and interrupted. "No, that's not possible."

Sending an unfriendly glance her way, the Scout shook his head as if to tell her to be quiet, and began once more spewing his opinion out into the world.

Louder this time, Lily interceded, "I'm telling you, this wasn't the Wolf Warband. They're to the east of the Heart of the Wyld and closing in from there."

"Well, just *maybe* they split up. Did you think about *that*?" the annoyed Scout practically spat at her.

Undeterred, Lily pressed her point. "This isn't their doing. It's too clumsy, too destructive for professional warriors like them. They're here to gather supplies, food and specifically *wood*, so they can make additional sea-worthy vessels. Burning the Wyld is directly counterproductive for them. If anything... I'm betting what happened was that the Coasties who were left in the Wyld as a distraction started a fire, and it got out of hand. They have no fire discipline, and their understanding of the forest is… well, they don't understand the forest."

Her words were logical, and she firmly believed them. Yet, they were not well received. Not only did her thoughts ring out to the councilors around her, she was speaking loudly enough that the evacuating civilians turned their attention to her. Among them were dozens of Coasties, who looked ready to run over and start throwing fists.

"Perhaps you save your *opinions* for another time," one acid-tongued councilor spoke at her in a soft, threatening tone. "You've already thrown our generosity in our face, but perhaps we dodged a deadly arrow. You certainly seem ready to slap away any hand extended in friendship, and in times like these, having the goodwill of the people around you can save your life."

Lily listened to his words then looked around at the large crowd of people who were throwing angry stares and glares her way. Ever so slowly, she began to shake her head and let out a deep scoff. "I can't believe I didn't see this until now. No job, no respect… *why* have I been trying so hard to join all of you? Grandmother had the right idea. Living as far away from *you* as possible."

As she turned on her heel, prepared to walk away from all of this and began her personal evacuation to the north, Red's mind was whirling with deep thoughts on her situation. She didn't care how speaking the truth had upset and frustrated the others. If they couldn't handle reality, it wasn't her fault. With her last living relative dead, she finally realized she didn't have any deep attachments remaining to the city-state.

Hot tears fell from her eyes as a deep sense of loss filled her—though she refused to let it overwhelm her. The thought of the woman who had raised her being cut down by an abomination, holding it off long enough to stop it growing into an even deadlier threat, only to be used as an insult against her? No. A far lesser, but still potent understanding struck her then: the dream she had designed for her life was gone. She no longer had any interest in being a Wyld Scout. She didn't want to work with these people, interact or be friends with them.

It was all... gone. Over.

Every ounce of trust she had for them had been burned away; frankly, they were lucky she didn't just storm off and offer her services to the invaders.

"As soon as this is all over, I'm rebuilding Grandmother's house and sending an arrow into the shoulder of any trespassers." She softly growled to herself, wiping away the last of the tears she would shed until she was able to properly mourn.

"No warning shots."

FOURTEEN

HER PACE WAS unhurried and steady, but Lily was ready to vanish into the underbrush and leave this mess of emotions and politics where it belonged: far, far away.

Yet, just as she reached the edge of the Heart of the Wyld and made to slip through the trees, a stern voice cut through the hubbub and landed directly in her sense of duty and meaning. "Lily Red! If you walk away now, innocent people *will* die."

She turned with great annoyance to stare at the imposing councilman who had shouted: Franklin. Her jaw tightened in defiance even as her feet felt anchored to the ground, unable to move an inch. "You seem to think we have no regard for our sacred duties, for the trust of the people of Canu Moch. But here *you* are... ready to leave them behind, just when the forest has become more dangerous than ever before. Are you going to abandon your ideals, all your years of effort, due to misplaced anger?"

Her lips pursed, and her eyes went dark as Lily realized the councilman was applying pressure directly on her by using Grandmother's teachings. For a long moment, she wavered, her silence the only external indicator of her internal struggle. Two more steps, and she'd have the solitude she so desperately desired right now. But if she refused to even hear him out, and people died because she only thought of herself, Lily would never live it down.

With a barely perceptible nod, she turned back to face the gathering crowd of nearly panicking people and walked closer.

The Councilman of the Druidic Grove wasted no time. Franklin pulled himself up a tree, standing on a thick branch and shouting for attention. "Things look bad right now, but fear not! An evacuation plan has been put in place, and we will begin immediately. Every last one of you will be escorted through the Wyld, to the north, with our final destination being Bleakrock. We don't know if they will take us in, but hopefully they will at least stand with us, providing succor against the invaders who are destroying, or in the case of the Coastals, *have* destroyed our homes."

At this, both Coasties and Wyldlings turned to each other in solidarity, tears openly running down some of their faces. After the momentary pause, the councilman pressed on, "Every Scout, whether they are officially employed by the Druidic Grove, or *not*, will be given a group of twenty non-combatants to escort. We cannot safely have more people at a time, due to the narrow paths, as well as the danger of drawing Ascended Beasts or Monsters to overly large groups in the untamed depths."

The announcement was met with a mix of relief and fresh worries. It was clear, no matter how gently he tried to state it, that the councilman didn't expect everyone to escape the forest. "Each group will be intermittently departing, along divergent paths, to give *everyone* the best possible chance of arriving safely and without interfering with each other's journey."

Having been awoken abruptly—the sun barely clearing the horizon—then informed of the need to flee, caused panic to claw its way through the crowd faster than the wildfire was burning through trees. The air was thick with tension and the scent of fear; people's eyes were wide with the primal terror of the hunted. Desperate cries filled the air as they pushed and shoved, scrambling to be the first to be allowed to escape.

As the noise became louder, and people began throwing fists and shoving—a minor riot forming—the Scouts employed by the Wyld stepped forward stoically, faces expressionless as they drew their blades. The naked steel gleamed brightly and cheerfully in the morning light, a stark contrast to the danger they represented.

Almost immediately, the crowd fractured into smaller groups, a semblance of order emerging thanks to the implicit threat. The Scouts left their formation, scattering among the clusters as leaders, their voices steady as they organized the evacuation, or at least where each set of people would be staged until it was their turn to run. Almost immediately, the first groups were hustled out of the city with a haste which spoke of the true seriousness of the situation—the representatives of the Wyld seemed to fully grasp that they were hanging on to control by the thinnest of margins.

As the first evacuees vanished behind the trees, those remaining watched them go with hooded gazes. Franklin saw their shivering and contemplation, shouting out for anyone who would listen, "We're going to give them ten minutes, then the next set will go! Get together with your families; hold each other for comfort! Find solace in our shared fear. The next several days will be hard, but we *will* get through this!"

The promise of only needing to wait ten minutes became a lifeline for those most frightened. It seemed like everyone was prepared to strike out into the only *lightly* patrolled and scouted areas near the center of the island, regardless of the danger they may find along the way. Seeing the determination on the faces of those around her, Lily felt ever more out of place. Before she became too uncomfortable, a smiling man waving at her wildly caught her attention, and she let out a long sigh before trudging over.

"Hello, Chuckles."

"*Hi*, Red! We were told we've been assigned to you, since we've followed your instructions before, and... for some reason, everyone else was really mad at you?" Chuckles nervously chuckled as he turned and motioned for her to follow him. "I'll show you where we're supposed to be... I think they called it our 'staging area'? It's in the red zone."

"Appropriate." Red nodded in understanding before following after him, soon finding a slightly smaller group of Coasties than she had taken charge of previously. With only a momentary internal grumble, she accepted her fate in the hopes that they'd be easier to manage than the last time. "Did they say anything else?"

"Oh, yeah! They're going around and dropping off supplies and such. When they do that, they'll let us know our departure time." Chuckles cheerfully collapsed onto the ground next to a roaring fire, mimicking the position of the other members of the group.

Shaking her head, Red quietly commented, "You know, I kind of envy how calm you can be during all of this."

"If we die, at least it won't be *sober*!" Chuckles called out, grabbing a jug off the ground and raising it, earning a round of cheers from the others in the small group. Red darted forward as he lifted the jug to his lips, yanking it out of his hands and smashing it into the fire.

A huge gout of flame shot into the air, causing the Coasties to shout in alarm and scatter away from the sudden wave of dry air. All of them turned to look at Red with confusion and no small amount of anger growing in their eyes, only to immediately back down as they saw her glowering right back at them.

"We will *not*..." Her words were soft, but caused the hair on everyone's neck to bristle in sudden fear, "I repeat, will *not*, have a repeat of the last time we were in the forest. You will most certainly *not* be following me while impaired. My goal is to keep all of you alive the entire time we are together. But here's the thing. It doesn't matter to me if you're eaten by beasts or monsters, slain or captured by the invaders, or even burned to cinders by the fire rushing toward us... if you put *my* life at risk, I *will* leave you to die."

Feeling she'd made her point, Red swept her eyes around the group, locking gazes with each of them. "Until we are given our leave time, I will be explaining how you *will* act in the forest. I'll show you hand signs for you to follow, just in case we run into situations where we can't speak. If you want to make it through this, treat the situation seriously."

So began Lily's first ever training session where *she* was the teacher. The information she laid out was the absolute basics, everything from walking in two lines, making sure they always had a clear line of sight to the person in front of them, and getting permission before eating or drinking *anything*. Once everyone had this information down, extremely begrudgingly in a few cases, she moved on to basic hand signs.

"When I make a hand sign, all of you do so as well." Even with the holdouts, Red was surprised at how easily the majority were accepting her tutelage. She made sure to take full advantage of their dedication, deciding the increasing level of danger had focused them like nothing else would. "That way, if you have a clear line of sight to the person in front of you, like you *always* should, right? Right. In that case, everyone will get the message within a second or so. Let's practice."

She marched them around the small, open space they'd been allotted, giving orders and offering constant suggestions.

Lily had two reasons for drilling this information into their skulls. One, it was actually necessary if they were going to avoid the very real dangers they would likely be experiencing in the near future. Two... she needed to keep their minds off the fact they *still* hadn't been told when they were going to leave.

The sun was nearly halfway across the sky, and the once-cacophonous sounds of the city had slowly vanished as the refugees emptied out of it. The air was now tinged with the scent of soot, and even her calm facade was beginning to crack under the grim reality of the situation. Red's eyes drifted to the greenery to the north of the Heart of the Wyld, "I guess this is what he meant by telling me how ignoring offers of 'friendship' would come back to bite me. Should we just... go? It's not like they're going to try and stop us if I just start shepherding them away."

Just as she murmured her thoughts, a small group of *extremely* sweaty people walked into their area.

"Lily Red?" one of them called out questioningly, "Good, you're here. We have your supplies and planned route. You have about... eight minutes to get in position and start moving. There's no one after you, so you won't have to worry about groups merging into yours from behind if you move too slowly."

Twenty large sacks were dropped, which she assumed had been filled with food and water for their journey. Immediately, she had to step forward and smack Chuckles' hand as he yanked it open and attempted to pull out some venison jerky. "What did I *just* get done telling you about asking me before you ate or drank anything? We need to carefully ration this. There's fifty miles of untamed forest between us and Bleakrock, and I guarantee you'll starve to death if you don't do exactly what I tell you. That goes for *all* of you!"

"Right..." the leader of the supply group muttered as they handed over one last forest-green backpack. "Here's your

Scout supply pack. It has a set of spare knives, thirty arrows, and a shortbow because someone noticed you weren't carrying one. Every bag has a small bedroll, but I recommend sleeping as little as you can possibly get away with. Fire doesn't slow down so you can rest."

"Thank you." Red was genuinely surprised someone had managed to be so thoughtful, even with their home being destroyed, and had to wonder who had gone out of their way to ensure she was properly equipped. "Coasties, let's go make you into Wyldlings!"

Her enthusiasm was as infectious as it was fake. As Lily led her group to their exit point, she watched as the last few people remaining in the city vanished in other directions. Taking a deep breath, she confirmed to herself that they were on their own and mentally accepted the burden of bringing these people to safety. Unfortunately, that deep breath revealed a sobering reality: a thin layer of smoke filled her lungs, and she frantically looked up and around, finding the wispy smoke in all directions.

It was already beginning to weave its way through the trees, and she could only hope the wind was pushing it far, *far* ahead of the inferno.

Either way, there was no time to waste. They began moving immediately, making no attempts at subtlety or stealth —not this close to the empty city. Right now, what they needed was distance at all costs.

They had barely made it twenty feet into the woods when System's Whisper flared up, and Red nearly automatically activated System's Echo. She didn't see anything right away, but held up her fist, and everyone behind her immediately stopped. "System... what's happening? I can see hundreds of footprints, so other people have been coming along here. There shouldn't be anything dangerous on this path?"

Taking a few more steps proved to be a mistake. Lily noticed she'd stepped on a tripwire so well hidden even *she* hadn't seen it, just as System's Whisper flared a brilliant crimson. In the next instant, the ground, the trees, and the foliage erupted with motion. Crossbow bolts *whizzed* through the air as a dense cloud of death arose. Branches whipped across the area at chest level—thick spikes driven into their wood—and tree trunks swung through the air as pendulums: her current least favorite hazard.

There was no logical way she should have been able to avoid everything. Yet, with System's Echo still showcasing everything around her, affording her innate understanding of their position relative to her body, she ducked, dove, weaved, leapt, and rolled. The soft sounds of the traps going off were eradicated by the calamitous noise of the swinging logs slamming into each other with thunderous retorts.

Her skill ended, but Red remained in place flat on the ground, shaking with nervous energy and hyperventilating as she waited for anything else to activate. Even though she wouldn't innately know exactly where it was coming from, she could avoid it if she was careful enough to-

"Red!" Chuckles' frantic voice called out, rushing forward to check her for injuries "By the *system*, Red, did you survive that? Please be okay!"

"I'm… I'm good. Stay back!" The surprise in her voice was evident to everyone, even herself, but Lily stood to her full height—such as it was—shaking as she slowly returned to the others. "I can't believe I'm okay, but I am. I don't… I don't understand."

"It's pretty obvious someone just tried to kill you," Chuckles growled in a low, dark tone. "Who'd want to do that? *Why* would they do that? Your death would mean our death, so whoever this was just… they tried to kill everyone here."

Lily's heart raced as she realized the man was correct. These traps were new, or at least newly reactivated, and designed with a clear, lethal intent which spoke of exacting knowledge of her path, and when she would be walking it. "The only person I could think of who would have enough influence to get the details of my route, or maybe even assign it, then have all the skill to set this up… is Reynard. He lost his position on the council because of his actions toward me, and believe me when I say there's no one more petty than he is."

"So, this isn't going to be the last time something like this happens?" one of the other Coasties flatly questioned, sidling away from Red slightly.

"Oh… it absolutely *is*." Red growled as she grit her teeth and scanned the area. "Listen up. I'm going to make sure you get to Bleakrock safely. But to do that, we're going to have to throw away the map they gave us. It's going to be harder, but we're leaving the path behind and taking a direct route through the Wyld. I'm not going to lie, it's going to be danger-ous… it's also the only way I know I can keep you safe."

No one could say anything against her, as Lily was the only one who knew how to navigate the forest in the first place. They followed along with varying degrees of reluctance or enthusiasm as the Scout caught her breath—realizing only then that something was pulling at her attention. Glancing down at her arm, she swiped her fingers across it and read the new, golden-glowing text forming there.

Skill increase! System Echo [Level 3 (Rudimentary) → Level 4 (Basic)]!

System's Echo is an active skill which allows you to [Basically] yet innately notice life forms as well as rapidly moving objects in a range of [40] meters around you for [12] seconds. Cooldown: [3 minutes]. Upon reaching Perfection, this skill becomes permanently active.

Requirement to advance to level 5: Use System's Echo to coordinate silent movement of a group of at least 10 people around a sleeping predator without waking it or allowing anyone in your group to become injured.

"I guess that counted as 'coordinating my group through a perilous situation, surviving a potentially deadly threat without any of them taking injuries'." Red chuckled darkly to herself at her next thought. "Reynard would be *furious* if he realized he was the reason I just became even more powerful."

FIFTEEN

ONLY A FEW DOZEN yards deeper into the woods, all traces of people passing were simply gone. As far as the forest was concerned, no one had walked across the mossy ground here —ever. Red led the way with quiet, measured, but swift footsteps. The Coasties kept up with her pace without issue, causing her to send jealous stares at their longer legs every once in a while.

As she sank into her forest-dwelling mindset, her eyes began slowly scanning the dense underbrush—fully understanding how allowing her eyes to dart around frantically would only cause her to miss important details—as well as keeping an eye on the smoky canopy overhead. As her grandmother had always taught her, most vision is drawn to motion, so if she conducted her sweeps slowly, carefully, even the most subtle change would rapidly draw her eye.

Even if her system-granted skills were in full effect, she had been trained better than to rely on any one sense unconditionally.

As the minutes rapidly passed and all too quickly turned into hours, Red found herself surprised at the Coasties following along behind her. They were pouring sweat, coughing, shuffling, their discomfort evident with every raspy breath and muffled, continuous complaints. But they hadn't slowed down even a little. Perhaps it was the looming specter of burning alive, or concern about being left behind, but there was a marked difference between the last time she'd led them and now.

Lily was touched by the trust they placed in her, and she simultaneously tried not to think about how much of a gamble this journey had become. She didn't know this part of the forest and had rarely had any reason to move north through the Wyld. Most of her efforts had been spent crossing the southern half of the island, and she'd only ever approached the city of stone directly when she had been completing Grandmother's challenge to collect one of their helmets—now more than two years previous.

Two years was an eternity in the Wyld, as the forest was constantly reshaping itself. Sure, the landmarks and the trees remained *mostly* the same, but the underbrush was always expanding and contracting, the territory of predators and prey shifting in ways which could confound even the most experienced Scouts. A flat piece of land one day could be overridden with burrowing creatures the next, leading to sprained or broken ankles if someone were running through an area not expecting the new holes.

Even though they kept to an outrageous pace, there was nothing the fleeing people could do about the passing of time. The sun eventually sank below the horizon, and they began making mistakes. She pushed the group as much as possible, but finally, reluctantly, she called a halt.

Nearly everyone let out sighs of relief, dropping to the ground wherever they were, and Red's eyes flared dangerously, "*No!* Not this time! Listen, I know everyone is tired. *I* sure am. But we're in unfamiliar territory. We need to set a watch rotation. There's twenty of us, so pair up, and I'll assign each duo an hour of watch. If we don't get to you tonight, you'll start tomorrow night off."

This, more than any of her other directives that day, brought on moans of annoyance and complaints. But Red wasn't having any of it and firmly stood her ground, and eventually everyone found a partner. After choosing who would stay awake and who would get to sleep, Red made a *safe* fire pit and allowed them to break into the rations they'd been given.

Which is when they found the next nasty surprise Reynard had left for them.

"Red, I think… is this meat supposed to be fuzzy?" Chuckles held up a slice of venison which had clearly gone bad and had a thick coating of mold on it. "Did they just not take the fur off it correctly, or what?"

Walking over, Lily inspected the meat with disgust, but somehow wasn't even terribly surprised. "That's mold, Chuckles. Eating that is no different than swallowing poison. Everyone, pull out all your food and show it to me."

After careful inspection in the firelight, she determined a little more than half of the total foodstuffs with them had been tampered with or were outright rotten. All of it got thrown into the woods, where it could safely degrade. Everyone watched her throw away their food with shock, prompting her to respond with her own confusion. "Have you never seen spoiled food before?"

"Not like that." One of the few women in the group spoke up. "As soon as our fish begins to smell bad back home, we return it to the sea."

"The waters feed us, and we return the favor." Almost everyone mumbled at the same time, leaving only Red to look around like she was surrounded by crazy people. At least she had some context, and had been given a deeper look into their lives recently, or she wouldn't have had a *clue* as to why they didn't use every part of every creature they killed.

Instead of scoffing at their lifestyle, as she would have only a few days ago, she instead pressed for more information. "Do you just dump it back in, or do you use it as bait?"

"We don't really *need* bait. Most fish are just scooped up by our nets, but the rest of them are perfectly happy eating whatever we toss in." Chuckles chimed in, scooting closer to her and the fire. "Sometimes, we take out extra sturdy bones to make tools or oversized fishing hooks, though."

"But... why bother?"

"Well, to get the biggest fish of the day, of course!" Chuckles' words brought a hoot of excitement from the rest of the group, who laughed along with a far-away look in their eyes. "If you want to pull in something really large, you have to fish in deeper water. That means a pretty nice fishing rod and a weighty hook. Otherwise, you won't get it past the smaller fish when you cast. Maybe, uh, I could show you some time?"

"I'm not interested," Red informed him as gently as possible, meeting his eyes to indicate she meant both fishing... and whatever *else* he might be fishing for. "I don't even particularly like fish. After eating creatures of the forest my whole life, fish has practically no flavor to me."

"Then you're making it wrong," Chuckles told her with a strained smile, quickly finding someone else to speak with a moment later. Lily felt a tiny hint of remorse for having to shut him down so publicly, but he'd been cozying up to her since she had fought the wolves on their behalf.

"Glad he can take a hint, at least," Red murmured before pushing herself up from her seated position with a deep, heaving breath, and brushed the dirt off her legs. Doing her best to forget how tired she was, she turned to the first people who were supposed to be on watch. "We hardly have any food left, so I'm going to go hunting. It's your job to keep everyone safe. In an hour, wake up the next group, but until then... if something goes wrong, it's on you."

Leaving on that less than encouraging note, Red stepped into the forest and activated System's Echo, hoping there would be some large game nearby, and she would be able to get back to the impromptu campsite and sleep soon. Unfortunately, the sounds of the Coasties and the light of the fire had driven off anything larger than a few birds. Having a range of forty meters in which she could see any living creature almost felt like cheating, but it also allowed her to move without fear of missing the prey she needed.

An hour passed, then two, she began to realize it was likely they weren't the only creatures who had begun fleeing the inferno. Even now, Lily could smell the smoke in the air, which meant the more sensitive creatures had probably been able to do so for half the day. Just before she was going to give up and return without any game, she spotted a sounder of boars sleeping around a tree. Taking careful aim, she put one arrow in the air, and another, and a third, before the first landed in a sleeping pig.

It let out a pained, startled squeal, not managing to alert any of the others before the other two arrows landed. The second caused a sow to shudder and go still after thrashing twice, but the third was *deflected* by a tusk.

That last creature immediately had all of Red's attention. The fact it could awaken, notice incoming danger, and block the projectile meant it was at the *least* an Ascended Beast—the equivalent of an Advanced Classed human—on the way to being a full monster if it ever got access to a Class Shrine.

Luckily for her, the swine scattered away from her, a few even running into the Ascended Beast a few times and causing it to lose track of Lily's position. After a moment, it followed the others—but it didn't run. It backed away, every once in a while grumpily sweeping its gaze in her general direction. Red gulped at the thought of having to fight such a creature without proper preparation or weapons, and promised herself she'd set a few traps around their next campsite.

After waiting for System's Echo to come off cooldown, and ensuring that the other pigs had left the area, she moved forward and began cleaning the slain creatures, spilling their offal without bothering to bury it—the fire racing toward them would take care of cleansing this area. Besides, leaving an easy meal out for a predator might lure them away from her own people. Next came the hard part: bringing the meat back to the Coasties.

It took a little while, but she found a fallen tree and managed to pull off a chunk of curved wood large enough to serve her purposes. Using her knife, she bored a hole through it, then looped a thin rope from her Scout's pack through it. Shifting the pigs into the makeshift sledge, she wrapped the remainder of the rope around herself as a harness and leaned forward.

Getting the sledge moving was difficult, but as she picked up speed, it became easier and easier. Her instincts as a Scout were scoffing at her; Lily couldn't help but stare at the huge trail she was leaving behind, which was the same as rolling out a red carpet directly to the camp. "There's nothing for it, I've got to feed them. If something comes after us, I'll just have to add it to our pantry."

Finding the pigs had taken slightly more than two hours, but returning only took approximately forty-five minutes, as she didn't need to remain quiet or carefully search the area while her skill was on cooldown. When she finally returned, dragging the fruits of her laborious hunt along behind her, she found a duo of Coasties staring in her general direction.

They appeared absolutely terrified, making Red realize just how much noise she'd been making. She got closer to the dying fire before speaking up. "It's just me. Also, you should sit away from the fire when you're on guard duty. It ruins your night vision."

"Little Red! You're back!" The guard on duty hissed at her in excitement, trying and failing to keep his voice down. "*I* didn't think you had abandoned us, but it had definitely crossed the minds of a few of the group. Are those... what are those?"

"Pigs." She told them, swaying on her feet. "Look, just think of them as really huge fish. Try to butcher them without wasting too much of the meat. I... I need sleep."

She wasn't sure if the exhaustion she was feeling was as etched into her features as she felt it was, but no one said a word to her as she pulled her bedroll off her pack and untied the harness, barely managing before collapsing into a dreamless, fitful sleep.

What felt like only minutes later, before daylight had arrived, before even the last few brave birds in the area began singing, Red opened her grimy eyes. After a moment, she realized she'd been awoken by the scent of sizzling bacon. "No~o... that needs to last us something like three days."

A hand reached over, helping her up to her feet. Chuckles showed her a small smile, though he still wasn't up to meeting her eyes. "Don't worry. We got them all butchered, and the meat is wrapped up just like the stuff in our packs that isn't spoiled. There were some leaves nearby that looked exactly the same, so we folded those around the pork. We're only cooking a little bit right now, just enough for everyone to have a couple mouthfuls. Then... I really think we need to run."

Red was surprised—almost embarrassingly so—by how much the Coasties had impressed her over the last day. She humored the Coasty by following Chuckle's pointing finger upward, immediately realizing what he was talking about. The light of their fire revealed how the thin smoke of the previous day had been replaced with a thicker, dark gray version.

The fire was closing in.

"Yeah... eat up. We're going to need all the energy we can get."

CHAPTER
SIXTEEN

THE FIRST LIGHT of dawn filtered through the dense canopy, through the smoke, before languidly splattering onto the red, swollen eyes of Lily and her group of Coasties. They'd been moving from the moment Lily had woken up and been able to check whether the boar meat was ready and hand it out. They were coated in dirt, soot, bugs, and worse; still, thanks to the urgency of their situation, not even the usual muttered complaints fell from their tired lips.

Compared to the Coasties, who were dealing with blisters on their feet for the first time in their lives, Red was practically chipper as she worked to keep their spirits and speed up through a mixture of encouragement and rewards. "Isn't this great, everyone? A stroll through the park with all our friends!"

"Is a park a place that's on fire, filled with monsters, and actively trying to kill you?" Chuckles shot back, earning a grin from Red, until she realized he was asking in earnest. "Why is there a *name* for that? Does this happen more than I expected?"

Several other people leaned in to hear the answer, and Lily's previous smile faded away slightly as she realized the

Coasties may not have the cultural background needed to understand her attempts at keeping their mood boosted. "You don't know what a park...? Okay, no, a park is a cultivated area where families and friends go to spend time together in a relaxed manner."

"Looks like you've thrown your net without knotting it first, 'Chuckles'. You see her smile vanish like a slippery haddock through the gap?" One of the few women in the group playfully slapped Chuckles' shoulder, earning a short laugh from everyone in the group who heard her—but leaving Red blinking in confusion.

The Scout nodded slowly, "I think I see how my words can be confusing."

Strangely enough, seeing Lily being absolutely nonplussed —specifically *not* perfectly grasping something immediately— somehow put the group at ease more than her previous attempts at levity. Some of the tension left their shoulders, they eased their grips on their pack's straps, and for some reason, they even began making less noise.

Discreetly activating System's Echo, Lily attempted to suss out the cause of this shift. Studying their movements, she noticed with a blink of surprise that everyone had fallen into a pattern of synchronized movements. Each of the Coasties were approximately the same height as the others, so as their pace began to sync up, their feet came down into the foot-prints of the person before them with remarkable coordina-tion and precision.

The resulting effect was startling: the *crunching* of leaves and *snapping* of twigs were nearly eliminated, only echoing out from the leading pair of Coasties, who broke the silence due to their lumbering. This minimized their footfall noise output, a completely novel group tactic for Lily, who was used to traveling alone—or with one other person at most. Intrigued by the sheer difference, she decided to push her knowledge of small group movement through the forest further. She began putting her full effort into studying how they moved, how to make even untrained civilians more efficient and soundless.

Having found a way to train even while on an escort mission, Lily's good mood returned with interest. Trusting her experience and system-enhanced skills to ensure they were going where they needed to go, the Scout began surreptitiously employing training methods she had learned long ago on the people following closely behind her. She would hold a fist up in one of the hand signs she'd taught them, increasing or decreasing their speed. Sometimes Lily would have them stop entirely or crouch and move forward as quietly as possible.

At first, the Coasties stumbled into each other when their walking speed changed, looked around in confusion when other people started crouching, or even dropped to the ground and curled up when they should've been moving forward quietly. Still, as the day wore on, they became more used to reacting appropriately. Not only was this good practice for her as a teacher, it genuinely ended up keeping the group out of danger dozens of times.

All manner of beasts were fleeing the flames behind them, everything from chattering squirrels to bears forced from their dens. What had started as a small trickle of creatures in the morning soon turned into stampede quantity as more and more of the forest was disturbed. Yet, the worst part wasn't the mindless animals running from a fiery death: it was the Ascended Beasts—the intelligent hunters—who took advantage of the plethora of prey to viciously hunt or just slaughter for fun.

Knowing the Coasties behind her would panic if they saw what was happening all around them, Lily was forced to weave through the forest, going around areas of large-scale fighting and bloodshed. System's Whisper highlighted the most direct path to her destination, but she had tweaked it for years to *her* standards. Narrow openings between trees, small amounts of climbing sheer cliffside, leaps across creeks. None of those were options—at least not *good* options—for a larger group.

Happily, System's Echo helped to make up the disparity, letting her find wider pathways and natural bridges, thanks to the ever-present moss which would grow across fallen trees and sections of flat ground at approximately the same elevation for long stretches without severe changes. Having to consider the physical needs of the people around her highlighted dozens of areas where she could improve, leaving Lily pleased with her newfound knowledge and giving her plenty of concepts to meditate on even as the long day wore all of them down.

By the time the sun was midway across the sky, they'd been relentlessly speed-walking, crouching, and tense for multiple hours. While the Scout had the training and wherewithal to keep this pace or a far more brutal one nearly the whole day, the Coasties were already stumbling and weaving back and forth. That, combined with one other factor, made Lily raise her hand and form a fist—officially calling a halt for the first time since they began.

Almost the entire group dropped to the ground without pause, breathing heavily but making very little noise due to their sheer fatigue. As she had the best relationship with Chuckles, Lily moved over to him and started whispering instructions. "I need you to make sure everyone gets some food in them. They need to have a hand-sized piece of jerky, no more than that for now. We'll have a heartier meal this evening, but we can't be weighed down right now."

"Why do you want *me-*" Chuckles paused as Red frantically waved her hands at him to get him to lower his voice. Trying again, closer to a whisper this time, he asked, "Why do you want me to be the one to hand out food? You usually watch us like a hawk whenever the packs get opened."

Red motioned him closer. "Don't spread this around yet, because I'm not sure... but I think we're going into an iron zone right now."

"That means nothing to me," he whispered back, though it was obvious by his expression he could tell it was something serious.

Sucking a breath through her teeth at how annoying it was to not share what she'd assumed was common knowledge, Lily quickly explained, "I've been having to shift our path pretty much constantly to avoid predators and beasts who're fighting. We've had to stay mostly northbound to stay ahead of the fire, but I think we've gone too far west. About an hour ago, do you remember when I guided us through a wide opening between rock walls?"

"Yeah, you were muttering about not having grappling hooks or rope ladders," Chuckles confirmed, smiling as he saw her roll her eyes and flush lightly. "You talk to yourself a *lot*."

"Hazard of being alone most of the time." Her hand cut through the air as if hoping to slay the embarrassment she was feeling. Lily bit her lip for a moment, ultimately deciding she needed to share the information, so she pressed forward. "Different sections of the Wyld are given different danger ratings. When I brought us in here, I thought we'd moved into a secluded area which would be fairly safe. There's even less smoke, thanks to the rock wall, but... have you noticed there are almost no animals here? At all?"

"Aren't they just fleeing the fire?" Chuckles tried to shrug off her concern but was clearly becoming uncomfortable. "What do you think is going on?"

"We are very, *very* off the beaten path." Red's gaze bore into his, steady and unflinching. "I think we stumbled into the territory of a proper *Monster*, not just an Ascended Beast. It's called an iron zone on our maps, due to needing at least purified iron to deal damage to low-level Monsters. The rating goes higher than this, silver, gold, magical, enchanted, and so forth, but nothing on the island has ever required anything more than *cold iron* at the maximum. But, look, I need you to make sure everyone gets fed and keep them calm while I scout ahead. Above anything else, keep them *quiet.*"

"Maybe you should just stay with the group…" Chuckles trailed off as he looked over his shoulder at his people, then turned back to Red, only to see her already marching into the underbrush. Shoulders slumping, he finished with a soft sigh, "Come back safe."

Instincts on high alert, the Scout carefully but steadily moved ahead, able to move easily five times faster alone than she had been with the group. There was another reason she wanted to search the area alone, something she couldn't as easily explain to Chuckles. System's Whisper, which had been unfailingly reliable as an indicator of danger and directionality, was sending her strangely ambiguous signals.

There was danger here, that much was obvious by how much red light was flaring through her vision. But it was hazy and dispersed, but not sparkling around her like poisonous air in a bog did—she knew that one from experience. There was nothing to do but carefully figure out exactly what was going on.

As she paced deeper, the forest around her felt increasingly confining. The air was motionless, and even the few birds she'd seen earlier in the area were now nowhere to be found. As she adjusted her path slightly westward, tall rock walls made an appearance. Combined with the fact they had entered through a gap in the stone, this showed Lily that she was most likely in a valley or perhaps a crevice where the forest had partially sunk into the ground. Another half hour of careful searching brought her to a quiet, seemingly peaceful grove with a single tree in the center, where she found her answer.

From the now-visible eastern rock wall to the western one, nothing but grass and flowers grew in a large circle around the central tree. Lily paused before entering the open space, as System's Whisper was indicating mounting danger. Before daring to move another step, she waited for her active skill to come off cooldown. As it did, she ensured that the central tree was within her forty-meter range before activating System's Echo.

The sight baffled her, the reason for the system's overwhelming warning of danger escaping her entirely. "There's a woman sleeping on one of the branches? Why is that an issue? Does she live out here, and why is she such a threat?"

Her skill being at 'Basic' meant she was able to see a fairly clear silhouette of the individual, but distinct details were difficult. Especially as the distant woman was laying on another source of shining vitality: the tree below her. Still, as Lily focused all of her considerable willpower intently on that specific space, various points of interest caught her attention. "She's holding flowers? No, there are plants growing… out of her? Is that a dryad? I didn't think there were any on the island."

That somehow didn't seem like the right answer, as her skills wouldn't be warning her of so much danger if this was a simple protector of the forest which had somehow managed to ascend to monster status. Dryads were territorial, but so long as they were left alone, they usually did the same for others wandering through their area.

Quack!

A flurry of wings beating against the sky overhead yanked her attention up, blood draining from her face at the sudden racket. A flock of ducks were on the wing, flapping frantically as if shocked that they had managed to get airborne—typical duck behavior.

Their calls to each other, combined with the flapping, caused the woman on the tree to stir. Just before Lily's skill ended, she saw the silhouette of what appeared to be an extremely beautiful woman. Then a sweet song rolled across the area, so bewitching and entrancing that the Scout couldn't help but listen carefully, wanting to know *so badly* what the words to the song were. She even took a few incautious steps forward, but luckily—for her—the birds had fully captured the attention of the monster of the valley.

Most of the ducks immediately broke formation and swarmed toward the tree, though all of the drab brown ones merely continued on their flight path after a moment of confusion. The affected birds landed on any open space near the woman, even her arms, shoulders, and head. They *quacked* loudly, as if to be the first to get the monstrously beautiful lady's attention. Almost as if she were trying to keep them calm, the woman of the tree reached her hands up to caress the first of them—only to tighten her grip and brutally snap its neck before reaching for the next of them.

Lily broke out of her trance as the *crack* of the bird's spine reached her ears. The loud singing had dropped to sweet murmuring meant only for the birds directly around the monster, giving the Scout enough of a respite to get herself under control. Shaking intensely, she moved all the way to the side of the valley and kept herself pressed against the rock face as she moved across the grove, hoping against hope that the monster wouldn't notice her presence.

Luckily, it appeared to be fully focused on its meal.

By this point, all of the waterfowl had been slain, and the creature had begun tearing chunks of flesh directly out of the creatures, loudly smacking her lips in satisfaction as she feasted. Lily glided on her toes past the grove, then hurried through the forest on the other side for another half hour before finding a point where the valley widened out, and she was back in the forest proper.

For a few long moments, she considered continuing onward. "There's a monster back there... not a dryad, not a siren, but with components of both? I bet Grandmother would've known what it was called right away."

As soon as her memory of her grandmother was at the forefront of her mind, Lily froze in place. She couldn't force herself to take another step away from the people who were counting on her—that would be throwing all of her mentor's teachings in the mud. With a deep breath and a firming of her will, she turned around and retraced her steps. Once more, she was walking through the forested valley, sneaking past the temptress tree, finally returning to the Coasties.

"Welcome back," Chuckles stated with far too much fervor. "Is everything okay up there?"

"No." Lily pointed in the direction they had entered the valley, which was beginning to clog with thick, black smoke. "But I think it's already too late to go anywhere else."

CHAPTER
SEVENTEEN

GATHERING the remainder of the group as close together as she could, Lily explained the situation clearly and concisely. Her voice was pitched to reach their ears, but no farther, making them unconsciously respond in kind when they spoke in return.

"There's a monster in there, a proper *monster*, and you want us to just... backfloat right on by it?" one of the Coasties scoffed at her.

Another had a more reasonable thought and voiced it to the group. "You don't know what it is, you don't know what it can do, except that it sings for its supper? How can you be sure we'll be able to get past it, or that it's dangerous to us in the first place?"

Red could only helplessly shrug and gesture around the area. "We're surrounded by steep cliffs on all sides, even if you can't see them from here. I'd say we could try to scale them, but by the time we did, we'd be in the middle of a thick cloud of smoke. There's a good chance we'd suffocate even while the fire is miles away, since we'd be breathing hard and needing more air than usual. We can't go back because, obviously, *fire*. The only way through is forward, and we need to make this happen before the creature is on the hunt."

"You said it woke up and hunted while you were there!" an accusing voice stated too loudly, causing Red's hand to twitch as if to grab some of her twine.

Deciding halfway through her action that gagging the man wouldn't keep his noise level down, Lily stopped her reflexive movement and nervously looked back toward the roiling smoke as she hurriedly answered. "Right, it *woke up* and hunted, because there was an easy, convenient meal right next to it. Before that, the monster was dead asleep, hinting at it being a nocturnal hunter. If I'm right, and we do this correctly, we'll gain a lot of ground and be able to slow down while still staying well ahead of the fire."

"But if you're wrong, we all *die*," came a sardonic, sneering comment.

Red leaned forward and replied with the rhyme all the people of the Wyld told their children: "Stay on the path, don't stray or roam, lest the forest decides you shan't go home."

Her sing-song warning caught the others off guard, so much so that they simply stared at her, waiting for an explanation. Shaking her head, she motioned for them to start walking. "It means no matter how brave you are or how knowledgeable you are, there are real dangers in the Wyld. You need to be prepared for any kind of... of... *chance encounter*. Even the most experienced Scout can run into something they can't handle, and no one will ever know what happened to them. Well, we're already off the path. If we don't get moving, we won't have any chance of survival at all."

With no small amount of fear, the others fell in line and began marching after her. Thanks to her warning, they did their absolute best to stay quiet. As minutes turned into an hour, then two, Lily began to despair of being able to escape the valley before nightfall. She had crossed the entirety of the monster's territory by herself, twice, in only a few hours, but that had been accomplished by utilizing all of her training and being able to pick out the best path for herself using her skills.

As hard as she tried, she couldn't get all three of the things she wanted from the group: speed, silence, and caution.

Thanks to her System's Echo skill, she was able to take care of caution for everyone involved. Speed was... an issue, but that was only due to her absolute *demand* of silence. They were maintaining a steady pace, but that was one of the only positive thoughts she had about their attempts at surviving the next few hours.

As for herself, Lily made sure to stay about ten meters ahead of the rest of the group, keeping her movements slow and deliberate, each step calculated not only to come down and make the least amount of noise possible, but to leave a visible impression in the dirt and moss those coming behind her could put their own feet into. Yet, even after having carefully detailed and demonstrated what they needed to do, the fact was... most people's feet were significantly larger than her own.

Even with trying to be generous with her measurements, the first person behind her would rustle leaves, snap twigs, or kick a loose stone. It didn't help that everyone was understandably tense, not knowing the exact position the monster had made its lair. Each sound triggered a chain reaction: a misplaced foot *here* created a sharp intake of breath *there*. The forest around the group was constantly squeaking, shaking, and rustling, with each person glaring at the original perpetrator as if it would be any individual's fault if the monster came sprinting toward them on all fours through the underbrush.

"It would literally be all of you who drew it down on us," Lily breathed with an incredulous shake of her head. System's Echo was activated as frequently as possible, giving her rock-solid confidence that nothing was in their direct vicinity. This allowed her to move without seeming to hold any fear, which she hoped the others would see.

It was only a few hours until evening when they arrived at the clearing, where she held up a hand to tell everyone to stop moving then crept ahead to confirm the monster was still asleep. With a single skill activation, she established its sleeping position on its side, one arm dangling from a branch as it breathed regularly. Looking closer, her eyes widened as she took in details which had eluded her previously.

The monster had shifted in size slightly, and it took a few moments of adjusting her perception through the skill for Red to realize that its stomach was greatly distended—it had clearly eaten every duck it had killed off. She could only hope it was sleeping off the banquet with a proper food coma. But what drew her eyes the most was how the beautiful woman had the literal face of a swine, her snout twitching in the air as a feather danced in the air over her nostrils.

Ever so carefully, she eased herself back to the group, nodding at their questioning stares and motioning for them to follow her even closer to the cliff wall.

When everyone had clustered together, Lily put one foot out into the open area and took a slow step forward. Then another, and another, until she was fully exposed. As she walked, instead of looking around or trying to do anything fancy, she kept her eyes on the ground, carefully reaching down and picking up every dry leaf or small branch along the path she was creating. Her hope was that, by mitigating all the risks, the people behind her wouldn't be able to mess this up, even if they tried.

When she was to the tree line on the other side, Lily finally turned around, after carefully setting her collected pile well off the path, then motioned for the Coasties to follow. Chuckles, who'd become something of an impromptu leader to the group, thanks to his familiarity with Red, stepped forward, attempting to appear brave. The way his hands shook and how his feet slowly eased forward as if the ground was covered in glass only proved how brave he actually was: being able to face this very real danger head-on, without freezing up or retreating, caused Lily's respect for the man to soar.

One by one, all the Coasties crossed the clearing, somehow managing to walk along the straight line she'd made without panicking. Once the last of them was at least out of the open area, she held her hands up, showing both her thumbs and nodding vigorously to express her approval. The next few minutes were incredibly tense, as they kept their steps so slow and light, it seemed to Lily as if she were at the head of a squad of trained professionals.

Then, at almost exactly the ten-minute mark after walking past the monster's lair, someone's foot came down and cleanly *snapped* a twig in half.

Everyone's head twisted to look at the perpetrator, blanching as they did so. Even Lily felt as though she were about to puke—it had been *loud*. System's Echo flared into existence in the next moment, and she waited five full seconds before finally allowing the tension to drain from her shoulders and motioned for the group to keep moving. A handful of minutes later, a quail suddenly erupted from the underbrush, the violent motion and sudden of whirring wings causing the nearest Coasty to directly faint from sheer surprise.

From then on, every so often, there would be rustling, movement, and other natural sounds. At those moments, the majority of the group would flinch, shiver, or freeze… but the more often it happened, the happier and more at ease Lily became.

If they were getting into an area animals still frequented, it was unlikely the monster had a way to sense prey at this distance. After forty minutes of walking, she finally increased their movement speed at the expense of silence—she wanted them *out* of this valley before dusk fell.

Another hour of careful, yet less-stealthy walking, followed by forty minutes of a louder speedwalk, and the end of the valley was in view. Glancing at the sky, Red saw that evening was quickly approaching, darkness coming early being a strong possibility with the amount of smoke rising from the Wyld. Everyone was wearing terse smiles as they hurried to the exit, quickly filing one-by-one into the non-crevasse forest on the other side.

As the first half of the group stepped past the natural stone barrier, Red felt a warm, heady tingling fill her. Her arm prickled with what must have been information about her skill increasing in potency and level. Beaming in excitement, she lifted her hand to swipe along her arm and read over the change, only to pause in horror as faint notes of beautiful music reached her ears. "It's *singing*."

The haunting melody wove a serenade of tragedy and pain through the trees, forcing unbidden tears from Red's eyes. Even worse, the effect on the others was immediate and terrifying. Every man in the group turned in the same direction at the same time as if caught by a fishing line; their eyes glazed over, mouths dropping open slightly. Then they lurched back the way they'd come, crashing through the underbrush without care for scrapes or hazards.

Bizarrely enough, the women in the group only took a few steps toward the singer before noticing the actions of the others and snapping out of the odd entrancement. Lily didn't have time to consider the oddity of the moment, instead immediately sprinting after the lumbering men. Happily, they were even worse at moving through the underbrush of the forest in this state than they were usually: attempting to push their way through bushes, struggling *over* obstacles which would've been easier to go around.

The first thing she tried upon reaching the nearest man was closing her fingers over his ears, completely sealing off the noise. "Come on, if you can't hear her, she can't control you!"

After several moments, she had to face the fact that her

attempt failed; there was something else, something magical, suffusing the cloying melody. "Well, this is gonna hurt, but better a headache tomorrow than dead today."

She didn't have anything as handy as some kind of alchemical sleep powders, nor anything as gentle as a bola to tie his legs together with a swift throw, so as to make it impossible for them to reach the monster. Instead, softly apologizing to the mentally captured men, she drew her dagger back— slamming the blunt pommel of her blade into the back of their skulls and knocking them unconscious, one by one.

For most, a quick tap to the correct spot was enough, but for others... unfortunately, a few of the Coasties were *very* thick-headed. Still, even after the first hit, they offered no resistance to the incoming blows; simply stumbling from the hit and continuing to lurch forward. She was thankful for this, though it made her wonder how long this monster had been active in the forest, drawing travelers in, without anyone knowing about it... or perhaps simply never living to tell the tale.

After double-checking that each of the people were accounted for, she began the laborious process of dragging them back to the exit of the valley. One after another, they were pulled along and deposited with the women of the group —who were each given a hefty rock and charged with ensuring that the men *stayed* unconscious for as long as it took.

Shortly after the first eleven men had been dragged back, the song filling the air took on a new tone. The lamenting melody shifted into anger and fear, unnaturally instilling equal amounts of those emotions in anyone in auditory range.

Though her hands were shaking, and her legs were trembling, Lily pushed through the unwanted emotional burden and hurried to complete her task. Only a dozen minutes later, the song cut off abruptly, replaced by a melodious, tri-toned scream echoing through the valley. Red stared into the distance, her eyes hard. "I guess there might be a silver lining to the forest burning: sounds like the flames are causing her to have dryad-out skin."

Just after muttering her thoughts, Red stumbled backward as the deepening darkness of the late day was driven back—a pillar of fire erupted into the sky, flooding the air with a deep, blood-red pulsing energy. The crackling magic of the burning monster and its tree only dissipated after a double handful of seconds, leaving the humans to silently stare at the horizon with wide eyes.

From that moment on, the monster's songs fell silent forever.

CHAPTER
EIGHTEEN

LILY AND THE other ladies of the group stood watch as the group of men slowly recovered from being knocked out with various blunt objects. There wasn't much they could do other than wait as soft groaning slowly filled the air, each of them waking at different times, depending on their resiliency and relative thickness of their skulls. The Scout took the time to try and relax, letting go of the tension that had been filling her for the last several hours.

No matter how narrow the escape from the monster's deadly song had been, they *had* gotten away without any serious injuries or losing people. Red shifted her stance slightly, adjusting the back of her shirt, which had been sticking to her skin from the buildup of sweat from both the heat of the day and nerves. With another deep breath in, and a long, drawn-out exhale, she reminded herself, "A win is a win... just take it and be happy."

She wasn't the only one enjoying a newfound, cautious sense of relief. The Coasties were smiling once more, now that they were outside of the valley. A few of the men were even making fun of each other for not having as large of a lump on their head.

"You barely have a *bruise*! What a wimp. I bet I could brush past you and knock you out by sheer accident!"

Scoffing in reply, the annoyed Coasty poked at the fist-sized lump on the skull of the first speaker. "You're just jealous I actually *have* a brain in my head. Looks like you're mostly bone—almost all the way down to the center. Not exactly a deepwater pearl we needed to dive for, eh?"

Deciding to ignore their antics, Lily turned her attention outward. The forest was once again alive with the sounds of nature, a calming chorus to someone like her who'd spent her entire life surrounded by these noises. Just thinking of the ominous silence which had filled the valley caused a chill to run down her spine, made worse by her sweat-soaked clothing. Remembering the self-cleaning function of her cloak, she pulled it tight around herself—both for warmth, as well as hoping it would siphon off some of the excess moisture.

She leaned against a sturdy tree, the familiar scratch of rough bark on her skin helping her to relax. With the group unable to move for the moment, and the men working on regaining their bearings, Lily decided to take a moment to go over the notifications which had filled her mind with information. At the time of receiving them, she'd been far too distracted to pay attention to what they said, but checking was only a swipe of her fingers away.

Glowing text scrawled down her arm, and for a long few moments, Lily could only stare in confusion at what she saw.

Skill increase! System Echo [Level 5 (Moderate) → Level 6 (Considerable)]!

System's Echo is an active skill which allows you to [Considerably] yet innately notice life forms as well as rapidly moving objects in a range of [60] meters around you for [18] seconds. Cooldown: [2 minutes]. Upon reaching Perfection, this skill becomes permanently active.

Requirement to advance to level 7: Leading a group of at least 15 people, detect and avoid an ambush from a safe distance, rerouting your group around the attackers without them realizing any of your group is in the area.

"Hold up... I gained *two* skill levels during all that?" Tapping at her arm, she tried to see what the previous message had been, to no avail. "What was the requirement for getting to level six? What did I do? How am I supposed to write a comprehensive guide of my class if I missed what I had to do for an entire level of it?"

Unfortunately, there was no way to read over her previous messages, as the information on her arm only showed her what *was* and what was needed to move forward. In fact, that was the entire reasoning for writing class manuals. Whenever someone got a unique class or skill, it was considered their duty to write it down to help plan the path of future generations. Seeing as most children tended to get their parents' class or skill, or at least some small variation of it, this tradition usually directly benefited the family of the writer the most.

Shaking off the slight discomfort of missing out on knowledge, Lily allowed the excitement of the moment to fill her. She was ascending through the levels of her class at breakneck speed and was now at a level on par with some of the highest-ranked Scouts on the island. "It can take anywhere from five to ten years to gain a level under normal circumstances... by the end of this crisis, how strong will I become?"

The shift in her focus toward pondering the future pushed a slowly dawning realization on her. "You know... now that I think of it... the requirements for my skill advancements are leading me down one of two paths. Either I'm going to Breakthrough to become some type of rescue operation specialist, or I'm going to see a sudden shift toward wartime tactics and maneuvering. I wonder what sort of future the system sees for me?"

Depending on her next few skill levels, Red should be able

to start getting a sense for what her Breakthrough Skill would end up being. If she went the route of helping and rescuing, which didn't sound like a bad life at all, she'd likely gain some type of focused and powerful method of enhancing her rescue operations. Going by her grandmother's power, Lily could only hope for some type of massively ridiculous physical boosting skill, which would activate when she was trying to help others.

But... if a lifetime of combat and survival situations was on the horizon, the Breakthrough Skill would likely be *much* different. In that scenario, she had no *idea* what her most powerful potential ability would become—especially because her Full Class so far had been aligned so powerfully with system-granted enhancements, unlike anything even Grand-mother had ever seen before.

Shaken out of her reverie by one voice rising above the low grumbling of the others, Lily looked over to see a duo of Coasties letting out deep guffaws as they took turns smacking each other on the lump of their head. A moment of watching caused Red to lift her hand and pinch the bridge of her nose in annoyance: they were trying to see how little force they needed to apply before they would knock the other out again. "Will you two knock that off? Anytime someone's knocked out, they have a very real risk of not waking up again. *I* wouldn't have done it in the first place if it wasn't absolutely necessary."

A few people grumbled good-naturedly about losing their entertainment, but Lily was pleased to note that everyone had a cautious smile on their face. They'd made good time, gotten past incredibly dangerous situations, even a *monster*; certainly, they had plenty to be happy about.

"What was that thing? I'll tell you this much, I'd offer a full basket of fish to be able to listen to that voice again." One voice, which cut through the others, was full of a dreamy remembrance, earning him a glare from everyone who hadn't been enthralled. "What? Someone sings to you and gets you all filled with nostalgia, promises you everything you've ever wanted in life, and asks for only one little favor in return? Why's it bad to want to hear that again?"

"You're the kind of fisherman who would sail a ship to siren-infested shores just to ogle the pretty fish women with sharp teeth." One of the Coasty women grumbled at him, landing a not very gentle slap on the back of his head and making him wince and cradle his head in his hands. "Don't go getting any ideas, they're certainly aren't going to be any monsters out there who're going to let you go as easily as you got away from this one!"

"Siren! That's it!" Another man snapped his fingers. "I knew there was something familiar about these things! I know what it was!"

Even Lily was drawn to the conversation at this point, leaning in to look at the man who was speaking. The Coasty was one of the older men in the group, and seemed to bask in the attention he was getting at the moment. Sitting up straight and puffing out his chest, the easy explanation he may have given was instead replaced by a puffed-up story.

"I've heard tales of these things, though not many people would be able to draw the same conclusion. After all, these are only a footnote in the stories of the true danger to all of us, the sirens. As I'm sure you all know, those are powerful coun-terparts to mermaids, carnivorous versions which lure men to their death by singing and getting weak-willed men to dive overboard and try to swim to them."

"Weak-willed?" One of the ladies snorted as she shook her head. "If only the weak-willed dive in, what does that make you? We can all see that bruise on the back of your skull."

The man flushed slightly as everyone around him let out a rueful chuckle, most of them reaching up to gingerly touch the back of their own heads. "A-*hem*, that is, this must be a land version of the sirens—far more tempting, can even get the strong of mind, like myself. It's called a Mavka, and it's essentially a nature spirit that got a taste for blood before ascending. Otherwise, it would've turned into a dryad of some kind, most likely."

"It had the face of a pig: tusks, snout, and all." Lily injected the information into the discussion, all eyes turning to her. After waiting to see if there was other incoming information, the others shrugged slightly and bobbed their heads in acceptance. "Still a Mavka?"

"Hmmm…" The older man considered, rubbing at his chin. "Probably, yes. When it's put like that, I bet it is a variant monster native to this island. We've all heard of this exact beasty before now, haven't we?"

Looking around at all the confused faces, he smugly crossed his arms. "Is this not Canu Moch? The island of *Singing Swine?*"

Realization dawned for everyone, and they nodded along in understanding. While it wasn't immediately helpful in the current situation to know what they'd just survived, understanding it had been seen before and others had lived to tell the tale—just as they had—had a calming effect on the group and bolstered their morale further. Another Coasty rubbed his hands together in excitement. "Being able to put a face and a name to it means we're gonna have a *fantastic* story to tell the next time we're around a fire."

Seeing how people were back on their feet and starting to get antsy, Red stepped into the group and clapped once. "Looks like everyone still has plenty of energy, so let's keep going. It's getting dark, but we can probably get another hour or two before we have to stop for the night."

Seeing some of their faces contort, she decided to offer some good news as well. "By the way, as far as I can tell, that detour through the valley saved us at least a day of travel. My estimation tells me that we'll have one more day of hard travel tomorrow, then we'll be arriving at Bleakrock the next morning. Most of the predators were fleeing north and east and avoided following along behind us. You know what that means —we shouldn't have much to worry about going forward! Everyone, grab a chunk of cooked meat the size of your closed fist, and eat it while we walk. Let's go!"

She wasn't sure if the cheer was for the food, or the fact there was only one more day of this misery for them. Either way, even as it got darker, the forest seemed less menacing to the Coasties, going by how they kept up a happy conversation while walking for the first time since this journey began. Red didn't mind; in fact, she encouraged it for the moment, as it allowed her to keep better track of everyone as evening turned to dusk. She removed herself from their bickering and bantering, still surprised and pleased by the fact that she hadn't yet lost anyone in her group.

"I can't believe we actually did that," Lily muttered to herself, shaking her head side to side as she recalled the murderous tree-woman. "What would Grandmother have told me…? She probably would've made me ask myself if that was the right decision. Hmm… it *seems* like it was the right decision, because nothing bad happened, but would I do it again, given different circumstances?"

Contemplating this conundrum gave her plenty to think about for the rest of the evening, until she finally called a stop for the night. For the first time, the Coasties didn't simply drop to the ground wherever they stood, instead getting together in a tight-knit group and laying their things around them. Red nodded approvingly, seeing they'd finally realized they should be minimizing the number of fires they needed to make while maximizing their body heat.

An uncharitable part of her mind asked why it had taken them *this* long, as every extra fire meant more work, both in getting it going and in collecting enough dry firewood to keep it going the entire night. For the chore-averse group of people, Lily would have thought huddling together for warmth would've been their go-to tactic, that she would have needed to force them to collect firewood and maintain the flames overnight.

But as little as she wanted to admit it, her respect for the Coasties had been growing over the last few days. Only as she shook herself out of her thoughts did the Scout realize exactly how mentally exhausted she was. Laying out her own bed roll, she shifted beneath her cloak fully, peeked around to make sure the watch rotation had been put in effect, then dropped off into a deep sleep.

CHAPTER
NINETEEN

RED WOKE UP COUGHING, throwing herself to her feet and looking around frantically. The false dawn filled her vision with a thin wash of pale, silvery light lancing through the dense foliage. The world was colored with constant shifting, swirling smoke as huge swathes of the Wyld continued burning. Frankly, it was a pleasant smell, reminding her of cooking in her grandmother's house, but the Scout pushed through the wooziness filling her mind at the moment and scanned the area.

"No one's awake? *No one's* awake! Who's supposed to be on watch right now?" Lily rushed around the area, not being gentle as she lightly kicked everyone who was snoring on the ground. "Wake up!"

Slowly, far more lethargically than any other morning so far, the Coasties opened crusty eyes and began sitting up. She counted heads as they rose to their feet, letting out a sigh of relief when she saw everyone was accounted for. "Who was supposed to be on watch?"

One man slowly lifted a shaky hand. "I was on watch? But... I don't know how, you just woke me up? I was even sitting up on that branch to make sure I stayed awake!"

A single glance at the speaker revealed many details to the trained eyes of the Scout, and she let out a grunt of frustration as she hurried over to him and palpated his skull. "It looks like you took a nasty fall. Do you remember much of what happened?"

"No, I was... I was looking around, and the next thing I know, I'm getting kicked?" He lifted his hands, palms up, his voice laced with as much confusion as his concussed eyes showed.

"Okay, looks like you were above ground level and passed out from smoke inhalation." After making sure nothing was broken, she gently patted both his shoulders and turned around to address the rest of the group. "This is why we're supposed to have *two* people at a time on watch! He could have bled out while we were all sleeping soundly, or we could've all died in our sleep from the gasses released by the forest burning."

"Ugh, does everything have to be a lecture?" A grumpy voice quietly reached her ears, and she looked over to glare at a man who was trying to whisper to the person next to him. He at least had the good grace to flush with embarrassment and looked down instead of meeting her eyes.

"Yes. *Everything* needs to be a lecture," Red tiredly replied, her voice raspy from breathing in the smoke all night long. "I'm doing my very best to keep you all alive, and if you aren't going to listen to my *lectures*, it's not going to work."

There was silence for a long moment, before finally it was broken by Chuckles speaking up. "Let's get going. It's going to be a long day, but the last one in the woods, right? The sooner we get there, the sooner you don't have to worry about us, and the sooner we don't have to remember any of these warnings."

That pulled a chuckle from the group and a resigned sigh from Red. Everyone gathered their belongings, moving slower than the situation warranted due to smoke-stained lungs, bodies weary from hard travel, and sleeping on the ground for multiple nights in a row. They soon fell into a determined march, quiet but for the constant coughing erupting along the double lines they formed for moving through the forest.

Once again, the sounds of nature were muted, most creatures having fled this part of the burning forest well before the humans managed to wake up. Still, Red led them forward with a measured pace across the mosaic of moss, dirt, and fallen leaves. Activating her newly empowered System's Echo, she closed her eyes and relied on the skill for a long few seconds, never slowing her pace.

Information flooded into her mind, all-encompassing without being overwhelming. Immediately, she saw a marked difference from yesterday to today: where before she'd been mostly seeing living things as outlines, now she was able to distinguish a much greater amount of detail. Snakes coiled around branches were clearly differentiated from the vines doing the same. When someone rested against a tree for a moment, they remained a distinct object, not blending together with the trunk into a single blob.

As they continued moving, she explored the ability further, slowly realizing the limitations and uses of the upgraded System's Echo.

The major limiting factor was: unless she was looking for something specific, like living creatures, there was simply a library's worth of data dropped in her mind, which was otherwise useless. Also, the farther out an object was from herself, the more hazy it became in her mind, unless she focused on it directly. Eventually, she was able to work out the fact that anything within ten meters of herself was absolutely clear in her mind. Each additional ten-meter zone, corresponding to each skill level, was slightly less perfect in detail, unless she was searching a small section of it with directed focus.

This was most noticeable in the zone from fifty to sixty

meters, similar to looking at something and only noticing it in the periphery of her vision. If she turned her 'eyes' and studied something, it would come into focus and become easier to understand than what she technically 'saw' out of the corner of her eye. Giving it some more thought, Red realized this was a perfectly understandable limitation.

"I know it's there, and I can turn more of my attention to it. But right now, I'm able to see over a hundred thousand square meters of area around me all at once… of course, I'm not seeing it all perfectly at the same time, especially that far out."

Everything had limits, but with training, Red was certain she could work to make those limits impact her less and less. For now, she simply continued fiddling with the skill, applying larger filters on the information it provided. This was as simple as subvocalizing what she wanted the system to stop showing her while the skill was active, mainly so she could test it and make sure she wasn't removing key functionality.

"Remove the inner parts of trees, leaving any creatures larger than my hand shown inside of them."

Immediately, Lily could no longer see the sap network of the trees around her, though she could see plenty of nests made inside their trunks—birds, squirrels, and all manner of fairly small creatures. She was going to make additional adjustments but flinched back as several of the creatures suddenly vanished from her mindscape.

She jerked her head up into the side, looking at the spot where a squirrel had been only a moment ago… finding that she couldn't see where it had been hiding through the dense smoke. "Did it just *die*? It must have, as I can see any living thing or moving objects. Okay, that's another thing to watch out for. Still gotta watch where I'm running, or I might trip over a carcass."

Happily, she only needed to wait another two minutes to

reactivate the skill and was able to continue fine tuning as the day wore on. They made good time, though the forest here was dense and untouched by man. Walkways between trees were often narrow, causing a slight accordion effect as the group in front continued walking after getting through, while those behind needed to slow or even stop to wait for their turn. Red never let the group stretch too far, knowing how easy it would be for them to get lost.

When tempers flared, she would loudly describe how excited she was to have a nice warm meal, and maybe even a soft bed when they got to Bleakrock the next morning. The reminder would help people cool down, keeping the mood fairly light and turning the conversation toward tentative plans and their hopes for the next few days.

Midafternoon, Lily noticed a rock formation which made her heart begin pounding. She was so excited she actually stopped moving, and Chuckles ran into her, sending both of them stumbling. "Red? What happened? Is something wrong?"

The loud questioning instantly caused the remainder of the group to tense up, many of them going still and having similar accidents play out—they stumbled or even fell. Lily turned around and lifted her hands to calm them down. "No, don't worry! I just recognize that rock formation. Now I know *exactly* where we are, and I can say for certain we're on the right path!"

No one cheered, but exciting murmuring certainly broke out. Chuckles tried to use the moment to wrap Lily in a tight hug, but she ducked away at the last second, making him laugh and snap his fingers. "Almost got one that time. Ah well. How far away is Bleakrock?"

Though she was raising an eyebrow at him and glaring, Lily fought a losing battle against a grin which kept trying to appear on her face. "Even with having to move at a snail's pace with all you Coasties... it should only be about six more hours of walking."

Everyone had their own reactions, some pumping their fist in the air silently, others grabbing someone in a bear hug and shaking them around. "Yes! We're getting out of this green abyss-hole!"

"Hey!" Red pretended to growl at them in anger, though she fervently agreed this was not the correct environment for them. "We're not out of the woods yet-"

This earned a chuckle, and she officially lost the battle against a wide smile which finally appeared on her face. "-so let's keep moving and get everyone somewhere that has very tall walls between you, fire, and raiders."

Adjusting their course slightly, Red continued leading the group, which now had pep in their step, eventually settling into a slightly faster march. Continuing to use the time to fiddle with her skill, Red reactivated System's Echo every two minutes when it came off cooldown, cheerfully working on toning down the kaleidoscope-maelstrom of positioning data.

Then, roughly at what would've been dinner time for the Coasties, the peaceful monotony of Red's marching was abruptly shattered.

As she reactivated her skill, she found a faint silhouette in the treetops above them, only distinguishable from the dense foliage thanks to the rapid leveling she'd undergone. Her heart was pounding in her chest as she focused on the incongruity, trying to match up what her skill told her with her own expectations, and coming up short.

"Everything okay? Are we stopping for dinner?" Chuckles inquired, ever the unelected spokesman for the group. At the same time, the silhouette far above them tensed up, and Red realized she'd slowed down slightly.

Making a snap decision, she shook her head and turned back to the rest of the group. "I know you're all tired and hungry, but we're going to continue on in a straight line for at least another hour! Push through, then we'll make camp!"

Instead of the groans she expected, she only got grunts of acknowledgment as the Coasties plodded forward. Before her skill went on cooldown, she watched the form above them relax and settle in to watch them.

Chuckles clearly sensed something was amiss, but seeing her firm-lipped expression and the way she kept her eyes locked forward, he had enough awareness to keep his own mouth shut. A few minutes later, Red reactivated her skill, watching as the silhouette in the treetops remained where it was. By the next activation, she was too far away—which meant she could speak without being overheard.

"We have a problem," she softly spoke into Chuckles' ear. "I saw a Scout back there, watching us from the treetops."

"A Scout?" Immediately, he started blatantly looking around, his wide eyes searching the branches around them as Lily facepalmed. "Where? Wait, no, that's good news... isn't it?"

"This is *exactly* why I didn't tell you when I first saw them." Red rolled her eyes as she watched the Coasty continue to ineffectually search the canopy. "Let me ask you this: why would a fellow Scout watch us from a distance, not offering any help or even saying hello? We could use the help, and no matter how much they trust me, I'm sure *proof* we're on the right track would make everyone happier."

Chuckles looked at her with clear brown, innocent eyes. As she waited, Red could practically see each thought going through his mind, as realization of the situation dawned on him. Chuckles gulped loudly, the cold knot she was feeling in her gut obviously being mirrored in him. "Then... that's not a friendly Scout? They're not out here to keep a lookout for us, they're probably here to watch for *you*?"

"I can't say for sure." Lily surprised herself with how calm her words came out. "All we know for sure is that they saw us, and they didn't seem very happy about it."

Turning around, she raised her voice so everyone could hear her. "We're going to stop early tonight, so we can be fresh in our last push! Eat everything you want, just make sure to save enough for breakfast. We'll be dining in Bleakrock by lunch!"

TWENTY

CHUCKLES' eyes bulged, and he sucked in a deep breath to yell for help as a hand clamped over his mouth. Red leaned in close, her left hand held up to her own mouth to indicate a need for silence. "Take it easy. Help me wake people up; we need to go. Now."

"But…!" The man trailed off as a glare drilled into him. Speaking much softer, he tried again. "Red, there's not even a hint of sunlight. It's got to be the middle of the night!"

"It *is* morning. Technically," she told him in the softest voice she could manage. "Remember what I told you before we went to sleep last night? If we want any chance of getting through here without a fight, we need to move completely unexpectedly. Tell everyone I saw some monsters, and we need to get out of here as quietly as possible."

Red was happy she didn't need to explain her real reason for the early departure, knowing she'd earned enough trust with them that they would take her at face value when she said there were dangerous creatures skulking around. The truth, there being Scouts out for blood—potentially even directly led by one of the most dangerous men in the entire Wyld—was a little secret she was happy to keep to herself.

She was afraid that if she let people know what was going on, they'd attempt to go out and reason with their assailants, walking directly into a trap, nabbed as a hostage, or worse: being slain directly so no witnesses would be left behind. The group was slowly woken up, but no matter how quiet they told everyone to be, whispering and muttering soon filled the air— to the point Lily needed to let out a sharp hiss between her teeth to get them to go quiet again.

"Everyone, let's get moving." Her voice barely carried in the heavy night air, yet the grumbles and muffled complaints announced that she'd been heard. Pulling out a coil of rope, she unspooled it as she went down the line, making sure each person had it in their grip before moving on. "Whatever you do, don't let go of this. It's pitch black, and if you get lost, we might not be able to come back for you. If I yank on it twice, that means stop immediately. After that, I'll pull on it again twice when we can move."

She was glad everyone in her group was an adult and understood the necessity of being as quiet as possible. Going to the front of the line, Lily made sure she was a little over fifteen feet ahead of the next person, just in case she activated a trap and needed to avoid it without getting one of them caught in it.

Beginning to walk, she found herself needing to pull for a moment, until the next person in line reluctantly began walking along with her. Satisfied that they were underway, she focused on carefully directing the group and fully opened her senses to the surroundings. The air was cool, containing a hint of humidity which pointed at an incoming storm. She could only hope it came soon, in an absolute deluge, as otherwise, there'd be practically nothing left of the forest to save.

The leaves on the ground were damp with morning dew, muffling their footsteps as they swept through the area. Beyond the soft rustling of feet being placed carelessly, the only other sounds were the occasional whispered curse as someone stumbled or was pulled too fast. It was too early for birds, and most other animals had already fled anywhere but south.

This meant only one thing to Lily: anything she heard out there right now was likely to be another person. At the same time, she knew exactly how loud her group was being, and how quickly they would be found if she wasn't the one guiding them.

With that thought, she activated System's Echo and adjusted her course to what System's Whisper told her would be the optimal path through the undergrowth. Comparing the two skills let her pick out what would be the best route for *everyone* involved, and with all of her senses—natural or magical—active to the maximum, she moved just a *little* bit faster. Lily acknowledged one small fact, speaking so quietly only she could hear herself.

"We need to be *past* Bleakrock by sunrise, or we're not going to make it. We can do this."

The rope keeping them connected was the only reminder she wasn't alone in the oppressive darkness. Every so often, even when System's Echo was in full effect, she'd pause and listen intently for any signs of a trap or ambush being sprung or prepared. The silence which echoed in her ears was not only relieving, but also a source of tension—like a spring being compressed, waiting for the pressure to come off so it could fling itself at her.

The first hour passed without issue, and people began to relax. Yet, before anyone could make the mistake of beginning to chatter among themselves, Lily gave the rope two sharp yanks. Immediately everyone stopped what they were doing, and most crouched down, even though doing so hadn't been part of their instructions. Red wasn't thinking about them at this moment, instead focused on a distant figure which had just barely entered the range of her skill. She considered the shape in the distance, watching until her skill went on cooldown once more.

"It's a Scout, that's for sure. Going by the way his head is tucked down, body tight against the tree... he's got to be asleep. Probably tied himself to the trunk so he wouldn't fall overnight." Red considered the route they were on, comparing it to the man in the tree. "Most likely, he's set himself up to be able to watch the area he trapped, so we should deviate around... this way..."

Another two sharp tugs, and the group was following after Lily, silent and careful once more. Swinging wide around the sleeping man, Red was never more thankful for System's Echo than she was at this moment. Knowing the position of her assumed enemy was extremely beneficial, especially in a low visibility area—doubly so when they couldn't find *her* location.

They began moving northeast, with a heavy emphasis on east. "If I can get us past the city, then backtrack from the north, no one should have had time to prepare for us or set traps to take us down out of sight. If we can just get close, Reynard will be defanged. He wouldn't *dare* risk his reputation by coming after us where other people could see what he's trying to do to us."

Approximately twenty minutes later, Red once more had to signal the group to remain still. Comparing the location of the newly discovered Scout to the previous one, she realized Reynard had woven a standard net grid pattern. Recalling her grandmother's lessons, as well as her own study of the Scout's manual she had practically memorized when she'd been attempting to join them, Lily realized the next Scout would be waiting for them at an angle between the two, farther north. The trio should make a perfect triangle, which they were currently in the lower left portion of.

If she had been planning to continue directly north, they would absolutely run into the next layer of the 'net'. Lily shook her head, amused at how insulted she felt by them using such a simple tactic. "Does he not expect me to have put any thought into the tactics they use as 'Official Scouts' since I was never on a Scout team? He *knows* I was trained by Grandmother, doesn't he?"

Once more she adjusted their route, only to pause and squint into the darkness. "No... he absolutely knows I was trained by her. I'm betting it's an offset pattern. He's expecting me to underestimate *him*, expecting me to think he's underestimated *me*. Straight north it is."

Forty minutes of walking later, Lily had to close her eyes and shake her head at what she saw. There, sixty meters due north of her, was the next layer of the net. "I... I can't believe it. I gave Reynard too much credit? He *wasn't* outthinking me; he actually *was* looking down on me. I know how he's acted over the last couple years, so why would I think he changed?"

Concerningly, this situation was different, significantly more dangerous. First of all, the man in the tree ahead of them was awake and alert, shown by the slow, constant turning of his head, which indicated he was scanning the area for intruders. Red could only blame herself, as she had allowed the people behind her to make a little more noise, thanks to thinking they were in the clear. She couldn't be certain if they woke him up, but she wouldn't be surprised if they did.

Secondly, she'd already found and disarmed two traps in the last few minutes. If there were so many obvious trip wires and activation sequences, it was highly likely there were going to be a myriad of better hidden and therefore more dangerous versions. With no other choice, Lily was forced to make the group backtrack along the path, then shift their heading and give the area a wide berth.

There was one positive outcome: if Reynard was going to use strategies against her that were straight out of the Wyld playbook, she would be able to avoid them without much further issue. As night rolled over into early, early morning, and the first rays of sunlight provided light for their journey, Lily had adjusted their path dozens of times, countering the net tactic perfectly—to the point where she hadn't seen another Scout with her skill for over two hours.

She allowed a few minutes for everyone to sit and eat their last bit of food then got them up and moving once more. This close to their destination, there was no chance she was going to give Reynard an opportunity to fix his mistakes and catch up to her.

As dawn became morning, and the birds began calling, the group of twenty-one total people had already had a full work day of careful navigation, heart-stopping close calls, and were swaying on their feet from exhaustion. Turning to face her charges, Lily looked at them carefully before speaking louder than she had allowed anyone to do the entire morning. "Does anyone need a break? I think we can keep-"

Twenty hands were in the air before she could finish her sentence, pulling a chuckle out of her. Before they could flop to the ground, she motioned them forward and stepped around a tree. There was a low chorus of groans, which cut off a moment later as they moved past the obstacle and stepped into an open, clear-cut area.

"We did it," Lily explained with a smug grin as they glared at her. "If you need a break, why don't we rest within the walls of Bleakrock?"

As the last of the group stepped into the open space, a call went up from the guards on the wall. "Make yourself known to the guard of Bleakrock! Are you friend or foe?"

"Coasties led by a Wyld Scout, seeking asylum from the invasion by Wolf Warband!" Lily called back at the top of her voice, a slight echo returning to her as her call bounced off the hard surface in the distance.

A few seconds later, a stern order came down from above. "We see you. Come halfway to the wall, then follow it to a gate for processing with the others. You will be under observation the entire way; do *not* do anything to give us cause to deny you entrance."

As soon as his words reached Red's ears, she felt a tingle on her arms. "By the system, that entire trek through the forest counted as one *single* ambush? I suppose... it was all coordinated and using a specific tactic. Looks like the system agrees with me that Reynard wouldn't put his own neck on the chopping block now that we're in Bleakrock's territory. How predictable."

Glancing down, she read over the information which was still in the process of being written into her soul.

Skill increase! System Echo [Level 6 (Considerable) → Level 7 (Proficient)]!

System's Echo is an active skill which allows you to [Proficiently] yet innately notice life forms as well as rapidly moving objects in a range of [70] meters around you for [21] seconds. Cooldown: [1 minute, 30 seconds]. Upon reaching Perfection, this skill becomes permanently active.

Requirement to advance to level 8: Successfully coordinate and carry out an ambush against either a group of hostiles or a leader of a hostile group, using System's Echo to detect the ambush from a safe distance. The group or leader who attempted the ambush must be either slain or rendered fully harmless.

Red looked over the new requirement for advancement with a sinking feeling in her gut, even as she led the others around the city while the guards watched them carefully. "Ugh... yeah... a clear shift toward combat-specific scouting. That doesn't bode well for Canu Moch."

TWENTY-ONE

THE GROUP of twenty-one people walked ever closer to the *open* gates of Bleakrock, a sight Lily had never seen in all her years. She stared at the walls, noting the incredible detail on them, as well as the perfect uniformity of the square stone the wall had been crafted from. As they cautiously stepped through the huge metal entrance, she gratefully realized she wasn't the only one looking around in curiosity and concern.

Her senses were going haywire, unable to rectify the utterly alien shift between her world and this one. The stark contrast between the organic chaos of the Wyld she had lived in her entire life, compared to the meticulous, ordered world within the city-state of Bleakrock made her stomach churn. The terrain had been altered completely, turned into something completely unnatural for the island. Firstly, after stepping through the gates of the wall, they found themselves in a vast, open space... with yet another wall between them and the actual city.

They were in a no man's land, a flat, stone space hinting at a community constantly prepared for war. Lily shook her head and murmured, perhaps too loud, "Why... *why* is there a fortress like this on Canu Moch, of all places? What are they protecting, or hiding?"

A plate mail-bedecked guard clattered toward them, a long halberd clutched in one hand being used as an impromptu walking stick. Lily swept her gaze over him, at first internally ridiculing the man for such an unnecessary, practically useless set of gear. Then, with a queasy feeling in her gut, she realized perhaps armor such as this *wasn't* as impractical outside of the forest. In fact, in an open space, his weapon would likely be far more devastating than the short swords favored in the woods. If he didn't need to constantly be moving on uneven terrain, or be concerned with sinking into mud-

"You there!" The guard shoved a gauntleted finger at her. "Keep sizing me up like that, and I'm going to think you're a troublemaker. You *don't* want me to think that about you, no matter how dangerous you might be. We just met, after all. Are you the Scout assigned to this group?"

More than anything, Red was taken aback by the seriousness with which she was being regarded. All her life, she'd been dealing with people teasing her or outright ignoring her, due to her stature. Yet, here, as soon as she stepped foot within the walls, the guard immediately realized she was not only dangerous, but in charge of the large group.

Frankly… she was flattered.

"I was. Having successfully and safely arrived, I hereby discharge my duty and turn over the safety of these Coastals to the city-state of Bleakrock. Do you accept this duty?"

"I, Captain Cliff of Bleakrock, accept these refugees and agree to take responsibility for them in the short term, until they have been informed of the rules and assigned housing." The man replied back to her just as formally, seeming to be put at ease by her professionalism.

He relaxed slightly, scanning over the others with hard eyes. "Welcome, everyone, to Bleakrock. Come with me to the secondary gate, where you can await entrance with the rest of your people. Before you enter our sanctuary, you must be made aware of the rules. Whether you agree to follow them or not, as soon as you step within the inner wall, you will be *bound* by them. Let's go."

He swiveled on his heel and began marching away, his metal-shod feet releasing an unpleasant, high-pitched scraping against the stone as he moved. Red turned to the Coasties, forcing a smile onto her face. "This is where our journey together ends. Thank you all for teaching me about your people and your ways. I hope to be able to visit you very, *very* briefly on the shores of Canu Moch someday."

Absolute silence met her, along with a score of blank stares. Chuckles shook his head and stepped forward with his palms up and arms akimbo. "You're not going to leave us just like that, are you? Red, you kept us safe for the last... for *days*! We trust you, but we don't know these people. Are you really going to just... hope for the best and leave us here? What if something terrible happens?"

Lily smiled and gently punched him. "What's going to happen, Chuckles? Are they going to chuck you in the pit?"

"I believe in the pit," he replied sincerely, referencing the assumption everyone had about the city of stone. "They've never grown outward, so where else are they going to go but down? They've never exiled anyone, which means they probably just throw troublemakers out into open air and let them go *splat* at the bottom."

"That can't possibly-"

Red tried to wave away his words, but Captain Cliff turned around and stared at the Coasty directly. "Follow the rules, and you will have no *reason* to be worried about the pit."

"It's *real*," came a horrified whisper from behind Lily.

"By the system, couldn't you have waited five *minutes* to terrify them?" Red hissed under her breath as the group stared at her with giant puppy eyes. "I'll walk with you to the next gate, but I'm not going to be bound by their rules. There's plenty of forest left, I'm getting back out there. I've nothing to fear from Wolf Warband, not when I'm alone."

The Coasties let out a cheer and started following along after the guard, forming a wide half-ring around Red as they walked—leaving her at the front of the group and huddling together to show their own solidarity with each other. They walked along the no man's land for a full three minutes before the secondary gate became visible. It was also wide open, though there were at least a dozen fully combat-armed guards blocking anyone from entering.

Not to mention there *were* people. *Lots* of people.

Lily and her group had entered from a more northern gate, while the entirety of the refugees from both the coast and the Wyld had poured through the southern one. Hundreds upon hundreds of people were packed into the open space, spanning from the currently blocked gate to the exterior one they'd entered through. Lily looked at the thick press of people, immediately uncomfortable with the thought of joining them, doubly so as the stench of such a large crowd —who'd been wandering through the woods for days without any way to maintain hygiene—struck her in the nose like a physical blow.

"Ugh, that's *rank*." She shuddered as they got closer, and the *otherness* of Bleakrock came into full view as she looked into their city. The only thought in her mind was 'straight'. The perfectly square blocks of stone which made up the walls were only the beginning; roads had been carved through the city in perfectly straight lines.

Even from here, she could see how they intersected at precise angles to create what must have been a grid pattern. The houses were uniformly constructed of the same mottled gray stone, boxy and square from start to finish, since there was no need to slant the roofs in a tropical zone such as Canu Moch.

As far as her eyes could see, everything was a square. A box. Utterly devoid of the natural curves of organic growth. Lily began unconsciously walking backwards when she realized there wasn't a single plant to be seen—only cold, hard stone. This place was anathema to her. After two steps, she backed directly into the close-knit Coasties and remembered where she was. "There you go! Look, everyone you've ever known is right over there. You're safe now. Everyone is good? Perfect. Goodbye."

"Are you sure you won't stay? Maybe just a *little* bit longer?" One of the ladies who'd been traveling in her group stepped forward and swept her into an unwanted hug. Lily pushed her off, only to find the entire group pushing in to show their thanks. She couldn't even be mad—much—as it was known how touchy-feely the Coasties were. They spent their entire lives showing love and appreciation with hugs, wrestling matches, and all sorts of minor things the people of the Wyld considered inappropriate in public.

"No, I will *not* stay." Red lifted a hand and stiff-armed the next man who tried to swoop her up and swing her around, sending him stumbling and tumbling to the ground, much to the appreciation and amusement of the others. "Look at that place. It's boxes and straight lines. In a place like this, my skills are... useless. Everyone can find everything for themselves. There's nothing to hunt, nothing to be wary of except other people. This is the worst type of prison I could find myself in."

The Coasties looked through the gate, then at each other while shrugging and mumbling. Chuckles summed it up best: "Doesn't look so bad in there. It's flat, but so's the ocean."

"Lily Red!" a powerful voice called out, pulling all their attention to five members of the Council of the Wyld walking toward them. Red could see the man at the head of the group counting the faces around her, then nodding approvingly. "We see you have fulfilled your task, even better than eighty-five percent of our official Scouts. Congratulations. We've been discussing your situation and would like to offer you a position on the council once more, now that you have some experience leading a group."

Looking at the press of people, the geometric city, then up at the sky—the only reminder she could see of nature continuing to exist—Lily considered her options. Then she met the councilor's eyes, and he knew her answer even before she started shaking her head. "This isn't the life I want. I'm going back out there. The forest is my home, and I'm certain to be safer there than anywhere else."

"You'll be *alone*." One of the councilors, who looked as though he'd been chewing on lemons the entire morning, finally lost his internal struggle and began spitting vitriol. "There's no one left out there. You will be cut down by the invaders the first time you come within range of them. If they can't find you, they'll burn you out just like they did to us! Do you think someone like you has a chance against them? A *little pink piggy* against the entire Wolf Warband?"

Rage tinted Lily's vision crimson, but as she stepped forward to give the man the verbal beatdown of his life, someone beat her to the punch.

Literally.

Chuckles stepped forward and threw a heavy haymaker, his fist distorting the councilor's face and sending the man flying with blood and a tooth erupting from his mouth. The Coasty bellowed at the tumbling man, "Who do you think you're talking to? If she wanted to, I'd bet Red could take out the entire warband by herself! It might take a while, but I've seen what she can do. We *all* have!"

The other Coasties piled on, needing to be pushed back to keep them from kicking the fallen councilor.

"We owe her our lives!"

"Where do you get off talking to her like that?"

"She's ten times the Scout any of your people could ever be!"

"Is this one Reynard? I owe him a punch if he is!" The last comment earned Red a few confused, angry glances from the shocked councilors, but several Bleakrock guards rushed toward them and separated the group before the situation could devolve further.

Against Lily's expectations, the man who appeared to be leading the council didn't get angry with her. Instead, he gestured to the Coasties all around her, who had already fought on her behalf without being asked. "Look at this, Red. How long have you been with these people, that you inspire such loyalty in them? Think of how you could use this to benefit *thousands*!"

"I say send her out to fight the wolves!" the bleeding councilor growled as he pushed himself off the ground, poking at his jaw tenderly. "She doesn't inspire *loyalty*! That 'Scout' is clearly *rabid* and is just spreading her infection to the people around her."

"Thank you for the offer." Red loudly and firmly stated. "This is the last time I'm going to say it. That's not the life I want; find someone else."

The head councilor reluctantly nodded at her, and Lily turned away to walk back to the distant gate. A deep voice shattered the air, drowning out all other noise and causing the assembled people of multiple city-states to go quiet instantly. "Enemy forces spotted!"

"Confirmed! Activate lockdown procedures!" Another voice came from the secondary wall, echoing in the sudden silence.

"No, no, *no*!" Lily broke into a sprint, rushing toward the already-closing gate. Just before she was in range to dive through it, thousands of pounds of metal slammed shut…

…but not before hundreds of raiders covered in wolf-adorned gear streamed through the trees like monsters appearing out of the mist.

TWENTY-TWO

RED DASHED TO THE SIDE, attempting to dig her fingers into the seam between the enormous blocks of stone making up the wall, only to find the rocks so perfectly joined she couldn't even fit a *fingernail* between them. Starting to panic slightly, she looked at the metal doors which had just shut, seeking any way to scale them or fit through an open space. Just as she had expected, and as she'd observed her first each time she had been in this area, there was no obvious way of getting through this barrier.

"Let me out of here!" She demanded as a guard patrol began walking toward her, clearly worried that she was attempting to sabotage the defenses. "I don't want to be here, and-"

"Look, kid, I don't know what you're playing at, but there's hundreds of vicious killers out there surrounding the city right now." One of the guards held up his left hand in a pacifying gesture. "Let's get you back with your group, maybe find your parents?"

Seething at the words, though it was clear he simply did not recognize she was an adult, Red looked around for a loose stone or something non-lethal to throw at the heavily armored man. Failing in that, she took a deep breath and steadied herself. "My name is Lily Red, I'm a Scout from the Wyld, and have had my Full Class for years. I was leading a group of Coasties into the city. I've no intention of staying here for any length of time. How do I get out?"

"Oh, sorry about the mix-up, miss." To his credit, the guard sounded legitimately chagrined. "I'm sure you get that all the time, but I apologize all the same."

Hearing the sincerity in his tone, Red slumped slightly, her anger sieving away. "I don't care about all that, I just need to get back outside."

"That's… well, I'm sorry to say that's not going to happen," the guard stated slowly, as though he were trying to calm a Wyld animal. In this case, he was at least half right. "The leadership of both city-states already agreed to the rules of hospitality, and by entering the first wall, you have implicitly agreed to them. With the outer wall closed, and enemies at the gates, we cannot in good faith allow you to exit. You would be going to your death, and that is against our ethos."

He shook his head sharply as Red opened her mouth, about to argue with him. Simply speaking louder, he finished what was clearly a prepared speech. "As exiting the outer wall is not an option, and remaining in the kill zone between walls with an active enemy outside is also not an option, only two options remain for you. Rejoin the others, enter Bleakrock, and live your life… or *don't*."

His tone as he finished his speech, and the way he gripped the shaft of his halberd, left no ambiguity as to his meaning. Lily replied sarcastically, "So, you're saying I have to go in, because I might die outside the walls. Or I can die for *sure* by your hand if I refuse?"

"Those are the rules. The rules are how the world *works*. The rules must be followed," the guard replied evenly. After a tense moment, he gestured down the open corridor with his weapon. "Please begin walking."

Unable to believe what she was hearing, Red shook her head and walked back toward the second gate, where people were still being blocked from entering. She glowered the entire time, even when the Coasties began cheering for her return. It didn't take long before a familiar face peeking out of a helmet appeared on the inner wall looking down at them, and a booming voice quieted the tired and exhausted crowd.

"Those of you who have arrived seeking shelter from the dangers of the outside world! My name is Captain Cliff, and on behalf of the city of Bleakrock, we thank you for choosing our home... to be your home." He waited a few moments as a cheer went up then quickly quieted down. "There are many differences between *our* lifestyle and the way you *used* to live. First of all, know this! As outsiders, once you've entered Bleakrock, you will never again be allowed to leave the city."

The announcement echoed twice through utter silence before a roar of disapproval went up. It took a dozen additional guards appearing atop the wall and shouting 'silence' in unison for the multitude of people to finally quiet to a bare grumbling.

Cliff pressed on, his voice as hard as the walls he was standing on. "Your children will have the option to leave, though they will never be able to return if they do so. The laws of the city are chiseled onto the wall of every building situated on an intersection. Ignorance of the law is no excuse for breaking it, and there are no second chances."

This time, the crowd simply stood there, the majority of them shaking their heads in confusion at what they'd gotten themselves into. Cliff nodded at the fact that they hadn't made the same mistake twice. "There is much opportunity in Bleakrock. We have prepared for your arrival for generations, knowing there would be an outside threat which eventually drew us all together. Every family will have their own home, a career, and plenty of mushroom popcorn."

No one really understood how to interpret the final bit of

his words, but Cliff didn't give them a chance to discuss it among themselves. "Entering the walls means agreeing to live as we live. Be judged under the same laws. You will find no favoritism toward residents who have been here longer than you, nor will you find leniency for your previous way of life. We cannot open up the gates and risk our city to the invaders, which means your only other choice is to remain between the walls."

"Anyone unaffiliated with Bleakrock in the killing zone between walls will be considered an enemy of the city and treated as such." His voice took on a darker tone at this moment, and Red felt a shiver go down her spine. When no one called out to ask further questions, he simply nodded and reached his fist up to tap against his chest. "Welcome to Bleakrock. Through simplicity, tomorrow is secured."

All the guards in the area, whether they were down among the people or on the walls, slammed a gauntleted fist to their chest and repeated the Captain, "*Through simplicity, tomorrow is secured!*"

"Be completely bored, for no real reason!" Chuckles mocked quietly, earning quiet laughs from everyone around him. Red tried not to show how much she agreed with him, keeping her eyes roving the area, ever on the lookout for a way to get out of this place.

The defenders of Bleakrock, which had been blocking the crowd from entering the city, stepped to the side, forming an honor guard and saluting the people who were now permanently entering their walls. Every thirty seconds, the group would bellow, "Welcome, new brothers and sisters! We've been expecting you."

Soon, the pace of people entering the city slowed to a crawl, but Red couldn't see why… as everyone blocking up the entrance was at least a foot taller than she was. Seeing how the day was going to go, she unhooked her backpack, pulled off her bedroll, and got comfortable.

The hours passed incredibly slowly, the highlights being lunch and dinner time, when new faces appeared on the walls only to lower massive vats of soup ever so carefully to the ground. There were a few issues at the start of meal time, as the uninhibited Coasties literally attempted to attack the food and needed to be shoved off by the guards. A few volunteers were put in charge of serving bowls of the soup and making sure everyone only got *one*.

Even Lily went over and tried what ended up being a type of mushroom soup—filling, if not particularly tasty—before returning to her relaxed position.

Dinner was the exact same meal, earning grumbles from the gathered people who were still waiting outside the gate. It was almost a full dark by the time the crowd had dispersed enough where Lily decided it was finally time to join in so she could get to a proper bed. Dozens of guards were on patrol and slowly closing in to make people move, which helped her make the final decision, but she still felt her lips twitch into a snarl as she stepped through the gate and thereby was considered to have accepted the rules of Bleakrock.

"Welcome, new sister!" A chipper female guard waved at Lily and motioned for her to step out of the crowd. It was at that moment when the Scout realized why this whole thing had taken so long. "I appreciate you coming in for in-processing. Unfortunately, there are several laws you would be breaking if you continued on from here. Let's get those taken care of, and you will be shown to your new assigned housing."

"What laws could I possibly be breaking?" Lily deadpanned as she gestured at the crowd she'd just stepped out of. "I waited patiently; I didn't cause any trouble. I just don't want to be here."

"Hopefully, you'll be able to get over that!" The full lips, which had been beaming a smile at her, turned downward for just a moment, and Lily felt a suspicious tingle of energy brush over her. "No weapons are allowed to be carried by any civilians within the city of Bleakrock. Only guards are allowed to carry anything which could be designated as a weapon or which you have been trained to use as a weapon."

"Great, so I have to join the guard?" Red's lips twisted in a half-grin. "A job offer literally out the gates. I like it."

"Unfortunately, no." Now the guard had fully lost her previous smile, instead having pressed her lips into a firm line. "First-generation residents cannot apply for a guard position, nor any other weapon-wielding profession. If you eventually have children, and they have completed their mandatory schooling period and earned a commendation from their professor, they can be considered for government positions such as the city guard."

"By the system, what are you even talking about?" Red was so shocked by the difference in culture—of someone who lived on the same island, no less—that she couldn't properly formulate a response to the ridiculous information she was hearing.

"That has been a common response today." The guard now seemed to be actively annoyed, rolling her eyes and huffing under her breath before sinking back into her trained professionalism. "Please hand over any weapons on your person. They'll be stored under your name for the use of any of your children who get such a position in the future. If, after twenty-five years, no such person exists, you'll be given the full value of the gear you're handing over today. On that note, do you have any active skills which could be used to harm other people?"

"No." Even Red didn't know if she was answering the question or refusing to give up the gear she was carrying. The guard lifted a hand, and half a dozen of her contemporaries rushed over, hands on hilts. "That is... I do not have active skills that can hurt people."

"Good." The lady gestured at a small table next to her. "Weapons, please."

Lily stepped closer, reaching for the short sword at her side. The guard, now stern-faced, raised a hand as a signal to stop, even as the others tightened their own grips on their swords or shafts of polearms. "Easy there... hard to take my weapons off if I don't reach for them."

With a resigned sigh, she began the process—and it was a *process*—of disarming herself. First came the obvious weapons, such as her short sword and bow. Then the knives from her belt, both the throwing version as well as the ones she used for butchering her kills. She paused, looking up at the guard hopefully, and felt another tingle on her skin. The guard lifted an eyebrow. "I was chosen for this task as I've earned an active skill called 'Sense Weapons'. *All* of your weapons, thank you."

Now more annoyed than resigned, Red reached in her cloak, producing additional blades, a small bag filled with ball bearings, three metal rods which could be used for hitting something or as a thrown weapon, twisted twine for snares or other various traps, then a few more small daggers, which had seen heavy use cutting vines or other rope-like items. Even as weathered as they were, an active skill would search them out without any issue.

The guard's eyebrows rose as the collection grew, and various muttering or chuckles came from the others. "I knew it was dangerous outside the walls... this seems a little... *extra*, doesn't it?"

"Failing to prepare is preparing to fail," Red spat as she stood back and crossed her arms. "Happy?"

For a few moments, the guard didn't reply, then Lily once more felt the tingling of the active skill searching her, and received a sharp nod. Once more, the bright smile was on the lady's face, and she motioned for Red to continue into the city. "Welcome to Bleakrock, officially. I think you, specifically, will like it here."

"Don't hold your breath."

"I won't, as there's no need to do something like that," the guard replied serenely. "There's no deep water here to dive into. Waist-deep at the worst. Your Coastal friends may not enjoy the city as much as you will, but they'll get used to it…"

"…they always do."

Upon hearing that final comment, Red felt a chill down her spine, suddenly filled with questions.

TWENTY-THREE

LILY WOKE up in the austere surroundings she'd been assigned, a one-room house—though calling it a house was generous. It was a large stone box, created with the same precision and clean lines as the outer walls. The door was made of metal, with a massive lever embedded which allowed her to lock it directly to the walls. Turning the lever caused metal rods to extend into matching stone holes in the wall, making it impossible to enter from the outside unless someone wanted to smash an entire side of the building to smithereens.

All in all, it was as secure as it was uncomfortable.

The bed was clearly something which had been secured through trade with the Wyld before this incident, and had equally obviously never been slept on before. She scanned the small space, which was lit by four tubes in the ceiling sealed on either end by quartz, which allowed daylight to sparkle into the room. The entire system was... incredibly impressive. It was a feat of engineering she'd never seen before, not in either of the city-states she had spent time in. As stark as the room was, she hadn't slept so well in days.

Still, no matter how secure she felt, Lily couldn't wait to escape this place. Getting up and placing her feet on the chilly stone caused shivers to run up her spine. "I'll take guaranteed freedom over guaranteed safety any day."

Letting out a long, low sigh, she pulled the latch of her door to the side, grunting with effort. She stepped outside, heading toward the communal wash house. Lily looked around, seeing only women approximately her own age in the area and rolling her eyes as she remembered one of the oddities of Bleakrock. "Oh, that's right. I'm in the 'unmarried woman' quarter. I can't *believe* I didn't punch that guard when he told me I could request a reassignment to a house nearly four times as large if I got married and started a family right away. 'For the future of Bleakrock'."

Snorting through her nose, she walked into the washhouse with only one further murmured comment. "I'm glad I wasn't too tired to convince them not to put me in the *children's* quarter. Don't think I could've held myself back from throwing fists at that point."

"Group DK-IS-GR-eight!" The words greeted her as she came out of the washroom, much refreshed. At first, Red didn't pay much attention, but the lady who was shouting into a strange funnel of metal to enhance her voice seemed to be staring at her specifically. "I repeat, group DK-IS-GR-eight! Your hospitality and familiarity-building tour of Bleakrock will be starting in ten minutes. Please be punctual, as they *will* leave without you. As you know, you will be expected to have this information. Remember, ignorance is no excuse!"

Wondering why she was being stared at so hard, Red looked down at a large medallion hanging on a long strip of thin cloth, realizing the medallion was shaped as the exact letters and numbers the lady had been shouting: 'DK-IS-GR8'.

With nothing better to do, Lily walked over and stood patiently in front of the lady, who gave her a thankful nod. Looking her over, the Scout realized this loud person was dressed almost exactly like every other city-employed person

—in undyed, grayish-white clothing. She'd noticed the guards wearing something similar under their armor and had wondered if it meant anything. "Apparently so."

Over the next few minutes, several other people joined. At the appointed time, the messenger stopped attempting to call anyone else over and immediately turned around and walked away. "If you are here with your group, please follow me! If you are in the wrong group, prepare to be turned away by the guards."

They followed after the plain-clothed lady, who led them through three intersections before coming to another, which had a pair of guards standing in the center of the road. "Assigned messenger Rita escorting group DK-IS-GR-eight to the tour guide."

"DK-IS-GR-eight?" The guard questioned, looking down at a chalkboard to confirm the date and time.

"Yes, DK-IS-GR-eight," the messenger confirmed. From there, she turned to look at the people following her. "You will be meeting up with tour guide Boren, though I assure you he's anything *but!*"

She paused, looking around the group as if expecting them to chuckle, shrugging when all she got was a weak smile at best. Without another word, she walked away, leaving the group members wondering if they were supposed to follow after her. Red took a step, but the guard leaned in front of her, locked eyes, and shook his head.

"Excellent! My group is already here!" A man in his mid-forties, practically vibrating with excitement over seeing them, ran up and clapped once in sheer exuberance. "Hello everyone in DK-IS-GR-eight, my name is *Boren*. Though, I assure you, I am anything but!"

The repeat joke only earned him cold stares, not even a weak smile like before. He squinted at them, then the guards, looking around until he saw the messenger vanishing in the distance. "Oh! I see the problem; you had Rita. She always steals my jokes. Well, don't you worry about that, I'll have plenty of fresh ones for you all day long!"

At that point, Red looked over her shoulder, trying to decide if she truly needed this information or should go back and hole up in her... 'house'. Before she had fully made her decision, Boren started moving along at a quick pace, motioning frantically for everyone to follow him. "You pulled the lucky draw, group DK-IS-GR-eight! By the way, you should all try and get to know each other. You were grouped by age, marital status, and a few other factors, so you should all have *plenty* in common."

From there, he launched into a long-winded lecture, even as the group members looked around at each other with wide eyes. "The opportunity to show off this city to such a large group, more groups over the next few weeks no less, is a rare treat for me! You may not believe this, but I've been an assigned tour guide since I was sixteen and have spent the last two decades guiding no more than five people at a time, incredibly intermittently! I've never understood why it took so long for you all to join us. The immigration policy is extremely straightforward. Anyone is allowed in, no questions asked, so long as they follow the rules! Sure, no one can leave..."

Boren paused for a moment, literally stopping in his tracks, "...you know, maybe *that's* why it's been so slow! No one left here to tell you all how easy it was! Look at that, one of life's great mysteries solved with my first group of the day."

Getting back on track, Boren began explaining the history of the city in great detail, his voice rich with pride as he spoke. "Before we get to any of the buildings, the history museum, the mage's tower, or *the pit*... let's discuss why Bleakrock exists in the first place! Long ago, generations upon generations, three groups of settlers arrived on Canu Moch. The first group was filled with a bunch of weak-willed ne'er-do-wells, who decided to build their entire society out of straw! Founder

Bleakrock watched them lose their homes every storm, having to rebuild from the ground up every time the wind blew."

Several of the people in the group were Coasties and glowered at the man, who blabbered along blithely, "The second group of settlers were mostly criminals other nations had exiled to this distant locale, and slunk into the woods where they could play with sticks, glare at each other, and build what has proven to be an extremely *flammable* lifestyle out of branches. It should come as no shock that the original founders of the Wyld wanted to have the privacy of the forest to hide their dark deeds."

Lily wasn't even upset at the callous speech, instead leaning forward to hear this version of events. A chance at learning the actual history of this island wasn't what she'd expected to get when she woke up this morning. Frankly, by looking around, she could only assume there were real records from the original founder still available to the city.

The Coastals had no written records whatsoever, their knowledge only being passed on in oral tradition, and the Wyld had only a couple generations of records—most of *those* being class advancement guides written by a family and passed through their line, information which was jealously guarded.

"Given the ephemeral nature of the first and the likelihood of the second eventually drawing an iron fist of retribution from the mainland, founder Bleakrock decided to create a fortress made of *brick* and *stone*. The city would, he swore, open its gates to its neighbors when they realized the truth of this world, when everything they had built fell apart or was destroyed by outsiders." Boren turned and flashed a smile at the group, "Well, DK-IS-GR-eight, as I'm sure you fully understand, that time is *now!*"

Though there was an obvious bias toward their own city-state, nothing Lily could think of would refute the information she was being given. The fact was, most of the history of the island was obfuscated either by the simple passage of time or purposely buried by those who had come before her. Lastly, even the obvious pride the residents of Bleakrock had in their city was justified. However long they'd been working on this project, their efforts were finally bearing fruit—the other independent groups on the island had fallen, and they'd rushed here for safety, just as the founder of the city had foreseen.

"Not exactly the way I'd want to live," Lily murmured to herself, apparently too loud as everyone turned to look at her, including the tour guide, who was waiting with a knowing smile on his face. Deciding to lean into it, she lifted her chin and expressed her thoughts more loudly. "How's this different than living in fear your entire lives? How many generations have come and gone waiting for this day? What would their lives have been like if they hadn't lived for an invasion that might never have come?"

Boren leaned forward, obviously happy to discuss and debate what must have been a common question within Bleakrock. "But it *did* come, didn't it? Our city is the most advanced defensive encampment in thousands upon thousands of miles. The mage tower within our walls produces the finest earth-magic users anywhere in the world. They, and others without magic-related skills, have been trained in the science of engineering, the combination of which has made all of *this* possible!"

The tour guide waved his arms out dramatically, as if to give the entire city a hug at the same time. Red swept her gaze around the area, unimpressed by the identical, boxy structures lining the streets. From wall to wall, there was only uniformity and hard angles—a testament to their devotion to efficiency and defense. "Okay… then, now what?"

Turning back with a smile, Boren looked at her with a slight quizzical expression. "What do you mean?"

"You were right. There was an invasion. You guys have made an impenetrable fortress and rescued the entire island.

Now what?" Red watched as the man cocked his head at her, clearly not understanding what she was getting at. "Isn't this the fulfillment of all of Bleakrock's goals? We are all safe, now how do we take back the island?"

"But..." Boren shook his head softly, as though preparing to reprimand a youngster asking silly questions. "Why would we ever do *that*? Everything anyone needs is already here or waiting to be pulled up from the earth below us! This warband will likely resettle the island and eventually possibly even become trading partners. Then, however long it takes, another group will invade, and the descendants of these invaders will rush here for safety! So, I suppose what's next is preparing for the next invasion. It's a foolproof rescue plan."

He continued walking, motioning for everyone to follow after him. Red stayed where she was, shocked at the man's cavalier attitude. One by one, the other members of the group walked past her, giving her understanding glances but not wanting to lose out on getting the information they needed. Slowly, almost mechanically, the Scout began following along, her mind still buzzing with what she'd just learned.

"This is a society of doomsayers. It doesn't matter what happens in the world around them... the response will be a smug, self-satisfied 'told you so'. They'll never do anything about it, never work to help people or make the world a better place outside of their walls." She fell silent for a moment before shaking her head slowly, letting out just one more thought.

"How terribly, *terribly* sad."

CHAPTER

TWENTY-FOUR

THE TOUR TOOK the rest of the morning, and Red made sure to learn as much as she could. No matter how badly she wanted out of here, it never hurt to be better informed. Their first stop was a fantastic sculpture of the original state of this area—and was apparently accurate down to the millimeter.

Just as they'd always been told, the city of Bleakrock had once been a single mountain, and over the generations, it had been quarried away to create the city and whatever other projects happened to need the stone. It was a rare piece of art in a city which didn't seem to put any value on beauty, but the sculpture also served as a point of pride for the city. Apparently, a new version was made every fifty years by the most skilled Stone Mage within the walls at the time, though all but this original were stored in a history museum.

"Don't worry *too* much; the museum will be one of our next stops. It has fascinating rock collections," Boren promised with a wink at them, as though he were informing them of a delicious treat coming their way.

From the sculpture of the mountain, their next stop was the duo of educational facilities: the college of engineering and the mage's tower. The names must have been for identifi-

cation purposes only, as both were identical, rectangular buildings. Just as the homes were austere, these were designed for
maximum utility only. Boren proudly announced the class-
rooms were equipped with only the necessities for learning,
absolutely *nothing* which could detract from the serious busi-
ness of educating the next generation.

They didn't go in, as that could be distracting to the
students, instead moving along through an entire district of
utterly empty housing areas. "Each class of graduates is tasked
with building twenty-five houses and properly connecting
them to the bedrock. This not only expands our city as our
founder directed, but it gives them practical experience while
paying the city back for their education."

After walking for twenty minutes and not seeing another
person except for a guard at every fourth intersection, Red
spoke up again. "How many people actually live in
Bleakrock?"

"I'm glad you asked! I'm certain, after taking a census,
we'll have *quite* a significant jump." Boren cheekily winked at
her, making Red's face twitch at the overly familiar and
overused gesture. "As we've had a sudden surge of new residents. But, as of our data from last month, we were at just
over nine thousand people."

"Nine-!" Lily's eyes went wide as she looked around the
area with a new respect, "That's less than a quarter of the
Wyld alone!"

"Less than a *fifth* of the Coastals," one of the other ladies
in the group stated proudly, before deflating slightly. "Or... it
was-"

Boren nodded along happily, winking at both of them in
turn. "Yes, it's been hard work making sure we've always had
new blood, but there have always been people excited to leave
behind their old ways and join us. When our city first started,
there were fewer than *thirty* total members. It was a good
thing most of them were powerful Stoneweavers, or none of

this would have been possible. We've come a long way since then."

"You've built a city that can house... how many tens of thousands of people?" Red shook her head in wonder. "I can't understand it."

"Only a few more stops before the museum!" Boren called out, having never slowed his pace. "I'm sure you have many, many questions, but I'm a tour guide! You're going to need to talk to a scholar for some of these more in-depth questions. You know what? I can even show you how to submit an application for a question-answering session with them! Later, of course. Now... behold... *the pit.*"

They moved past a final structure, coming up to a wall which was almost neck-high on Red. On the other side of the wall was a vast pit which she couldn't see the bottom of—not because it was so far down, but because she didn't want to embarrass herself by having to clamor up the wall to see. The others were making noises of appreciation, easily able to peer down. One of them looked at the guide in confusion. "Isn't this just a hole in the ground? That's supposed to be... exciting?"

"Yes! It's a fantastic, *immensely* useful location." Boren was practically rubbing his hands in glee. "It serves dozens of purposes. First and foremost, the branching caves which have been safely carved and reinforced serve as our mushroom farms. This provides sustenance and healthy nutrition for the entire city. If you're lucky, you'll be assigned to one of the farms—a high honor. Not many people show the necessary talent and dedication to the city to bring up all the food we need!"

"Wait... that's not the *only* type of food you have, is it?" Red was the first to make the connection, but as everyone remembered the mushroom soup they'd been given the previous day for lunch, dinner, then breakfast this morning, their faces blanched. "That was just emergency rations so you could make sure everyone got to eat while they got settled... right?"

Boren's smile became slightly strained as he pressed on, ignoring the question. "This was also the location of the core of the mountain! It's filled with metals, precious gems, and is the source of all the densest and durable stone around—which all of our buildings are made from! Over the years, we've replaced weaker, more brittle structures with this upgraded material and used the excess stone as trading goods with your previous city-states."

"No, you need to answer-"

Lily was cut off as Boren pushed onward, speaking slightly louder to drown her out. "Lastly, it serves as an active training area for our spellcasters and engineers! If you think about it, the pit is a microcosm of founder Bleakrock's philosophy, a place where truly every inch serves a practical purpose. This echoes our mantra of preparation and austerity. Why don't we swing over to the history museum and let you admire the *exquisite* work of our Mages."

"*Wait.*" This time she got in front of the tour guide and blocked his path. "Are you trying to tell us this is all we can look forward to, for the rest of our lives, because we aren't allowed to leave, since it isn't 'safe' out there?"

"What more could you possibly *want?*" Boren quizzed her almost sadly, as if he was going to have to be the one to tell her a great truth when she'd been believing a lie her whole life. "Anything you want to know, you will be able to learn. You are safe, and you will have food and meaningful work. We have *purpose* in life, and so will you."

"But what about..." Red struggled to put her swirling thoughts into words. "Quality of life and beauty?"

"If you have talent as an artist, I'm certain you'll be allowed to join their ranks." Boren gestured to the wall, drawing Red's eye to the intense, intricate embellishments that had been carved into nearly every surface. "We're always looking to make the city more beautiful."

"I need plants, *greenery*." Lily was shaking, starting to panic at the thought of never being allowed out of this place.

Boren reached out to try and pat her on the shoulder, his hand slowing and stopping, then retracting as her glare intensified. Instead, he nodded slightly and sent a conciliatory wink her way. "Many of the mushrooms in the pit are green; I'm certain you'll be able to make a case for working among them."

"You have a very unique way of life here." Red took a deep breath and slowly shook her head, keeping her eyes locked on the man in front of her. "I can't live like this. I can't have the same buildings over and over. I can't eat the same thing day after day. I don't want to be *assigned* a career which I will have to work until my dying breath. I want to make my *own* choices."

"That's just how life works here." Boren kept the same measured cadence to his voice, no longer excited, but not showing any anger. "Don't worry. We've had hundreds and *hundreds* of people join us over the years, both from the Wyld and the Coastals. Everyone gets used to this and eventually comes to accept it. Then their children love it, and their grandchildren even more. Remember... through simplicity, tomorrow is secured."

After waiting for Lily to reply, which she failed to do, although her jaw kept working, Boren nodded, winked, and continued on with the tour as if he hadn't been interrupted. "Now, why don't we all go over to the museum and see how the area has changed over the decades! Whoever figures out how long Bleakrock has stood, based on what I've told you on the tour, gets a special treat with dinner tonight—mushroom popcorn! That's a specialty item you'd usually need to trade in a full day's work tokens for, but we've been given special dispensation..."

At that point, Lily simply stopped listening. "So. This place is a cult. Great. Now I have *another* reason to get out of here as fast as possible. On the plus side... I'm not going to have to do anything. There's no way everyone is going to be fine staying here. As soon as they realize they're only going to be eating nutrient-dense mushrooms for the rest of their lives, the riots will start on their own."

Thinking through that further, Lily began putting together a strategy for what her next few days would look like. She assumed there would soon be a breakdown, and the massive swell in population meant the original inhabitants wouldn't be able to stop them if the new arrivals worked together to make changes. Adding on the fact of only a small percentage of the locals being allowed to carry weapons, Lily assumed they would be overrun in minutes.

After the tour had concluded, she returned to her assigned house, only leaving it to use her assigned washhouse or eat meals at the assigned time. As the first day turned into the second, then the third, she started wondering if perhaps she really *was* different than everyone else from outside this city. "Not a peep from anyone? No signs of anyone being upset with their treatment or wanting to leave. *Why?*"

As far as she knew, Wolf Warband hadn't stuck around after seeing the fortress of a city. There'd been no announcements, no shouted demands, nothing at all to indicate the island was currently being overrun. Or... nothing she'd heard.

Lily stepped outside of her house, finding only a few other people bothering to go outside and walk around. Waiting for something to happen wasn't what she needed, so the Scout began walking around and doing what she did best—figuring out who was doing what and where they were doing it. "System's Echo."

How she perceived the world around her changed drastically, Lily had known the place was barren of plant life, but what she hadn't expected was absolutely *nothing*. Every crack where a weed could put down roots had been sealed and smoothed over. It made her stomach turn. On a positive note, suddenly she didn't feel anywhere near as alone. Never before had her skill shown her *only* people.

Yet, even that made her deeply dissatisfied with the situation. Almost everyone was listlessly laying around on their beds, waiting for someone to come and give them instructions. Those who were moving around were doing so in a *very* agitated manner, prowling back and forth like tigers trapped in a cage. Still, before she could decide on a plan of action, she noticed a large group of people approaching and turned to watch them as they rolled down the street.

They had a large metal disk suspended from a rock frame, the entire thing on wheels so they could move what had to be thousands of pounds of material pulled from the earth. Lily watched curiously, having never seen a contraption like this before. Her head tilted to the side as the group came to a stop, and one of the people pulled back a huge staff with a ball at one end. "What could they possibly be do-"

The stick swung forward, hitting the metal circle and creating a sound, a cross between thunder and a tree crashing to the ground. Lily yelped and sprang away from the sudden, horrible noise, but distance didn't help. A second strike landed on the metal, then a third, before the newcomers shifted into a relaxed, waiting position. All across the area, people began throwing open their doors and stepping into the open to see what had been making such a terrible hullabaloo. After realizing it had been made on purpose, they began gathering in the open area.

Once enough people had arrived, a man got on top of the stone portion of the noise maker and began to shout, "Thank you all for attending this meeting so quickly! We are here to give out your permanent work assignments. Please form an orderly line based on your group. Please do not get in line until you have every member of your group, or you will be turned away once you get to the front."

Awkward shuffling ensued, but soon the man was shouting out orders with a beaming smile. "Group GSTL-IS-BD, you have been assigned to quarry maintenance! Congratulations, you will be assisting our brightest minds by helping them return their practice areas to pristine condition each day."

"Group RPNZL-TWR-zero-one, you will gain glory by helping to maintain air shafts which will bring clean air to those assigned to mining operations!"

"CNDR-BLLA-zero-two—Mushroom spore sorters!"

"—sewer tunnel scrapers. It may not sound impressive, but you will be the envy of the entire city with nearly triple their luxury good tokens!"

"—rodent control squad!"

"—ration packer."

"—water reclamation worker! You'll be working closely with the sewer tunnel scrapers, expect fantastic benefits!"

On and on the assignments went. The more the man spoke, the wider Red's smile became. "That guard was right... I *specifically* find this interesting. I'm betting no one else does."

Dissatisfaction was brewing in the air like a storm along the shore. The Coastals were horrified, already balking at the prospect of toiling in the mines for the rest of their lives. All of their classes and skills were geared toward living along the open ocean, and being told they would spend their lives underground, in the confines of cold, unyielding stone, was no different than a death sentence.

As for the Wyldlings, she didn't need to make any guesses at how they would react. All of them were used to some degree of solitude and a high amount of autonomy in their decision-making processes. Those two facts together made for a population who wasn't afraid to speak their mind in the slightest.

"I need the freedom to roam; I'd rather be thrown to the wolves out there than stay caged like an animal!"

Lily let out a sigh of relief as someone broke under the pressure—she'd been worried she would be the first.

"Enough of that," the man shouting their new assignments called out indifferently, his voice as hard and unforgiving as the stone they were surrounded by. "This is your life now. No one leaves Bleakrock. Not for any reason. That's rule number one, written right there."

"To the *abyss* with your rules!" A Coasty howled, lifting a pouch and hurling it at the wall the announcer was indicating. It stuck and released its contents, a brown smear splattering out from the point of impact and trailing down the wall.

"Uhh…" Lily edged away from the wall.

The man giving out assignments was absolutely thunderstruck. "You… you threw that against the wall? You just *wasted* your entire breakfast? During a time of belt tightening and rationing for the good of the new population?"

"Oh. It was mushroom soup. Thank goodness," Red murmured with a sigh of relief. Taking in a deep breath, she squared her shoulders and shouted, "Let's take back our *homes*! Follow me, and let's get *out* of here!"

Dozens of the ladies in the area shouted in agreement, and they began rushing down the streets toward the city gates. As they moved, handfuls, hundreds, then *thousands* of people who'd been learning of their bleak futures around the city began to join them.

TWENTY-FIVE

THE AIR WAS riotous with noise as pressure between the three factions began to reach a boiling point. Not a single Coastal or Wyldling had remained behind to wait and see what would happen. They were hungry, angry, and ready to take control of their lives once more. The prospect of living a life *assigned* to them within these walls had driven the entire group, en masse, to make a break for it.

"Better a quick death by an invader's sword than a slow death in a stone grave!" One Coasty was trying to start a chant, not realizing it didn't flow off the tongue well enough to be picked up by the rest of the crowd.

Lily was right near the front of the rushing group, though she had fallen behind slightly, thanks to the height difference between her and the people around her. Activating System's Echo again and again, she searched for anyone who had fallen and was at risk of being crushed, diving in and yanking them to their feet wherever she could. As they approached the gate at speed, she felt her heart sink. It appeared that the rulers of Bleakrock had realized this was a possibility and had prepared accordingly.

Rows of plate mail-clad warriors stood between the ragtag mob and the exit to the city, their metal armor gleaming in the early morning light. A single glance at what was waiting for them caused the momentum of the charging crowd to shift.

As the metal-wielding warriors settled into an aggressive position, moving with fluid motions indicating a high level of training and practice, the angry cries turned into concerned, frustrated murmuring. Even worse, in the next moment, a horrid *cracking* sound came from behind the warriors, and dust began swirling off the ground.

This was followed shortly by boulders being torn from the street, which floated overhead menacingly—clearly, the Stoneweavers of Bleakrock had been deployed to quash any burgeoning uprising. Lily prepared herself to fight, no matter the odds, and called out at the top of her lungs, "They can't stop all of us! We outnumber them a hundred to *one!*"

While this did put a little pep in their step once more, there was a general feeling of unease, despite their sheer numbers. The city's residents held all the weapons, Mages with the power to crush opposition, and a fierce belief that they were doing the right thing.

Captain Cliff appeared on the wall, shouting down with an amplified voice, "Enough of acting like *children*! I'm going to give you one chance to end this conflict before it truly begins, then I'm going to give the order to begin cutting through. We can always rebuild the population with whoever among you has the good sense to calm down, return to your homes, and have a peaceful life."

The demand from the Captain of the guard had the opposite effect he was going for, causing everyone to remember exactly why they'd come here. Tempers flared, and tension mounted as people shouted at the top of their lungs. Red shouted along with them, feeling as though her voice was rising above the others.

"Why would you kill us all instead of just letting us *leave*?"

The Captain slammed his fist down on the wall in front of him, causing the stone to shatter with an explosive retort. "Because you are now all *security risks!*"

His bellowed, furious words were the first time any of them had seen a member of Bleakrock respond with anything other than happiness or at worst a neutral reply. This, more than anything else, caused most of the hubbub to die down for a moment, giving the Captain enough time to launch into an unhinged rant.

"Allowing even a single person to leave the city compromises our entire way of life! You could reveal our defenses, resources, and *perceived* weaknesses." He snarled the last as if there wasn't any *true* weakness in the city. "Every person who leaves could provide valuable information to our eventual jealous enemies. Not only that, we can and *will* be self-sufficient. We are prepared for any catastrophe, and by making sure everyone is here, we know all the skills, resources, and the population will remain intact! You walking out of here is a drain on our human resources and will directly impact our ability to grow!"

"We're not *resources!*" a Coasty screeched furiously. "You can't just make us stay here, you-"

Ignoring the protests, Captain Cliff continued, now walking back and forth on the wall in agitation. "The outside world is corrupt! Dangerous! You've all agreed to the rules and requirements of Bleakrock. Trying to subvert this is no less than treason. Go back to your homes, and settle in for the long haul… or we'll drop you in the pits to help grow mushrooms."

"I *knew* it!" Chuckles' harsh whisper cut through the silence, though Lily couldn't see where he was standing in relation to her.

The bizarre threat caused people to blanch, wondering if they'd already been eating mushrooms grown from bodies. A voice Red recognized, Franklin, the new leader of the Wyld council, stepped forward and coldly responded on behalf of the entire city-state, "I think we're just going to have to take our chances."

Spurred on by this cold declaration, the crowd surged forward once more... only managing to move two steps before the air was shattered by a deep, gravelly voice.

"Little pigs, little pigs, let us come in." It took a moment for Lily to place the voice, as it was slightly distorted, but it originated from outside the walls.

"Big Bad Wolf?" she barely managed to whisper before the voice shook the air once more.

"City of Canu Moch!" Big Bad's roared through the open air, "Open these doors and send the ones who fled here out. I specifically need-"

"Shut down the outsider!" Captain Cliff barked at a group of Stoneweavers, who punched forward with their fists, sending dozens and dozens of boulders flying over the walls toward the origin of the shouting. Then the Captain turned his furious eyes back to the near-rioting crowd. "What do you want? *Luxury*? Fine! Caterers, bring out the truffles and popcorn!"

A sweet scent filled the air as dozens of doors were flung open, and trolleys laden with sweet roasted mushrooms were trundled out among the crowd. Cliff angrily gestured around, "Look at all this! We prepared a holiday to celebrate your lifestyle assignment day! Bleakrock *wants* to take care of you; it wants to guide you, protect you! Stop this pointless-"

"You missed!" Big Bad's voice echoed through the air once more, sounding smugly amused. "Whoever is in there shouting, you know we can hear you, right? Your entire city is surrounded, and this is me officially declaring a siege against you. There will be no food, no water, no supplies, until you meet our demands!"

Cliff turned and faced the outer wall, shouting into the distance, "Keep them! We need nothing from you, nor the tainted land around our city! We will happily live on mush-rooms alone, as we have for generations! Abyss, we will live *like* mushrooms if needed—in the thick shadow of our walls! Our Stoneweavers can repair any damage, and our warriors are highly trained! We can and *will* survive *anything* you attempt."

"This guy is cracked in the head." Red eyed the raging Captain, slowly realizing this man was likely the leader of the entire city, if no one was speaking up against him.

There was a long delay, but Big Bad finally spoke again, this time without a hint of playfulness in his tone. "Let us in, or send them out. Otherwise, we will destroy this city. It may take a few weeks to prepare, but we are experts at siege weapons. We *will* get through your walls. You have mages who can repair the damage we do? Sure... but *we* can bombard you day and night."

Big Bad paused to let the echoes die down, then carried on, "I *guarantee* we will get through. You have warriors who can defend against *us*? How adorable. I'm leading an entire nation of battle-tested Wolves, and you have 'trained' warriors. Not to mention, the entire time you are waiting for us to break through, well. As I had mentioned, we can hear you. It appears to us that even as you defend from without, you'll need to defend from within. Fighting a second battle against the very people you allowed into your fortress of stone? How long can you last?"

Captain Cliff didn't respond right away, though even from a distance, Lily could see him clenching and unclenching his fist, contemplating his options as he heaved for breath. Finally, he raised his amplified voice once more, though he sounded calmer this time. "They understand what will happen if they go out to you. A guaranteed life of servitude or death awaits them. All you've done is give us a common enemy to rally against! Canu Moch stands united against-"

"I'm going to fight my way out of here, no matter *what!*" Lily didn't even realize the piercing cry had escaped her lips until she felt the eyes of the crowd turned to her. Stepping forward, the Scout lifted her hands, "If I have to *punch* my way through the walls… well, if that's what it takes, I'll *do* it!"

Unable to hear her unamplified words, Big Bad replied to Captain Cliff with his characteristic blend of boldness and simplicity. "Listen up, whoever you are. From now on, this island is *our* home. We are going nowhere until it is fully under our control. It's a land of abundance. There's as much fish as we will ever need, a difficult-to-invade location, and enough wood remaining to make the fleet we need *dozens* of times over!"

"*But.*"

Big Bad let the word hang in the air for a long moment before finishing the thought. "The continued existence of this city is a *problem* for us. We don't want to settle into our new home, then need to deal with constant hostility, skirmishes, and-"

"We've never left the city, and we're not about to start!" Captain Cliff shouted back, a glimmer of hope coming through his voice. "Take the island. *I* don't care!"

Lily could practically see Big Bad shaking his head in her mind's eye as the raider spoke. "Too risky. I'll make you a deal instead. An offer, a chance. If anyone in there will face me in single combat—and by some miracle they win—I will swear by the system to leave the island forever, taking all of my people with me. If they lose, *when* they lose, you will send out everyone you took in. They will come build our fleet, feed our warriors, and they will be well taken care of."

"Pah!" Cliff scoffed loudly. "What of Bleakrock? You expect us to simply hand over generations of effort?"

"No!" Big Bad called back without pause, having clearly planned this conversation in advance. "*When* they lose, so long as someone shows the courage to fight in the first place, you will realize the futility of acting against us. You will swear by the system to become active, pleasant trading partners, allowing people to come and go as they please. If you are not a good neighbor to us, how can you expect us to be a good neighbor to you?"

"I expect *nothing* from you," the Captain stated frostily. "Officially, on behalf of Bleakrock and all of its *permanent* residents, I unequivocally *reject* your offer."

CHAPTER
TWENTY-SIX

EVEN BEFORE CAPTAIN Cliff's words finished echoing through the air, Red and hundreds of island dwellers had thrown themselves at the guards. The silence turned into furious roaring, the sound of feet on stone, fists meeting armor…

…then the meaty tearing of blades slicing through flesh, and boulders raining down on bodies.

Crimson blood splashed over Lily's bright red cloak, making her clothing appear mottled, as if she were attempting to create a camouflaged outfit of crimson. None of the lifeblood was hers, but the warrior who'd swung the halberd down with a grunt had definitely been targeting her. She'd managed to drop into a deep squat—so low her rear brushed against the ground—as the heavy weapon sailed past her and slashed into multiple people.

From her position low to the stone road, Red sprang forward like a cat pouncing on a mouse, through the small gap in the ranks which had formed due to the warrior's overextension. No matter how intense the cacophony of shouting, clashing of metal, and *thud* of bodies were, no matter how much she wanted to tear through these people standing between her and freedom, she had no illusions about her ability to take on the heavily armored fighters in a direct fight.

No, her strengths lay elsewhere—in a much more important task.

Rolling into a forward somersault as she landed, Lily pushed up, shoving against a leg that felt like an immovable pillar of metal, all to get past the final ranks of the startled city guards. "*System's Echo!*"

Almost overwhelmed with the sheer multitude of thrashing bodies and rapidly swinging weapons, Lily nearly lost herself. Then, a huge *woosh* in the air above her made the Scout flinch, but also helped her center herself. Her eyes trained on her true targets, singling out the dozen Stoneweavers ripping enormous boulders out of the bedrock of the street and launching them into the charging crowd.

"A blade can only cut a few people at a time, a five-hundred-pound rock launched as if from a trebuchet can pulverize *dozens*," Red murmured to herself as the Stoneweavers casually continued to raise their hands, commanding stone to flow—or *tear*—out of the bedrock below them, depending on their skill level. As they'd been standing behind multiple ranks of heavy armor, all their focus went to putting down the insurgents, and not a thought was spent of their personal safety... and she was going to make sure their reliance on the guards cost them.

Just as she had swiftly maneuvered past the slow, metal-clad fighters, Red now slipped seamlessly into the ranks of the mages. Her small, agile frame allowed her to weave through the gaps in their meticulously practiced formations. After avoiding the last desperate lunges from the technically-skilled citizens of Bleakrock, her system-enhanced skills guided her to the highest-priority targets: the Stoneweavers. Once she was within the midst of the unarmored spellcasters, the warriors who turned to pursue her found themselves body-blocked by their own allies, their warning shouts lost in the chaos.

At this point, the Scout had many factors working to her benefit: not only did her small stature allow her to move quickly among these people, she Lily had always favored non-lethal techniques. Being so highly trained allowed her to fight exactly as she preferred without having to worry about sending the locals into a rage if she were to overstep and kill their people.

Lastly, but just as important, her slight frame also caused them to *greatly* underestimate her.

Red dipped down, scooping up a rock which had fallen from one of the boulders torn from the ground, and ironically used it to bash the first of her targets into unconsciousness. The mage had been so engrossed in his spellwork that he'd barely registered her approach before she was on him, not able to send more than a confused, questioning glance at her before Red swung the rock with her full strength.

Before her first victim had even hit the ground, Red was moving again, her eyes locked on the next closest mage. He was a young man, likely having only recently graduated from the mandatory schooling they practiced here. The Scout's searching scan took in many details about him, such as the thick beads of sweat on his brow as he shakily levitated a boulder three times his own body weight. There was also his plain, undyed clothes, marking him as a person in service to the city. Yet the most useful detail—to her—was the sharpness of his cheekbones.

Their rigidity combined with his weak chin flashed a warning to Red that a full-force blow would likely shatter his skull. Adjusting her strength, she hit him with what was only a *tap* compared to the **wallop** she'd given the first, and he collapsed just as easily, eyes rolling up into his skull. The huge boulder dropped out of the air, shouts of alarm warning the other mages and causing one of them to lift his arms and activate his skills, managing to slow the tiny meteor enough for people to get out of its way as it landed.

"Which of you lost control?" the mage who'd intervened shouted, his voice shaky. "That's three months of three-quarters rations and a revoking of your truffle allotment!"

Finally, one of the warriors had the wherewithal to shove a finger in her direction, pointing out the person garbed in bright red already swinging her rock again. "You pompous fools, a *Wyldling* is among you!"

The reaction from the mages wasn't what Red had expected. Those closest to her let out a high-pitched squeal of terror and attempted to furiously backpedal, only to find themselves trapped between the metal gate and the metal shells of the warriors being pushed back by the mob. Second by second, the citizens of Bleakrock were being forced closer to her. Deciding to play along, and perhaps amplify their fear, Red hefted the slightly bloody stone in her hand and put a vicious smile on her face.

Without a word, she rushed forward, causing at least two mages to trip and a third to swing around in what almost looked like a dance. Stone flowed out of the ground near him, shaped into a spike, and was flung through the air nearly as fast as an arrow.

"Abyss!" Lily hissed as she contorted her body to avoid the large shard, her training overpowering her surprise enough to completely avoid taking a hit. The formation of warriors wasn't as lucky. The rock smashed into their backs, causing the armor of the man struck to crumple and sending him reeling forward, knocking another *four* men out of position.

The rioting people took advantage of the distraction, forcing themselves through the hole and pushing against either side of the guards so others could pile in to the gap, then *onto* the fallen men.

At this angle, Red could either fall or potentially hurt herself by forcing her body back into position. She chose to tumble, rolling back to her feet after bouncing once and skidding slightly, scuffing the surface of her left knee and elbow enough for blood to start oozing out. It was a minor pain, but any distraction in combat had the potential to be life-ending. Pushing through and doing her best to ignore the sudden soreness, she ducked and kicked out, hooking her foot behind a mage's knee.

Bracing and pulling, she caused him to stumble, then falter and fully drop to the ground. Now back on her own feet and feeling confident in her footwork, Lily kicked the man in the side of the face, just above the jawline, immediately causing his body to go limp. "Three down, *way* too many to go. Good thing I'm not planning to take them all out by myself."

Her actions had been having the desired result, causing the area of effect damage from the mages to be completely disrupted and giving the mob the confidence they needed to throw themselves against the huge men holding sharp weapons. Even with their advantages, the warriors were being overwhelmed. Slowly at first, but picking up speed as more of them were forced to the ground, and their halberds or swords were confiscated and turned against them. Powerfully muscled Coasties were swinging the oversized polearms with no skill, sending the citizens of Bleakrock reeling and stumbling with each hit.

Wyldlings who managed to get their hands on weapons were using them to just as great an effect, though they tended to target joints and seams in the armor of their opponents. Less disruptive to the lines, but far more deadly to those targeted.

Glaring at Lily, the middle-aged Stoneweaver who had been shouting directions stomped forward, his arms spread wide to the side as if he were a bird about to take flight. As his foot landed, he swung both hands together until his palms met with a sharp *clap*, and only Red's System's Whisper skill flaring a warning at the same moment allowed her to dodge out of the way.

Even after her initial escape, some internal part of her

warned that touching the ground was a bad idea, so her sideways leap ended with her grabbing onto a nearby man, swinging herself past him, and throwing him backward to gain additional distance. The stone rumbled and shifted slightly, not sounding terribly menacing. Still, as Lily touched down and rushed at the nearest unarmored man, she glanced at where the spell had been cast.

A hint of fear *zinged* through her spine as she saw the man she'd tossed: he had sunk into the stone to his shoulders —head first. His legs and hands were frantically flapping back and forth, and a couple men were weaving their hands rapidly in front of themselves, clearly trying to save their contemporary who was currently suffocating in the resolidified stone.

Now her eyes were on the middle-aged mage, who seemed to be the oldest among the group and therefore likely the most experienced. *Certainly,* he seemed to be the most powerful. Without an outward hint of hesitation, she sprinted toward the dangerous man, staying low to the ground and causing her red cloak to flare into the air.

His eyes narrowed slightly, and the man contemptuously crossed his arms, simply lifting his right foot and stomping it, then his left, back and forth again and again. Each time one of his limbs came down, a rock no larger than Lily's fist shot out of the ground at a forty-five-degree angle from the stone road in front of him.

She dodged the first, and the man's eyebrow arched slightly over his narrowed eyes. As the second and third sailed past her with less than an inch to spare, he picked up the pace. Sucking in a sharp breath, Lily met the mage's eyes and tipped her head forward slightly, making the smile on her face appear cruel and dangerous. Then, making sure he was staring into her eyes, she closed her own in an effort to bluff that his efforts were futile.

"System's Echo."

The next projectiles were moving too fast for her eyes to

track; what with all the other commotion, not to mention the thick dust rising into the air from all the stone shaping going on. Yet, with her skill active, she could perfectly see the fast-moving boulders as they peeled themselves from the ground and were launched unerringly at her center mass. One after another they missed her, until she was only three feet from the older man.

Then one stone ball grazed her arm, causing her to slip slightly on the loose gravel strewn across the road. Before she could recover, another slammed into her gut and sent her tumbling backward, hitting the ground and being dragged along for a moment. Gasping in an ineffectual attempt to replace the wind that had been knocked out of her, Lily tried to roll to the side to avoid any follow-up attacks. The pain wasn't too bad, and she was ready to make a second attempt.

The Stoneweaver had a different idea. With a twisting gesture of his fingers, the ball of rock which had impacted her melted, forming into an arch over her torso and connecting to the ground. She quickly struggled and attempted to slip out of the sudden bar which had formed, but couldn't muster the power to get away before another rock landed on her legs, arms, and torso once again, shifting and shaping until she was firmly connected to the stone.

"The ringleader is captured; let's deal with the rest of this rabble!" the apparent leader of the Stoneweavers barked out, returning his attention to the ongoing conflict.

CHAPTER

TWENTY-SEVEN

ONLY A MOMENT LATER, the middle-aged mage let out a sharp, squealing shriek as the mob finally overran the last of the warriors and surged toward him. Stomping his feet, clapping his hands, and whistling sharply enough to make the bedrock tremble, the Stoneweaver and his entire group threw everything they had at the crowd.

It was all for naught.

No matter how many people fell, groaning from the blunt damage inflicted by stone balls, or trapped up to their waists in stone which had turned liquid for a bare second, dozens more people were able to take their place and continue pushing forward. Now that the defensive line had broken, the mages were dog piled, rendered fully immobile in under ten seconds.

At that point, a ragged cheer went up, quickly echoed more energetically by the people who'd been unable to be a part of the fighting. In all of the calamitous noise, Lily clearing her throat at some nearby Coasties nearly went unheard.

"Hey, a little help over here?" She was almost embarrassed

to need to be saved, but the hulking Coasties only had wide grins on their faces.

"Is that Little Red Riding Hood? By the system, I never expected *you* to be a damsel in distress!" The first laughed as he lifted his newly acquired weapon, slamming the metal end cap of the halberd into the stone near her waist, cracking the thin shell of bedrock on the first hit. On the second, it crumbled on that side, but shifting her weight didn't allow Red to break free.

"Careful with your words, buddy." The other Coasty let out a dark laugh. "I've been hearing a whole bunch of stories, and I saw what she did back here. There were at least twenty people, guards and mages, with their heads cracked open before we got over here. If anything, she's a damsel *of* distress."

"Yes, that is *entirely* accurate information. At least twenty. I lost count after that many," Lily deadpanned as they worked to smash her free of her restraints. The instant she was able to scramble out of her earthen prison, she didn't pause to catch her breath. Instead, after nodding her appreciation at the Coasties, she hurried over to where the Stoneweavers were being gathered, finding most of them groaning and whining. Scanning the faces, a frown began to grow on her own. "Where's the older one? Who has him?"

There were a few confused murmurs, but it was the soft chuckle coming from one of the young, captured Stoneweavers that truly drew her attention. Feeling her eyes on him, he smugly jutted his chin out and proudly stated, "Master Mage Martin managed magical makeshift mineshaft, must make Miss mad. Muahaha."

"Don't hurt him!" another captured Stoneweaver frantically muttered as Lily took a step closer. "He took a nasty hit to the head. Master Martin has reached Mastery with his Stoneweaving and has been practicing instant escapes for nearly a decade. We've been trying to figure out how to apply that to beds in houses, so we could drop everyone down into a safe house chamber below the city."

"So he's... gone?" Red confirmed, not overly pleased when she got only a hesitant nod in reply.

"He dropped into the stone below us, but I'm certain he can control how far he goes and what angle he moves at. Most likely, he will be able to rejoin the city forces elsewhere."

Red considered the man's words. "You seem pretty chatty about all this."

The young man shrugged as well as he could with his arms tied tightly behind his back. "I mean, let's be real here, Martin was always pushing unity as the highest form of duty to the city. Then... then he left us here—without *him*—at the first major setback we've ever encountered. I'm not exactly in a good mental place right now."

"Fair enough. You're gonna be okay." Red gently patted the young man on the shoulder, then walked away, considering the new information. "Master Mage... that means he must have his Stoneweaver skill up to level nine. If that's true, he's a single step away from not only level ten, but gaining access to a Breakthrough Skill. I'm living proof that skills increase fastest in combat situations, which means he could become extremely dangerous over the next few minutes. Who knows, his leveling requirements might have just gotten met, and he's even *more* powerful already. We *really* need to get out of here."

Looking at the gate revealed their next objective: the gatehouse. Controlling the gatehouse meant being able to open and close the first point of egress from the city whenever they needed—the first step toward freedom for all of them. A large group had clustered around the base of the narrow stairs which led to the gatehouse atop the wall, arguing back and forth over who would go first.

"There's definitely going to be guards protecting the mechanism!" a scholarly Wyldling was cautioning. "First person up the stairs is going to catch a spear in the gut!"

"In that case, it should *absolutely* be one of you," an over-sized Coasty stated, to the agreement of all the other bulky fishermen around him. "We won't have the space to swing these big sticks, and you forest dwellers are used to fighting in close quarters."

It looked like the bickering was going to extend into harsh words, as tensions were still high, and adrenaline was pumping through everyone's veins. Lily stepped forward, short sword lifting into the air and catching the attention of the flinchy men. "If you're not going to get a move on, when this is an absolute win for us, then get out of the way so *I* can get it done!"

They hesitated for a moment, only for one of the Wyldlings, a Scout, to snort and push his way through the door. "I'm not going to let her take *all* the credit for our win today. Someone follow me."

"Then you're admitting I have *most* of the credit, at least?" Red called after him, earning a sharp laugh from the Coasties who'd remained at ground level. Deciding against letting them go through the dangerous staircase without assistance, she activated System's Echo to find the position of the people above them. "Fifth flight of stairs, two guards! Eighth flight, one guard! Two people waiting in the gatehouse! Then…"

She trailed off as her skill revealed a horrifying situation. Lily's head jerked to the side, staring into the distance, but having her vision blocked by the buildings in the way. "People are being *pushed*? What's happening?"

Taking a few steps closer, Lily found that dozens of people were being pressed back by… something non-living, so her skill couldn't give her a great explanation. There was a gap between the press of bodies and another small group, which was walking at an unhurried pace, allowing Red to make an intuitive leap and realize what was going on. "I need everyone who has a weapon to get over to the next street! Stoneweavers are shoving our people back; they need help!"

"What do you mean *shoving* them back?" A few people, less concerned than they should be, jeered back at her, still high on their current success. "We had mages throwing boulders at us, and they're just being pushed? They'll be *fi~ine*."

For the first time, the straight lines of the city were of use to Lily, as she was able to calculate the eventual destination of the people being pushed. "Bleakrock is corralling innocent people with a moving wall of rock; they're going to shove them into *the pit*! We need to save them! Spread the word, go, *go*!"

That got people moving, though there was plenty of confusion. Letting out a huff of annoyance, Red hurled herself across the street, maneuvering herself across the torn-up landscape, pushing past small groups of people huddled together for security until she'd fully crossed the street. She looked up, annoyed at how very *tall* the uniform, boring house-boxes suddenly seemed. "Right, now I just need to figure out how to get up there so I don't need to find an inter-section."

The same problem she had when trying to scale the wall reared its ugly head here: there were no seams in the sheer stone face, no window sills to use as hand holds. With a soft curse, she turned to make a break for it, hoping she'd be able to figure out how to handle the mages when they could see her coming. A small handful of Coasties were blocking her way, a familiar face at the front. Chuckles gave her a half-hearted wave. "Hey there, Red! We saw your cloak flapping in the wind as you ran over here. Thought you might need a hand."

"Unless you can get me over the building, I'll be fine. Glad to see you're all safe." She tried to push past, only for his hand to shoot out and block her way.

He yanked it back as she lifted her short sword, though even Lily wasn't sure what she was going to do with it. "Hold on a second, I think we can actually help with that. Do you trust us?"

"*No*. Move." Red barked at him without hesitation, pausing and letting out a tiny growl of frustration as she amended her answer. "Okay, you've earned *some* trust from me. Speak quickly, lives are on the line."

"You just need to get on top of the building, right? We can do that. Come on, boys!" Chuckles held out a hand, and Red hesitatingly took it. His other meaty paw came forward and clamped down on her wrist, then she found hers both arms and legs clamped in vice-like grips. "Just like daybreak fishing. *Long cast!*"

"Hold on, what are you about to-" The four men lifted her into the air, swung her back, then forward, and did it again, grunting with effort as they put as much force into the forward momentum as possible. All of them released at the same time, and Red found herself in reverse free fall. The stone wall of the building streaked past her, Lily's nose almost brushing the upper edge of the stone box as she sailed over it. At the apex of her motion, her arms were pinwheeling, and the Scout only held on to her sword by sheer force of habit.

Then she started falling, and her rational mind took over once more. Lily had fallen hundreds, *thousands* of times. Out of trees, down from rocks, jumping from waterfalls—this was familiar territory. She shifted mid-air, getting her feet under her as the flat top of the structure loomed large underneath. She landed awkwardly, stumbling and dropping her weapon with a **clatter** as she frantically pushed forward to land on the flat surface instead of falling off.

After just a moment, she stabilized. Looking back over the edge, Red waved down at the Coasties, who were staring up with no small amount of concern. "Thanks! ...I think."

"Told you it would work!" Chuckles nudged the man next to him. "You owe me at least-"

"Not exactly happy you were betting on whether that would work or *not*!" Red shouted down, turning away to refocus on her current objective. She recovered her weapon and crawled to the opposite edge of the roof, poking her head over as minimally as possible. With her bird's-eye view, she watched as screaming Coasties and Wyldlings were shoved, scooped, and battered along by a wall of stone spanning the entire street.

Six Stoneweavers were actively walking forward, each of them holding one hand out and moving in time with the others. Several warriors, as well as at least three additional mages, were walking behind them, not doing much other than providing security for the group. Lily took several deep breaths, trying to push back her fatigue and plan a proper ambush. "I'm still ahead of them... should I hit the Stoneweavers or the warriors?"

Each second she agonized over her decision was another few steps closer for the powerful skill users. Eyes focusing on the mages, who were callously joking with each other, she made her choice. Pulling herself up into a crouching position, she waited, timing her movement to the walking speed of the men below.

"Three, two, one..." Lily stood and stepped off the roof almost casually.

"*Now.*"

TWENTY-EIGHT

AT FIRST, her fall was silent, simply a rush of motion and sensation as the wind streamed past her face. Then Lily's cloak caught the air. A single, sharp *flap* was the only warning her target had before she shifted her knees to be under her and smashed into his shoulders, riding the mage to the ground and possibly breaking his spine in the process. The way he thrashed around in pain meant that was unlikely, though he went still after she delivered a sharp rap to the back of his head with her shortsword.

The moving wall of stone significantly slowed without his assistance, but didn't stop. Instead, the other five Stoneweavers controlling it grunted with sudden strain and leaned forward as if they were physically pushing against the barrier. Pushing herself off the fallen mage, Lily leapt toward the next in line, swinging the flat of her blade against the side of his head with a meaty *smack*. The edges of her sword still caught skin, drawing thin lines of blood on his cheek.

The mage let out a sharp cry of pain, collapsing to the ground howling as he clutched his face. Deciding against pausing to ensure that he was out of the fight, Lily simply continued gliding forward. The unexpected agony was likely enough to keep the man from concentrating on any spells for the next few minutes. As her blade met the next mage's shoulder with a *crack*, followed by the pommel swinging around and finding a temporary home against his temple, the guards following behind finally got close enough to engage her in direct combat.

Luckily, they were shouting warnings and war cries as they closed in on her, giving Lily plenty of time to prepare herself. As the third of six Stoneweavers went down, she rolled in the same direction, using his body as a shield to force the warriors to check their blows.

Then she was on her feet, turning to face them while releasing a rock from her off hand. It *pinged* off a plate mail helmet, not dealing any permanent damage, but clearly ringing the man's bell by the way he rapidly shook his head. This gave Red just enough time to feign a movement toward the next mage in line, causing the guards to stumble. She instead backtracked and swung her blade at the off-balance warrior's knees, striking his right leg and causing it to buckle. Between the hit and the vertigo, the warrior was unable to maintain his balance, and the weight of his armor took him to the ground.

To her great annoyance, the other Stoneweavers had stepped forward and joined in with the others to keep the wall moving instead of working to engage her. Two other warriors, each with a sword, started swinging powerful blows at the small woman, a calm killing intent clear in their steely eyes. Lily's world became centered on evading, using minimal contact to guide each weapon away from her and acrobatics she'd trained for use in avoiding limbs of trees whipping at her as she chased after beasts she was hunting. Something needed to change, quickly, or she'd be cut down. Then hundreds if not thousands of people would be fed to the pit to grow bland, nutritional mushrooms.

Reinforcements arrived at that moment. Unfortunately, they weren't reinforcing *her*.

Pounding, metal-clad feet announced the arrival of a surge of city guards flanked by another handful of mages. Most concerningly, Captain Cliff was at the forefront of the group, sword out as he barreled down the straight road. Their eyes met, and Red did *not* like what she saw there—not one bit.

Pushing into the air, she flipped back, landing with both feet on the chest of one of the armored warriors and kicking off as hard as she could manage. Though she couldn't see it, she knew the man fell to the ground thanks to the clatter of metal bouncing off the stone street. Feeling petty, she internally mumbled, "I hope it's *really* expensive and difficult to get dents out of plate mail."

"You, *again*?" Captain Cliff's words carried a predatory intensity, his grip on a sword showing that he was a man ready to shed blood for the safety of his city. "I asked you when we first met if you were a troublemaker, and you said *no*! You *lied* to me!"

"Who says *yes* to a question like that?" she shouted back, frantically searching around for a way out of the situation. Her eyes landed on the mage who was still clutching his face, drawn by his attempt to get to his feet and target her with an outstretched hand. Acting on her instinctual desire to put wounded animals out of their misery, as well as not wanting a ball of rock to dent her forehead, Lily ducked around him and brought her short sword up to the neck of the young man.

She saw him go stiff with fear, even as she resigned herself to not getting out of this situation without bloodshed. Trying to ignore the sinking feeling in her gut, Lily tensed her arm and began to *pull-*

"*Dad, help!*" The young mage screeched as the edge of her blade began to part the skin of his throat. Lily went stock-still as she saw his outstretched hand shift to grasp at Captain Cliff, whose expression had shifted drastically from one moment to the next. She scanned the man in front of her, then the still-distant Captain, and realized she had accidentally taken the leader of the city's son hostage.

Everything went very quiet and still at that moment. The guards and mages who'd been barreling down the street quickly slowed, then screeched to a halt as they took in the situation. The Stoneweavers and warriors near Red stopped, their faces filled with confusion as they looked to Captain Cliff for orders.

Lily felt the young man swallow hard, his bobbing Adam's apple causing his skin to be nicked by the sharp blade once more, and a fresh trickle of blood traveled down the hollow of his neck. Instantly, Captain Cliff took a single, sharp step forward, caught between paternal instincts and his duty to the city. In the next moment, he froze in place once more. His voice, hardened and sharpened by years of command, filled the space around them.

"You will let him go, this *instant*." System's Whisper flashed a warning in her vision, causing Red to instinctively tighten her muscles as what must've been a skill-empowered order impacted her. The young man must have expected her not to be able to resist in the slightest, as he tried to duck away, only to choke as blade only pressed even more firmly against his flesh.

Red locked eyes with Captain Cliff. "Try something like that again, and I might not be able to stop myself. Speak slowly and calmly, or my decades of butchering deer might just force my hand. Accidentally."

Captain Cliff let out a long, slow breath through pursed lips, slowly lifting his sword and sheathing it before holding both of his hands in the air. "What do you want, number seven of DK-IS-GR-eight? What's that? You didn't think I knew who you were, or that I would keep tabs on you?"

Lily had scowled as he began speaking. "No, I just don't

want you to refer to me by a designation. My name is Lily. Lily Red."

"You haven't *earned* a name-" The Captain clenched his teeth together, wincing as he bit off his instinctual reply. "Right... Lily, is it? What will it take for you to release that young Stoneweaver?"

"It's pretty simple, Captain." Red spoke firmly yet respectfully, knowing a man like this couldn't bear any insult to his pride, especially not in front of so many subordinates. "You seem quite unhappy with my people being here. They're *very* unhappy being kept here. Let us go, and both our problems are solved."

She had kept her voice steady, feeling as though carrying the weight of all of her people's lives had lent her words gravitas.

So it was *extra* surprising when the Captain clenched his jaw and slowly began lowering his hands. "I *can't*. It's against everything Bleakrock stands for. Our mission, our ethos, *the rules*. I can't so flagrantly disregard everything we have ever worked for. You are telling me to give up our entire way of life for one person. A person who is *beyond* significant to me, but... whose loss would *not* damage the foundation of Bleakrock."

The world felt like it was tilting, and Red blinked owlishly as Captain Cliff's words sank into her mind. Not helping the situation, the young man she was holding a blade to stood *straighter*, as though ready to accept his sacrifice for the greater good.

"Then your city will be destroyed," Lily firmly stated, knowing better than to hesitate any longer. She could see the mages making subtle motions, as if trying to figure out a spell to cast against her to put an end to the situation without her noticing.

The warriors were inching closer, ready to put her down as soon as they were given the command. She didn't let it issue forth, pressing the issue harder, "We have weapons inside the walls, and the first gate has already fallen to the unified city-states of the Coastals and the Wyld. When the bombardment from Wolf Warband begins, and they pour in, my people are *absolutely* vindictive enough to make sure they take you down with them."

Instead of righteous vindication, now her words were dark, a clear, threatening foreshadowing of the near future. Going by the way everyone stopped once again, this had gotten through to them where nothing else she'd stated had worked. Captain Cliff hesitated, his expression entirely neutral. "It's too late. We've put too much into this. There's no way out of this situation, not with the honor of Bleakrock intact. I'm sorry it has come to this... my son... but no matter what it costs-"

Realizing the Captain was about to order his own son to fall on her sword, which would certainly mean she would be torn apart in the next second, Red shouted at the top of her voice. "Stop! You can keep your honor intact *and* let us go. Let me explain, so we can stop this bloodshed before it starts. Just let me talk."

"Then..." The Captain took a sharp, shuddering breath, his lip curling slightly as an internal battle waged within him. Finally, mercifully, he ground out a single word. "Speak."

"You've been offered an *honorable* deal from an external enemy who has the means and experience to destroy you, and everything your society has built." Red spoke clearly, yet rapidly. "Drwg Mawr has offered to leave this island if he's bested in single combat. *I can beat him.*"

"Ridiculous," the Captain instantly scoffed. "He's a murderous invader, with a reputation for unthinking violence. Do you truly think a rabid dog like that would follow through on his offer of single combat? Whoever steps out there will be cut to ribbons by dozens of his followers the instant they are exposed."

"Well... I suppose that would still solve *one* of your problems," Red countered with a dark laugh. "Let me go fight him. If I win, you'll swear to release everyone who wants to go. It'll be a magnanimous, honorable gesture from a powerful leader who successfully turned away an invasion of tens of thousands of raiders… and nothing else. Everyone will remember the safety you provided them, and how you nobly released them once the danger had passed."

"And *when* you die," Captain Cliff darkly rejoined, "I will be the man who sent tens of thousands of people into servitude under a nation of raiders. The ships they build will be used to invade neighboring countries, and the death toll will climb into the hundreds of thousands. All because of *you*. That is what you are asking me to risk."

Red let out a soft sigh and eased back on the pressure she'd been applying to her blade. "Either take a chance to get rid of them now, while you can, or accept *guaranteed* destruction. The longer you wait, the more inevitable your defeat becomes. Is there *honor* in being the one overseeing the city when it falls?"

"Captain." As a warrior stepped forward and addressed the man, Red nearly cut open her hostage's throat out of sheer surprise of the interruption. "If I may be so bold… by the system, I swear I would only be happier and more proud of you if you removed these ungrateful, murderous, rampaging, *vile* people from our city."

"I want to have a happy, simple life again," a mage joined in weakly. "I second the opinion."

The Captain swept his gaze around the area, finding every one of his people vigorously nodding, even pleading with their eyes. "This… this is unexpected."

Finally, his eyes came to rest on his son, and they exchanged a wordless conversation through that stare. The Captain sucked in a deep breath and spoke more powerfully, "You will swear to go and fight their leader in single combat?

And either way, I get to rid my city of these... dissident elements?"

"So long as you give me back my gear and swear to release me without harm and leave me alone afterward, I swear I will accept the challenge of single combat, so long as you swear to release everyone from the city who wants to go. I will never willingly return to this city." Lifting her off hand and shifting her weight so her hostage had to move along with her, Lily showed the front of her torso and made an 'X' over her heart. "Cross my heart and hope to die."

Golden light flared from the mark she'd drawn on her chest, earning a gasp from everyone assembled as the stone of the city around them grumbled in recognition of the over-flowing power. The system had borne witness to her oath, and failing to follow through would ensure her death.

"On these terms, I accept and so swear," Captain Cliff solemnly replied, mimicking her motion. "Cross my heart... and hope to die."

TWENTY-NINE

LILY IMMEDIATELY RELEASED HER HOSTAGE, knowing she was as safe from these people as could be reasonably expected. The young man walked away, trying to maintain a brave face as crimson fluid dripped down his throat. By the time he'd crossed half the distance between himself and the main group, Captain Cliff had swept forward and yanked him into a desperate hug. No one said a word, and a moment later, the Captain took a step back, hands on his son's shoulders, and reached out to straighten his undyed uniform.

"Congratulations, you are now one of the elite few mages who can say they were in combat with a foreign, body-focused adversary, captured, and lived to train future generations." Cliff gruffly stated, nodding sharply before returning his attention to Lily.

While the Captain had been focused on his son, Lily had turned her attention away to give him a moment of privacy. The system was tingling her senses, so she'd swiped her fingers across her arm to see what had changed.

***Skill increase! System Echo [Level 7 (Proficient) →
Level 8 (Extensive)]!***

System's Echo is an active skill which allows you to [Extensively] yet innately notice life forms as well as rapidly moving objects in a range of [80] meters around you for [24] seconds. Cooldown: [1 minute]. Upon reaching Perfection, this skill becomes permanently active.

Requirement to advance to level 9: Enter and exit an enemy encampment which is on high alert without being seen, resupplying yourself with any necessary food or equipment for survival, and rendering their supplies useless.

"Huh... I suppose I wouldn't have considered him helpless at that moment, but maybe getting him to back down and... *oo~oh*. It must have been when he swore the oath that he was considered no longer any threat." Lily etched this memory into her mind, promising herself she would write everything down as soon as possible. She had already missed one requirement, she certainly wasn't going to fail herself twice. Looking at her new requirement, the Scout let out a small wince, "Yikes... not many chances to practice that one. Either get it right the first time or get stabbed to death."

"Are you done muttering to yourself?" Captain Cliff grumbled at her, clearly eager to get moving so he could rid himself of her presence. Lily nodded, remembering he'd only sworn not to harm her, not to be happy she was still here. "Excellent. If you would follow me to the wall, so we can make a proper announcement and get everyone to calm down for a little while, that would be *wonderful*."

Red fell in step behind him a moment later, but she couldn't stop herself from pushing his buttons, "I didn't realize sarcasm and passive aggressiveness were considered 'simplicity securing tomorrow'."

"There are many things you've never bothered to learn about Bleakrock," Cliff derisively countered, not bothering to rise to her bait. "Wonders, knowledge, *potential* which you and your people will never again have the opportunity to behold.

It took half a week for you all to decide you'd rather serve as indentured servants—at *best*—under a force who will be a danger to dozens of countries... instead of being patient, being *bored*, for any length of time whatsoever."

Turning to look at her, his eyes were disappointed, as stony as his namesake. "Here I thought Wyldlings had more fore-thought than *Coasties*."

Half a month previously, those would've been fighting words for Lily. Now she only shook her head and didn't bother to keep a smile off her face. "I've learned many things about people living outside the forest recently. The Coasties have their own way of life, you have yours, even *Wolf Warband* has good reason for what they do. I don't know, Captain. Perhaps conversation and perspective is the death of disgust toward the lives of other people."

The Captain rolled his eyes while minutely shaking his head. "What utter nonsense. There are thousands upon thousands of cultures out there. They *can't* all be right, and they aren't. They are poison, as clearly shown by trying to bring you into our fold. No longer will we accept large groups who are looking for safety. As of today, a new law will be inscribed on our walls: no more than five percent of our population—in terms of refugees or immigrants—will be accepted at any one time, under *any* circumstances."

His proclamation turned many heads, and Red noticed with concern that a zealous light had appeared in the eyes of the people around her. They began to applaud the Captain, who shook his head sadly and waved for them to finish. Red's eyes darted around, trying to figure out what was going on. "That was... odd?"

"Not that *you* deserve to know this," a nearby warrior sneered at her, fondling his weapon as he looked at the sword she was still brazenly carrying. "But the Captain of the city has one duty. That is the preservation of our ways. To that end, in their entire tenure as Captain, they may make only *one* law. If they do not make any at all, their names are placed in the hall of justice, to be remembered as someone who was able to preserve the city *perfectly* while they lived."

"Captain Cliff just gave up his opportunity to be remembered among the best leaders of our city," another broke in, appearing solemn but gleeful. "Only under the most extreme circumstances would any Captain give up the greatest honor they could achieve. He will be remembered only by us. His name will never be added to our records or associated with his law, except by the people who were here to witness it. Within a generation, he will be forgotten."

Red looked back at the Captain, who had a stern, yet slightly hollow expression on his face. A begrudging respect for the man began to seep into her mind, and she tried to ruthlessly clamp down on it. "Seems harsh."

"No. It's *simple*," Cliff replied tiredly, "If we follow the rules and do our duty, we live good, safe, happy lives. What more could anyone want?"

"*Through simplicity, tomorrow is secured.*" The group of warriors and mages chanted at the Captain, who looked back at them, surprise evident on his face as they saluted him. He inclined his head slightly, acknowledging the respect they were showing, and motioned for Lily to follow him up a set of stairs leading to the top of the wall.

A few minutes later, they were stomping along the inner wall, walking toward a section of the stone where a series of metal tubes were stationed. Cliff pointed at a strange funnel. "When we speak into this, various tubes we've placed throughout the walls, streets, and buildings will carry the message across the city."

Curiosity piqued, Red spoke without thinking. "I thought you'd activated a skill to be heard at such a distance. A spell, perhaps?"

"No," Cliff haughtily replied, his lips twitching with disdain. "As I said, wonders you have never imagined before *fill* this city. This is simply a result of training the best critical-thinking engineers this world has ever seen."

Several people among the escort puffed up their chests proudly, basking in the praise Cliff was offhandedly showering them with. For his part, the Captain stumped over to the tubes and took a deep breath, then commandingly bellowed into the tubes.

"Citizens of Bleakrock! Wyldlings. Coastals. After speaking at length with a representative of your people, Lily Red, we have come to an agreement. She has offered to accept the terms of the honorable duel with the leader of the invading force. If she wins, thereby removing the threat to your lives and reclaiming the island on your behalf, I have sworn by the system to allow you egress from Bleakrock."

Lily stepped forward as the Captain sharply walked away, adding her own words to the tubes and causing the Captain to falter for a moment. "The honorable Captain Cliff has been working to guarantee our lives and health. When this threat has passed, please make sure to respectfully leave the city, and everyone can return to their lives. As simple or complex as you want them to be. For now, everyone should rest assured that you will be able to go home soon. Please cease all hostilities *immediately*."

Slowly at first, but rapidly increasing in volume, a cheer went up across the city as thousands of voices were raised in excitement. Red turned and glanced at the Captain, who was glaring at her, though there was a large amount of surprise in his eyes at how she had shown him such respect. He quickly turned away, taking a few more steps before coming to a halt at another set of tubes, which had been set up on the opposite side of the walkway.

"Invaders! Wolf Warband." Cliff's voice echoed from the edge of the wall, filling the area surrounding the city with his words. "After careful deliberation, we would like to accept your terms of individual combat. We will patiently await your instructions."

Just after Cliff finished his shouting into the distance, a muscled young man ran across the wall toward them, carrying a large, familiar pack. Slowing to a stop, he cautiously handed it over to Lily, who flipped it open and found all her knives, as well as the rest of the Scout kit intact. She nodded at the runner and quickly began strapping the knives into their original positions, placed ball bearings and metal rods in her cloak, and swung the rest of the pack onto her back, extending straps from it which wrapped around her body and were tied together in front to help secure the load.

All of this was accomplished in only a double handful of seconds, the fluid motions and familiarity with which she handled the gear earning her blank stares from the group as a whole. After a moment of discomfort, she decided they were impressed, and tilted her head slightly. "Thanks."

Motioning for Red to follow him, the Captain walked along the wall for another fifty feet or so, then he nodded at his son who was standing among the Stoneweavers. The eager young man stepped forward and made several slow, intricate motions before exhaling sharply and *pushing*. A section of the wall began extending across the open area, creating a huge stone bridge from the inner wall to the outer.

"Even if you *had* taken the entire city," The Captain proclaimed without looking at Red, his arms folded behind his back as he stood in an 'at ease' position. "The *only* way to open the second set of gates is to be atop the outer wall. There are no ladders, no trees... nothing you could use to get across without the aid of a Stoneweaver. As you've already seen, they would all rather die than betray the city. The outer wall is made from the densest, most durable stone we have. Without *siege weapons*-"

He sneered as he said the words, as if he was still wavering on if he should believe the invaders could actually bring them to bear or not, "-there would be almost no method of scaling the outer wall to get to the gate house. Even if you did, it requires four mages working in unison to lift the stone plugs from their casing to open the metal gates. The best you would have been able to do is eventually get to the top of the walls, then fling yourself over in hopes you wouldn't go *splat* when you hit the ground."

"Lucky for us, it never came to that," Lily replied as evenly as she could, though she was internally wincing at the information. Her mind began to replay every item she could try to use to make a ladder or a staircase, such as beds.

A frown tugged at her lips as she realized the bedframes had been melded with the stone. They would need to shatter the legs in order to move them. Even then, the beds were designed to be too large to fit through the doors. Clearly, they'd been sculpted by the mages inside the houses. No matter what other tactic she could think of, it seemed the city had engineered a solution against it.

Then an idea came to her, and she perked up slightly. "Human pyramid. The walls are only about forty feet tall, and there's thousands of us. We could stack ourselves up, then hold on to each other's arms and legs to get people over the other side. From there, it would be a simple matter to cross the island, retrieve tools, and come back with the necessary equipment for a safe exit."

"Yes, that is possible." The Captain nodded, his smirk turning ugly as he looked at her. "All you would need to do is trust every person involved to the utmost degree. Then you would need to wait patiently as they ran off to get their tools and ladders, trusting them to come back and do what they said they would. If it were me, looking at the track record of your peoples, well... I don't have much faith in their follow-through."

Deciding against getting into an argument, especially since she couldn't help but unhappily agree with his assessment,

Red merely lapsed into silence as they waited for Wolf Warband to finally respond.

Happily, only a few minutes later, a familiar, enormous man stepped out of the tree line, flanked by dozens of warriors dragging an immense horn cut from some unfortunate beast. The leader of the raiders leaned toward one end of the horn, and a moment later, his voice boomed through the air out the other side.

"We are ready. Send out your fighter."

"I want to discuss the terms of our combat!" Red shouted across the distance. She waited for a reply, only to feel her heart sink as Big Bad's voice came once more.

"Whoever is trying to yell at us, you *do* know we can't hear you from this distance, right? If you have something to say, come down here and say it to my face." Mocking laughter from the warriors around the enemy leader faintly echoed through the horn, and Red flushed crimson as the people around her mimicked them.

"You want me to come down and talk face-to-face?" Red growled deep in her throat, "*Fine.*"

Spinning in place, she reached out and yanked a halberd away from a startled warrior, then leaped off the wall headfirst.

CHAPTER

THIRTY

As she descended, Lily swung her short sword behind her, turning it horizontal and using it like a scraper against the wall. It didn't slow her very much, if at all—the blade was unable to dig into the dense stone—but it helped stabilize her fall like the rudder of a ship at sea. With her other hand, she pulled the halberd beneath her feet, sharp top pointed downward at a forty-five-degree angle.

The long polearm hit the ground well ahead of her, its momentum stopping instantly. As it did so, the back of the weapon tried to jerk out of her hand, but Lily forcibly guided it to hit the wall. For just a moment, it had two points of contact and was stable. Her feet—already on the metal-banded wooden shaft—pressed down, and the weapon bent *almost* to the point of breaking before rebounding and flinging her out and away from the wall. With *most* of the force of her fall arrested, she tucked forward and rolled as she hit the ground, bruising her shoulders and tailbone as she flipped toosh over tea kettle.

She sprang to her feet on the first bounce.

"I'm so glad that worked," Red muttered under her voice, silently swearing to herself she would never tell anyone she hadn't expected her spur-of-the-moment decision to end so well. "Maybe Franklin had a point, and I *should* try to get my temper under control. Eh... I suppose even the tide can be counted on to come in twice a day."

Activating System's Echo, she was able to see the people up on the wall staring down at her with their jaws hanging open, several of them making frantic, confused motions toward her as she walked away, seemingly entirely unharmed. Thanks to her skill, she didn't need to look back, allowing Red to move casually, as if this had been the only possible result of her jump. Inspecting her Bleakrock-made short sword with a critical eye, she shook her head and tossed it to the side—it had dulled to the point of being no better than a stout steel stick.

"Drwg Mawr!" she bellowed after crossing half the no man's land between the wall and the forest. "I've come to accept your offer of single combat!"

The seafaring fighters exploded into laughter as they registered her words, bending over and slapping their knees as their howling turned into convulsions. Red didn't care about them; her eyes were firmly locked on Drwg Mawr, who had a deep scowl on his face. Still chortling, three warriors casually strode into the open, walking toward her with annoyance in their glances and condescending smiles on their faces.

"Little pig, the offer was not for one such as you! Drwg Mawr does not fight tiny little tweens!" As the words finished spilling from his mouth, the warrior collapsed to his knees, then to the ground, his eyes rolling into the back of his head.

The laughter cut off as a ball bearing un-suctioned from the man's forehead and rolled across the ground, coming to a stop in a small divot. Calculating, angry glares moved to Red, who'd stopped moving, freezing in her throwing position to ensure everyone knew who had taken down the leading member of the Wolf Warband trio. The other two stepped forward with angry grunts, only for another ball bearing to be thrown at them. Both of them dodged the first toss, only for the follow-up of metal rods to the throat to bring them to the ground, clutching at their windpipes and desperately gagging as they tried to force air into their lungs.

"Those could easily have been knives, and you certainly wouldn't have recovered so easily," Red coldly and loudly announced. "Is this the extent of the *honor* Wolf Warband shows? You, Drwg Mawr, swore we would engage in single combat. Yet *three* of your subordinates are on the ground in front of me after showing clear hostility and refusing combat on your behalf. How do you respond?"

Moving slowly, as if to avoid startling the red-cloaked, fierce woman glaring him down, Drwg Mawr walked into the open area. Grabbing the unconscious man by his leg, he casually lifted and tossed him, one handed, behind himself and into the woods. Then he paused as he got between the other men, who were already starting to get back on their feet. Letting out a deep, primal growl, he first looked at one, then the other. "You have *shamed* me."

Both immediately dropped to their knees, yanking out their weapons and offering them to their leader. Drwg Mawr looked up at Red. "As you are the one wronged, you may make the choice. These men have sullied my honor and are offering to wash away their debt with their blood. Do you accept their death?"

"What? No! If I *wanted* them dead, they would've been dead already." Red recoiled from the scene as the kneeling men quickly put away their weapons, relief evident on their faces. "Instead, I want a small alteration to the terms of our combat."

Not saying a word, Drwg Mawr simply crossed his arms and waited. Lily took a deep breath and clearly laid out her demands. "I still want single combat, but I don't want to have to face you in a small space. Let me fight you in the forest, as a hunter would a wolf."

"Acceptable." Drwg Mawr lifted a hand before she could say anything else. "With a time limit. If you do not defeat me within the time limit, it will be considered my win. You are also not allowed to accept help from any other person, and I will not allow my warriors to offer me any assistance in turn. Single combat, on my honor... and yours. I will hunt you relentlessly, but if all you do is run away... well, you know this island, this forest, better than I. I'm certain you would be able to hide long enough to make me want to give up."

"That's..." Red hesitated, trying to figure out if she had any other options. "Fine. How long? What sort of time limit?"

"Twelve hours."

Lily shook her head instantly. "I know of your skills, Drwg Mawr. Your regeneration would keep you healthy, full of vigor, far beyond my capability to match. One week."

"I still have physical needs." The leader of Wolf Warband shook his head instantly. "Getting food from my people would count as assistance, and after a week of hunger, I would be shift from predator to prey, too weak to continue. One day."

Cursing internally, Red tried to think of any other way she could gain an advantage. Seeing the two men who were still kneeling next to their leader, her eyes brightened slightly. "Three days! One for each of the men who came forward to attack me. One for each city-state I am fighting for."

Drwg Mawr frowned, grinding his teeth as he considered her words. He looked down at the men next to him, who trembled under the weight of his glare, then back at Red. Nodding and speaking slowly, he concluded their negotiations. "That is acceptable. Three days, during which I will do my best to continuously hunt you. If, at the end of this time, you have not defeated me, it will be considered my win. I will accept no help from an outside source, nor will you. The time will start as soon as you enter the forest. Do you agree?"

Red hesitated slightly, her mind spinning with ideas as she tried to find anything else to add to the agreement. Unfortunately, there was nothing. Very cautiously, she nodded in return. "Yes. Cross my heart, and hope to die."

"As do I," the warrior replied with a hint of surprise in his voice. Golden marks appeared over their chests as the world acknowledged their words.

"Then, all that remains is for the ruler of the city to agree to my terms as well." Drwg Mawr backed away from Lily, moving over to the horn and explaining the terms of their combat to Captain Cliff. After a few words back and forth, both of them swore on the system to honor the terms Drwg Mawr had laid out. Enormous golden X's appeared in the sky above them as the system confirmed it had witnessed their agreement, enlarged so both parties could witness them.

"Then, let us engage in glorious, honorable combat." Drwg Mawr blinked in confusion as he looked around for the red-cloaked Scout. "Where...?"

"Time begins now!" Lily's voice floated through the air as the last hint of her garment vanished into the tree line. There was a wild smile on her face as she dashed between the trees. Several of the other warriors had seen her rushing away, but they had been forced to hold themselves back from pointing out her movement, as that would've been considered as their leader accepting their help.

Contrary to her expectations, as she passed through the trees without rustling a leaf, her feet leaving no trace of her passing on the thick moss, the only sound she heard from Big Bad was a distant...

"*Ha!*"

Lily was slightly concerned to hear that he was as excited about this situation as she was. "What advantage does he think he has? I'm untouchable in the forest. I have the training, the skills, and an edge provided by the system. Plus, now I have a lead."

The answer came moments later, with the huge man entering the forest. Red could tell the exact moment he did so, because the sound reaching her was reminiscent of a boulder crashing through the underbrush. Without regard to plants, branches, or small obstacles, the warrior sprinted at full speed after her.

After a flash of smugness, Lily's smile faded away. "Oh no... for a second, I thought he could only keep that up for a short while. But his health and stamina are going to regenerate endlessly. He doesn't care if he gets beaten up smashing through stuff, he'll be as untouched as a lotus by morning."

Gritting her teeth, she began adding turns and shifts through passages between trees which were too small for him to directly follow her. The familiar scent of earth and musty moss was filling her lungs, filling her with nostalgia and calmness despite the situation. "*Way* better than sterile stone and mushrooms. It's *good* to be home."

Her cloak was a blur of red against a green and brown backdrop, her feet flashing over the forest floor as she ran like she was angry at the ground. Already, she was forming a plan. Even with the switchbacks and looping path, Lily couldn't move in too direct a path, if she wanted to hide her destination. "Unless it got caught in a fire, I have a supply cache about twelve miles from here. I made the rope and bought the gear; nothing in there should count as me accepting help from an outside source."

Mentally double-checking the inventory she'd left there, Lily nodded and confirmed her plan within her mind. Deciding she wanted to get a bead on where Big Bad was, she subvocalized, "System's Echo."

Immediately, her eyes went wide, and she threw herself off the path, barely managing to dodge out of the way as the huge man sprinted through the area she'd just been standing, tackling a bush instead of her and snarling in frustration as it was ripped from the ground, sending a cloud of dirt into the air. "*Abyss!*"

"Avoid any and all straightaways, got it," Lily shakily swore to herself as she returned to her maximum speed. Now, however, she made sure to bound through the forest like a rabbit, zigzagging and choosing new directions constantly. She leaped over logs, bustled along branches, and altered her momentum by thumping into trees. Each minute, as her skill came off cooldown, she made sure to activate it and ensure Big Bad wasn't homing in on her at an oblique angle.

After what felt like an eternity of the most intense silent running she'd ever performed, Lily noticed a camouflaged mark she had placed on a large boulder and instantly adjusted her direction once more. Confirming her adversary wasn't within eighty meters of her, she slid to a stop and yanked open the hidden deposit, quickly pulling out all of the materials she needed, or at least those which wouldn't slow her down.

Just as she bundled the last coil of twine into her bag, she heard the riotous crashing which had preceded Big Bad for the last ten miles. Eyes wide, she grabbed the last item she needed from the cache before slamming it shut: a bow and quiver of owl-feather fletched arrows. Immediately, she began running once more, this time without a direction in mind, as she contemplated a single thought she was certain would haunt her for the next three days.

"By the *system*... how does he keep finding me?"

THIRTY-ONE

LILY WORKED to keep her breathing strong and steady as she rushed across what felt like the entirety of Canu Moch. In reality, she was simply flitting across a patchwork of green forest, ash-coated glades, and diving through sunbeams, leaving swirling patterns in the air as she disturbed the residual smoke from the embers of the intense forest fire which had swept through the Wyld.

The Scout was drawing on all of her knowledge of the woods to lead Drwg Mawr on a wild chase, trying to shake him off her trail... and it wasn't working. Anytime she got to the point where he was outside the range of System's Echo, the warrior suddenly put on a burst of speed and turned leaves into mulch, branches into splinters, in essence creating a man-shaped hole in the underbrush wherever he passed.

"What is *up* with this guy?" Red finally spat in frustration as the leader of Wolf Warband *hopped* over a gulch she had needed to use a large stick to pole vault over. "I knew he'd be hard to tire out, but where'd this ability to find me no matter what come from?"

Lily tried to think through the situation as rationally as possible and kept coming up with only one answer. "He must have some kind of skill to either track me, or he put a mark on me he can follow no matter what. It wouldn't be something someone else did, or the system would've informed me of him having already lost the battle. Top priority is going to be working out how he's doing that... but for now, I can use it to my advantage."

The man was moving in as straight of a line as the forest would allow, which meant he wasn't relying on finding traces of her passing. Lily would still need to ensure she was changing directions frequently, or his far longer legs and seemingly endless endurance would allow him to grasp onto her in no time flat. She had no illusions of her ability to escape his grip if he managed to catch her, which meant she needed to avoid that outcome at all costs. Taking a deep breath, Lily began the first stage of her next plan. "System's Echo."

Immediately, she innately understood Big Bad's position relative to her and adjusted her course to put a thick copse of trees between them. Then, having a moment to move without fear of being tackled in the next second, she swept her attention around the area her skill reached. The forest here was absolutely *teeming* with life... and death.

Predators and prey, fleeing for their lives from the fires to the south, had been forced into close proximity. All around her, she could see territorial disputes between apex predators, miniature stampedes as herds of animals ran from dangerous beasts, but most importantly... a clear path through them.

Before her skill went back on cooldown, Red adjusted her path once more, this time getting something much *less* innocuous than some plants between her and the charging brute: a bear. As far as she could tell, it had been forced from its slumber then harried by a pride of cougars after it lumbered into their territory. It was moving aggressively, lunging at any creature who dared to come close, and was a perfect distraction.

"The agreement said no assistance from other people. It

never said anything about Wyld animals." Red chuckled to herself as she skillfully pushed through bushes, foliage, and nettles. A minute later, she reactivated her skill and took a moment to make sure the warrior and bear had clashed. With her skill now being at level eight, she could clearly distinguish the two, even though they were practically hugging as they yanked each other back and forth.

Lily let out a grunt and pulled her pack open. "Yeah, that dude can wrestle a bear. *Don't* let him get his paws on you, Red."

While he was entangled with the creature, she spun the twine out of her pack. Using her nimble, dexterous fingers—as well as lots of experience—she quickly looped the twine into an oversized snare trap, knowing it would have to have an extra-large opening to catch the man who would no doubt be *sprinting* through the area. Lamenting the lack of proper rope, she set and armed the trap, needing to scurry up a tree like a squirrel to loop it properly above a stout branch.

Activating System's Echo as soon as it came off cooldown once more, her jaw dropped as she sensed Big Bad rushing toward her once again, with no sign of the bear in her senses. "He wrestled it and beat it to death? In under a minute?"

With no time to test the trap, she put herself in a straight line moving away from it. As expected, Big Bad picked up speed since he was able to move in a straight line, and less than ten seconds later, thick branches behind her *snapped* back into position as the snare activated.

"Wha—*ahhhh!*" His deep voice echoed through the forest, and Lily felt a smile grow on her face as she imagined him bouncing up and down In the air like a fish hooked on a pole. "Clever! Yet ultimately *useless!*"

Lily had slowed her pace for a moment, contemplating returning to claim victory, but she sprinted off as she heard the unmistakable sound of taught twine being cut through, followed a second later by a crashing noise, which must've been the fighter hitting the ground and destroying the stinging nettles he would've been dangling above.

"That might not stop him, but he's not going to be very happy."

Indeed, moments later, a strangled, confused cry went up. The sound of thrashing echoed through the woods, returning to the already too-familiar noise of the warrior rampaging through the forest. Chuckling to herself, Lily decided to go *up* instead of continuing along the ground. "A normal person would be scratching at the welts left by those nettles for a week. I wonder how long it'll take *him* to heal?"

Now deep enough in the forest that the trees were old growth, meaning spaced apart and sturdy, remaining on the ground would've basically *ensured* she was caught by the long-legged individual behind her. It took longer than she wanted, but soon she'd scaled one of the trees and was able to begin rushing along the branches. Luckily for her, Lily had exquisite balance, and the branches were thicker than her entire body —plenty of room for her to run at full speed.

The grin dropped off her face as the bulky form of Big Bad suddenly burst through the underbrush in the distance and sprinted through the suddenly clear area, passing directly beneath her and continuing for dozens of meters before slowing down hesitantly. Lily narrowed her eyes as he turned and scanned the area, hardly daring to whisper her own thoughts to herself. "Whatever is letting him find me, it isn't accurate at close range. So... I *can* hide, but I can't run. Good to know."

"You can save us several days of effort by just giving up now," Drwg Mawr called out, pausing for a moment after speaking as though expecting an answer. Lily was neither foolish nor prideful enough to answer him and give away her exact location, and the rueful grin she could see on the man's face showed he knew it as well... but had been hoping she might slip up. "I will not tire; I can, at *most*, be slowed down."

Lily lifted her bow, slowly drawing an arrow and nocking it. With slow, steady motions, she pushed the leather-coated grip of the weapon upward to assist in drawing the string back, then slowly settled it in place. The tip of her arrow was aimed directly at his overly muscular thigh, and she ever so slowly began to loosen her grip.

She had been trained to just *relax* when attacking, ensuring the release of the string didn't bounce the bow. This meant that when the projectile jumped away from her, it was almost as much of a surprise to her as it was to the man who suddenly had an arrow in his leg. He folded over, his hands pressed to his leg to stem the bleeding. Staggering back and forth, Drwg Mawr bellowed in agony, "*Gahh*! You shot me!"

"I'll do it again if I have to! That could just as easily have been your heart or your eye!" Red confidently responded, a second arrow already pointed at a more lethal part of his body. "Admit-"

"Heh, *he~eh*..." Drwg Mawr's head snapped in her direction as he let a drawn-out chuckle escape his lips, eyes latching onto her red silhouette among the boughs of the trees. The pitiful expression on his face vanished instantly, replaced with utter glee. "*Gotcha.*"

Casually plucking the arrow out of his leg, he tossed it to the side as he sprang forward, running to the nearest trunk and scaling it as though he'd been born among the trees. Lily launched another arrow at him. It sank into his arm... and was promptly ignored. Slapping her bow into place on her back, she turned and started scampering away. "Yeah, that's a *nope*. Go, go, *go!*"

"Trees aren't any harder than the rigging of a boat!" Big Bad laughed as he pounded along the complex deciduous highway. "Time for this to end!"

He grabbed a branch and swung, flipping in the air to maintain his momentum as he came down and hurtled along the path Red had taken. As he pushed through a thickly-leaved area, he came almost face to face with his quarry, who was waiting only a half-dozen paces away.

"Better luck next time, Big Bad."

She let go of the huge limb she'd been dragging along with her, and it sprang across the distance faster than the eye could see to slam directly into the warrior's chest. The branch combined with his forward momentum to send the man flying, shattering the wooden limb and leaving the raider without a handhold to grasp or catch himself with. Red gave a mocking salute as Big Bad tumbled through the air, ignobly falling to the ground with an enormous *thump*.

"Ha! Ha, *haa*!" Laughter had *not* been what she was expecting, and Lily's grin turned grim as she peeked over the edge of the wooden path and saw him already getting back to his feet. "This is the most fun I've had in years! Everyone always either fights to the death or surrenders immediately. *You* hit me with a *tree*!"

"You like that?" Lily scoffed, turning away to continue her escape attempt once more. "Great. I'll keep it coming."

CHAPTER

THIRTY-TWO

"System's Echo."

For the next twenty-four seconds, Lily gravely examined eighty meters of life around herself. No matter how she waited, no matter where she looked, it appeared Big Bad Wolf had officially been left behind. She waited a full minute so she could activate the skill again, but once more, the warrior was nowhere to be found. "Did I finally give him the slip? Was he using some sort of magical artifact to find me, and now it's out of power? Is... is that how those things work?"

The only magical item she had experience with was her own crimson cloak, with its cleaning and self-repair properties. Those were passive effects, continuous, and as far as she knew, permanent as it was actually *enchanted*—as in, given by the system or created by a Fairy or Hero of the system. Unfortunately, without knowing for sure if he could find her, meaning he could pop up at any time day or night, she would need to be exceedingly careful.

Her speed dropped as night fell, the dense foliage and underbrush she'd needed for cover now replaced with the shadow of the planet. The chirping of birds and calls back and forth between different herds of animals had been replaced with soft calls from nocturnal creatures as they began their hunts. Without the plethora of daytime beasts moving around, each misstep or rustle Red contributed to the ambiance would draw attention. Every sound felt amplified, even Lily's breath, which was coming in measured pulls instead of gasps, only thanks to her bodily control and intense focus.

Exhaustion was pulling at her, and at this point, moving through utter darkness would guarantee mistakes, even with her level of skill. Lily softly grumbled to herself, "Who would've thought being chased through the woods with your life on the line would make someone so much more tired than crossing the entire island from start to finish over the course of a day?"

No matter what the risks were, she kept moving. Even if she couldn't see him currently, Big Bad was relentlessly pursuing her, just as he had promised to do. Late evening turned into full night, and the forest began filling with fog as it slowly cooled down.

Lily finally decided to find a place where she'd be safe enough to sleep when midnight approached. With a practiced eye, she scanned the enormous trees around her, finally choosing one with the densest quantity of branches and began slipping up and through them; inching ever closer to the cloud-covered moon. "I'll just go *all* the way up, to the point the branches wouldn't support his weight. That's gotta be enough... wait, what am I saying? He's too big to get up here without *smashing* his way through these in the first place. It's basically a built-in alarm."

Lily winced as she examined her thoughts, realizing they were nearly deluded from adrenaline and exhaustion. "I've got to give myself a break. This morning, I led a revolt against a city and made them cave to our demands, then convinced a warrior to fight me in familiar territory, and have been running ever since. Start to finish, no matter what, I should be proud I even made it *this* far without rest."

No matter how sleepy she was feeling, Lily didn't allow herself to leave behind any obvious signs of her passing. She climbed through the branches, slipping past dried leaves—not to mention twigs which were ready to snap with the lightest of touches—all while digging her fingers into the rough bark *just* enough to maintain her position without tearing it off and dropping remnants which could be found at the base of the tree.

Up, up, up.

This deep in the forest, the wooden sentinels had never been felled, nor had they been trimmed or maintained. The ground became a distant concern, soon hidden by the rising fog. Finally, so high up that her every movement caused the top of the tree to sway back and forth, Red wrapped herself in her cloak and nestled herself among the branches.

As soon as she was in a secure position, she activated System's Echo once more. Ever so carefully, her mind flowed over the world around her. "Nothing. Somehow... I got away. As soon as I wake up, we're going to get to the cache and start setting up some *real* traps. He thought a branch was fun? I'll hit him with a *tree* and see how he likes that. He's... too sturdy to... *yawn*... take it easy on."

Sleep claimed her, the tree gently swaying with the breeze rocking her to sleep.

Light.

Before her eyes were fully opened, or her mind was cognizant of her surroundings, light filled her mind. It wasn't a pleasant pre-dawn light filtering through the clouds above, nor was it the flickering, concerning flare of the forest being on fire. No, this was deeper, more primal... a light ingrained in her soul.

System's Whisper was *screaming* at her.

Her eyelids slammed open, and Lily's vision was filled with

the image of a massive hand reaching toward her throat. A scream wanted to erupt from her throat, but she managed to just barely hold it back. The hand was inching closer, but clearly the warrior thought she was still asleep and was trying to ensure he had a good grip before allowing her to wake up. If she let him know she was aware... Lily knew he would lunge for her.

Thankfully, her cloak was moving in the wind slightly, allowing her to carefully shift her position and get her feet under her without alerting him. Ever so carefully timing her next motion, she waited until *just* before the man was sure to clench his fingers before pushing up and away. The wind worked in her favor, a strong gust blowing the top of the tree in the opposite direction of her leap.

"*No!*"

The roar of annoyance followed Lily as she fell through the air, thin branches turning to splinters as she passed through them. Her cloak was billowing around her, but Lily yanked it close to protect her skin from the shattering wood. As thicker branches appeared in her vision, a concerning sound reached her ears: a similar snapping of twigs and branches, but not from her passage through the canopy. "Abyss, I have practically no lead!"

Her momentum was already being arrested, but with his size, and her already having caught against many of the small branches which would have been in his path, Big Bad was falling far faster. Sucking in a quick breath, she wrapped her cloak around both hands and reached out, grabbing onto a limb as she fell and pulling hard to shift her direction.

An instant later, the branch bounced back up, and she heard an almost immediate, ominous *snap* as Big Bad tried to follow her example with the grab-and-swing motion. Luckily, this time his weight and momentum was working against him.

Lily shot to the side, but Drwg Mawr continued in a

straight line toward the ground. Knowing she was still in an extremely dangerous situation, she began reaching her hands out, letting go of her cloak as she slowed down enough to catch branches without tearing her palms open. The warrior finally fell far enough to find a branch large enough to support his weight and was already beginning his pursuit.

The Scout grit her teeth and growled deeply in her throat. "I am *unhappy* with how much damage you can shrug off."

"Now we get to do this all over again, but you will get less sleep the next time you rest, for now you know I will be there when you awaken!" Drwg Mawr called up and after her, not slowing down in the slightest as he shouted. "I am the paragon of endurance. I will *not* stop. You will not have enough time to execute a strategy. You will lose, and if all you can manage is to run for the next three days, you will still lose, but you will be tired doing it."

Red's feet finally found purchase on a particularly thick branch. Without missing a beat or bothering to waste her air on bantering with an enemy, she began running along the new path among the treetops. "Gotta take stock of my situation… I've had at *most* three hours of sleep. I have no idea how he got that close without me noticing. What do I have going in my favor? It's still dark. With the fog, visibility is near zero. This means he's still tracking me magically, or I would've already lost him by now. Holding back as he did must have been a ploy to lull me into a false sense of security. Lovely. Who needs sleep, anyway?"

"Not me!" Behind her, the scraping of bark grated on her nerves. Leaves cascaded from branches as the huge man displaced them with his less than graceful pursuit, turning the silent night into a cacophony of forest destruction. His sheer size and attempt at following the path she was treading made subtlety impossible—but it appeared he had fully thrown in the towel on 'subtle'. "I'm onto your tricks! I won't be slapped to the ground by another branch."

Between his disregard for personal injury and his desire to end this combat quickly, Drwg Mawr recklessly barreled through the canopy.

"Say that all you want, doesn't mean it's true." Red murmured as she continued slipping through the trees far above the ground. "Gotta kick this habit of saying my thoughts out loud."

She settled into a continuous movement pattern, only picking up speed when she felt the long boughs she ran upon shake under the bulk of her pursuer. Finally, the Scout found what she'd been looking for—the edge of a glade. She ran along a branch, and it slowly dipped toward the ground. Just before she got to the final few steps on the wood, she ducked down, crouched, then flung herself forward as the tree limb rebounded upward.

Lily flew across the open space in a long arc before tucking and rolling, managing to grasp a branch on the far side of the clearing and pull herself up on a new path a dozen feet closer to the ground. "Come on, come on…! He's too close to have my exact location. He only has a direction…"

"*Wahhh!*"

"Got 'im." A near-feral smile appeared on Lily's face, fading slightly as she heard an explosive splash. "Aww… he fell into a pond? Abyss, that's barely gonna put a dent in his speed."

She'd been hoping that, by falling from so high, the warrior might have broken a leg or an arm, giving her enough time to get a lead while he healed through it. Even so, Lily wasn't about to waste the opportunity. Big Bad was momentarily out of the chase, so her mind was already racing ahead to try and determine her next steps. "Even if he *did* get hurt, he's going to get back on his feet and after me in no time flat. I can't outrun him forever, and the more tricks I use on him, the fewer options I'll have to use when I need them."

As she came to a fork in her path, Red hesitated for a bare

moment. If she went to the right, she'd be able to reach the next supply depot and just *maybe* have enough time to set up traps, which would be enough to tie him down. But that meant heavy, thick rope. Preferably nets, pits, or deadfalls. She needed more than a few minutes to get those ready; she needed *time*. "I need to use the rules of engagement against him, so he loses on a technicality... how can I make that happen?"

Lily's foot came down, and she made a choice, shifting to run along the left side of the tree, her path beginning a long loop back the way she'd come. The first glimmerings of a plan began to form, slowly trickling out to create a strategy which would use her knowledge of the forest, skills as a Scout, and the nature of her pursuer against him.

"If I can't hide from him in the forest, then I need to muddy the trail." As the light of dawn began to reach the remnants of the verdant forest, Lily's eyes fixed on a thick column of smoke lazily drifting upward. "Let's see if he can magically track me among his own people."

THIRTY-THREE

"COME ON, I know they can be found in this part of the forest," Lily grumbled as she frantically searched the under-growth. "How can something purple and bright red hide so well among green leaves... wait. I wonder how many people have said that about me?"

Lily giggled slightly, realizing how sleep deprived and manic she was starting to sound. The thought sobered her up, and she pushed through leaves and plants with more intention until she finally found what she'd been looking for: clusters of berries she was hoping would turn the situation in her favor. Her fingers began plucking the luscious fruit, easily avoiding the prickly thorns around them since she knew what to watch for.

A crashing in the woods, far distant for the moment, made her eyes widen. Abandoning her attempts at caution, she grasped the woody interior of the bush and firmly shook it, causing berries to fall and scatter across the ground. She swept them up, handful by handful, dropping them into one of the water-resistant compartments of her scout satchel. "This is going to have to be enough!"

Lily knew she was playing a dangerous game, but the lives

and freedom of thousands were resting on her shoulders; now wasn't the time to worry about the well-being of her enemies. After casting the imminent moral quandary to the side, she was on the move once more, calculating how this portion of her goal would fit in with the entirety of her plan. "It's not much, but if I want to muddy the waters, anything I can do to make the mud *thick* will help. *Hee…* gross."

The plume of smoke rising in the distance came closer, and Big Bad would have some idea of where she was going, but she hoped the man assumed she would avoid the rest of Wolf Warband. Unfortunately for him, and them, avoidance wasn't her goal. Not today.

Her current strategy relied on the warriors messing up and causing the system to call the trial-by-combat in her favor because of it. Even the *thought* of what she was about to do sent a thrill of excitement *zinging* through her heart, the rush of adrenaline sharpening her senses and clearing away some of the fog of sleeplessness which had been accruing.

System's Echo informed Lily that she had plenty of time, as Big Bad wasn't yet within eighty meters of her. Taking all the time she needed to approach unheard and unseen, Lily swept her gaze over the Wolf Warband camp. It was *alive* in a way she hadn't seen since visiting the Coasties next to the ocean, but in a way far closer to her liking.

Instead of lazing around and shouting at each other, playing games, and being foolish, the warriors were completing all sorts of tasks in a lively manner. They argued and laughed, sharpened weapons and practiced skills, all the while keeping their eyes on their surroundings; as they knew they were deep in enemy territory.

This was a group who was highly disciplined, extremely proficient in what they did. As much as she wanted to see them as terrible, destructive invaders who'd wrecked her home and life, all she saw were people who combined the best qualities of all three city-states on Canu Moch. "Yeah… if they stay here, this island is fish-*boned*. They have the camaraderie of the Coasties, the skill of the Wyldlings, and the armor and weaponry of Bleakrock. No wonder Captain Cliff took their threats of siege weaponry seriously."

With a deep breath, Lily activated her skill and stepped into the open area between the forest and the camp. System's Whisper highlighted the best path for her to move along, just as System's *Echo* ensured she moved when heads were turned away from her. Lily slipped into the camp without a hint of noise, her bright red cloak always just beyond the periphery of the next warrior's vision. Once she was past the outer line, with the most alert warriors and posted sentries, it became even easier to penetrate to the core of their defenses.

Face calm, but heart pounding, Lily moved into the central area of the camp, which had been set up in a circular pattern. Barrels and crates were in neatly organized patterns. Frustratingly, they were out in the open and not hidden under the canopy of a tent, leaving her exposed as she sidled up to them. She licked her lips as she forced the lid off one of the water barrels, suddenly realizing exactly how dry her tongue and throat were. Dipping a ladle which had been conveniently left near the water barrel, she lifted it and drank her fill of the spring water, which was too fresh to be anything but recently collected from the island.

"Ahh... tastes like home." With one of her basic needs met, the Scout found her rapid heartbeat calming. Feeling much refreshed, Lily quickly moved to the next stages of her plan. After refilling her waterskin in the clean water, she pulled a handful of berries out of her bag and *squeezed* until fresh juice flowed out and into the water. Then she dipped her hand in, swishing around until her fingers were again more clean. "Hope the raiders love six hours of intense intestinal scouring each time they take a sip."

The last time Lily had seen this type of berry, she'd been slapping it out of the hands of a Coasty she was leading to the

Heart of the Wyld. The two people who'd already eaten their fill had left literal trails pointing at their destination—the traces she hadn't been willing to hide even for the benefit of the city-state. Luckily, all evidence of her 'dereliction of duty' would have been eradicated in the fires farther south.

With the first task complete, Red wasted no time moving among the rest of the supplies. She crushed the berries, moving quickly and efficiently between water and barrels of mead, even managing to mix the pulp into the large pots of stew she assumed the warband would be consuming for their next meal. Dry rations got a trickle of the fluid mixed in among them, but even that should be enough to cause terrible discomfort. The berries were *potent*, and consuming any part of them would be enough to restart the *emptying* process once more.

Her bag was refilled with clean jerkies and water, enough supplies for several days on the go, as she wouldn't have enough time to hunt. Satisfaction filled Lily as she cast her eyes over the now-poisoned rations, knowing there would soon be chaos and terrible smells filling the camp. Most importantly, it should slow down the warriors and *hopefully* require the attention of Big Bad himself.

Then the Scout stepped over to her true destination: utility crates.

"If you won't let me get to my supply depots… I'll just raid yours." Red chuckled darkly as she quickly filled the remaining space in her pack with everything from daggers to thick wire, which could be used in anything from traps to weapon repair. Then came the most burdensome articles, as Lily tossed three entire coils of Coastal-made entwined-straw rope—approximately a hundred feet each—over her head before wiggling her arm through to wear them like an oversized sash. She immediately felt the difference as she began moving to the opposite side of the camp: her steps were heavier, her motions less smooth.

"This doesn't count as me accepting help from someone else, right, system?" Lily muttered into the empty air. "I'm taking supplies from my enemies. I'm not getting help from someone who *wants* to help me. It's totally justified in my head, but if it's going to make me lose, I'll drop it all right now."

The system stayed blessedly silent, and no warning colors flashed in her vision from her always-active skills. System's Echo slipped into place once more, the information it provided causing Lily to blanch and roll under a table loaded with furs and armor in need of repairs.

Drwg Mawr sprinted *around* the camp, causing the members of Wolf Warband to shout in concern, then in greeting as they recognized their leader. At best, the huge warrior sent them glances of annoyance as he barreled past... only to re-emerge from the forest as he got far enough away from the camp to gauge that Lily hadn't continued on past them.

"Mawr!" A warrior shouted, "Have you completed your single combat already? Why are you...?"

"He's on the hunt!" Someone else shouted, interrupting the first. "His quarry must be nearby; sniff 'em out!"

Immediately, all of the men in the area had their head on a swivel, their eyes roving over the camp—inspecting every nook and cranny. Her own eyes went wide, and a bright smile appeared on Lily's face. Just as she was about to roll from under the table and expose her presence to the nearest invader, Drwg Mawr's voice boomed out, anger and horrified realization filling his words.

"Wolf Warband! Eyes *up!*" There was a long, tense moment as the raiders instead glanced over at him in confusion. Big Bad snarled and reached for the huge cudgel swinging off his bandolier. "Don't be fools! She's trying to get one of you to alert me to her position! If you assist me, I will need to admit defeat, even *if* the system itself did not declare it on her behalf, and it *would!*"

With her skill still active for the moment, Lily saw as expressions shifted in understanding, jaws dropped, and Big Bad lifted his weapon as though he were going to smack the nearest man with it. "I said, eyes *up*! On the *sky*! If someone sees her, I'm certain they will react and draw my attention!"

The huge man began stalking into the camp, flipping tables and yanking down tents with a single pull as he went. There were a few murmurs of discontentment, but no one actively impeded his search. With a soft grunt of annoyance, Lily took the opportunity to casually walk out of the camp, knowing no one would see her—likely not even out of the corner of their eyes. "Annoyingly *tall* warriors, these. Ugh... why does Drwg Mawr have to be so frustratingly good at figuring out my next move? I almost had him. If I would've stepped out *two* seconds earlier...!"

She had stopped herself from *trying* to get their attention, barely, when she realized doing so intentionally would be the same as requesting the help of an outside source. They were actively attempting *not* to see her, which would've made any such action immediately lead to her loss. "By the system, he's too clever by half!"

Lily circled the camp, slowly moving through the forest around and around the area. If she got too far away, his tracking method would alert him to her distance and direction —while also eliminating any possibility of him eating some of the poisoned food. She'd been able to resupply from her own cache and had to wonder if there was anything in the camp he could consider his and his alone, with no outside assistance. The Scout was fairly certain she had managed to insert some of the berry juice in every possible edible substance, and so she waited.

Ten minutes later, Big Bad had successfully tossed the entire camp, letting out a roar of frustration before throwing his head back and releasing a deep belly laugh. "I don't know what game you're playing, Red! I'll tell you this, wasting my time is not the same as defeating me."

Finishing his thought, the huge man let out a soft sigh, then turned and ran into the forest. Lily narrowed her eyes as she watched him go. "At his speed, I can assume five meters every handful of seconds."

She began counting down, reaching twenty-two seconds before the sounds of the warrior in the distance suddenly halted, then began returning, getting louder over time. "Accounting for the distance between us and him needing to go around obstacles… once he's outside of a hundred meters, he's shown my direction in relation to him. That's a good data point to have."

"I guess he's gone?" The words floated to Red where she was waiting just outside the camp. "Lunch time, then?"

Even as Big Bad came sprinting toward her in a straight line, Lily couldn't manage to keep herself from snickering. "Eat up, boys."

THIRTY-FOUR

RED EXPLODED out of the underbrush, a shower of leaves slowly falling to the ground behind her. Her breath was coming in ragged gasps as she pushed into and through the next underbrush in her way. Her cloak was snagging on thorns, roots felt like they were reaching up to try and trip her, branches reached like grasping hands in an attempt to slow her down. "Abyss, *abyss!*"

A moment later, the bushes she'd disturbed practically *exploded* as Big Bad burst through them, pumping his arms and legs like a trained sprinter. His breathing was also altered, but instead of gasping, it was sharp inhales and bursting exhales as he fueled his massive body with air. Lily had waited too long, hoping to be around to see the mayhem of her actions against the camp. Unfortunately, she had misjudged how effective Drwg Mawr's tracking magic was—as well as the fine-tuned senses of the man himself.

The Scout had been crouched, watching the first among the enemy sip their stew, as she practically convulsed with suppressed laughter. She'd heard Big Bad crashing through the underbrush in the distance, but a tingling sensation on her arm had caught her attention, and she'd swiped her fingers along her skin to see what the system wanted to tell her.

Skill increase! System's Echo [Level 8 (Extensive) → Level 9 (Master)]!

System's Echo is an active skill which allows you to [Masterfully] yet innately notice life forms as well as rapidly moving objects in a range of [90] meters around you for [27] seconds. Cooldown: [30 seconds]. Upon reaching Perfection, this skill becomes permanently active.

If that would have been the only information, she would've been able to quickly recover and get back on the move. Unfortunately, there was one more piece: the final requirement for her to go from level nine to level ten with the skill. Upon reading it, she had frozen as her mind drank in the realization that she had only one real chance to achieve her Breakthrough Skill.

Requirement to advance to level 10: Single-handedly end a war.

From the moment her eyes traced the lines of the words, there was no other choice but to defeat Drwg Mawr. It was a deceptively simple task, five words which would determine if she achieved greatness at an age where she would be considered a prodigy among prodigies. By the time she'd pulled herself out of the spiral of shock and brought her focus back to the present, the huge warrior had already been reaching for her. Lily had needed to scramble out of the way, hopping for the first several feet like a rabbit as she got her body in alignment and started running.

From that point on, she'd been doing her best to escape, but hadn't managed to get more than five full feet away from the Big Bad Wolf.

"I suppose... the skill leveling requirement is only *four* words, if I consider the hyphenated portion as a single one.

Ha, *haaa*!" Lily shook off the bizarre, intrusive thoughts as she pumped her legs, pushing through thorny weeds and trying to ignore the lactic acid building up in her calves. "Well... unless I want... to go join a war.... in some distant country, and figure out a way to end it myself... this is my only chance to achieve *Breakthrough*!"

Unfortunately, Drwg Mawr wasn't going to play nice and *let* her win. Over and over he swung at her, his grasping hand nearly closing around her cloak, hair, or limbs far too frequently. Lily found herself playing the most frantic game of forest tag of her life, dropping to the ground, rolling, ducking, jumping, flipping, and evading by a *literal* hair's breadth as his enormous hands squeezed down on empty air time and time again.

Finally, she managed to leap across a small ravine with a creek trickling along at the bottom, catching an overhanging branch—only to reverse course midair to land nearly exactly where she'd leapt from.

Drwg Mawr, on the other hand, could only bellow in frustration as he wheeled around, frantically trying to turn and get back to his jump point. He struck the ground on the far bank and skidded, falling and bouncing only once before immediately returning to his feet. For a long moment, they simply stood there, on opposite sides of the drop, staring each other down without moving.

Taking a long, shuddering breath, the warrior broke the silence, "Truly, I have never seen someone move through rough terrain as you do. It is almost as if you are part Dryad, and the forest bends around you."

"I can also honestly say I've never seen someone able to keep up with me." Red paused for a moment, tilting her head forward to indicate his legs and lower abdomen. "You have enough dirt, blood, and pulped plant matter on you where I might consider *you* to be part of the forest. On that note, you're tall and thick enough to be a tree."

"Your skill and wit are admirable." Drwg Mawr let out a heavy sigh as his hand reached toward his belt, wrapping around the handle of his cudgel. "I would appreciate your surrender. I'm certain we could come to favorable terms. By the system, I am impressed enough where the last thing I want to do is hurt you. I must forewarn you... while it is right at the bottom, it is still *on* the list. For my people, I must succeed."

Lily shook her head, her rapid breathing slowing as she used the small break to recover to the best of her ability. "I have no choice *but* to win. For so, so many reasons."

"Then, I hope you are able to deal with the consequences, and I can only request your forgiveness for what I must do." The huge warrior's voice was a low rumble reminiscent of an earthquake as it escaped his chest. He tilted his head forward, eyes locking on her with deadly intent as he gripped the cudgel and lifted it. "I cannot allow my growing respect for you, my opponent, to cost my people the resources of this island. I had wanted to succeed without bloodshed, but I will do what needs must."

Everything which needed to be said between them had been spoken, so Lily turned and flitted into the woods. Moments later, her pursuer was across the gap and sprinting after her. Yet, one major thing had changed in the last few moments: the Scout was no longer frantic. Instead, there was a cold dread filling her gut.

The chase had evolved; it was no longer a simple game of predator and prey, where Big Bad managing to grip her meant the end of their duel. It had become a full-blown death duel, with the leader of Wolf Warband prepared to go to any lengths to secure a victory. System's Whisper flashed a warning, almost too late, as his cudgel swung through the air swiftly, a blurry streak she barely evaded.

As the heavy weapon struck a tree, releasing a spray of bark-turned-shrapnel, Lily unconsciously gasped aloud,

"Celestial feces, you can swing that thing faster than you can *grab* at me?"

"I am not unskilled in grappling and hand-to-hand combat," Drwg Mawr calmly stated, wrenching his weapon out of the tree, where sap was flooding from the new crater in its side. "Yet my focus has always been on *obliterating* the enemy standing before me. With each swing, I can put all of my body's strength into my blow, knowing overextending or injuring myself will be a condition which fixes itself in moments."

"That explains how you managed to put so much muscle on your frame." Lily nervously laughed as she circled around him, her eyes able to remain fixed on his thanks to System's Whisper having already highlighted the optimal pathway. "What do you eat, an entire boatload of fish each day?"

He tilted his head slightly as he paused, "Is this your attempt to figure out how to surrender? Or is this you circling to get in position, to try and run... abyss it, get *back* here!"

Lily dove through a gap between trees, the world around her warning the Scout against staying upright. His cudgel smashed into the trees, one of them reduced to pulp and falling to the ground in the next second, and the other beginning to tilt.

"That would've taken my head off!" She looked back, expecting the warrior to be nearly on top of her, but her jaw dropped as she realized he had *thrown* his weapon. Snapping her chin back up into place, Lily turned and ran. Behind her, she heard a deep sigh before a sound of splintering wood informed her that Drwg Mawr had retrieved his cudgel from the tree trunk it had embedded itself into.

"You will need to sleep eventually, and I will be there."

Though both his chilling words and massive form were pursuing her, the Scout ran on without hesitation. As she moved, now secure in having a slight lead, she pulled apart the first coil of rope wrapped around her shoulder and began weaving her hands along it deftly. Evasion was no longer a real option; if he got within striking distance of her again, there was a good chance a single blow would shatter her spine.

"Definitely can't allow *that* to happen."

With the warrior having drawn his weapon, and severe injury—at the minimum—now on the table, she also set aside her life-long compunctions against truly injuring another person. Lily shook her head even as she had the thought. "If I even *can* hurt him. This man must be part troll or something similar, if he's able to regenerate so constantly."

Now she felt as if she were allowed traps she'd previously dismissed as too dangerous. She hadn't wanted to finish the man off, *just in case* his people wouldn't be bound by his promise to leave. Lily finished tying off the knot, creating a wide-set snare funnel. Activating System's Echo, she looked ahead for both a sturdy branch, as well as the conditions she needed for the trap either to deal enough damage to put the man down for good... or break him enough to give her a chance to make something that *would* finish the job.

"There!" The ability to see anything living from such a great distance allowed her to find the target points for arming, setting, and activating her newly-minted trap before she was even fifty meters out. Lily dropped the open loop on the ground, swirling the rope to widen the snare out further, then ran slightly up a tree, pushing off a low-hanging branch while trailing the rope coil behind her. At the apex of her jump, she flicked her wrist and sent the remaining length up and over a branch, where it unfurled and fell in front of her, slapping the ground just as she touched down.

She grabbed the dangling rope, swinging it forward and around a tree trunk which had fallen, mostly, but ended up being supported by two other trees before it could descend fully to the ground. Lily had seen how the living trees were bent and warped by its weight, and she knew where she could press to make them spring back into shape. The sound of Big

Bad crashing through the forest behind her filled her senses as she frantically tied off the knots, then climbed the trunk of one of the living trees.

Placing her back against the trunk, she put both feet on the dead tree in a squat position, and began to shove.

Just as Big Bad came into view, the dry wood *cracked* and shifted, hundreds of pounds of dead tree finishing its long-awaited plummet toward the ground. The rope went taut, and the snare opening on the ground suddenly yanked closed. For a moment, she thought the trap had failed, but then Lily met Big Bad's eyes as they widened in surprise.

The trap was simple, yet effective. Both of his feet were snagged in the suddenly tight rope, and he was yanked side-ways, rapping off the ground with a grunt of surprise before being hoisted violently into the air. He shot up feet first, wrapping around the wrong side of the branch once, only to be *whiplashed* back around in the opposite direction as the rope followed the momentum of the falling tree.

Lily had only intended for him to be left dangling in the air, but instead he hit the branch with a *crack* that didn't sound like *wood* breaking. His arc spun around once more, completing a full rotation around the limb before being sling-shot forward, slamming into a tree at full speed before being dropped nearly thirty feet to the ground.

From her vantage point, the Scout watched with her heart pounding, seeing no movement. "Well… that would've killed *me* for sure. Maybe he's-"

"*Unngh.*" A deep groan floated up from the pile of bleeding meat, fur armor, and frayed rope. "I actually felt that one."

Drwg Mawr slowly, painfully, got to his feet while dizzily looking around until he saw her perched above him. More than anything else, there was deep annoyance etched into his face as he took a step toward her, wincing as his foot came down. Another step came, slow and painful, but that still meant progress toward her. Lily nodded slowly, starting to understand exactly how durable this monster of a man truly was. By his third step, it seemed some of his pain had ebbed, and he began moving more confidently.

Deciding against waiting around until he was back to full strength, Lily bounded down the tree limb, jumping in the air and catching the other tree which had been supporting the fallen log. Her weight and momentum pulled the top of it free from where it had been caught against its neighbor. It dipped and shifted, and for a long moment, she hung in the air, unmoving.

Then the ancient oak groaned, wanting nothing more than to stand tall and proudly once more. The tree whipped forward and up, sending Lily flying above the canopy and away. It would've been a perfect escape, had it not been for the words floating through the air alongside her.

"You can vanish as impressively as you desire... but your time is running low, Lily Red!"

CHAPTER
THIRTY-FIVE

As FAR AS Lily could tell, she'd been working on her current trap for over an hour before Drwg Mawr came *bounding* through the woods toward her, now visible to her system-granted senses at ninety meters distant.

Currently, she was standing in the entrance of the valley where the Mavka's territory had been, rushing to finish rigging the trap while needing to maintain caution; the setup was incredibly precarious. "Tie off the trip wire to the counter-weight, don't pull on it... step back, *good*."

Lily turned and ran into the valley, the way mostly open, due to the cliffs of the space having trapped the fire within its walls. She was taking a severe risk at the moment: if the trap didn't bury the warrior sufficiently, he would be able to cross the open space far faster than she could ever hope to manage. Still, her concern turned out to be for naught: once she was a quarter of the way through the valley, the sharp ringing of stone sliding and collapsing echoed through the natural hollow.

She chanced a glance behind herself, watching as the entrance to the valley collapsed inward as a landslide of rock and loosened dirt. Lily had easily been able to discern how the stone had barely been holding together; *especially* near the entrance. The intensity of the fire, spurred on by the death of the monstrous Singing Swine in its center, had completely burned away the plants which had been growing along the cliff face from stem to root.

Not only had the supporting plants been incinerated, the moisture had evaporated, leaving only brittle rock and charred dirt. After removing a few key boulders, and ensuring the rest of it was barely supported, Lily had put the wire she had liberated from the warband's camp to good use.

Lily had been meticulous in avoiding the use of wire until now, leaving Drwg Mawr with no reason to anticipate it. After being flung around by rope traps several times already, she knew he'd be on high alert, especially in a burned-out area like this. He was surely expecting some sort of trick—though nothing on this scale—but by introducing wire into the equation she had all but ensured her victory.

Going by the plume of ash and dust rising into the air behind her, the trap had been even more effective than she'd expected, likely collapsing more than twenty feet of stone on top of the man.

"I can only hope he's buried in a stone coffin." Lily didn't slow down in the slightest, in fact picking up speed as she hit her stride. "The system hasn't informed me of a victory, so he's alive for now, at the *least*. If he suffocates, I guess that counts as a win. Otherwise, I need to plan my next move."

Twilight was arriving as she got to the other end of the valley, bursting through the opening and looking around sadly at the utterly *removed* forest. Lily had expected the devastation, but what she saw still nearly floored her. Charcoal tree trunks were all that remained as far as the eye could see, and a thick layer of ash across the ground guaranteed that it would be impossible for her to move through this area without leaving a path for the warrior to easily follow—not that he needed it.

Lily ran on, not stopping until true darkness had arrived.

Unlike the last time she'd slept, there were no trees with long branches to nestle in, no places for her to hide or escape if she backed herself into a corner. Instead, the Scout darted through the area several times, making double handfuls of false trails before wrapping around back near the start, and fully burying herself under the ash.

With her cloak wrapped closely to her head, she was able to carefully breathe below the blanket of fine particles, and so quickly fell into an exhausted, dreamless slumber.

Heavy footsteps woke her an unknown amount of time later, though it was still night, going by the darkness around her—early morning at best. The sounds could've easily been made by a lumbering bear, but Lily was wise enough to understand that every animal had vacated the area. There were no plants for the herbivores, and no herbivores for the carnivores.

Only Lily was in the area, being hunted by the Big Bad Wolf.

"I know you are somewhere around here." Drwg Mawr suddenly called out, his voice still as relaxed and fresh as it had been at the start of their clash. It was so shocking in the otherwise absolute silence that Lily almost reflexively flinched, which would certainly have given away her position when ash plumed from her location. "Come out. I just want to *talk*."

Hidden beneath the cover of darkness and the burned remnants of the Wyld, Lily arched a disbelieving eyebrow. Moments later, the warrior's voice came, this time trembling with barely suppressed rage.

"You dropped a *cliffside* of stone on me! It took me *hours* to push those rocks off and half the night to heal enough to give chase. Congratulations. You have officially lasted longer than anyone else has against me. Accept your small victory, and I will allow you one *last* chance to discuss the terms of your surrender. I cannot, in good faith, make this offer another time. Not without you managing a significant victory against me. I tell you now… you will *not* have another fortuitous success."

His foot planted itself directly adjacent to Lily's face, and her eyes went wide as he stooped down slightly. For a moment, she considered bursting up and running, but a hasty activation of System's Echo showed his left hand drifting down and touching a track she'd intentionally left behind. It hadn't rained, and there were many similar trails in the area, so she had no idea what benefit he could get from tracing her small footprint.

His hand passed over the small air hole she'd left for herself, and her eyes went wide as they caught on a small patch of glowing red fabric.

There, on his wolf-paw gauntlet, was a scrap of her cloak. Several things clicked into place at the same time. It was obvious now that Drwg Mawr had been using whatever magic was imbued in his gauntlet to sustain the enchantment on the torn piece of fabric. Her cloak was meant to repair itself over time, so he was likely boosting the magic remaining in that scrap so it would reach out in an attempt to grow in her general direction.

The hundred-meter distance requirement also made a… *fuzzy* sort of sense, as the cloak was meant to heal itself using the largest remaining portion of cloth available. If a scrap was too close, its magical pseudo-intelligence would cause the smaller chunk to go inert, expecting the remainder of the cloak to already be putting itself back together. In other words, normally a problem like this would never be possible: the magic within the small part would fade rapidly. Yet, somehow Drwg Mawr was preventing that from happening.

Big Bad suddenly shifted, sprinting forward as if he'd seen something. Lily almost poked her head up to see what it was, only to realize at the last moment the man was attempting to startle her into giving away her location. It didn't work, so he slowed down after a few seconds of pounding over the charred dirt. System's Echo allowed her to keep his location in her mind's eye, which suddenly gave Lily an interesting idea. "I can use this against him... the range of my skill is ninety meters. He'll only find my location if I let him get approximately a hundred meters away."

Seeing how the huge man was currently moving away from her, Lily pushed herself to her feet, a soft cascade of ash falling around her. "No going back into hiding now. I've got to keep him in sensory range at all times and get him moving where *I* need to go."

Feeling as though her mind had been sharpened by the simple act of making a decision, cold determination filled her heart. She'd been acting as prey for too long, and it was time to return to her strengths. Lily had dealt with beasts, Monsters, and natural disasters. Just because the Big Bad Wolf was a combination of all three didn't mean she needed to stay on the run.

She just needed to stay ahead of him, *leading* him where she wanted him to go instead of fleeing. A quiet voice in the back of her mind had been urging this strategy for over a day now, and it had already paid off in the form of both of her exceedingly successful traps against him. Now, it was time to clear the board and start a new game.

Drwg Mawr's voice cut through the silence in the distance, and though she couldn't hear him, Lily assumed he was repeating his demand for her to give up once again. "Just more proof you have no idea how to actually find me without magical assistance."

Until this moment, she hadn't recognized how badly his ability to track her no matter how she worked to evade him— *her*, Lily Red, now arguably the best Scout on Canu Moch— had been messing with her head. Somehow, realizing the fact that he had just salvaged a scrap of her cloak, most likely from when she'd fought the Skinwalker, allowed her to regain full confidence in her abilities. "Let's see how long it takes for the Big Bad Wolf to howl with frustration."

She began moving in a circular pattern, keeping Drwg Mawr just over eighty meters away at any given time. When he went the wrong direction, she needed to turn and follow for a short while, but he always returned to moving south and west—which Lily realized was the straight-line direction from the mouth of the valley he'd been buried in earlier that day. "South and west... I can work with that."

Drwg Mawr drifted back and forth, a beacon of life to her system-granted senses in the burned-out charcoal forest. She always allowed him to come closer, as close as seventy meters, just before System's Echo went on cooldown. Then, there were thirty seconds of gently ramping concern as the skill cooled down, only for her to reorient her position as soon as it could be reactivated.

His proximity was a palpable force in her mind, almost like the heat of the sun on a bad sunburn. But as she continued leading him, creating false trails, sometimes even circling him entirely, Lily slowly became more comfortable. After all, she was used to sometimes needing to hunt a large creature for days at a time, until it either returned to its burrow to rest... or finally made a mistake. In this case, she knew she'd have to count on the latter.

Darkness was her ally in this endeavor, and Lily continued stepping through the ash carefully, quietly, making sure her feet were coming down on solid ground instead of lumps of brittle remnants which would *crackle* if stepped on. Lily dropped into a concerned crouch as she heard a growling shout, followed by a heavy *thump*... then the unmistakable sound of a tree trunk collapsing. "Hiding among the graveyard of the Wyld? No."

From that point forward, each time Drwg Mawr came near what was left of a tree, he would casually smack it with his cudgel and send the weakened wooden husk collapsing to the ground—kicking up a huge cloud of ash with each falling trunk. It seemed counterintuitive to Lily, "What is he up to? All he's doing is making sure I know where he is at all times."

She resumed pacing, back and forth, watching the huge man take out his frustration on the landscape. Just before her skill went on cooldown, she took a sharp breath of surprise as the warrior turned on his heel and sprinted *away* from her. At that moment she lost her extra sense and needed to make a snap decision. "He doesn't know I can detect his life force; he must've been trying to obscure the area, and make a bunch of noise so I wouldn't realize he was running away. All so he could determine my location?"

Without hesitating, she followed him at a dead run. His legs were longer than hers, allowing the man to cross the distance faster, but as the seconds ticked by until System's Echo could be used once more, she could only follow after the huge man. "Three, two... *System's Echo!*"

Drwg Mawr was right at the edge of her perception, at least eighty-nine meters away. Strangely enough, he was starting to slow down. Soon he'd slowed to a jog, then a walk, before finally coming to a stop. She couldn't hear his rumbled, muttered words, but she was able to discern him staring at his left arm, tapping, then *slapping* the gauntlet, as if wondering if the magic had been broken.

"Come on, big boy," Red called under her breath. "We need to find the edge of the wildfire before there's enough sunshine for you to see me out in the open like this. You said you would be relentlessly hunting after me... so do it!"

THIRTY-SIX

THE NIGHT FLEW BY FAR TOO FAST, with Red needing to resort to standard attention-*gaining* tactics to keep the huge man moving. Frankly, it was satisfying and relieving to be able to throw a rock or chunk of charred wood into the distance and have him eagerly chase after it. "When I see him like this he's not so bad. Kinda like a puppy being thrown a toy. Oh, is this what 'keep your friends close, but your enemies closer' means? Never realized until just now. I'm learning so many new things these days."

She'd spent the entirety of the night working to remember the area; walking along paths which had been eradicated from visibility by fire but ensured firm, packed dirt to trek on under the thick layer of soot. Every step, every sound she made, was calculated to frustrate Drwg Mawr, keeping him at the edge of her range in an attempt to convince him his magic had failed. Yet, her hopes on making him ignore the magic seemed to be impossible, as the warrior almost constantly—to an unhealthy degree, in her mind—lifted his left arm in hopes of seeing the scrap of enchanted cloth reacting.

Now the night was waning, with the first hints of dawn painting the sky in gray, pale blue highlights showing where the first rays of the sun were filtering over the horizon. Still, they hadn't found the edge of the fire in the Wyld's range, and she was beginning to sweat over the fact that not even a *potential* safe haven could be found.

Taking a deep breath, Lily prepared herself for the next stage in this deadly game of cat and mouse. Instead of being able to casually walk around, as she had all night, Lily needed to stay low, darting from tree to burned out tree when she was able to determine that Drwg Mawr's head was turned away. "System, I need a path to the closest part of the forest not destroyed. That would be the optimal path."

The lights of System's Whisper which always filled—but rarely obscured—her vision, began dancing as she shifted her intent. She had long ago reached level ten, Perfection, with the skill; allowing her to make requests like this without needing to spend days or weeks practicing just to adjust it ever-so-slightly. Over the course of the next few seconds, the current optimal path between good hiding points melted away, each distinct light melding into a single beam traveling in a straight line: *far* into the distance.

"Okay... now I at least know where I need to go." Lily inspected the path with a critical eye, wishing it gave her a distance indicator as well. Unfortunately, that was outside the purview of the scale. All she could do now was continue moving, drawing attention, and ensuring she stayed out of sight. Lifting a rock, she threw it with precision, curving it around a tree trunk in the distance—where it hit something hard and loudly shattered.

Less than eight seconds later, Drwg Mawr went barreling past Lily's current hiding spot, literally causing a wake of ash and soot to swirl up behind him.

Brackk! The sound of his cudgel slamming into the tree husk was almost instantly drowned out by the sound of the trunk falling apart and scattering to the ground. Letting out a bellow of frustration, the huge man swung his weapon in an

arc over the ground, generating enough wind to blow the soft carpet of dust into the air in front of him. "One day remains, Red! I'm doing *my* part. I will hunt you, as *tedious* as it has become. You will then *surrender-*"

Lily's lips curled upward, ignoring the rest of his posturing as she decided how she would have responded if she wasn't so concerned with giving away her location. She practiced it in her mind for when she had beaten him and could taunt Big Bad from a safe distance, "Pretty sure our agreement never said anything about *me* surrendering to you."

Then she'd vanish into the woods, after making sure his tracking gauntlet was either destroyed or the scrap of cloth had been removed. After that, she would once more be unfindable, *untouchable*, in the woods. Using the thick cloud of particles in the air as cover, Lily walked down the path of light her skills were projecting, pausing only when she'd gotten behind a charcoal trunk thick enough to fully hide her from the warrior's perceptive stare. "System's Echo."

Dawn fully broke at that moment, their position close to the midpoint of the planet making it seem as if the sun had been suddenly catapulted into the sky. Sunrise and sunset in this zone were both very sudden, something she was used to… but apparently Big Bad was not.

"This place is bizarre!" he spoke to himself, though loudly enough for her to hear, knowing she was *somewhere* in the area. "In the far north, we are lucky to get five hours of full sunlight. The mountains, capped with thick snow, cause the start and end of day to last for hours at a time. Storms are ever-present, cold enough to force us into our longhalls for weeks at a time. All this to say… doing nothing with my time is a learned pastime of mine. You can't make me forfeit out of boredom. At least I have plenty of things to *smash*."

He punctuated his words by obliterating another tree, letting out a grunt of satisfaction as he did so. "I'm still willing to discuss… *feces*."

Lily had seen the same thing at the same moment, but her reaction was vastly different. There, in the distance, bright green was showing through the somber gray and black landscape. The edge of the fire's destruction was looming ahead, far enough that it would take several hours to reach it at this pace but close enough to give her hope.

Unfortunately, this final stretch would most certainly be the most perilous portion of their little game of hide and seek. Before Red could react, Drwg Mawr raced ahead, running, sprinting, *leaping*; forcing her to do the same lest he suddenly learn her location. His erratic movement, the unpredictable cunning of the warrior, caused adrenaline to race through her.

Lily's heart was pounding in anticipation of the fight or flight to come.

The huge man turned and revealed his plan with a swing of the cudgel. A tree went down, and he leaped to the next and battered it down with yet another single swing. One after another, he created a long line of open ground—trying to ensure that Lily had no possible cover for her attempt to escape into the forest in the distance.

Even so, before the dust had settled, she'd made it halfway across the sudden clearing. System's Whisper flashed a warning, and she dove to the ground, tucking her cloak around her and intentionally grinding the fabric into the dust as she rolled. Barely daring to breathe, she felt the remaining particles in the air settle over her, helping to cover up and secure her position.

System's Echo came off cooldown, and was reactivated once more.

"What now, Red?" Drwg Mawr smugly shouted, twirling his cudgel around in great satisfaction. "At some point, you *will* have to leave your hiding spot. Or... don't. Yes, let's stay here the rest of the day. I'll talk, and you can listen."

Lily immediately put her hands over her ears, digging the

tips of her index fingers in just in case he had some sort of active ability to control people or influence them using his voice. As uncommon as skills of that nature were, they did exist in all aspects, from terrible, *Villainous* powers meant to control people's minds, to Heroes literally inciting courage, to guardsmen generating obedience to the law—as she had almost learned the hard way when Captain Cliff almost succeeded in a demand for her to give up his son.

She felt the air trembling ever so slightly as his words echoed through the area, but all the Scout cared about was the movements of his head and eyes. With System's Echo at level nine, therefore giving her a *Masterful* amount of detail and control, she was even able to track his pupils as they scanned the dead environment. Annoyingly, he was extraordinarily well-trained and effective, leaving almost nothing for her to exploit.

Almost nothing.

His attentiveness to the scrap of magical cloth on his gauntlet bordered on obsession at this point. Every few seconds, his eyes would flick to his left hand, no matter where else he had been looking. "Must be worried I already got past him. If I were him, I'd be worried about that, too. I'm *that* good."

Carefully timing her motions, Lily waited until he had scanned to the left once more, crawling forward a few feet as his eyes continued onward. Once more his gaze flicked to his left arm, then swung back up and continued his visual assessment of the area.

Minutes began flowing by, marked only by System's Echo going onto cooldown and coming off of it. Dozens of starts and stops later, her body was fully behind his standard line of sight. Unless he suddenly decided to turn around, an action he hadn't taken in the nearly two hours since his manual clearing of the area, Lily decided it would be safe to move a little faster.

Using every skill to remain as silent as she had at her disposal, every trick she'd learned and not drawing attention, using only her fingers and toes... Red continued crawling forward.

Fifty meters past him. Seventy. *Ninety.*

As she got to the very outermost edge of her ability to sense the mountain of vitality which was the warrior behind her, the Scout took a moment to rest and recover her energy. She ate some of the jerky, sipped on the water she'd retrieved from the warband camp, and gave herself a few minutes to digest it before finally lifting herself from the prone position, coiling her legs under herself like a cat about to pounce.

"Maybe... a tenth of a mile to go?" she promised herself under her breath, psyching herself up for the next few minutes. A deep inhale, a gentle exhale, and Lily reactivated System's Echo for the last time before she would begin her escape attempt. "He's looking around, looking around... eyes on his gauntlet... looking up! *Go!*"

It might not help much, but there were always a few seconds between when he looked around, then back at his armor to see if the tracker had reactivated. She counted down the average time, pouring on the speed and getting to a full, maintainable sprint before a sudden shout of surprise echoed through the air around her. Then Lily stopped thinking, her mind focused on the narrow line drawn by the system—the path toward the *only* possibility of safety even the world itself could find.

The ground beneath her feet blurred into a mix of crimson and ash, her cloak flapping forward against her as the wind blew against her back, acting as a sail and giving her just a *hint* of a boost in speed. Seconds later, the edge of the forest was now a tangible goal and not just a distant green mirage. A distant sound floated on the wind to her ears, but Lily managed to ignore her instinctive reaction to activate her skill, knowing she would need it to determine a safe course through the forest as she got closer.

Lily's lungs were burning with the effort, especially with how much soot had made its way into them. Her entire body —particularly her legs—joined in on complaining, but she pushed forward, driven by intense determination and willpower... with just an *inkling* of fear as the pounding foot-steps of Drwg Mawr echoed ominously behind her.

Keeping her focus on the path, the light of the system which shined only in her own mind, she did her utmost to ignore the menacing steps growing louder and closer as the immense man activated every muscle in his body to close the distance between them; probably tearing himself apart to reach his inhuman straight-line speed.

He shouted with excitement, hot breath practically washing across Lily's neck. "It's *over!*"

A massive shadow loomed over Lily just as she was about to break into the greenery. Even with her lead and prepara-tions, Big Bad had closed the distance, his longer legs and powerful physique granting him an advantage in a direct sprint. The blaring light of the system and the shadow of his swinging arm were her only warnings—all told, just *barely* enough for Lily to *screech* to a stop and push backward.

The warrior was overambitious with his swing and overex-tended. Such a hefty weapon, his intense momentum, and the treacherous sliding surface of soot converged to send Drwg Mawr bellyflopping to the ground. A garbled sound escaped his lips as his attack missed, and it may have been her imagi-nation, but Lily felt like the ground trembled as he impacted.

She had already recovered her footing and was darting forward as he began to struggle up; but as Big Bad yanked his head out of the ash and sucked in a breath, she saw an oppor-tunity she couldn't pass on.

The huge man who'd caused her to get almost no sleep in the last two nights had just half-buried himself in mud and ash. Even as his frantic eyes darted around, seeking her out, Red's feet came down on the back of his skull and smashed his face into the ground as she used his head as a springboard to dive into the forest.

A moment later, a choked scream erupted from the man— less anger or rage, being composed solidly of disbelief and incredulity. His frustration warmed Lily's heart, comforting her almost as much as the leaves of the forest closing around her.

"Ahh… a big green hug welcoming me home. This day is off to a good start."

THIRTY-SEVEN

MANEUVERING through an area of the Wyld she was familiar with filled Lily with bittersweet emotions.

Sweet, because she knew all the important locations around her, such as where to find the resources she'd need to finally defeat Big Bad, not to mention her knowledge of excellent choke points where she could strategically place traps to counter his physical advantages most effectively. Bitter, due to the forest she'd known her entire life being drastically altered by the destructive fire which had swept through it.

Strangely enough, it was the brightness of the day which caught her attention the most. The early morning light was filtering through the trees at nearly three times the intensity she was used to—at least this deep in the forest. The canopies of many ancient arbors had been burned completely away, even if what must've been a *torrential* rainstorm in this part of the forest had saved their trunks. Not *all* of them, certainly. There were plenty of new clearings with charcoal tree trunks marking where proud sections of the forest had once stood.

Lily kept System's Echo active as often as possible, making sure to avoid any type of clearing, even if it took her on a circuitous route. "As soon as we're on an open field again, there's no way he's letting me out of it. Not again. I won't be able to count on his misstepping and..."

She swallowed a lump in her throat as the memory of his cudgel *whiffing* past her left ear rose up. Shaking off the fear, which felt like lead shoes wrapping around her feet, the Scout focused on slipping through the forest like an errant gust of wind.

As Lily came close to an unnaturally fire-eaten grove, she ran sideways up a tree trunk for three steps before pushing off, barrel rolling, and landing on a low-hanging branch. Using her well-practiced method of springboarding off of it, she crossed the open space without remaining on flat ground where the long-legged warrior could catch up.

As she sailed through the air, a dappled pattern of sunlight spun across the ground as the trees were gently shaken by a steadily increasing wind. Her eye caught on a small, *vibrantly* green leaf as it fluttered to the ground. "Why is the forest looking *healthier* than it used to? Besides the completely destroyed sections, that is. Is it just the fact that there's more light, so I'm seeing it in a different way? Or is something *else* going on?"

Her feet touched down on a branch, and philosophical musings on agriculture were forced to the side as the wood beneath her shattered into wood shavings and soot. Letting out a yelp, Lily fell half a dozen feet before crashing into the thick underbrush, which had thankfully escaped the inferno that had swept through the treetops of Canu Moch. Groaning at the new bruises, Lily sucked wind for a moment as her gaze swept over the forest floor, alighting on a clear stretch of packed dirt.

"This is... if I take that path, we'd arrive in the Heart of the Wyld in less than an hour. Has he really already chased me this far?"

She forced her breathing back into a pattern to better fuel her body, finding herself being swept up in the nostalgic scent of decomposing leaves and the earthy smell of the forest floor. There was only a slight tang of fresh smoke still hovering in the air, but already it had mostly been hidden behind smells of nature as it worked to heal the fiery scars.

Lily decided that, since she had returned to the ground, she would make the most of it. Pumping her legs, the Scout kept her speed high and steps light so she wouldn't sink into the loamy dirt. Her small frame allowed her to run atop the soft soil underfoot without leaving obvious tracks, though she didn't mind so much at the moment—it wasn't as if she were being tracked in a *normal* way.

Behind her, the near-continuous sound of leaves and branches slapping against a body was suddenly interrupted, and Lily reflexively reactivated System's Echo... just in time to watch as Drwg Mawr pushed both hands down, his entire body moving on a perfect horizontal plane as he extracted his foot from a small hole.

His legs swung forward, and the man started running after her again, but the distance between them had increased by about eight meters. It continued climbing for several long seconds as the warrior hobbled along, clearly having badly turned his ankle. Still, Big Bad quickly regained his normal pace without showing another hint of discomfort, indicating to Lily that his regeneration must have fully repaired him.

"Thanks for helping me gauge what sort of time you need to heal from minor injuries. Every little data point helps. Seems like, even though you can chase me in a straight line, you're unfamiliar with the forest. Even a minor misstep is going to cost you badly." Lily chuckled as she flowed over the ground, intent on not allowing the warrior behind her to make up the distance he'd lost. "I'll make *sure* of it."

A sharp bird cry pierced the silence, acting as an alarm clock for the rest of the forest, which seemed to instantly wake up and fill with the chatter of animals. The sudden transition from near-total silence to the sounds of a forest bustling with life relaxed her, and Lily's strides grew wider as she took less care to be quiet. Conversely, the sudden burst of noise had taken the warrior behind her off guard, and he'd swerved to the side as if expecting a trap to be flying toward him.

It had only cost him approximately a second and a half, but Lily pushed herself harder to make sure she took advantage of his flinch. He was moving with less confidence now. The deeper into the forest they went, the more Big Bad's nerves seemed to be on edge. As she watched on—thanks to her skill—a squirrel scampered up a tree, startled by Drwg Mawr's presence. The sudden motion and angry chattering drew the man's eye and caused him to stumble over an exposed root.

"Eleven-meter gap increase in total." Lily cheerfully gauged the distance, finding the man behind her had fallen back to a comfortable fifty-three meters. Understanding struck her as she realized the forest around her wasn't as devastated as she'd feared. "He's afraid of traps right now? Perhaps he has good reason to be? Maybe he's getting to the edge of what his body can regenerate without proper food and rest. It has to have *some* kind of limit. Right?"

She evened out her path, now running in a mostly-straight line toward the Heart of the Wyld. "If the place didn't burn down, there's going to be plenty of traps still active I can use against him. That's not accepting help, is it? Nah... that's using the terrain to my advantage. Heh."

Though Lily was more tired than she'd ever been in her life, the fear and tension which had been her constant companion since the start of this battle of endurance had begun to flow away. Here, among the trees, she lived and moved with *purpose*, instead of frantically fleeing and running in circles just to stay ahead of her pursuer. A flash of red to her left drew Lily's eye as a fox popped from the underbrush, locking eyes with her for a brief moment.

For a moment, a smile touched her lips as she saw a

kindred spirit, a hunter cloaked in red who had survived against all odds.

Then the fox was impacted from the side as first one, then *three* rabbits leaped out of the bush and tore into it with sharp, carnivorous teeth.

"*Wah!*" Pumping her arms, Lily ran from the area before she could draw their attention. "Right…! No Scouts in the area are hunting down critters before they become Ascended Beasts or stumble across a Class Shrine and reach Monster-classification. Abyss, it's been only a few days, and even the *bunnies* are turning."

She shuddered to think what the forest would look like in a few weeks, with all of its Class Shrines unguarded and exposed to the elements. Thinking back on the fox, which she'd felt a moment of kinship with, Lily winced and glanced to the side, wary of hungry bunnies in the greenery. "Yeah, let's just hope that wasn't a premonition…"

Trying to keep her mind off her own superstitions, knowing it was just her exhausted brain making her feel uneasy, Lily threaded her way through the forest, drawing ever closer to the Heart of the Wyld. To her *great* concern, the closer she got, the more scars from the recent inferno could be found. She grit her teeth as she tried not to worry too much— it was unlikely that the fire had swept *all* of the traps from the forest, so long as rain had arrived in time.

Just before the midpoint of the day, she found a snare hidden beneath a layer of ash and debris. Luckily, a small rune which *considerate* Scouts would place on trees near active traps warned her in time to keep her ankle from getting caught. It wasn't a strong enough trap to harm her, as it was meant for rabbits—the non-carnivorous type—but would be enough to trip her or bring her to the ground. "Can't get caught in the traps I'm trying to use against him. Big Bad can blast through as many as he likes, but if I make one mistake bad enough for him to catch up, that's it for me."

She hopped over the loop of twine, running for another ten seconds before activating System's Echo to see what would happen to Drwg Mawr. As she'd hoped, the warrior's long strides, confident and unyielding, dropped him right into the center of the trap. On his next step, the snare tightened around his ankle, and he jolted slightly before continuing as if nothing had happened. A pair of sounds reached her ears near simultaneously a second later: a grunt of surprise and the *snap* of fire-damaged rope bursting into flailing strings.

"I knew he was durable, but how strong *is* this guy? Or maybe that snare was more fire-damaged than I expected." Lily grumbled with a mix of frustration and grudging respect, which she tried to ruthlessly stomp into non-existence. "Okay… let's see how he deals with *this* one."

They'd gotten much closer to the Wyldling's city, and she had been scanning the canopy for minutes at this point. Finally, Red found what she'd been looking for: a lethal swinging tree trunk trap, the kind which had slain six of the Coastals she'd rescued from the shore. Even the thought of using it against her enemy filled her with a slightly sickened sensation… but she held her breath and forced herself to remember: as singular and personal as the duel seemed, this was *war*.

Dashing straight through the bottleneck between trees— meant to guarantee the trap's effectiveness against whoever sprung it—Lily lifted her knees high, putting down her feet just before and just *after* the tripwire. "Can't jump over every trap, or he'll figure out a pattern to use against me."

At least, *Lily* would figure out a pattern. Against a battle-hardened, cunning veteran like Drwg Mawr? She couldn't take any chances.

Her heart began to race as Big Bad pushed between the trees, running forward seemingly without a care in the world. She watched as both his feet hovered in the air, his sprint allowing him to cross a half dozen of Lily's paces at a time, only for the front one to slam down directly on the tripwire. It snapped, and the counterweights shifted, the logs in the air beginning to swing.

Even with his prodigious speed, he wouldn't be out of the way of the ten trees lashed together as a pendulum. They closed in on him from either side, and Red's heart leapt in her chest as she watched Big Bad falter slightly. She refused to look away, knowing whatever happened had been her choice, and–

Snap. Crash!

The trap failed, the flame-damaged branches it'd been hooked onto snapping beneath the weight of the logs as they moved; dropping them to either side of the path where they landed upright. Lily's mouth twitched into a scowl, even as a broad grin broke out on Big Bad's face as the trees stood in place like an honorary salute to the leader of Wolf Warband as he wove forward.

"Abyss… I had even been *expecting* that to happen with some of the traps." Undeterred, if slightly disappointed that the first attempt hadn't worked out perfectly, Lily pressed on, choosing a winding road which would take them in a near-full circle of the city. "Well, if at first I don't succeed, I'll just try, try again."

As midday came and went, Lily had led the man behind her along a deadly route he didn't *bother* to deviate from. The first series of traps she had attempted were various camou-flaged pitfalls, some even having spikes or other unpleasant surprises at the bottom. Every single one completely failed to catch or even slow the warrior. Against all common sense, whether it was luck or some niche skill, Drwg Mawr managed to avoid *every* pit.

It didn't matter if Lily hopped across them, ran over a central beam which spanned the hole, or simply brought him close, there was just no catching the wolf in a pit trap.

Even though it was a bizarre inconsistency, there were plenty of other opportunities for her to succeed. One after another, Lily ran the huge man into traps. Some worked perfectly, but far too many were surprising failures. Sharp, metal-studded branches tore gashes open across his body, even impaling him in some instances, but the only indication they had affected him even slightly was the slowly widening gap between the raider and the Scout.

With each successful or failed iteration, Lily was able to compile a bit more information. "Seems like traps requiring rope are almost always failing. Twice as much if they were high above the ground. Must've burned or warped in the heat, even if their trees didn't collapse. The metal-based ones seem fine, but it's hard to say if that's because they were low to the ground or just better able to survive the intense flames which must've filled the air around here."

The forest around the damaged city had become a kaleidoscope of blood and calamity. Every step Drwg Mawr took was a gamble for him, but even with the damage and pain he must've been enduring, he *still* seemed fresher than Lily—who was heaving each breath into lungs which felt like they were burning. Then there was the stitch in her side that had grown beyond painful and directly into *concerning*. She frantically searched for yet another thing to hit the man with, voicing her thoughts around gasps, too tired to keep them quietly in her head. "Need something... big!"

Unfortunately, all of the 'big' traps faltered and failed without fail, and Lily had no idea where she could go to try and find another. That despairing thought gave her pause, and her head ever so slightly turned to look due east of the city. "Reynard knew I'd be coming back to the city... if he tried to set something up to slaughter me as I left the Heart of the Wyld... wouldn't he also have tried to make sure I didn't get here in the first place?"

Hoping she was right, but also wishing she hadn't made such a terrible enemy for no reason, she broke off her loop and ran through the now-charred double tree which marked the start of the path home.

Behind her, Big Bad stepped on the packed dirt trail and picked up speed. Three minutes, five, and Red was beginning to doubt her intuition. Drwg Mawr was starting to make up the distance he'd lost, her large lead consistently dropping as they ran down the open path. Just as she was about to give up and shift off into the forest once more, Lily's eyes landed on a root path extending from a nearby tree.

As she got closer, she squinted at it with a hint of confusion, hoping it was what she thought it might be. "I know every *inch* of this path... those roots never grew across this section."

System's Echo didn't highlight the raised dirt, showing that whatever was there wasn't alive—unlike all the *other* roots threading through the forest floor. Not knowing what would happen, she stepped *off* the path and ran alongside it, costing her a small amount of speed Drwg Mawr unknowingly began to capitalize upon.

After a handful of seconds, she got back on the main path, but only after the ground returned to its untampered state. Moments later, a deep **twang** reverberated in the air, followed by what sounded like the sky collapsing to the earth. She fully turned around, skidding to a halt to see what was happening.

Drwg Mawr had stepped on a wire buried just below the surface, causing a net mesh of metal threads to spring out of the ground. Both his legs were caught in the holes, and he'd been painfully slammed to the ground. As if that wasn't enough, a clatter of falling logs, branches, and stones dropped from the canopy above, a large net holding all of it together and dropping it as a unit onto Big Bad.

The initial trap had been meant to disorient and slow whoever set it off, while the second was clearly meant to splatter whoever it landed on with a *vengeance*.

"That was meant for *me*." Lily could only stare at the ingenious, devious work in horror. Slowly, her lips closed, and her eyes hardened. "When this is all over, I need to do something about Reynard. Something *permanent*."

"Uuu-*wahh!*" Nearly half a minute after the trap had collapsed on Drwg Mawr, it began to shift to the side, with the warrior trapped underneath bellowing in exertion as he shifted hundreds of pounds of rock and stone off of him.

"This is starting to get ridiculous."

Even as she spoke the words, the exhausted Lily was barely even surprised at his survival. She simply shook her head and let out a defeated sigh. Turning on her heel, she began running down the path once more.

"Guess there's only one chance left. Over the river, and through the hills. To Grandmother's house we go."

THIRTY-EIGHT

THE AFTERNOON SUN was baking Lily's skin as she hurried along the path, now no longer able to maintain a full-on run, let alone sprint. "So... *hot*... without the shade!"

Her vision was wavering, and she found herself half-blinded by the constant, searing light. The Scout's feet were moving mechanically, lifting and falling, only pushing forward and doing it all over again thanks to her deep well of willpower. She'd gone beyond exhaustion at this point. As her eyelids fluttered to moisten her burning eyes, her body betrayed her.

Red wasn't certain if it was a root, an uneven patch of dirt, or just her imagination, but her eyes snapped open as her center of balance shifted. The world came back into view as the ground rushed up at her, and the Scout barely managed to get her arms out to protect her face from the sudden fall. Pulling herself back from the precipice of unconsciousness, Lily forced herself to keep moving. She managed to get back on her feet and stumble forward even as her body whispered sweet lies of resting for 'just a moment'.

"N-no." She spoke aloud to herself, the words slurring thanks to a dry tongue that suddenly seemed twice as large as usual. "That's sleep talking. Once it has me, it's not letting go for at least a day."

Lily was running on fumes, but she had a task which needed to be completed before she could allow herself to pause. For the last two hours, Drwg Mawr hadn't come into her perception, but he had to still be coming after her. There was no way the system would consider him to be 'relentlessly pursuing her' if he'd stopped and taken a nap. "I bet he broke his legs and spine, and is just crawling toward me using his fingertips while he waits for the bones and damaged nerves to heal. *Bleh.* He's gross."

The path curved, and Red's gaze traced along it, finding that excitement was beginning to wake her up a little. This was the last stretch between her and the only home she'd ever had. Not only was it a beacon of safety and sweet memories, it had the bulk of all the trap-making materials, weapons, food, and all sorts of other quality-of-life items she'd made or acquired over her entire life.

"Just need to get into the storage room and get to work. If I can't hurt the Big Bad Wolf enough to make him howl and give up, I'm going to have to figure out how to make it impossible for him to keep fighting."

She made her way around the final loop, nearly dropping to her knees as she took in the huge pile of still-smoldering coals—all that remained of Grandmother's house. "By the system, why can't I catch a *break*? It would've been hard enough to get everything I needed with the building collapsing from the Skinwalker smashing itself around, but now... oh, *that's* not good."

One section of the house remained, a space which was immutable as far as humanity was concerned. Lily's eyes traced the familiar Class Shrine standing in what was essentially an open-walled gazebo now that the protection—built by the people of the Wyld, and guarded by her grandmother—had been stripped away by the inferno. "This couldn't be where the rabbits were upgrading themselves, I'm sure that had to be in the Druidic Grove. Which means… I should *probably* keep my eyes peeled for other monsters who took advantage of the easy access."

It was easier said than done. Even at that moment, Lily was needing to be careful with how frequently she blinked—her eyes kept trying to remain closed.

Lost for a moment in her memories and her plans to figure out if any Ascended Beasts had become full monsters, Lily didn't notice her body was swaying. Her knees buckled, and this time, there was no sudden jarring return to awareness as she fell—only the soft grass of a lawn which had been well-kept until earlier this week and hadn't yet been reclaimed by nature.

Only her System's Whisper sending strobing warning lights into her brain saved her. Not from any impending monster, but from fully succumbing to sleep and rolling eye-first onto a thick nail which had been knocked out of the wall and bounced over here. The spike was an unhappy reminder of the battle against the Huntsman, but served to get her motivated to trudge along once more. Absolutely *sick* with exhaustion, Lily shakily crawled away from her landing site, not daring to lay back down or blink until she was able to push herself all the way up to her feet. "I don't need the house… there's… yeah."

System's Echo still showed no sign of her dogged pursuer, so she pushed herself to move around the ruined house, past it, behind it, into the Scout-training sanctuary her grandmother had crafted. It was a hidden gem in the forest, encased in natural stone walls similar to the Singing Swine's territory, but much smaller for obvious reasons. Scouts had been trained in this oasis of the Wyld for more than three decades, honing their skills in an area considered safe—at least compared to the rest of the forest.

Now, she could only hope that making her last stand

where her grandmother had spent the majority of her life imparting her wisdom would somehow help her succeed.

Stepping through the entrance, which was hidden from the untrained eye, the air immediately felt different: cool, moist, *normal*. Seeing the mossy ground, trees which hadn't changed in centuries, a dense canopy above her head... Lily nearly broke down from sheer relief. "This is it. Only one way in, no way out. If I fail with this, I can only hope he'll give me another chance to surrender."

Whether it was the lack of constant light, the dewy moisture soothing her burning skin, or simply being back in an area she was intimately familiar with, Lily felt her fatigued mind clearing. "This isn't just Grandmother's garden, or some trees..."

Red grabbed a handle hidden behind a bush, pulling a hatch open silently, thanks to the well-oiled hinges she'd been tasked with maintaining for nearly fifteen years. Inside the space was hundreds upon hundreds of feet of tied-off ropes, nets designed for capturing large animals, shovels, kits for making or extinguishing fires, chalk for marking trees when moving through an unfamiliar area, bows and quivers of arrows, a few short swords, and scores of weapons for throwing—everything from marbles to javelins.

In short, everything she needed.

This was her personal supply depot, filled with everything she had bartered for over the years of hunting and live-trapping for wealthy parents who wanted rare creatures for their children to train. A glance at the far corner showed a metal helmet, putting a soft smile on Lily's lips, "Everything in here I either made myself, bartered for it, and in only *one* case... stole."

Taking a deep breath of satisfaction with the tools at hand, she reached over and firmly grasped a long, coiled rope. "Thanks for giving me enough time to get ready, Big Bad.

Every extra moment is a gift... that's why it's called the present."

Pulling everything she needed out of the supply depot, she took a moment to plan out how she would neutralize her enemy. By the time he got here, Drwg Mawr would certainly be on high alert, knowing he'd given her enough time to create a labyrinth of traps. "How can I use his *knowing* I'll be ready to my advantage?"

After a minute of serious contemplation, she jolted herself into moving once more, just before she would have fallen asleep. "Nope, need more doing, less pausing and thinking. He's going to be expecting me to put together something horrifying in order to take him down, because that's the only thing that has slowed him down so far. In that case..."

She reopened the hatch, pulling out far more dangerous, scary-looking implements than she had requisitioned for her *real* plan. Knives, spikes, thickened wires—sharpened on one edge to create a thin but durable cutting tool, as effective on flesh as it would be on cheese. Hauling everything over to an open area nearly halfway through the training encirclement, Lily began putting together a convincing fake of a fiendish trap.

Collections of snares hanging down from tree limbs, caltrops scattered among the grass, tripwires which didn't actually connect to anything, all of it was woven through the small clearing's foliage, underbrush, and even left lying seemingly-yet-*actually* innocuously on the ground. All of it was put together to create what appeared to be an absolute *blender* of potential death, hidden just enough to make it look as though she'd tried to hide it perfectly, but simply lacked the skill or time to do so.

Only someone who took the time to follow the 'traps', especially the wires, would be able to discern their true nature: the entire clearing was filled with decoys. Every last one of them was meant to draw attention, hinting to Drwg Mawr that Lily had become overconfident and expected him to barrel through the area without thought of consequence to himself.

She paused after having that thought and reluctantly reached down to *actually* arm several of the traps—just in case. "I don't want to make him *think* I'm getting overconfident, then *actually* be so overconfident he won't fall for the trap, that he *does* fall for the trap and nothing happens. Then he'll know the trap isn't a trap, and be on the lookout for the real trap. ... trappy trap. I'm *way* too tired for this."

Casting one last glance over the decoys, she pulled a face at the sloppy work, a stark contrast to her normal, meticulous crafting. Even though she wanted to project the desperate last stand of someone too exhausted to care, it bothered her to leave a mess like this out in the open where someone else was sure to see it and judge her.

Lily paused for a moment, stifling her laughter as she turned to begin work on the *real* project. "*Pfft*. Why do I care if he thinks I make sloppy traps? If all goes to plan, he'll be sailing away from Canu Moch by midday tomorrow, never to return."

She turned and paced away from the decoy area, moving back deeper into the enclosed training space. Climbing a tree, she gauged her line of sight, shifting slightly until she found a branch large enough for her purposes, while also being visible from the clearing. Then she got to work, placing traps around the base of the tree with the precision and caution only someone who had mastered the most advanced Scouting skills available on the island could match. With her grandmother having been slain, Lily was loath to admit, but only Reynard could likely match this setup.

"He never would, though. I've never seen that man do anything in a less than lethal way. 'If they don't die without knowing what killed them, what's the point'?" Lily's lips pulled back in a feral grin as she thought about catching the rival

Scout in her traps and getting a chance to properly… *thank*… him for his contributions to the defense of Canu Moch, as well as the boost to her skill levels.

After the real traps had been set, she gently pulled on one of the tight ropes to test its tension, nodding happily as she heard the needed *click*. After resetting and arming the final wire, Lily searched the area with System's Echo once again— still no Big Bad Wolf creeping up on her. "Hmm… okay… I'll just keep adding more on until either he shows his face, or it starts getting dark. Whichever comes first."

Layer after layer of defenses sprung up around the tree, all of them tied to a single point of activation. Minutes turned into hours, and one trap turned into twenty-two. Surprisingly, as dusk turned into twilight, Drwg Mawr still hadn't shown up. "Did he really break his spine, or… what?"

She surveyed her handiwork leerily, honestly concerned about getting down from the tree without accidentally setting something off. Lily shook off that concern, reminding herself that nothing would activate without the main line on the tree losing tension. "Time for the final touch."

Even knowing it was integral to her success, and Drwg Mawr was literally only able to follow her because she hadn't taken it off, it still took the remainder of Lily's willpower to pull off her red cloak and wrap it around the target practice dummy she had settled on the branch. The hood came up, wrapping over the metal helmet she'd purloined from an unsuspecting Bleakrock guard before her eighteenth birthday. The entire arrangement was settled in the same sleeping position the warrior had nearly managed to catch her in a day ago… or was it two days?

She climbed down from the tree, making sure the bait was settled so as to be almost, *almost* perfectly hidden. Checking on the fake traps, she could barely catch a glimpse of the pseudo-sleeping form. To anyone with a keen eye, everything should appear as if she had positioned herself to lay in wait in such a way as to watch Big Bad get caught up in traps, only to succumb to her exhaustion before he arrived.

Not wanting to admit how close that situation had come to reality, Lily moved to be at a point between both trap zones, creating a triangular line of sight. Checking her scouting gear, now only browns and greens which would actually *help* her blend in, Lily slumped back against the tree supporting her.

Instantly and irresistibly, the Scout succumbed to sleep.

CHAPTER
THIRTY-NINE

DANGER.

Lily tried to instantly open her eyes and scan the area, but could only manage a painfully slow version of the act. Her eyelids were heavy, her mouth felt as dry as the ashes she'd been running through for the last few days, and however much sleep the Scout had managed to get wasn't *nearly* enough to recover from her exertions. Still, it was enough to barely function, which was all she needed for the moment.

Now begrudgingly awake, she melded further against the tree trunk, barely moving, ensuring she didn't make any of the mistakes she wouldn't have control over while asleep. Her gaze wandered around the area, trying to find what the system had warned her about, had woken her for.

Nothing, as far as she could see.

Then, realizing she wasn't using her greatest advantage, Lily activated System's Echo and searched the area once more. Her heart started *slamming* in her chest as the beacon of vitality that was Drwg Mawr appeared in her mind's eye— almost *directly below* her current position.

Stifling a squeal upon remembering how he'd crawled up the tree and barely missed getting a hand on her *almost* made her tuck and roll off her vantage point. Just before she let her body take control, her mind pointed out the fact that the huge man wasn't *climbing* her tree, but only standing near her. In fact, he wasn't even looking in her direction.

It was just before dawn with only hours to go before she automatically lost the battle. Just the barest hint of light was illuminating the area, meaning she'd been given far more time to sleep than she'd expected. Lily had to force herself not to squirm as a gruesome thought crossed her mind. "If he gave me this much time, is it only because he'd been terribly broken? Was he just out there suffering until he could finally put himself back together?"

Inflicting needless pain on another creature was absolute taboo in her mind, not to mention being one of the strongest and most heavily punished laws of the Wyld. A second thought popped into her head... specifically, she was wondering if she should've waited around and taken advantage of his weakened state to claim victory. Reluctantly, she shook the thought away. "Can't go back and change what I did. Plus, there's no guarantee it would've worked."

Her spiraling thoughts paused as Big Bad stepped forward, an enormous silhouette silently sliding through the area. Practically holding her breath, she watched him navigate the open space. His movements were deliberate, slow, *cautious* as he slid forward a few more feet, ensured he didn't have any branches above himself, and stood to his full height. She watched him from her position in the tree, able to see the back of his body with her eyes, while simultaneously being able to watch his facial expressions and track every fractional shift of his vision thanks to System's Echo.

A glint of light caught Dwrg Mawr's attention, and his head slowly shifted until he was staring at the clearing filled with the decoy traps she had meticulously and sloppily prepared. His chin tucked down slightly as he glowered at the area, noting the 'lethal' constructs; their placement, design, and… a small frown appeared on his face when he realized he'd been able to see the traps in the first place.

Words, whispered so softly she wouldn't have been able to hear them had the forest not been so still, drifted up to Lily's ears. "Why? Was she trying to scare me off instead of…? No, this is an arrangement of desperation… a ploy not fully realized. Which means she can't be far."

After double checking the area again, he glanced down at his gauntlet and outright dismissed the idea of walking into the clearing. Instead, the huge man began scrutinizing his surroundings. Lily shivered at his genius-level insight, hardly daring to believe how quickly he picked out the open spaces in the clearing, tracing sightlines across the ground, into the trees at eye level, then far above his head. If he'd been a Scout, he would've been near Mastery with his skills.

Only ten seconds had passed from the point he had decided she must be nearby until Lily saw him pause, his head tilting slightly.

Even before checking with System's echo, she knew Big Bad was staring at 'her' sleeping far above. As soon as he was certain he'd found his target, the man *flowed* forward, moving through the forest in a manner completely different from Red's style. It was a study in silent efficiency: the predatory grace of a wolf, combined with the deadly intent of a warrior who'd been tried and tested in battle.

He treated the ground he was walking on as an enemy as much as an ally. Leaves which would crinkle if brushed were instead firmly *crushed* into the ground, giving them no opportunity to sound off. Branches which could handle his strength were pushed away steadily, while the smaller ones were woven around so as not to break them and alert his quarry.

All the while, his piercing stare never wavered from Lily's red cloak, and soon he was directly below that tree. As he reached up and began to scale it, she was finally able to see how he'd managed to get so close to her once before without

being noticed. It was an odd way to climb, as he never negoti-
ated a limb of the tree; instead, he wrapped his hands in a
tight grip around the trunk directly, pulling himself up as if he
were ascending a rope. His legs curled out and behind him,
carefully not touching *anything* as he silently maneuvered
upward.

All too quickly, he was at the same level as her mannequin
and slowly came around the tree from the back. Finally, he
settled his feet on a branch, drawing his cudgel with his right
hand and lifting it into the air. Lily leaned forward, excited to
watch her pursuer enact his own downfall. "Do it, Big Bad.
All you need to do is make the line go slack. Go on... hit it.
Knock any part of 'me' off the branch-"

Her smile froze, the glimmer of excitement fading into
confusion. Instead of smashing the training dummy as
expected, Drwg Mawr lowered his cudgel until it was resting
gently atop the crimson cloak, then he spoke in a loud voice,
practically announcing his presence to the entire forest. "Lily
Red. At this moment, I could have slain you. But... I find that
would be a terrible waste. As much as it hurts my pride, I will
even *beg* you. Please. I give you one last chance... surrender. I
would like to talk."

"Well, *that's* not gonna work for me. I have *way* too many
taunts and one-liners ready to go for when you're all tied up."
Lily grumbled as she reached to her back, unhooking her bow
and smoothly stringing it. "Plus, an empty cloak isn't gonna be
much of a conversation partner."

"I saw your work down below, and know how much it
must have pained you not to be able to reach your usual standard." The warrior stated somberly, as if having noticed a
dirty secret of hers. "Believe me, it is no small feat to have
managed to come this far. No one else has *ever* lasted a full
three days against me. Enough of this game. It is now time for
me to accept your..."

Big Bad went silent as he pulled back the hood of her

cloak, only for the heavy metal helmet to fall out of the assemblage and clatter to the ground, sounding as if it had hit every branch on the way down. After allowing himself a single second of shock, watching the item fall, Drwg Mawr's reaction was immediate. A swift turn of his head, his vision sweeping out to encompass the entire clearing as he searched for the *real* Lily. His body tensed, his muscles beginning to coil in preparation of springing into action.

Suddenly the cloak he had a loose grip on was jerked out of his hand as an arrow flitted into it and *thunked* heavily into the mannequin the garment had been wrapped around. The warrior hadn't been able to react to the incoming projectile, unable to hear it thanks to the owl-feather fletching smoothing and silencing its movement through the night.

**Sss-pip.*"

The tripwire activated, followed by a barrage of twanging, clattering, shifting and rustling, as if the entire forest around the tree Big Bad was standing on had come to life. His reaction was a testament to his instincts, but unfortunately for him, Lily had expected him to do exactly what he did next. Instead of getting close to the tree trunk and hoping nothing was coming at him, the warrior launched himself out and away, shifting in midair to get his feet under him.

In any other situation, he would've been able to evade the unseen dangers, but Lily had put all of her *Perfected* skills to the test, setting up a web of traps around him. As the tension left the tripwire, twenty-six different slingshots launched a set of three round stones. The stones spread slightly as they flew, the cables woven between them revealing each of the projectiles to actually be a bola, triple weights which spun wildly through the air.

Although most sailed past the falling giant, one after another met their mark and bound Big Bad's limbs to his torso. Though he tried to shift around, the warrior was unable to avoid becoming snarled in sinews as he dropped.

The constricting embrace would've immobilized almost anyone else, but by the time he landed heavily on the ground—struggling to his feet and trying to hop away from whatever else was coming—the huge man had already snapped through two of the entangling weapons. Luckily for Lily, she had more planned than simply trying to slow him down. Moments after the last of the bolas had launched, the air was filled with creaking and groaning as a massive weighted net swept through the open space between trees, dragged by a large bough as it swung back to its natural position.

The net wrapped around Big Bad as he tried and failed to dive out of the way, pulling him along as he grunted with the impact. Red watched him twist with maximum exertion, attempting and succeeding at keeping his feet under him. As the net came to a stop, it set off yet another tripwire. A second net shot *up* from the ground, closing over the first and being tightly drawn like a purse string as the two trees pulled the opposite sides of the net to reset themselves.

For a few heartbeats, the air was still, broken only by the harsh breathing of the wrapped-up warrior. Then he let out a shaky laugh and shouted into the darkness of the night, "This isn't enough to *defeat* me, *Lily*!"

"Good thing it's not over then, isn't it?" the Scout murmured, not giving up her location even though she was at least eighty percent sure she had already won. "Give it a second... here we go. *This* one wasn't damaged by fire like the others."

Even though he was wrapped in layers of nets and hidden from normal vision, Lily was able to watch him thanks to the system's help. Branches snapped, and the air howled as the crescendo of her trap swung through the canopy: a huge log released from a hidden cradle high above. The pendulous blunt wood smashed into the ball of netting as if the wrath of nature itself was being unleashed on the invader, sending him spinning through the air as the ropes holding the nets aloft were ripped from their anchor points.

Exactly as they were designed to do.

The entire bundle hit the ground, spinning and rolling until finally tipping over the edge of a pit trap Lily had originally dug when she was fifteen. The Scout watched Drwg Mawr drop in the first pit she had managed to wrangle him into; only to almost immediately begin shaking back and forth violently, trying to throw off the bindings and netting.

Concerningly, he started to have some small success.

She hopped out of the tree, running across the rough terrain until she was standing casually at the top of the pit. "Finally, *I* get to ask *you* this. Want to surrender?"

"Not happening," his muffled voice floated from the bottom of the pit. "I'll be out of here shortly. Then I'll deal with *you*."

Lily shrugged, jogging over to a wedge which had been placed in front of a log. She turned back to the pit, raising her voice once more, "Last chance to surrender! I'll even help you up."

"Don't worry, I'll be *right there*." Big Bad chuckled darkly as he thrashed more violently, actually managing to stick his feet through the holes of the nets and stand up.

"I tried."

Yanking the wedge out, Lily jumped to the side as the log was pushed away by a huge wall of gravel. The small stones and dirt slid into the pit, filling it completely over the span of only a few seconds. Letting out a small sigh as the last of the stones cascaded onto the rest, she waved at the pit. "I'd say this was fun, but… no. It wasn't. Now, I don't think you're going to be able to get out of… oh, come *on*."

As the last of the dust settled, and silence echoed away from the pit, she found Big Bad's eyes locked with hers. As a final act of defiance, he had shifted his body and managed to swim slightly up the stream of stones like a salmon up a waterfall. Big Bad was buried up to his nose, but somehow seemed pleased with himself over the outcome.

Even as Lily watched on, he shook back and forth, causing small rocks to fall away from the net wrapped around his face and give him some breathing room.

"I'm *incredibly* frustrated by you." She let out a defeated sigh as she crunched across the gravel, bending over and retrieving a large jug from behind a bush before walking back to the buried man. "*Please* surrender? I really don't want to add to my future nightmares just to put an end to this."

Without waiting for an answer, she began pouring the thick, viscous liquid out of the jug and onto Big Bad's head. "Before you ask, this is a type of torch fuel my grandmother was particular about. Whenever it showed up in the market, I was sent to buy as much as I could get my hands on. It burns hot... for a long, *long* time."

"Mmphh."

Lily moved a scoop of gravel away from the warrior's face, grasping the rope and shaking it side to side to ensure he had enough room to breathe and speak.

"Ah. My thanks. Listen, like I said to you only a few moments ago... to your *cloak*, I suppose... I would like to talk to you."

"Get to talking, then." Lily stepped back and pulled out a flint and steel, striking it a single time onto a torch coated in the oil she had just described to Big Bad. It flared up, a deep blue at its base, with orange and yellow flames flashing upward for several feet before calming and burning down, but only slightly. "Now, if the words coming out of your mouth are anything other than your surrender, they'd better be worth hearing."

"Fair enough. Lily Red, this is the most fun I've had in my entire life, and my first resounding defeat since I had my father to test myself against." Even as his eyes tracked the flame she was waving back and forth, Drwg Mawr never lost the bright grin on his face. "I had been expecting this to go another way, with plenty of time to explain my reasoning, but..."

He took a deep breath as the torch came closer.

"Let me try this again." His bright blue eyes locked onto a pair of bright green ones reflecting a wavering flame. "Lily Red. Become my wife."

FORTY

THE CRACKLING torch was now the only sound in the area as both people simply stared at each other, one in expectation, one in blank shock.

Lily finally broke out of her stupor, a frown appearing at the same moment. "I'm... not sure if this qualifies as 'words worth hearing'. There's no way you expect me to actually say 'yes', right? Look, if you're gonna stall for time, I'm gonna light you on fire just to see if the damage sticks."

"See, this is exactly why I had been wanting to talk and explain more clearly." Drwg Mawr grumblingly sighed as Red tipped the oil container over onto him, drenching him with a second liberal coating. "Hey! I'm- *glub*, *plahh*, let me-"

He went silent as Red brought the torch a little too close for comfort. "You say you want to talk to me. Does that change the fact I've caught you, trapped you, rendered you at least temporarily helpless, and can keep finding new ways to try and kill you? I'd... rather not. I'll have to try everything I can think of. You'll suffer, at least until you die, or the system decides who wins at the end of our three days."

Big Bad gasped for air as she pulled the container back, allowing him a moment to respond. "No, it doesn't change that, but I'd like to have the opportunity to *discuss* this without a constant compulsion to leave the island tugging at my soul."

Red sent a dazzling smile at him, showing perhaps a little too much of her teeth. "You won't be going anywhere until I dig you out of there, and I won't be doing so until I know for a fact you won't be doing anything to try and hurt me. Just surrender, or I'm going to assume you're saying anything you can think of to try to buy yourself time to escape."

He didn't say anything, instead heaving for breath and furrowing his brow while thinking, even as liquid dripped from his curly brown beard and pooled around his mouth. Red sighed and shrugged dramatically, wincing as she slowly brought the flame closer to his exposed, drenched head. Drwg Mawr struggled mightily, and Lily closed her eyes as the torch came closer, not wanting to see the moment he-

"*Stop*! You win. I surrender!" He barked with great concern as sparks leapt from the torch, flaring out just before touching the liquid on his head. "By the system, I swear to uphold the terms of our single combat!"

Lily jerked her hand back, relief flooding her as she stuck the torch in the ground. A golden 'X' appeared over her chest, fading after a long moment into a clear, pearlescent version of itself which floated up and sank into her skin, permanently tattooing itself on her left cheek.

She knew what it would look like, but hadn't ever expected such an honor: the mark was a system-honor, indicating a sworn promise being fulfilled. All unfulfilled yet unbroken promises were inscribed on someone's heart and remained after death, a well-documented phenomenon, which had given rise to a popular compliment about someone who always kept their word: 'that person has a heart of gold'.

In contrast, a *golden* 'X' mark on the left cheek was a system representation of a person who had a system-witnessed marriage, and had gained a Conjoined Skill, a symbol which could never become pearlescent unless one of the married duo died.

The golden 'X' on the *right* cheek meant something entirely different—that was the mark of a leader of a nation who'd been recognized as a worthy leader, and granted a blessing by the system. Lastly, a pearlescent 'X' on the right cheek was the mark of a Hero or a Fairy: a man or a woman who had maximized their positive reputation with the system.

Rumors stated that each of these marks would grant the person acquiring them an additional power, though as she had always lived on Canu Moch, she'd never met someone with such a mark. Becoming a system-recognized Hero or Fairy wasn't an opportunity often bestowed, and it had never happened without achievements at scale.

Her finger traced over the raised line on her face, even as she looked curiously at Big Bad's face to see if he had any such marks... or worse, a sickly green 'X' indicating a deeply negative reputation with the system: someone known as a Villain, or Witch.

Happily, he only had two marks, a golden 'X' on his right cheek—the mark of a system-recognized leader of a nation—as well as the same mark she now possessed of a completed system-oath on his left.

Lily wasn't sure at first why she stared at his left cheek so long, but felt herself flushing slightly when she realized it was because she was looking to see if there was a golden marriage mark hidden under his beard—even though she knew it could never be hidden without magical means if someone was looking for it. "Well... thank you for surrendering. I suppose now would be a good time to let you know that I only poured watered-down mead over your head? To be frank, the real oil is *far* too expensive to waste on trying to cook something that refuses to stay cooked."

"You...! That was a bluff?" Big Bad stared at her in shock, his mouth working as he tried and failed to find something to say. Then he began chuckling, a rueful laugh at first, turning into a full-on roar as he got going. When he finally managed to get control of himself, he tried again, "She's even *frugal*! Father, I've found the perfect woman. I never expected the prophecy to be fulfilled this way, but the whims of fate are ever opaque until the moment has arrived."

"I would've burned you if I really needed to do so. Also… *ew*? Don't tell me you proposed to me because someone once mumbled over a crystal ball and told you what the various fumes were making them experience." Red chuckled as she adjusted the ropes to give him slightly more breathing room. "I'd be terribly disappointed to have yet another reason to get you off the island as fast as possible."

"No." Big Bad shifted slightly, his best attempt at shaking his head. "Not at all. The proposal is entirely *my* desire. I will say, my initial pursuit of you was spurred by an oracle, but… everything about you has called to me since the first time I chased you into the forest. Become my wife?"

"Romantic, and perfectly delivered. Even a question this time. Improvement." Lily patted him on the cheek, grinning as he tried to suggestively bite her hand in response. "Look, I'll be digging you out for a while here. Go ahead and talk. I'll try not to laugh at you… too much."

So saying, she got to work, grabbing a shovel and starting to scoop gravel out from around the defeated warrior. For his part, Drwg Mawr remained perfectly still as he stared at her with hungry eyes.

"Allow me to list your achievements. You've bested *me*, in the area I have the most confidence in: extended combat." The man stated the words as if he still couldn't quite believe them. "Escaping me in the woods showed your immense dedication to your class and skills. Surviving against and helping me defeat a Huntsman, a Skinwalker no less, proved your ability in combat. Leading people away from my initial entry to the island? Holding off twenty of my warriors at the same time with your well-placed projectiles? Being chosen by *three* separate nations to represent them against me?"

He shook his head in admiration, though his eyes remained locked on her, to the point that Lily was beginning to become uncomfortable as she worked, feeling as though her hands and body were betraying her by becoming clumsy. Even then, he didn't stop speaking, "Then... evading and tricking me. Infiltrating my camp, full of my most skilled and trusted men? Creating traps *as you ran*? You remained hidden in an open field without even grass to hide behind... all while dressed in a bright red cloak?"

He locked onto her green eyes with his bright blues, "Must I go on? I have more."

"Oh, I *insist*. Please keep telling me how awesome I am." Red grumbled, trying to make her voice gruff but only managing to blush harder, turning her eyes to avoid his.

"Very well."

"I'm not-"

But Drwg Mawr wasn't about to stop, though his shoulders had been exposed and he could have started wiggling to aid in freeing his body. "The way you found and exploited loopholes in our agreement was masterful. No one can say you got *help* from my people, yet you have many days' worth of food and drink taken from my camp."

"About that..." Red started speaking sheepishly, but he merely shook his head.

"The supplies you pulled out of nowhere? How long have you been preparing for my arrival, to be able to rearm yourself anywhere you tread?" His smile was full of heat, so Lily busied herself with digging, scraping the shovel against his skin in a few areas—not that he complained. "Then, the traps? Ugh, the traps... over and over, you risked your own health and safety to ensure that the use of them against me was fair. Lastly, you led me here, to a place I've *been* before, and utterly vanished, even though I knew where you should be."

"Vanished? Is that why it took you until almost dawn to find me? You couldn't find the entrance to this training area?" Lily chuckled and looked directly at him, a mistake, since she couldn't stop a bark of laughter at his expression.

"There's an entrance? I climbed three trees to even *start* on the cliff face!" The utter indignation in his words struck Lily, and she needed to step away for a moment to get herself under control. "Listen… all of this together shows me a woman I've been searching for my whole adult life. One who is smart, resourceful, and at *least* my equal in a variety of ways. The fact you are astonishingly confident and eye-catchingly beautiful certainly doesn't hurt."

"Oh, good. I just so happen to be pretty." Lily shook her head disbelievingly as she pulled on the net around the trapped man. "I was worried about that."

"You have no reason to be." Drwg Mawr informed her without a hint of humor. "As I said, this your beauty is a happy coincidence, but the other aspects are far more important to me. My people's lives are changing, as is the world. Villains and Witches killed my father, our leader. For this, they must be eradicated. I need someone who can teach my warriors a new way of living, and help us adapt to new situations and terrain. I'd like that to be you."

"You want me… for my skills." Red blinked at him, the shovel in her hands all but forgotten. "Because you want me to help train an entire nation of people."

"Yes."

"Huh." Lily sat down and stared at him, finally starting to take the man seriously. "In that case, why the marriage offer? Well, marriage *statement*, originally."

He didn't flinch away from her penetrating stare. "I know better than to ignore the opportunity of a lifetime. If the idea is absolutely repellent to you, I will still beg you to join me as the well-paid lead instructor of my people."

Blinking rapidly as she thought over the new information, Lily fiddled with her arm to buy herself a moment. She swiped along her forearm, bringing up the new information.

Skill increase! System's Echo [Level 9 (Master) → Level 10 (Perfection)]!

System's Echo is an active skill which allows you to [Perfectly] yet innately notice life forms as well as rapidly moving objects in a range of [100] meters around you. This skill has reached Perfection and has become permanently active.

As soon as Lily read the notification, her senses expanded and settled into place with a mental *click*. Nothing around her could now hide from her senses, and Lily took a deep breath as the system smoothed the final edges of the skill, ensuring the permanency caused her no issues, but felt as natural as if she'd been born with the skill active. There was one last line of text, which wrote itself out, vanished, and appeared again.

You have earned access to your Full Class Breakthrough Skill. Touch a Class Shrine to activate it!

Seeing the text, Lily was flooded with the desire to rush over to the remains of her home and slap the shrine. Only the current situation with the trapped and staring raider kept her in place. "Drwg Mawr. I can't do anything with you; it would be a betrayal to the people of Canu Moch. Your people invaded my island and killed so *many*-"

"No." He instantly denied, cutting her off as thoroughly as a knife to the neck. "We killed no one. This was a bloodless endeavor on our part. As soon as we walked up to the coastal towns, fully planning to trade for food, the locals ran away squealing at the top of their lungs. They knocked over torches, setting their homes alight. We rushed in to pull people out and save whatever food and drink we could manage. Anyone who remained was rounded up and tasked with pulling in fish for us to begin restocking the fleet's rations."

"You didn't kill any of them? Not one?" Red's voice was incredulous.

"I will swear to it, if I must," Big Bad solemnly stated. "First, we never got the chance, nor did we meet with resistance. Second, we were here to restock and gather a workforce. Killing them would have been counter to our goals."

Red winced as he casually implied that he *would've* killed the people if needed. "Not… the best reasons for not slaughtering innocents I've ever heard. Still… I'm guessing you'd also swear to not destroying the forest by setting it on fire?"

"We need boats. The loss of easy access to wood from the shoreline is incredibly frustrating." Drwg Mawr growled at the reminder. "I'd have to check with my people, but I can state with reasonable certainty that it was not us."

Lily thought through the rest of her issues with working with Wolf Warband. "I was right, then. Fearing the Big Bad Wolf, the three little pigs turned on each other. The Coasties burned down their homes and ours. Wyldlings killed off Coasties and Citizens of Bleakrock. The latter group tried to trap the other nations and force them to convert to their bizarre customs, no matter what it cost them. My home is gone, Grandmother subsumed without a body to bury. What… do I even have left, if I remain here?"

The warrior's eyes widened fractionally, practically vibrating with excitement, but held his tongue as she voiced her thoughts.

"The Coasties make a game of annoying me. I've made dangerous enemies among the leadership of the Wyld, and Bleakrock would likely feed me to the pit and make me into mushrooms if I showed my face there again." Big Bad's head tilted, confused at the last musing thought. Lily didn't even notice. "My home has been burned down. My only remaining relative was killed by the experiments of a foreign Witch Queen. I have no strong attachments remaining. If I *did* stay… it'd be a life of solitude and watching my back."

A full minute passed in silence as she wrestled with her thoughts.

Finally, she looked at the partially freed man. "You mentioned something about a prophecy. What was it?"

"When I became the Mawr, I consulted an oracle. A Fairy Godmother with a connection to the stars. She told me the solution to most of my problems would be found here, on the far-distant shores of Canu Moch." His lips twitched as he watched Lily raise her shovel again. "I asked her what I should do when I got here, and she told me I only needed to do one thing."

"Which was…?" Lily rolled her eyes when he paused, clearly baiting her into raising the question.

"She told me, when I landed on the island, I needed to do the first thing I was told, by the first person I met. Do you remember your first words to me?"

"No…?"

"You said, 'Come and get me, if you can'." Drwg Mawr swallowed hard, his wolf grin turning sheepish. "I've tried very hard to get you. My offer of marriage is my last chance, and I hope I won't fail yet again."

CHAPTER
FORTY-ONE

As she pulled the second net off the now-only-bound warrior, Big Bad flexed and grunted. The four remaining bolas *snapped*, falling to the ground and leaving the huge, overly muscular man in arm's reach. At that moment, Lily was distinctly aware of how dangerous this man was, yet was strangely comforted by his presence.

Even though he was at least two feet away, his body heat radiated off his skin, warming her up as the chill of the morning sank into her bones. The sweat she had worked up was practically freezing, now that she was no longer shoveling gravel out of the pit. Clearing her throat, she looked up, and up... "I hope you realize I haven't agreed to anything yet, least of all marriage."

"Yes." He stretched his body, the small bruises across his neck and torso already fading, now that the rocks were no longer actively crushing him. "This is an important decision. I don't want you to rush it. I simply needed to be the first to make the attempt, so you would see my sincerity."

Slowly, she backed away from him, and he waited patiently until she was at a comfortable distance. Then she started leading him though the area, retrieving her cloak before doing anything further. Once the familiar, warm material was once more wrapped around her, Lily finally allowed herself to relax slightly. "I actually won. Even the system acknowledged that I single-handedly stopped a war."

"A war?" Drwg Mawr shook his head. "We had never intended to wage war on your people."

Both considered his words, and the truth slowly dawned on the Scout. "Was it the war between the city-states? Captain Cliff called a ceasefire and told me that he would end all hostilities and release the people if I won. *That's* the war I stopped?"

"It must be," her too-warm follower firmly agreed. The excitement of winning had filled Lily with excitement and adrenaline, but it was rapidly fading away, reminding her exactly how tired she really was.

As they approached the rock wall surrounding the training grounds, she barely noticed the warrior tense up, only faintly chuckling as she heard his cursing about 'tricky islanders' as they walked through the camouflaged passage carved into its base.

Lily took the most direct path toward the Class Shrine, aiming herself directly at her old home. Only as she got close, and realized Big Bad had slowed down, did she turn to see why he was hesitating.

There was a faint, confused smile on his lips, "The shrine? I had thought you were uncertain? I'm ready right now, but... I want this to be a choice you never resent me for."

She blinked at him owlishly, taking far too long to remember the fact that system-recognized marriages, just like class advancement, could only happen at a Class Shrine. "Ah! *No!* I mean, no, I earned my Breakthrough Skill, and I'm going over there to gain access to it."

"*Breakthrough?*" He sucked in a breath, leaning forward slightly in excitement as his gaze became even more fervent. "I mean no disrespect, but I had assumed you were younger than me. I am twenty-eight and have only increased my Full Class Advanced Skill to level seven, even with a life full of combat. Are you older than...?"

"I'm twenty." She flinched as he instantly slammed his hands together in a thunderous clap.

"My future wife is a genius among geniuses!" he bellowed to the sky, practically hopping in place as Lily's eyes went wide. While he was focused on his own thoughts, the Scout edged away from the gleeful man, wanting nothing more at this moment than to get to the shrine and realize her full potential—earning the skill bought by hard work, war, and the death of her only relative.

Codex Arcane Ledger access requested.

C.A.L. is assessing...
requirements for Breakthrough have been fulfilled!

Checking all system merits.

Basic Class:
-Basic Skill: 10/10.
-Advanced Skill: 10/10.
-Breakthrough Skill: 0/10.
Total: 20/30.

Advanced Class:
-Basic Skill: 10/10.
-Advanced Skill: 10/10.
-Breakthrough Skill: 0/10.
Total: 20/30.

Full Class:
-Basic Skill: 10/10.
-Advanced Skill: 10/10.

Total: 20/20.

Bonus points

-*System merit (Uncommon): Fulfilled System Oath. +5 points*
-*System merit (Rare): Adult Prodigy (Achieve Breakthrough in Full Class before 22nd birthday) +10.*
-*System merit (Epic): Young Adult Prodigy (Achieve Breakthrough in Full Class before 21st birthday) +15.*
-*System merit (Legendary): Achieve Breakthrough in a combat class without killing another human. +20.*
Total class points to be applied: 110/80.

Generating Full Class Breakthrough Skill...
Skill generated!

Breakthrough Skill: System Ordained Scout 0/10.

The user of this skill can choose a task, offering it to the system as a level-increase requirement. If the system accepts the task, all stats of the user will be increased by base x (2 x [Level]) while actively working toward the completion of the task. The system may assign an additional task if the local area is unfavorably balanced between good and evil, but these requests will always be optional.

A single task may generate more than one level, or none at all, depending on difficulty. Once this skill reaches Perfection, the selected task will generate rewards from the system in lieu of level increases. Rewards can range from Magical to Enchanted items, depending on the difficulty of the task.

Tears ran freely down her face as Lily read over the skill, recognizing a hint of her Grandmother's Breakthrough Skill, which must've been passed in her bloodline. She touched her heart. "I'll always remember you. Goodbye, Grandma."

After unlocking the skill, many things clicked into place for Lily. If she wanted to progress this skill and reach her full potential, she'd need to leave this small corner of the world behind. There was no way there would be enough happening here that the system would reward her with skill levels, not when the most dangerous threat to the people of the island had turned out to be themselves. With this realization, she took a deep breath and put her thoughts in order before opening her mouth.

"Big Bad. Dwrg Mawr."

"Yes, my betrothed?" The huge man stepped forward eagerly, perhaps a little *too* sure of his upcoming success.

"Is your regeneration your highest skill?" At Lily's words, the man gained a wild smile, knowing there was only one reason she would be asking.

"Oh, it is," he promised, swiping his fingers along his arm to allow Red to read the details herself if she so chose—a deeply personal offer, as exact information on someone's skills gave valuable information on their weaknesses. "The skill is called 'Constitution of the TrollWolf'. So long as I have my fill of food and drink, I will constantly have the energy I need to continue, even eventually healing through almost any wound. At Perfection, I'll become nearly unkillable... with flames being the one glaring weakness, as you somehow determined."

"If... as the only dowry I could bring..." Lily swallowed hard as the warrior went utterly still, as though any motion might make her change her mind.

She cursed under her breath, barely able to believe the words she was about to put out into the world, "If I could offer you a Conjoined Skill, where all your physical stats would increase by a multiplier of your skill level... would you personally guarantee I wouldn't regret you becoming my husband?"

"I would swear to it." Drwg Mawr lifted his hand to make an 'X' over his heart, but she reached out and abruptly stopped him.

"I'd rather you didn't do that. You'll never be able to

swear to a perfect happily ever after. Plus, that's *not* what I want." Her voice became stronger as she finished her thought. "I want adventure and new experiences. I also… I want revenge. To hunt down the Witch Queen who killed our family. I don't want you to be forced by the system to keep me perfectly happy. As my… as Grandmother often told me, a relationship is not a problem to be solved, but a tension to be managed. Is that a life we can live… together?"

"I believe it is." Drwg Mawr's voice was so low it made *her* chest buzz as he spoke. "As for revenge… that part I know I can promise. Would you be willing to teach my people, as I had hoped? They are my responsibility, and I have sworn to lead them as best as possible, even at the cost of my personal happiness."

"The fact you want me for what I can do for your people *instead* of only for you is why I'm even considering… that is, why I'm *doing* this. Celestial feces, I'm about to…" Lily paused, swallowed, and worked to force out the words which had caught in her throat, the words which felt utterly strange —almost, but not *quite*, a betrayal to the islanders of Canu Moch. "Then… if you're still willing, join me at the Class Shrine, and let's… get married?"

She'd seen Dwrg Mawr move fast before, but the way he *lunged* to get to the shrine made it truly appear as though he was angry at the world itself for allowing distance to *exist* between him and his goal. Lily waited to hear why he was acting like this, but he only showed her a wide, wolfish grin.

Still, she hesitated, wondering if she was making the wrong decision. "I don't want to be destroying people's lives for us to travel. Is raiding the only option you'd consider?"

The warrior's smile dimmed, but only slightly. "War is all we know, and has always been the whetstone we've improved our lives upon. If there's another way, I'd consider it… but we *must* leave, and soon. Already my oath calls at me, barely allowing me to stand still."

Red blinked rapidly as multiple scenarios played out in her mind. They'd be hunting the Witch Queen, and who knew how long that would take, how distant they'd need to roam. "War… yes. *War*, but not raiding. If we're *raiding*, every place we set foot will fight against us, slowing us further and further. But what if we were *invited* into their lands? Even more, what if they *paid* us to be there?"

"I… don't follow." Drwg Mawr admitted, his eyes slowly drifting to the sea as his off hand came up to rub at his chest, specifically the space over his heart, with discomfort.

"If this Witch Queen has been the cause of so many issues for *us*, so far removed from the world, certainly the mainland is having all sorts of problems. What if we went there and solved those problems for them… for money?" Lily flashed him a vicious grin, fully capturing his attention once more. "What would you say to acting as a hired blade instead of a raiding nation? Instead of Wolf Warband, we would introduce ourselves as Wolf Mercenary Company."

She trailed off as his smile changed, his eyes glinting. "What?"

"You said 'we'. If *we* went there." He leaned closer, the heat rolling off his body crashing into her chilled frame. "In your head, we're already married, and you're planning our future conquests. I am merely excited. Happy. As to the change? That sounds… like something we should have already done. Unsurprisingly, your wisdom has incredible depths. Our arrival to this island was truly what my people… *our* people, and what *I* needed."

Lily swallowed, hard, as he sidled closer, knowing she wouldn't run. Not this time. She placed her right elbow on the table, raising her arm as if she were challenging him to an arm wrestling competition. Drwg Mawr adjusted his position to stand directly in front of the shrine, leaned down to match her stance, and clasped her hand in his—pressing their forearms together as closely as possible. Seeing her entire hand be swallowed by his, being held firmly yet gently, Lily's mind began spinning up wild ideas of what the next few years would look like together with this immense, powerful figure.

"T-then… in that case… Dwrg Mawr, witnessed by the system, would you become my husband?" Before he could answer her, Lily whispered in wide-eyed shock, "Life will never be the same."

"It'll be so *much* more." He promised as he met her eyes, giving Lily two points of intense blue to focus on and stopping her thoughts from spiraling away. "It would be my honor, Lily Red. Witnessed by the system, I desire nothing more than to have you become my wife."

Codex Arcane Ledger is responding to your request to become married to Drwg Mawr of the Wolfman Nation!

Scanning…. Assessing… you are not being coerced or forced into making this choice. You are at least at the legal age for marriage for your kingdom. No skills or foreign substances are impairing your choices or altering your thoughts. Your exhaustion level is high—temporarily adjusting. Be aware, this incoming state will be reverted as soon as you make a choice.

Lily felt a jolt of energy, and her tired mind and body were instantly rejuvenated. Gone was any hint of sleepiness, and in its place was sharp, *wonderful* clarity of thought.

Please think through this choice carefully. The effects of a system-witnessed marriage cannot be undone. Whom you marry matters greatly, as your highest unlocked skill in your most potent unlocked class will be combined with theirs to make a Conjoined Skill.

You may only ever have a single Conjoined Skill. It will increase in potency in a similar manner to your other skills but will require the presence of your marriage partner to do so, unless they have died in a manner unrelated to you. Killing them or having them killed will forever halt the increase in skill level of your skill.

The system cannot be deceived.

If you choose not to continue this marriage witnessing and feel you may be in danger because of it, you will be instantly transported to a different Class Shrine with your safety guaranteed by the system for 24 hours.

With this knowledge, and with a clear understanding of your own thoughts, do you wish to marry Drwg Mawr, of the Wolfman Nation?

"I do," Lily Red stated at the same moment as Drwg Mawr, as if the system had aligned their thoughts and movements to be perfectly synchronized.

Marriage witnessed! Congratulations on this immensely important, irreversible choice! Generating Conjoined Skill.

They glanced at each other, amused by the choice of words the system used to describe the situation.

Conjoined Skill: Constitution of the Red Wolf. Level 0/10.

Like any other wolf, so long as you have eaten enough food and drank enough water, you are well satisfied and ready to continue. If your body has the resources to support it, your stamina and health will regenerate 100 + (100 x [Level]) % faster than your baseline. When your Conjoined partner has chosen a task aligned with your goals and accepted by the system, both of your physical statistics will increase by 1 x [Level].

Requirements for Skill increase: Choose a task with your Conjoined marriage partner. Once this skill has reached Perfection, you will gain system rewards instead of further levels for system-accepted tasks.

*Special modifier applied: You have been granted a modifier '**Damsel of Distress**'.*

Against seemingly insurmountable odds, you transformed a set of skills or circumstances which nearly guaranteed failure or even death into a foundation for success with far-reaching and profound effects. By taking your fate into your own hands, you have broken free of the Codex Arcane Ledger's predicted outcome for your life.

Effect: When in the presence of another 'Damsel of Distress', you will be able to recognize each other as kindred spirits and [Minimally] share the benefits of your skills, if so desired, while in range. This will increase in potency with the skill it was acquired in tandem with.

The system messages faded away, leaving only the two newlyweds, who blinked away the afterimages before locking eyes and awkwardly waiting for the other to say something. Lily felt heat rushing to her cheeks and shyly pulled her hand free from Big Bad's. "Um... so, now what?"

"I know what *I'd* like to do." He stepped close, swept her into the air, and planted a firm kiss on her surprised lips. Then he brought his mouth close to her ear and whispered, "After crossing this island and chasing you for several days... I could *really* go for a bath."

"After that?" Lily laughed dizzily, her head swimming and her lips tingling.

"Hmm? Then?" The corner of his smile twitched upward. "Many, *many* fun things. But also plentiful work. There's much to do."

"A nation to convert to a mercenary company," Lily added in, *just* to make sure.

Drwg Mawr bobbed his head in happy agreement. "First, we must get our people off this island."

"Then we start the hunt." Lily's eyes flashed with dark

promise as she agreed. "There's a Witch out there who needs to pay for the evil she's inflicted on the world."

"Thanks to you, we'll get paid for doing exactly what we were going to do anyway." Drwg Mawr chuckled as he went in for what was only ever their second kiss. He looked at her glowing arm, the new golden mark on her left cheek, then back into her eyes as he lifted her into his arms and carried her toward the distant shore. "Already, you have changed the way I am thinking about the future. I cannot wait to see what other wonderful things you make happen…"

"…My Damsel of Distress."

Continue the Damsels of Distress series on Patreon.com/ DakotaKrout - or order on Amazon, geni.us/DamselsSeries.

Cinder X Bella
Beauty X Beast
Rob X Punzel
Snow X Dwight

ABOUT DAKOTA KROUT

Good. Clean. Fun.

Dakota Krout is a celebrated author known for infusing fantasy novels with fun, punny, and clean humor. With multiple best-selling series—including "Divine Dungeon", "Completionist Chronicles", "Cooking With Disaster", and "Full Murderhobo"—he brings joy and laughter to readers. Dakota's work, renowned for its wit and creativity, earned a place as one of Audible's top 5 fantasy picks in 2017, a top 5 bestseller rank featured on the New York Times, and was chosen by Audible as among "the top 100 fantasy books of all time" in 2024.

Dakota's journey in publishing has been filled with gratefulness, and a deep desire to continue bringing smiles and laughter to the readers. *"I hope you Read Every Book With A Smile!"*

Connect with Dakota:
MountaindalePress.com
Patreon.com/DakotaKrout
Facebook.com/DakotaKrout
Instagram.com/DakotaKrout
Twitter.com/DakotaKrout
Discord.gg/mdp

ABOUT MOUNTAINDALE PRESS

Dakota and Danielle Krout, a husband and wife team, strive to create as well as publish excellent fantasy and science fiction novels. Self-publishing *The Divine Dungeon: Dungeon Born* in 2016 transformed their careers from Dakota's military and programming background and Danielle's Ph.D. in pharmacology to President and CEO, respectively, of a small press. Their goal is to share their success with other authors and provide captivating fiction to readers with the purpose of solidifying Mountaindale Press as the place 'Where Fantasy Transforms Reality.'

Connect with Mountaindale Press:
MountaindalePress.com
Facebook.com/MountaindalePress
Twitter.com/_Mountaindale
Instagram.com/MountaindalePress

MOUNTAINDALE PRESS TITLES
GAMELIT AND LITRPG

The Completionist Chronicles,
Cooking with Disaster,
The Divine Dungeon,
Full Murderhobo, and
Year of the Sword by Dakota Krout

Metier Apocalypse by Frank G. Albelo

A Touch of Power by Jay Boyce

Ether Collapse and
Ether Flows by Ryan DeBruyn

Unbound by Nicoli Gonnella

Lion's Lineage by Rohan Hublikar and Dakota Krout

Wolfman Warlock by James Hunter and Dakota Krout

Axe Druid,
Mephisto's Magic Online, and
High Table Hijinks by Christopher Johns

Tower of Jack by Sean Loomer

Dragon Core Chronicles by Lars Machmüller

Pixel Dust and
Necrotic Apocalypse by D. Petrie

Viceroy's Pride and
Tower of Somnus by Cale Plamann

Henchman by Carl Stubblefield

Artorian's Archives by Dennis Vanderkerken and Dakota
Krout